Rookie Year: Journey of a First-Year Teacher

Rookie Year: Journey of a First-Year Teacher

a novel by
Kelvin L. Reed

Peralta Publishing Company
Boston, Massachusetts

"The Greatest Love of All" by Linda Creed and Michael Masser
© 1977 EMI Gold Horizon Music Corp. and EMI Golden Torch Music Corp.
All rights reserved. Used by permission
Warner Bros. Publications U.S. Inc., Miami, FL 33014

First Edition

Peralta Publishing Company
P.O. 35407
Boston, MA 02135-0007

Printed in Canada

ISBN 0-9667631-2-2
Library of Congress Catalog Card Number: 98-96642

Copyediting services provided by Rider Associates in Watertown, Massachusetts and Jack Pudney & Associates in Schenectady, New York.

Cover and interior design by Archer-Ellison Design, Winter Park, Florida.

Acknowledgements

A writer more talented than I would be able to compose adequate words to sufficiently thank the people who have assisted me in transforming this project from a dream into a reality.

First, I am indebted to my wonderful and understanding wife, Marieta, who consented to sacrificing so much of our precious time together so that I could write this book. She was one of my initial reviewers and one of my best critics. Without her support in this endeavor—and others, there would have been no novel.

I wish to especially thank a good friend, Mary Ellen Stokes, for being another early reader of *Rookie Year: Journey of a First-Year Teacher*. Over the course of a year, she sat down with me after reading each chapter and gave me honest feedback, charging no more than a glass of lemonade (with a splash of pineapple juice). Her astute criticism kept me on course.

I also wish to thank a fellow teacher and dear friend, Tony Rome, who selflessly read my entire manuscript and provided me with numerous suggestions, rescuing the reader from my frequent short-sightedness and long-windedness.

I express my appreciation to another fellow teacher, Ramona Arroyo, who offered assistance with the Spanish expressions that appear in the book.

Finally, I wish to thank Joseph Hill of Madison, Wisconsin, whose generosity on my behalf years ago helped me to finish graduate school.

*T*his book is dedicated to John Taylor, Arvid Goplen, Jacqueline Oliveira, George Morten, Josiah Dilley and to the many other wonderful teachers I have had.

September

Date: The Present

The tall, muscular young man slowly approached the steps with apprehension. He had found the side door to the school. The two-story building, made up of red brick, now faded pink, had obviously seen better days. No visible parking lot existed for the staff. The playground, which could temporarily host their cars, bore no markings. Several feet of the fence around the perimeter had been stomped to the ground. The six-feet, four-inch former football player paused, reluctant to interrupt the busy man blocking his path, but the sign reported that the front doors were being repaired.

"Hello," he said to a short, older man in a white T-shirt. The man's hairy arms swung fiercely as he swept the top of the crumbling concrete stairs. Little pieces of cement tumbled downward, bouncing alongside the dry leaves deposited by a nearby oak tree. They joined the candy wrappers dropped by the children who lived across the street. "A little warm today, isn't it?"

"Shown 'nuff is," the man answered. Sweat poured from his forehead. He stopped sweeping and allowed the new teacher to hop up the stairs. The sun punished both of them, but not equally. The gruff man, just a few months from retirement, chuckled when he raised his head and matched the voice with the man. "But I'd rather be out here with what I got on than in there with what you got on," he joked, smiling and raising his gray eyebrows. "Waitaminute," he commanded. "You gonna be in 217. Good room. Bad kids, though." He scratched the ash-looking stubble on his face and shooed away a fly. "Name's J.J. Head custodian here. You need anything, you come see me. That young fella working your floor's just part-time. 'Kay?"

"Okay," replied the younger man.

J.J. noticed other teachers approaching. His smile disappeared as he returned to his task.

Thomas stepped inside, procuring some relief from the sun. He turned right and heard the echo of his lonely footsteps as he crept up a few worn wooden steps, then pushed open a set of mix-matched double doors; the left one obviously brand-new. At the opposite end of a freshly-waxed path about thirty yards long, separated by a dark corridor with walls the color of cooked bacon, he could see a comforting light beaming from his destina-tion—the school's office.

The first day of school had arrived—but not for students. Teachers re-ported for duty right after Labor Day, a day before the children. Thomas entered the office sanctuary and stood in front of the counter. On the other side, protected by a three-and-a-half-feet-high pressed-wood fortress, a big-boned woman with honey-blond hair atop black skin peered over her glasses, staring at a computer screen. She glanced at Thomas, then back at the machine. She shook her finger, brandishing bronze polish covering mani-cured glue-on nails, and threatened the contraption. Her nemesis replied with a low, unwavering hum. Without moving, she finally called, "Can I help you, dear?"

"Thank you," he replied. "I'm Thomas Payne. I'm a new teacher here and I—"

"Oh, nice to meet you, Mr. Payne. I'm *Miss* Marilyn Walker, the school secretary," she said, examining his towering frame appreciatively. He was just like she liked her men: tall, handsome, clean-shaven and *young*. His brown skin matched the color of maple syrup, probably just as sweet, the woman guessed. She removed her glasses and sauntered closer to the counter. "Mr. Dorn told me about you," she said. Her recently pruned eyebrows arched upward. "So you're going to try your hand with the Wild Bunch, huh?" She quickly cupped her hand over her wide mouth and blinked her eyes. The embarrassed woman looked around, struggling for something to say. Saved by her mechanical tormentor, she rushed out the words: "Do you know anything about computers, honey?"

Ten minutes later Thomas climbed a flight of stairs in search of Room 217. His mind backed up to Ms. Walker. ("Marilyn," she had insisted.) "The Wild Bunch" she called them. He played back his brief exchange with J.J. ("Bad kids, though.") Again he hit the reverse button in his mind and saw himself a week ago in the principal's office, seated in a chair with one bad leg. Sitting across from him was a pear-shaped, arrogant man named Mr. Dorn, the ten-year headmaster of the school. To his left sat Ms. Garcia, a Puerto Rican woman with a thick accent and dark-brown hair, an obvious dye job; she taught the third-grade bilingual class. Ms. Mustafa, a much younger woman who taught kindergarten, took notes and asked only one question. The young bachelor didn't have to strain remembering that one, with her fine self.

Thomas recalled that Mr. Dorn had done most of the talking. The principal had examined the candidate's résumé and background, and seemed impressed with the applicant's 3.7 undergraduate grade point average. The interviewee had proudly told the gray-haired, mahogany-colored man with the receding hairline about his degree in elementary education and history from Ohio State University and master's degree in education administration from Boston College. He had mentioned growing up in Cincinnati and playing a little football at Ohio State when he was twenty pounds lighter. Nothing fancy, but a starter in the second half of his senior year. The interviewers had appeared to be politely attentive. Thomas remembered that the energy level in the room had risen considerably when the subject of classroom management came up.

Thomas reflected on his decision not to disclose his ideas about using ceremonies as tools in building a classroom community and maintaining discipline. The candidate had not yet found the words to explain his six-month involvement in a self-exploration, self-enrichment program offered by an Oregon-based company called Revelations, Inc. He had enrolled in the Columbus, Ohio, program during his senior year in college and participated in all three "courses." He underwent Phase I, Basic Discovery; Phase II, How Others See Me; and finally, Phase III, Plan and Take Action. Thomas had been greatly affected by the exercises he had encountered two years before and planned to adopt some of them for use in the classroom. The exercises were not common stock in the school of pedagogy, but the rookie teacher viewed them as having potential in a low-achieving, inner-city school.

Thomas's thoughts were interrupted by the realization that he had reached his destination. He switched his leather briefcase to his left hand and lightly touched the door that displayed "217" in faint letters on the scratched glass. He reached for the doorknob and turned. With a creak and a whimper, the door opened. Excitement and fear stirred Mr. Thomas Payne as he stepped inside the very first classroom of his own.

Fear remained, but his excitement dissipated upon inspection of the room. The shiny floor glistened with several coats of fresh wax, but numerous potholes stretched from wall to wall. Thomas could barely see out of the windows, because they were scratched or dirty. Pounds of plaster were scattered across the floor, having obviously fallen from the ceiling. Huge, dark stains on the ceiling provided evidence of a leaky roof. Six of the twelve light fixtures overhead remained uncovered, exposing long fluorescent tubes. The teacher's desk, his desk, had a missing drawer, and his chair tilted sideways, absent a caster. One of the six student-closet doors had fallen to the floor. When the new tenant attempted to turn on the sink in the back of the room, a foul-smelling brown liquid oozed out.

"Hell," Thomas muttered to himself, holding his smooth face in his hands. "What a dump." He was spared from further horror by the sound of footsteps. The door swung open and a short lady in jeans rolled in, bearing a smile and a handshake.

"Hi, I'm Ms. Patterson. I teach fourth grade. I'm in 214 right down the hall," she announced, placing her hand on her forehead and pushing a handful of enhanced blond hair out of the way.

"Nice to meet you." Thomas replied, trying to hide his surprise at seeing a White woman. Because of his interview, he had been under the impression that the John Adams School was staffed totally by people of color. "Thomas Payne," he said.

"I had this group last year in fourth grade." Ms. Patterson confessed with an embarrassed smile. She giggled nervously and examined her new colleague's physical presence. "Is that what you're wearing?"

The man looked himself over and frowned. He modeled one of his newer suits; a blue pinstripe deal with a red silk tie and silk handkerchief in the jacket pocket. The fresh polish of his shoes reflected the sunlight that could fight its way into the room. Now he felt embarrassed. "I've got some overalls in the car," he replied.

"Well, you should go get them," Ms. Patterson admonished, pointing her finger and surveying the room. "You'll need them." She turned and started toward the door.

"Um, Ms. Patterson?" Thomas heard himself call out. For some reason, he didn't want to be alone just yet. His new neighbor turned around. He took three steps to get closer to her. "What happened to the fifth-grade teacher who had this room last year?"

"Oh, Ms. Blufford? She couldn't get a transfer to another school so she decided to take early retirement."

"Why?"

Ms. Patterson glided backwards out the door. "I guess she thought the time was right." Now she could be heard but not seen. "You'll be fine." Her echoing footsteps gradually grew distant.

"Right. Couldn't be better," Thomas mumbled.

The John Adams Elementary School was an old structure within the Boston Public School Department. It rested on a narrow street with little traffic and plenty of trees. With two floors and half a basement, it served children in the Boston community of Roxbury. Of the 350 students who attended the Adams last year, 327 had received free or reduced-cost lunch based on household income. The school contained one bilingual class and one English-speaking class for each of its six grades (all-day kindergarten to fifth). Two Advanced Work Classes, one for fourth grade and one for grade five, brought additional bragging rights. With no gymnasium, physical education classes were conducted outside or in a classroom.

Every winter the children and staff complained about the cold indoor temperatures. The year before Thomas arrived, the school had been promised gallons of gleaming white and bright blue paint, new light fixtures and new windows, but for some bureaucratic reason the improvements never materialized. However, because of the vociferous demands of the administrators, teachers and parents, the Adams did receive several visits in the spring by an exterminator.

A male voice on a static-heavy loudspeaker announced that the entire staff should meet in Room 203, the school library on the second floor. By 9 o'clock, Thomas found himself at the other end of his floor inspecting a room about half the size of his. Over a dozen large boxes of books and other library materials occupied the back corners. Three boxes of new books were stacked on top of each other, serving as door-stoppers. Empty and dusty wooden shelves leaned against the walls, having enjoyed an unburdened summer. The staff of the Adams squeezed into the room at a leisurely pace due to the heat and their own excess body fat. Thomas perceived quite a mixture of colors among their faces, after all. A table stacked with coffee and donuts greeted them, and several women eagerly descended on the treats like vultures. Soon they all found a seat and listened to the principal trying to inspire the troops. The man's words generated a few nods in agreement and some polite applause.

Thomas observed the way the crew had voluntarily arranged their temporary lodging. The Black teaching veterans sat among themselves, while the White professionals likewise congregated together. The Hispanic members of the staff—both teachers and paraprofessional aides—coalesced around an invisibly demarcated area, whispering in Spanish. Thomas recalled his football-playing days at OSU. His teammates, although indiscriminately cooperative with each other during games, divided themselves in similar fashion on the sideline and during social events. Thomas cut his eyes around the room. He was one of only three men present.

"We've got to rethink what we've been doing and make some changes," Mr. Dorn insisted. "We've got to …"

Thomas visually perused his immediate environment again. He noticed that not many attractive women taught at the Adams.

"The 350 kids we have here deserve our best efforts," the principal declared. "They need …"

Thomas gradually swung his vision over to Ms. Mustafa. The twenty-four-year-old man observed her posture. She looked straight ahead at Mr. Dorn, occasionally nodding her head. Thomas subtly adjusted his eyes from the unblemished copper skin of her face to her square shoulders, then surreptitiously appraised the two well-crafted curves on each side of her necklace. Very nice indeed, he thought. Regaining his proper frame of mind, he looked back at the principal, who seemed to be wrapping up his soliloquy.

"Now I'd like to introduce some new members of the Adams family," he announced. A few of the older teachers laughed. Mr. Dorn, catching his unintended joke, chuckled at his wittiness. He took out a white handkerchief and wiped his shiny face. "First of all, as some of you already know, Ms. Knowles had her baby, a little girl, so she won't be back for a while."

This brought a mixture of "ooohhs" and "aaahhs" from the audience, bringing the members to life. A few in the room broke into applause. Eventually, everyone joined in. Thomas spotted a couple of teachers snickering. He didn't understand it at the time but later would be told that Ms. Knowles was the *unmarried* youngest daughter of Reverend Jeremiah F. Knowles, the distinguished senior pastor at the First Roxbury Baptist Church, one of the largest churches in Boston.

Mr. Dorn continued. "So I'd like you all to make Ms. Bishop feel real welcomed, as she takes over the second grade—until Ms. Knowles comes back." The teachers broke into sincere applause as the principal motioned towards the back of the library. An overdressed, cream-colored woman in her early thirties stood, smiled and waved to everyone, then quickly sat down, somewhat flush-faced. Apparently, all new staff personnel received a similar introduction, their fifteen seconds of fame, so to speak.

Suddenly, Thomas felt self-conscious about how he looked. He felt silly in his suit and tie, while almost everyone else wore jeans. He felt self-conscious about being a man. He felt self-conscious about being over six feet tall. Thomas Payne had been a successful wide receiver for the Ohio State Buckeyes, admired for keeping his cool in front of 50,000 screaming fans. Now he had broken into a sweat at the prospect of being inspected by two-and-a-half-dozen teachers.

After three more introductions—two paraprofessional workers and another teacher—the dreaded moment arrived. "And I'm very happy to welcome a new man to our team," Mr. Dorn declared with the emphasis on MAN. "He'll take over the fifth grade in the place of our dear, beloved Ms. Blufford who, as you all know, retired. Please make Mr. Thomas Payne feel welcomed."

The room broke into applause. Thomas stood and waved. Mixed in with the noise, he heard voices offering encouragement and admonition.

"Good luck, honey."

"Maybe a man will keep that group in line."

"You let 'em know who's boss, right up front."

The rest of the meeting spun as a blur to Thomas. With so much to do, the staff spent most of the day packed in that hot library listening to dry information about bureaucratic matters: The superintendent's video introduction. A review of last year's poor standardized test scores at the Adams. The revised school calendar. Bulletin board assignments. The revised curriculum standards. Words from a soft-spoken Hispanic woman named Abigail Flores—who turned out to be the Adams second-year assistant principal— about new state requirements for the bilingual students. New referral forms for the school special education evaluation team leader (who would be at the Adams only one day a week). The new Boston School Department disciplinary code.

The list went on and on until noon before Mr. Dorn dismissed the obviously uncomfortable and agitated group for lunch. He insisted that they meet back again at 12:40 for just a few more minutes to discuss the new school mission statement and the new teacher evaluation forms. After the principal gave his blessing, everyone bolted out of the room. Several murmured about another beginning-of-the-year waste of time. Thomas mulled the best route to his car when he was met by a dark-skinned man in his late twenties.

"So you're the new kid," the man said, holding out his hand. "I'm Glen Bennett. I teach first grade—right underneath you."

"Nice to meet you, Mr. Bennett."

"*Glen*, my brother, please. We better not stand on ceremony, given that there's not much testosterone around here." Thomas laughed and the two men shook hands. The "new kid" began to say something, then stopped when he noticed his colleague looking cautiously from side to side as if they had been followed. Three women walked by speaking Spanish, oblivious of the two men. When they passed, Glen spoke again. "I've been here about six years now. You new to the system?"

He didn't know why, but Thomas looked around suspiciously, then simply nodded.

"Okay," the veteran teacher said. "The first rule when you're new here or anywhere—but especially here—is keep your eyes and ears open and your mouth closed. The whole place's got loose lips. Tell one person something in confidence at noon, and it'll be all over the building by 12:30 in English, Spanish, Creole and Chinese."

They walked down the hall to the first-grade room. After a click of the light, Thomas froze in amazement. The area came alive with pictures of dancing bears, floating butterflies, hopping jackrabbits and a whole zoo of wildlife in bright colors extolling the wonders of the alphabet. The walls had been painted a cheerful baby blue. The smell of fresh paint still hung faintly in the air. In one corner lay a plush carpet on which children could sit. In another stood several waist-high bookshelves loaded with children's books. Many other wonders accosted his senses, too numerous for Thomas to process.

"Wow!" he exclaimed.

Glen smiled with pride. "Like I said, I've been here for going on six years. It takes time to get things for your room. Yours'll look like this in a couple of years." He stepped closer to his mentee and reached for the lapel of his suit. "New kid on the block, huh? I've got a smock you can have, if you want." He paused, then nodded his head approvingly. "Nice suit, though." Again, they laughed.

"That's okay," Thomas answered. "I brought some overalls with me in the car. I just wore these for the morning meeting." He tried to sound convincing.

"Smart," Glen said. "Well, I'll let you go eat and change. There's all kinds of cheap restaurants down on Washington Street. See you back upstairs in half an hour." He reached for the parts to assemble a cardboard train set with big letters printed on the side.

The new fifth-grade teacher didn't really want to leave but knew not to overstay his welcome. He said good-bye, turned and walked out the door, which had been sprinkled with about two dozen large, yellow happy-face circles.

Thomas opened the trunk of his car, grabbed his overalls and weighed them in his hand. They were clean—he had never actually worn them—and heavy. He decided to just take off his jacket and tie, roll up his sleeves and try to not do any damage to the pants of his suit. He returned to the building, climbed the stairs and approached his room. Two women stood together directly across from his room, one short Asian, wearing glasses, and one Hispanic, wearing incredibly long hair that successfully fought the bracket on her head. They whispered to each other and eased over to him.

"Hi," the woman closer to him said softly. Thomas did not notice an accent at all when she spoke, as he had expected. "I'm Ms. Sanchez-Taylor. I'm your neighbor across the hall. I teach the fifth-grade bilingual class." She looked at her colleague.

"Good afternoon," the other woman joined in. "I'm Mrs. Chang. I'm in the classroom right next to yours. I teach fifth-grade, AWC," she added proudly with just a trace of an accent. "Advanced Work Class," she explained. "Although sometimes…" She chuckled. So did Thomas and Ms. Sanchez-Taylor. "It's too bad. I end up taking the high-achieving students who would be in your class. It's not fair," she admitted, flashing a smile. "But thanks!"

Thomas became intrigued. "So the kids who do well leave the regular education classes and go into a class just for them?"

The bilingual teacher spoke again. "That's right. Three students who would've been in my room this year will be in AWC instead because they scored high on the test they took last year."

"That's right," Mrs. Chang offered. "In fact, I think I got four who would've been in your class, Mr. Payne."

"How many do you have this year?" Ms. Sanchez-Taylor asked.

"I'll have fifteen," she answered. "Mr. Dorn let me take a peek at my class list." Mrs. Chang turned to Thomas. "There can't be more than sixteen in AWC," she explained without a hint of guilt. Wisely, she changed the subject. "Mr. Payne, we're all pulling for you with that group you've got—or should I say praying for you."

Thomas looked her straight in the eye. "You mean the so-called 'Wild Bunch?' I've heard a little talk. What's the story on them?"

The two women glanced at each other. Ms. Sanchez-Taylor broke the silence. "No one's told you about them?" Again, silence. This time Mrs. Chang provided the information. "That group's been the 'Class From Hell' since kindergarten. They started off on the wrong foot with some young gal right out of college. She came here with her head all filled up with that nonsense they teach those kids in school nowadays about discipline, you know." She waved her hand and rolled her eyes toward Ms. Sanchez-Taylor. They both nodded in agreement.

Thomas joined in the nonverbal acknowledgment. After all, he was the son of an award-winning teacher from Cincinnati, Ohio. He could hear his mother's voice: "Lord, Lord. I've got to unlearn another student teacher out of all of that mess she learned in college." Mom told him stories of student teachers reduced to tears inside of a week from taking the advice of professors, usually White professors, who hadn't taught school in twenty years and never taught at an inner-city school.

Mrs. Chang continued. "The next year, instead of giving those students to Mr. Bennett, who knows what to do with obstreperous kids, Mr. Dorn put Glen in second grade and gave them to another woman who couldn't even make them sit down for five minutes. They've been trouble for one year after the next ever since."

"Until this year," Thomas declared flatly.

The two women exchanged glances. Ms. Sanchez-Taylor clapped her hands. "All right, *amigo!*" she exclaimed, then took her turn to testify. "Mr. Dorn and Ms. Flores spent so much time dealing with that class. Poor Ms. Patterson. Last year she came this close to resigning." She held out her thumb and index finger about an inch apart. "I'll tell you this: If you can make that class fly straight, Mr. Dorn will make you permanent right away, and the rest of us will build a shrine in your honor." Her shoulders shook as she giggled.

"I'd prefer cash," Thomas retorted. All three laughed. The young man's spirits perked up. He loved a challenge. Also, the thought of being successful where others had failed appealed to him. "Thanks for the info," he said. "It was nice meeting you, Ms. Sanchez-Taylor and..." He paused for a brief second to jar his memory, "Ms. Chang."

"You too, and it's *Mrs.* Chang," she cautioned. "I'm naturalized but I've still got my Chinese ways."

"Sorry, *Mrs.* Chang," he corrected himself. "See you two downstairs in about..." He looked at his watch and frowned, "Fifteen minutes." All three dispersed into their respective classrooms. Thomas grew angry at himself for not getting any work done and swore that he would stay at school all night if necessary.

Back in the library, he endured another hour of business with his colleagues. He studied his watch every few minutes as the parade of forms, procedures and paperwork crept one by one through the stuffy, small school library. A little after 1:30 Mr. Dorn dismissed the teachers while reminding them that they were contractually obligated to stay in the building until 2:45 p.m. Thomas walked straight past a group of loitering teachers, down the hall and into his room.

After a few hours, he had reason to be pleased with his progress. The room had not been unclean, except for the windows. They had actually been stained from age and an assault of school-issued cheap, clear tape for over a generation. Apparently, Ms. Blufford was fond of covering the windows with cutesy knickknacks. Thomas tried to visualize her; probably one of those old-fashioned teachers who liked to keep things clean. She evidently did not want whoever took over the classroom to spend time cleaning up after her. She had cleared out almost everything and had even left a note:

Dear Room 217 Teacher:

You are welcome to keep whatever you find of use. Throw out what you don't want or take it down to the teacher's room for community property. Good luck and God bless.

Sincerely,

Pearl Blufford

Thomas foraged through six huge boxes sitting on the side counter of the classroom. He found mountains of useful materials: learning games, worksheet duplicating masters, bulletin board objects, transparencies, science kits, and computer software. At first, he thought that the previous tenant had left the objects behind by mistake. But, he reasoned, probably after a long and distinguished career as a classroom teacher, Ms. Blufford simply wanted to leave that life behind her and chart new waters.

After claiming those items of value to him, the new Room 217 occupant quickly repacked the boxes. He kept three and stuffed two boxes with materials to be thrown away. He carried one down to the teacher's room and stuffed it into a large shelf actually marked "Community Property."

Four teachers, all middle-aged, had gathered in the teacher's room chatting about how much they had to do. One asked Thomas how he was getting along. He answered that he had made progress and should get back upstairs before he got tired. After brief introductions and amenities, Thomas bought two fruit punch drinks at a soda machine, then left the busy teachers to their arduous tasks. As he closed the door, he could hear one of the teachers—the one sitting down—complain that there just wasn't enough time to do all that had to be done.

At about 6:30 Thomas declared aloud that his room was shaping up. Ms. Blufford had left a bucket, some towels and half a bottle of disinfectant cleaner by the sink. The new teacher filled the bucket with water from the boys' bathroom and washed off all of the furniture in the room. Then he organized the layout of the room the way he wanted it. Eventually, the discomfort of hunger began to creep up on him. While considering his dinner options, the door swung open, and the loud creak it produced startled him. J.J. appeared, jiggling a large set of keys.

"Sorry," he said. "Didn't mean to spook ya." He took two paces inside, inspected the surroundings and nodded his head. "Startin' to look all right in here." He turned his attention back to Thomas. "I just came to tell you that I'm gonna lock up soon." The short man reached in his pocket and put a cigarette in his mouth but didn't light it. As he talked the cigarette bobbed up and down on his lips, just like in the old black-and-white movies. "Something else, Mr. Payne. Everyone else is gone and you don't wanna leave your car in the back all by itself 'round here. Last year, a coupla teachers got their cars stolen or busted into. If you gonna work late, it's okay with me but pull your car onto the front so's it'll be safer."

"Thanks, J.J. I'll do that." Thomas replied. He remembered something the senior custodian had told him earlier. "Say, J.J., what happened to that young guy on your crew you told me about this morning? I don't recall seeing him today."

J.J. frowned. "Oh, Tony? Punk-ass White boy is 'bout as lazy as they come. Called in sick—again. When he's here he don't half work, with them damn earphones stuck in his ears, listening to that shit." The exasperated man parted his lips, revealing his clenched yellow teeth. Thomas tried to understand and wanted to exhibit his gratitude in some way. He noticed the floor again.

"Say, brother. The floors really look great."

The short, tired man broke into a half-smile. "Well, I try to do the best with what I got. The kids deserve that much." He moved to leave. "Don't forget to close your windows. You gotta go out the front door 'cause the back one's locked and the alarm's on. See you tomorrow—dressed smart this time." He laughed and disappeared down the hall.

Thomas closed the six huge windows in the room, grabbed his personal belongings and turned out the lights. He descended down the center stairway and exited the building, making sure to securely shut the huge, slightly warped, newly repaired front door. The evening air had turned a bit cooler. Some girls jumped double-Dutch across the street. One little girl in pigtails saw Thomas and said hello. He returned the greeting and walked around to the back. His ten-year-old red sportscar—a one-year project personally restored by his father and bestowed as a college graduation gift—awaited, conspicuously alone. Thomas staked out the area to make sure he had no company, took out his key ring, pointed it at his car and disarmed the security system. He entered and drove off in a hurry.

His apartment in Jamaica Plain, an integrated neighborhood in Boston adjacent to Roxbury, was in a simple three-family dwelling with a small living/dining room area but a large bedroom. The owner lived downstairs, while two smaller units occupied the second floor. The relatively new tenant climbed the stairs, balancing a box of still very hot Chinese food as he unlocked the door and turned on the lights.

He inspected his castle for a few seconds. A mound of dirty dishes accumulated from the past three days soaked in the kitchen sink. Three living room tables hosted stacks of mail, books and discs—both music and computer. Recently ordered movies (vintage stock from the 1950's) had been precariously stacked on the top of a large television. Thick computer manuals and software filled a plush, black swivel chair near an old desk with a ketchup-stained cordless phone perched on top of the pile. Peering into the bedroom, Thomas spotted his king-sized bed, which hadn't been made since the last time he changed the sheets—a week ago. A tall wicker basket next to the bed overflowed with dirty laundry. On the floor lay an open guitar case; the electric guitar leaned against the wall. The shirt he had worn to church on Sunday relaxed over the amplifier. Two suits he had decided not to wear posed with open arms on top of the bed. A set of clean, blue socks lay next to them.

He closed the large picture window and turned on the air-conditioner, then threw his mail on the center living room table. It was all junk anyway, he thought while hunting for the remote control to the television. Frustrated after a five-minute search, he reached and turned it on by hand. An attractive woman stood in front of an old school pontificating about the upcoming first day of classes in Boston. Thomas frantically foraged for his remote, finally recovering it under a pile of books, but by the time he turned up the volume, the reporter had given her name and signed off. "Hell," he muttered. He searched for his telephone so that he could retrieve his messages and ate while listening.

"Hi, honey. It's Mom. How'd your first day go? I know the kids weren't there but I'm sure you had fun. Give us a call when you get in. Have you heard from your brother lately? We got a letter from him today. He's doing as well as can be expected. Well, I'd better go before I get cut off again. Your dad and I are very proud of you. Bye!"

Two more messages followed; one from a college friend, reminding Thomas about playing basketball on Saturday and another from the pastor of his church, thanking him for agreeing to teach Sunday school. Then came the final message. The second her familiar voice stung his ears, Thomas sat up. He laid his beef with broccoli on top of an uneven pile of newspapers on the floor.

"Hi, Thomas. It's me, Laura. I just wanted to call to say hi and see how you are. I spoke to your mother earlier. She said today was your first day at school. I hope it went well." The voice paused. "I know I shouldn't be calling, but I just wanted to see how you were getting along. Call me—no, don't call. I-I'm going to go. Bye."

Energy returned to Thomas's body. He picked up the phone, dialed the unforgettable number and listened. His heartbeat intensified with each ring.

Laura wasn't in and he couldn't think of what to say so he hung up rather than leave a message. The excited man looked at his watch and surmised that she was probably at the library. He turned off the TV, grabbed his jacket, stuffed his dinner in the refrigerator and bolted out the door.

A half-hour later Thomas drove into the parking lot of the Boston College Law School Library in Newton. The semester had not yet resumed so only a handful of students lurked about. The lone non-law student searched and recognized his former fiancée's car. He was delighted and a little embarrassed at the same time. Still, he pushed open the right double-door in the back of the building and quietly trudged in. His hands scanned the marble walls as he slowly climbed the stairs to the second floor where Laura usually studied. His heart pounded fiercely at the thought of seeing her again. Thomas stepped past the electronic scanner to the left of the reference desk and slowly moved towards the back of the room. He became aware that the floor of the room squeaked, something he had not noticed before. He peered through a shelf full of books on tort laws and saw who he had come to see—and someone else.

His Laura, dressed in designer jeans and a designer white cotton blouse sat at a table accompanied by a stack of books and a handsome, young African American man, not a law student but certainly cut from that mold. He seemed to be about five years older than Thomas. He wasn't as tall, at least from what anyone could tell sizing up a seated man. He had very short hair and a thin beard. His blue silk tie hung about two inches from his neck. His expensive-looking leather briefcase rested at the corner of their battered wooden table. The jacket to his expensive-looking suit hugged the chair to his right. Laura, as lovely and poised as ever, whispered something to her companion and silently laughed. They sat together close enough for Thomas to recognize that they meant something to each other. Exactly what, he did not wait to find out.

Driving home two minutes later, Thomas chastised himself for jumping offside by racing to Newton and making a complete ass out of himself. He took some comfort in the fact that no one had seen him. It was nearly 9 o'clock, and he still had to cut out pictures for his bulletin board. The night air had turned cooler, and the stars shone brightly in a cloudless sky. The moon was barely visible. Thomas could see several constellations posing in the dark heavens. He put on some Miles Davis and let his mind drift to

Laura's words on that momentous day nearly four months ago. "I love you but I can't marry you," she said. "I need someone more mature," she said. "I think you should want more out of life—not that I don't respect your mother and her profession," she said. Thomas shifted into fourth gear and sped home. All of a sudden he was very hungry.

Cooler and less humid air greeted the next morning. The meteorologists predicted a partly cloudy day and rain for the afternoon. Although he had slept very poorly, Thomas went to work at 7: 30 a.m., forty-five minutes early. Throughout the morning, he heard a few teachers griping about the news report on Channel 9: how poorly the students in the Boston Public School system were doing, according to the latest test scores. Several teachers at the Adams called the whole news story biased and racist.

Thomas worked in his classroom while listening to "oldies" music on a small radio. He brought tools from home and successfully repaired a few broken student desks, his own chair and two of the windows. The latter opened with ease but refused to be so agreeable in closing. He did not possess the talents of his father, a former mechanical engineer, who took his pension and opened his own booming auto garage in Cincinnati, but Thomas thought that his dad would be pleased that at least one of his sons had listened to him.

The outside world notwithstanding, at 8:15 everyone received a summons to the school library. At least this time, a stand-up oscillating fan offered relief to the agitated group, courtesy of Ms. Higgins, the school "librarian." (She was actually a paraprofessional aide with a year of community college training in liberal arts. The Boston Public School Department employed few full-fledged college-educated librarians.) Thomas's thoughts faded in and out during the meeting. He could not devote his full attention to the issues presented, due to lack of sleep and haunting images from the previous evening. He had little experience with being the jealous one but could not escape replaying the image of Laura sitting in that room enjoying herself with another man. Was he a successful corporate lawyer who made a six-figure salary? How long had they been seeing each other? Had they spent the night making love? Thomas shook the last question from his head.

At 8:35 he stood in the schoolyard with all of the other teachers clutching his class list as if it were the Holy Grail. The air was warm but dry, and the sun easily avoided the few clouds in the sky. Almost everyone except Mr. Dorn, Ms. Flores and Thomas emerged unadorned by the accouterments of an outer jacket. In fact, Thomas expressed silent surprise at the casual dress of several teachers. Some wore jeans! He shuddered to think what his mother would say if she bore witness to such behavior. Thomas felt conspicuously tall again. At an elementary school, with the population almost exclusively small children and women, a six-feet, four-inch, 220-pound male could hardly go unnoticed. Yesterday, he had overheard two of the female para-professional aides (referred to as "paras") comment about him being so cute. The athletic man took it all in stride. He had gotten used to such talk from his college days. He knew not to investigate further because his father had often warned him not to let flattery go to his head and not to shit where he ate.

Thirty-two names appeared on Thomas's class list. Earlier, Mr. Dorn had assured him that some on the list would not return to the Adams this year. In fact, the principal knew of one who had been arrested for setting fires and was being detained at a juvenile detention center. Yesterday, the Boston Teacher's Union building representative had advised each teacher about the class size limit according to the contract. Thomas could have no more than twenty-eight students. The building rep repeated Mr. Dorn's assertion that not all of the students on the list would return. Thomas told her he knew of one who would not.

One by one, the parents of several fifth-grade students approached Mr. Payne, introduced themselves and presented a child who would be in his class. Thomas found himself meeting almost exclusively with women. Most of the them acknowledged the difficulties from the previous years. Several expressed relief that a male would teach the fifth grade. Of course, privately they assured the new teacher that their child had not been the cause of trouble; the disruptions had originated from others in the class.

Thomas was pleased to see so many children frolicking about like the little ponies or tiger cubs he watched on televised documentaries. He counted maybe a dozen or so White or Asian students in the yard; most looked frightened and clung closely to their parents. (Later, Thomas discovered that every one was a fourth- or fifth-grade Advanced Work student.) As he inspected the playground, in the corner of his left eye he caught the glimpse of one very cute, well-dressed but diffident Hispanic girl slowly approaching him. She wore a powder-blue skirt with a white blouse. Thomas suspected that the child was new to the Adams and confused about where to go. She seemed upset. When she finally reached an audible distance, she spoke hesitantly and softly.

"Excuse me, Mr. Payne, but I'm not supposed to be in your class. I'm supposed to be with Ms. Sanchez-Taylor," she announced in a sad and lonely voice while pointing to a group of students about ten feet away.

Thomas gave her his full attention, then examined his class list. "You are? Well, let me see, honey," he replied. "What's your name?"

"Maria," she answered. "Maria Colón."

"Well, Maria. It says here that you're in my class. See?" He shared his list with the obviously frightened girl.

Her eyes began to fill with water. "No, Mr. Payne," she stated incredulously. "I was in Ms. Valdez's class last year. I'm supposed to be in a bilingual class." Her cheeks soaked with falling tears.

Thomas understood and tried to comfort her with the encouragement of his voice. He spoke quietly. "Maria, I'm sure that you're a very good student. Is that right?"

The young girl nodded.

"Well," he continued. "It looks like you've done so well that they thought it was time to move you out of a bilingual class and into my class full-time." He paused and smiled at her. I bet you won a lot of awards last year in school, right?"

"I was on the Honor Roll all year in Ms. Valdez's class and in Ms. Garcia's class too," she answered proudly, her voice stronger.

"Sure, sure, I knew it," Thomas replied. "Now, I'll tell you what. I promise that if you work hard for me like you've always done, you'll have a good year. I'll bet that—"

They were suddenly interrupted by two tall African American boys who ran near them playfully shouting at each other. Maria became fearful again. Thomas scowled at the two boys and motioned with his hand for them to move on—*immediately.* They did. Standing in the middle of the schoolyard with scores of bodies moving about, he resumed his private talk with Maria. "You're probably worried about the class. I promise you, there'll be no trouble out of them this year. Will you trust me?"

Maria moved her head again.

"Now, honey, look at my list. Is there anyone else's name you recognize who was with you in Ms. Valdez's class—or someone who's your friend?"

Maria examined the list. "Him, Hernando," she replied, pointing. Her breath smelled pepperminty from toothpaste. "And her, Carmelita!" Her voice suggested pleasant surprise.

Thomas looked around. "Do you see either of them?" Maria perused the area and pointed at a taller girl standing only a few feet away. She wore a dark-blue skirt with a sky-blue blouse and struggled with the decision of whether or not to wear her glasses. "Carmelita," Thomas called gently. The girl put on a pair of wire-framed glasses and walked slowly towards both of them. He spoke gingerly. "Carmelita, I'm Mr. Payne. You're in my class, this year. You know that already?"

"*Si*, yes sir," she answered. "My mother told me." She did not show emotion about the class assignment one way or the other.

"Fine, fine. It's going to be all right. We're going to have a great year, I promise. But do something for me, *por favor*? Stay with Maria here until we go inside, okay? She's a little nervous about the first day of school." Thomas then placed Maria's hand in Carmelita's. He primed himself to offer further reassurance to Maria, but the two girls ran off together, laughing and speaking in Spanish.

Within twenty minutes the schoolyard emptied. Thomas and his brood filed into their classroom. Inside, a huge banner above the chalkboard exhorted, "WELCOME TO FIFTH GRADE AT THE ADAMS." Thomas had arranged the desks, broken and bent as they were, so that the class divided into two equal sections facing each other. A vacant center runway separated the two sections but provided the teacher with easy access to both. His desk, already covered with books and papers, had been pushed into a far corner away from the students. A large table, also covered with books and papers, kept it company. The clean room bore countless markings from decades of use.

Unoriginal but meaningful artwork graced the walls and doors. Pictures of famous African American and Hispanic American heroes and heroines hung all over the room. Icons like Booker T. Washington, Harriet Tubman and Cesar Chavez watched over everyone who entered. Posters displaying sagacious words from revered living and departed souls reminded the new Room 217 tenants of their mission. "Determination + Discipline + Hard Work = Success," admonished famed teacher Jaime Escalante. "Education is our passport to the future, for tomorrow belongs to people who prepare for it today," cautioned Malcolm X. "If there is no struggle, there is no progress," pronounced Frederick Douglass.

After everyone claimed a seat, Thomas took preliminary attendance. Most seemed to know about one lad's brush with the law and its consequence. Several students offered remarks about other absent students when Thomas called their names. Two students had come to the wrong class; one large boy abdicated to the fourth grade, and one doe-eyed Caucasian girl received an immediate transfer to the Advanced Work Class. The latter seemed profoundly relieved when she left. Within twenty minutes, one boy entered Payneland from the bilingual room and another girl from Mrs. Chang's. After all movement ceased, the final count for Room 217 came to twenty-four pupils, every one Black or Hispanic.

Thomas gave each student a handout of a short story to read and five questions to answer, partly busy work to get them settled and partly to see how well they could read and comprehend. He was then able to tape a three-by-five-inch name card onto the front of each student's desk. After exactly twenty minutes he announced that time had expired. Several students pleaded for just a little more time but to no avail. Thomas noticed that Maria had finished completely and asked her to collect the work. When she gave him the papers, he winked at her and she smiled back.

After going over the *Boston Public School Disciplinary Code* and instructing the students to return it signed by their parents by the next school day, Thomas came to the most important part of the day. He would submit the classroom ground rules and the "Introduction to the fifth grade with Mr. Payne" remarks. Two people had influenced his choice of how to begin the school year, his mother and his college football coach.

His mother, an elementary teacher beginning her twenty-first year, had brought Thomas to school with her on numerous occasions. Regardless of what grade she taught—and she had taught everything from kindergarten to eighth grade—Mom was firm. She had grown up in Tennessee and attended an all-Black Catholic school. (Thomas, his sister and his brother had all attended private Catholic schools before college.) "Never let your students see you smile until Thanksgiving," she would admonish her son. But he also recognized how much his mother loved teaching and loved her students. At the end of every year, she cried when they left, as did they.

"In all my years of coaching, I have never seen such sorry sacks of shit and I've been doing this for twenty-three years," Benjamin "Brick Wall"

Wahlberg, head football coach for the Ohio State Buckeyes, announced shaking his head. "You lazy, tit-sucking mamas boys think you can play football? I've seen better hustling from the cheerleaders!" he bellowed. "All of you think you're hot shit because you were big-time stars in high school or made the team last year." He ripped his sunglasses off his face and banged them on his clipboard. "Well, I've got news for you: On my team EVERYBODY starts over! Nobody's gonna be given nothing. I don't give a damn what you did last year. Most of you rat fucks'll be cut in the next two weeks. You're the lucky ones." The coach cleared his throat. His face grew red and sweat beaded on his forehead. "Because those of you who make the team are gonna wish you hadn't. I'm gonna kick your sorry, lazy asses all over this field until you drop!"

Thomas had decided to start out tough. He knew that a tough teacher found it easier to lighten up after seizing control of his class, while a light teacher found it difficult to get tough after having lost it. He took out the class ground rules and gave them to a tall boy to distribute, one of the rambunctious ones he had met outside while comforting Maria. Unfortunately, the boy could not seem to avoid the feet of several classmates while making his deliveries. Thomas approached him.

"Thank you anyway, Asa. I'll take them." He held out his hand.

"I didn't do nothing. It was them. They got big feet!" the boy answered with a hearty laugh and thorough scan of the classroom audience. Thomas said nothing but stood before his student with his hand open. "I didn't even do nothing. I swear. It was them!" Asa protested. Thomas continued his stance, displaying no emotion at all. "Okay, okay," the youngster conceded. "I'll be more careful." He attempted to position himself on the other side of his teacher but found the path blocked. At first, most of the spectators laughed at their classmate's antics, but soon the room grew silent. The two stood in the middle of the runway staring at each other. The boy's smile evaporated and he gently placed the papers in the man's hand and sat down, mumbling about not even doing nothing.

"First down," Thomas thought to himself. He chose a small boy with a closely cropped haircut to finish the task Asa had started. When everyone had a sheet, the rookie teacher stood in the middle of the room again.

Thomas believed that securing informed consent of the classroom rules provided everyone involved with a mutual starting place. In this case, the kids and their parents would be aware of teacher expectations—and the expectations would be in writing. The presentation of written ground rules was a procedure he had appropriated from his association with Revelations, Inc. during his senior year in college.

He waved a sheet of paper in the air and delivered his introduction. "What you have in your hands are the ground rules for the class. All classes have rules. These are ours. It's important to—"

"Mr. Payne?" An innocent-looking, hazel-eyed girl held up her hand. Thomas looked at her name card.

"Please don't call my name, Christine," he instructed. "I can see your hand."

Her eyes grew as wide as plums. "I'm sorry," she said genuinely. "I just wanted to know will we get to vote on these?"

"We?" Thomas furled his eyebrows. "We?" he asked again. "*We* don't need to, Christine," he answered. "*I* already did." The man continued. "As I was saying, it's important for you and your parents to know what I expect of you. With the class ground rules here in writing, now you do. You'll get two copies of these rules; one for you and one to take home. Make sure your folks get them. Read them to yourself silently. Then we'll go over them one by one." The entire class grew quiet as they studied.

Ground Rules, Room 217, Grade 5

1. *Attendance*: Be present every day. Be on time. ALL absences require parent or doctor's note.
2. *Homework*: Checked first thing in the morning. Complete every day by deadline.
3. *Food, gum*: Eating only allowed in cafeteria during lunch period or special events. Gum chewing not allowed on school grounds. No food in the student's desk. (Students caught eating during class required to bring same treat for the entire class.) No food outside in the playground.
4. *Bathroom*: Only during morning and afternoon breaks, taken by the entire class *in silence.*
5. *Point system*: One point per day per student for Movie Day at end of month. 80% of total possible points needed for movie. Point for every day of the week puts student on "All-Star List." Point for every day of the month puts student on "Superstar List." All students present and with homework completed is an "All-Star Day," earning an extra recess.
6. *Talking*: Raise hand and wait to be addressed.
7. *Leaving seat*: Request permission.
8. *Materials*: 2 pencils, eraser, crayons, scissors (optional). Important: Pay for all lost school materials. Hardcover books must be covered.

9. *Library cards*: Every student MUST have a Boston Public Library card (due last Friday of September). Card must be free and clear of all fines, overdue books, etc.
10. *Entering, leaving building*: Enter building only with class in the morning. Remain until end of school day. If dismissed early by parent permission, must have parent or note from parent.
11. *Entering the classroom*: Must be accompanied by another student or teacher.
12. *Emergency cards*: Teacher must know how to reach parent or guardian during day and evening.
13. *Hallway behavior*: Quiet at all times, walking only.
14. *Cafeteria behavior*: Well-mannered, respectful to adults. Stay in the cafeteria.
15. *Special classes*: Total respect, obedience (Art, P.E., Music, etc.).
16. *Student of the Week*: Has total authority in teacher's absence.
17. *Buddies*: Student will choose own buddy. Check homework, assists each other for entire year. To be chosen Student of the Week, buddy must have point for every day in school that week.
18. *Class meeting*: Can be requested by any student for good reason.
19. *Class project*: The entire class will be involved in a "giving" project, performing community service for the school.
    Special Issues:
20. *Lying*: Automatic "grounding" for one week.
21. *Fighting*: Teacher supports principal in issuing suspension.
22. *Bringing of weapons*: Automatic suspension.
23. *Play items during class*: Taken by teacher and NOT returned.
24. *Stealing*: Automatic removal of seat from class space.
25. *Refusal to obey order from teacher*: Left behind on next field trip, possibly all future field trips.

Thomas could hear the youngsters gasp and whisper to each other as they read the document. Each new line brought further shock and dismay. Every few minutes a student's eyes would widen and a hand would rise. The fifth-grade instructor matter-of-factly announced that questions would be answered when he reviewed the rules with the entire class and not before.

He took the opportunity to glance at the reading exercise the students had completed, or attempted to complete. Only a handful answered all five questions. Most printed their responses. About half gave short answers to open-ended questions. The majority got no further than the third item. One student's paper was virtually blank. Thomas looked up at the clock, set the papers on his desk and called for their attention.

"Class," he said. "If you look at rule number four, you will see that we will go to the bathroom as a group and return as such. That means, you will go then and only then. There will be no students from 217 wandering around the halls alone."

Thomas instructed that they form two lines by the door; one for girls and one for boys. He chose a well-groomed girl named Deborah to supervise the girls and a well-groomed boy named Angel to take charge of the boys. He admonished them that their individual recess time later depended on leaving and returning quietly. While leaving their seats to gather at the door, the students casually conversed with one another. Thomas casually strolled over to the door. He smiled at his pupils. A few smiled back.

"Everyone sit down," he calmly commanded, pointing behind them. Complaints surfaced before most complied. A few standing in the front of the line closest to the door looked imploringly at their teacher. His lack of expression advised them that such performances were futile. "I said *everyone* sit down," he repeated louder. Gradually, they all did. Thomas smirked. "What's it to me if you go to the bathroom or not? If you want to go, you'll line up with your mouths closed. We'll not disturb the other classes. Do I make myself clear?" A few half-hearted responses drifted toward him. He pushed farther, exclaiming, "I said, do I make myself clear?" and received unanimous acknowledgment.

The youngsters gathered and returned to their seats twice more for the same infraction. The third time occurred after a few members had walked down the hall and reached the bathroom door. The students became very frustrated, tired, hot and now angry at this tyrant. "Don't be angry at me," Thomas rebutted. "Talk to Maurice and Asa." Several students eyed the two boys with seething rage. Some told the boys that they'd *better* be quiet next time or else.

"Mr. Payne," Maurice said earnestly. "I just told Asa to move up a little 'cause—"

"I don't know what you were talking about. It's none of my business. I said line up quietly. Either you can do that or you can't!" Thomas shot back. Maurice lowered his head. Asa, seated at the back of the room, endured a host of dirty looks.

"Okay," Thomas commanded. "Let's try it one more time." He thought for a second. "And one more thing." He looked around. "Make sure you stay in a straight line the whole time, or we'll spend your recess time practicing forming a straight line. Wouldn't that be fun?" No one replied but a few shook their heads, apparently voting no. The man turned to Deborah and stretched out his muscular arm. "Ladies first." This time, the entire group made it into the bathroom without being stopped.

"Another first down," the rookie teacher thought to himself.

Thomas stood in the middle of the hall and watched his students standing straight as soldiers and quiet. He praised them in a hushed tone while they waited for their classmates to join them. "I'm proud," he whispered. "You're going to be a terrific group."

The boys finished first. One of them stood in the hall directly in front of a huge bulletin board displaying several airplanes loaded with books. The boy, Gary, loved airplanes. He had decorated his room with model airplanes of various sizes, shapes and material that took hours to assemble. He stared at the impressive scene and reached for one of the cardboard airplanes to see how it had been constructed.

"No, don't touch it," an adult voice snapped.

The boy jerked his hand away and held it at his side. In a few minutes Deborah came out with the last of the girls. She stepped to the head of the line. Thomas did not speak but pointed at her, then towards the classroom door at the other end of the hall. The girls moved. Thomas motioned for Angel, heading the boys' line, to walk behind the last girl.

While the class plodded along, Mr. Dorn and Ms. Flores appeared from the other end of the hall. They had come to check on the bottom third of the Adams's senior class. Perhaps they could assist Mr. Payne by reading the riot act to these historically troublesome youths on the first day of school—sort of a pre-emptive strike. While rehearsing and choreographing their performance, they were suddenly seized with awe at the spectacle approaching them. Mr. Dorn put his hands on his face. Ms. Flores put her right hand on her heart. The students they had come to forewarn walked past the two administrators without uttering a word. They marched into the classroom with shouts of "excellent" and "wonderful" following them from the principal and assistant principal. Thomas, standing next to his desk, heard a remark from an unknown student.

"Not yet," he barked. "I'll tell you when." He turned to Deborah. "Everybody quiet?" Deborah shook her head from side to side.

"Cleo and Christine were talking," she reported. The two accused girls protested immediately.

"Quiet!" Thomas ordered. He gazed at Cleopatra with steel-cold eyes. "Okay, you first."

The very tall, thin girl with her hair in lavish braids pointed at her alleged co-malefactor. "Christine cut me in the bathroom, and I told her that I was first." She scrunched up her mouth and put her hand on her jaw. "That's all I said."

Thomas turned his face towards Christine. She was a heavy-set girl wearing brand-new blue jeans that made noise when she made the slightest movement. "And you?"

"I was first," she answered. "I told Cleo that she had to wait her turn. She always be cu'in people." At that point she folded her arms across her developing chest.

"Sounds like you two were talking. Both of you stay at your desks during recess."

The boys faired even worse. Four of them received instructions to stay in their seats during recess for similar small but technical infractions. Thomas was determined to maintain a "zero tolerance" atmosphere, at least for the time being.

The new teacher turned to address Mr. Dorn and Ms. Flores but they had vacated the doorway. He gave all but the six marked students five minutes to get out of their seats and talk to each other. After exactly five minutes he resumed reviewing the classroom ground rules. Another student recommended that they vote on the rules, but Thomas dismissed the idea with a short reply.

"Almighty God did not give Moses the Ten *Suggestions*," he said.

From time to time throughout the morning, frequent interruptions echoed from the intercom. Thomas became annoyed but understood. However, he fostered less understanding about the shortage of textbooks for every subject. Expecting that at least four more students would appear within the next few days, Thomas had no idea how he would adequately progress from day to day. He made a mental note to speak to Mr. Dorn after school.

The young teacher gave the entire class an impromptu multiplication quiz of twenty-five single-digit problems to complete in two-and-a-half minutes. He watched them. His mother had taught him to observe not just the product but the process. Thomas shook his head in disbelief. Many students used their fingers to count to the answers, obviously not knowing the facts from memory. Some attempted to figure out the problems by drawing numerous slashes on the back of the paper. Most did not complete the quiz. After time had expired, each student received another's paper, and they corrected the quiz in class. The minimum passing mark: fifteen correct. Only nine of them had passed.

Later, right before lunch, Thomas strongly suggested that each student thank the lunch server after being served. Then he escorted the class down the stairs to the cafeteria, only to bring them back to the classroom twice, once for talking in the hallway and once for pushing and skipping past each other in the lunch line. Because they were the last group to eat, no one from Room 217 stepped out into the schoolyard for recess.

More interruptions sprinkled the remainder of the school day. Thomas finished reading only half of a mystery story aloud and assigned that every student write a full-page ending. He gave the students ten math problems to solve on a worksheet and acknowledged that the first day of school had all but come to a close. The bell rang for dismissal preparation at 2:30. Fifteen minutes later, all students had vacated the premises. Two hours later, Thomas finished his first day as a teacher.

That evening Thomas called his parents. He enjoyed a close relationship with both of them. He appreciated his mother's passion and dedication to education—passion and dedication which had inspired him to pursue the same career. His mom never yearned to become an administrator, but Thomas believed that the best way to influence a system was to become a leader within that system. His senior-year enrollment in the Revelations programs had, among other matters, helped him become clear about his professional vision. He aspired to be a principal. He admired his mother's openness and zest for life.

His father, on the other hand, was more subdued, more thoughtful. He smiled a lot but not broadly and enjoyed solitude and working with things more than people. A mechanical engineering graduate from Ohio State, Gabriel Payne used fewer words than his wife but always managed to get his point across. When he decided to leave a well-paying job after twenty years—and take his pension with him—to open his own auto garage, Thomas remembered how his mother fretted and worried, while his dad calmly assured her that everything would be all right. With business booming because of his father's reputation for honesty and high-quality work, both father and son now regale each other by exchanging glances and smiles whenever they hear his mother assure her friends that she always knew "Gabriel's Garage" would be a hit.

Thomas loved his parents for their support and friendship. He didn't understand his friends who frequently spoke disparagingly about their parents. He always expressed shock to hear about a family's drinking, drugs, or other problems based on parent selfishness, abuse or neglect. To him, his parents were the tops. They had sacrificed and freely given so that their three children would have ample opportunities in life.

The last thought lingered in his mind as he opened the letter from his brother, the one that had been waiting on his living room table for twenty-four hours. Thomas still harbored resentment at his brother for hurting his parent's with his recklessness. He ripped open the envelope, grabbed the paper inside and unfolded it.

Dear Little Brother,

Things are going better for me these days. I'm still waiting to hear about my appeal. My lawyer says that I've got a good chance. I expect to hear something by the end of next month. There's not much of a life here for a cop on the inside. I'm praying that God will be merciful and let me have just one more chance.

I haven't heard from April or the kids. I write but I never get a reply. I guess I can't blame her for being angry. Mom said she would look in on the kids for me. If you are in town for Thanksgiving, maybe you can pay me a visit—if I'm still here, that is (I hope not). Maybe we'll both be at the house enjoying Mom's sweet potato pie.

How are you doing? I hope this letter reaches you in time for opening day at your school. I know you will be a great teacher. Well, I'm not much for writing so I'll end here. Take care of yourself, little brother. God bless you.

Love,

Edward

Thomas put the letter back in the envelope and threw it back on the table. He promised himself that he would write his brother back during the weekend. He got up and began straightening up his apartment. Tomorrow, some of the guys were coming over to play cards after they all shot a few hoops.

Thursday got off to a rocky start between Thomas and his students. First, eight of them brought excuses instead of homework. To his request for a one-page ending to the mystery story, most brought far less. Too often, as he stood next to each student and examined the contents of his or her desk, he counted at least one missing item. In all, he kept fourteen in for recess and angrily promised that their parents would receive a call that evening. The first-year teacher added that he would surely keep them after school if they chose to be so derelict again.

To make matters worse, the next day Mr. Dorn all but guaranteed that no new textbooks would be ordered. Also, another new student came to school, leaving only one empty desk. Thomas had no idea what to do if more than one new pupil showed up for school on Monday. Somehow, he got through the day. A few minutes before dismissal prep he had the class form a circle in the middle of the room. Every Friday he planned to gather his team. He clenched his teeth and spoke forcefully.

"The first three days of school have come and gone. So far, I do NOT like what I've seen." He squinted as he scanned their faces one by one. "You think you can come into my classroom and get credit for just showing up? Forget it! Nobody's getting a free ride in my classroom!" The students were taken aback by their teacher's crescendoing voice. "You had a good time last year, huh? You showed Ms. Patterson how smart you were, huh? You thought it was funny wasting Mr. Dorn's and Ms. Flores's time last year, huh?" He kept slapping them in the face with his cold, icy stares. "Don't make the mistake of thinking that I'm Ms. Patterson. You're going to leave fifth grade as winners, who've given your best, or you'll be back here with me next year, so help me God!" Several students glanced at each other fearfully.

Abruptly, the head coach changed his tone. "Listen, we come from a great people. We do. Maybe no one's told you that. Take a minute and look at the pictures of these heroes and heroines around you." He pointed. "They fought and died so that you'd have a chance at an education that doesn't cost your family a dime." Thomas thumped his chest. "Our people have been kings and queens, scientists, mathematicians, artists and inventors." He lowered his voice solemnly. "Ladies and gentlemen, you ARE the senior class this year. The little kids here from kindergarten on up are watching you. They want to be like you." Thomas continued earnestly. "Let me ask you this: There are two other fifth-grade classes here. Which class is going to walk out of here in June known as the best fifth-graders the Adams has ever had? Will it be 219, 216 or 217?"

"Two-seventeen," the class shot back.

"Can't hear you," Thomas replied, putting his hands to his ears.

"Two-seventeen!" they said louder.

"Okay, that's better." He extended his strong right arm into their midst. "Everyone put your hand in here and let's tell everyone who's the best class at the Adams." With some contortions, they all put their hands in the middle of the circle and called out their room number one more time. Thomas felt much better about the day.

That weekend he called the caretakers of almost every student in his class. *Almost* every student because three did not have working telephones. Too often the calls lasted far longer than Thomas had intended because so many had a tendency to launch into what he would later coin the "Soap Opera," the sad saga of bad luck that had befallen the family. Thomas always listened politely when the caretaker launched into the story. He felt compassion for the teller and the child involved, but did not see how a father abandoning the family years ago meant a fifth-grader could not do homework to the best of his/her ability.

Also, Thomas had acquired his mother's tendency to believe that people often created their own bad luck. He had heard Mom utter comments like "She should have thought about that before she had all of those kids with no husband," or "Shouldn't have been there in the first place and it wouldn't have happened," or "Go out and get a job and get a life." Thomas believed that everyone deserved a helping hand, but no one should expect a free ride. No story would persuade him to let any of his students off the hook.

The following week continued to be a struggle. True to his word, Thomas kept several pupils after school, and he skipped lunch to stay in with students who had not completed assignments or had not done well on them. (He refused to place an F on a homework paper, instead marking it with the initials "DA," for "Do Again.") Eventually, two more new students arrived. Serendipity arrived with them; chairs and desks were found for their benefit.

The second Friday of school also arrived, and Thomas chose his first class leader as Student of the Week. Out of twenty-seven students, only a few had shown enough consistent leadership and responsibility to be trusted with so important a position. About a half-dozen had come to school every day, ready and willing to work, in Thomas's judgment. He chose a handsome, white toothed, dark-skinned boy named Melvin Dilettante as his first Student of the Week. Melvin's family originated from Haiti. His father and mother were together and legally married, a rarity among the families of Room 217 children. The entire Dilettante family had come to the Adams on the first day of school; dad, mom, grandmom and the two older sisters, both very pretty. Melvin, the youngest, had only a trace of his family's regal-sounding accent. They all exuded a proud but unhaughty air about them.

First, Thomas approached the bulletin board especially created for the honor. In big, multicolored letters the words "Student of the Week" stretched across the board. Underneath the words, seven criteria were listed:

1. Leadership
2. Responsibility
3. Plays to win
4. Attendance
5. Behavior
6. Homework
7. Takes care of buddy

A blank spot for a name had been left in the center of the display, soon to be revealed. Thomas gathered his team into a circle and described what he expected from the class leader. He called on a volunteer to read one of the seven requirements, then another until all had been proclaimed. To everyone's surprise, the man played soft music and turned off all the lights. Then he placed Melvin in the center of the circle and announced his appointment. The class broke into genuine, respectful applause.

The first-year teacher hung a laminated gold sign around Melvin's neck that read "Student of the Week" and informed everyone that for the duration of his one-week term, Melvin would be addressed as "Captain" because he served as captain of the team. Thomas presented the new leader with a small cardboard box filled with a collection of gifts, from which he could choose one. Melvin chose a new pen, then changed his mind and chose a fancy, bright red ruler. Thomas explained that the Captain had his total trust, and anywhere on John Adams School territory he was to be obeyed without delay or argument.

Thomas had also set up a bulletin board honoring the first all-stars, those who had earned every point for the week by attending school every day, bringing in their homework and exhibiting exemplary behavior. Nine students saw their names included on the All-Star List. The list would be posted every week, Thomas declared. Next week everyone would start all over again. After the final wrap-up and group cheer, Melvin dismissed the class.

After all the students had gone, Thomas sat at his desk, scanning and wincing at the results of the first spelling test. He heard a loud creak by the door, then a soft voice called his name. He looked to the left and saw Maria standing in the doorway, as unassuming as ever. He glanced at the papers once more, furled his eyebrows and shook his head, then greeted her with a smile.

"Yes, Maria. Did you forget something?"

"No, Mr. Payne." She did not meet his gaze. "I wanted to ask you something."

"What is it, honey?"

"If I work real hard like you told the class . . . " She paused and her voice trailed off. Thomas said nothing but waited patiently. She started over. "If I work real hard like you told the class, do you think I could be Student of the Week someday?" She looked down at her new sneakers, obviously embarrassed.

Thomas found it difficult to retain his self-protective, cautionary air. He stood and stepped closer to Maria. "Sweetie, of course you could. Why, when your time comes, I know you'll make a fine Student of the Week—and I expect your time to come very soon. You just keep on working hard and making me proud, like you always do, and your name will be on that board before you know it."

Maria turned to leave and Thomas escorted her down the center stairway. When they said good-bye at the front door, she flashed a beautiful, sweet smile, tempting Thomas to offer some sort of contact but he resisted.

The following week Thomas required that each member of the class choose a buddy. He reminded them that they would be buddies for the remainder of the school year. He placed the entire class in a wide circle and encouraged them to form meaningful pairs with the song "Lean on Me" playing in the background. Maria and Carmelita chose each other right away. Toward the end of the process some of the less popular students, hurt and embarrassed, chose each other by default. Thomas made a mental note to make sure that they received extra praise and encouragement for the next few days.

The notion of being required to choose a buddy was not original. While a participant in the Revelations Phase II and III programs, Thomas had been so obligated. He and his buddy still maintained their friendship, although it spanned several hundred miles. His buddy, Peter, a blond-haired attorney who had recently move to California, had sent him an e-mail message just a couple of days before. Although he had immediately replied, Thomas made another mental note to place a call to California when he got home.

Later in the week, on the third Friday as promised, Thomas took his students to the public library. Nature produced a beautiful morning for walking. The air was cool and a kind breeze gently coaxed tree branches to hypnotically sway from side to side in unison. Thomas left three students behind in Glen's first-grade room; they had failed to present him with a valid library card. One of the three had brought a note from his mother saying that she would meet the class at the library (only a ten-minute walk from the Adams) and pay her son's fine for a library book he had lost two years before. When she arrived at the library and learned that her son had been left behind, she slammed the money on the counter and stormed out of the library in a huff. The first-year teacher turned to his class and stated resolutely, "*I* make the rules for my class."

At the end of every day since the first day of school, an X or a check had been placed next to the name of each student on a huge calendar called September Sam. On the last school day of the month, the first Movie Day arrived. Thomas had stopped at the grocery store the night before and bought bags of natural fruit punch, popcorn, chips and assorted treats. On M-Day, as he called it, right before lunch he reminded the class that a student needed eighty percent of the total possible points available for the month to stay and watch the movie—in this case, seventeen points.

Thomas went down the list one by one, calling each student's name and announcing the verdict. Fifteen students received permission to stay and enjoy a half-hour film based on a story discovered during Reading class. Ten long-faced students were dispersed to other rooms to get an early start on homework (a couple of exiles had not come to school). Three of the "in" students had earned all of the possible points for the month. Their feat was noted by a separate display next to the All-Star List. Also, they could choose any seat in the house. Maria received lavish praise as one of the "Superstars." It lifted her spirits about still not having been selected Student of the Week. For an hour Thomas catered to the "in" group like a humble servant.

At the end of the day Thomas attempted to clean up from the festivities. It took him twice as long as it should have because he spent several minutes politely forcing Maria to leave the building. She had begged him over and over to let her stay to help but finally took "no" for an answer and let her teacher return to his tasks. While arranging paper plates in his closet, Thomas mentally assessed the progress of the class. With the first month of school having come and gone, he saw potential in his students and in himself.

October

Thomas sat comfortably in his living room reading the Sunday paper. The sports pages rested atop the scattered *Boston Globe*, which occupied half the sofa. He had gotten home from church an hour before and relished taking time just to relax. The sound of grunts and the sight of crunching bodies provided him with entertainment as multimillionaire professional football players attacked each other on television. The drapes nearby had been drawn to clarify the images on the screen. The smell of hot-buttered popcorn permeated the air throughout the entire apartment. The first Sunday in October offered somewhat cool air but sunny skies; a perfect day for playing or just watching a game. As a former football player and now teacher, Thomas loved the fall season.

On third down, the Chicago Bears offensive cast crouched near the goal line, threatening to score. The defensive linemen of the New York Giants had positioned themselves so close to the enemy they could each smell what the other had eaten for breakfast. Thomas fixed his eyes on the twenty-seven-inch screen and predicted the outcome. He grabbed another handful of popcorn and pushed the tasty butter-drenched kernels into his mouth. The Bears' quarterback smashed into the line of three-hundred-pound goliaths and across the invisible plane for a touchdown. Thomas had predicted correctly. He cheered for the Bears, one of his favorite teams, and for himself for his play-calling acumen.

The former Ohio State Buckeye fondly remembered his own days as a player. He had never deceived himself into dreaming that his destiny entailed becoming a star professional athlete. Many of his teammates had fallen into that trap. They blew off a college education—often tuition-free—in spite of warnings from their parents, other teammates and even Coach Wahlberg (who claimed he didn't want any "dumb-ass jocks" on his team). When these improvident young men got injured or became scholastically ineligible to play, they fell flat on their asses because they had no back-up plan. Thomas considered himself a pretty good but not a great wide receiver. He would have spent the entire senior year riding the pine if "Lucky" Lou Washington hadn't gotten his leg broken running a reverse halfway through the season.

The wounded-bird sound of the telephone interrupted his memories. He grabbed the remote control but decided not to mute the sound. "Damn," he swore. He scanned the digits on the caller-identification box but could not associate a name with the number; whoever was calling would get the bum's rush anyway until the game ended. He picked up the telephone. "Hello?"

"Hello, Thomas? How are you?" a woman on the other end inquired, with just a touch of tentativeness and timidity in her voice.

"I'm fine, thanks," the young man answered slowly. From embarrassing college experiences, he had learned to avoid guessing at a female caller's name from the sound of her voice. The television being on and the volume high provided him with perfect cover. "I'm sorry, I've got the television a little loud and I can't find the remote. Would you speak a little louder, please. Who is this again?"

"Oh, sorry," answered the voice, a little disappointed. "This is Sherice."

"Sherice!" Thomas answered in a high voice. "I'm really glad to hear from you. I was going to call you soon," he added without the slightest hesitation, "but I'm afraid that I'm in the middle of something. I've got some buddies coming over to watch the game, and I gotta get ready. Can I call you back later? Thanks. I'll talk to you then. Bye." He hung up and returned his attention to the television. The Bears had the ball again already—an interception or fumble or something. "Shit! Shit! Shit!" he exclaimed. "I missed it."

A commercial spouting the features of a foreign automobile he certainly could not afford provided Thomas with an opportunity to roam around the kitchen searching for another root beer. He almost never drank alcohol except on special occasions, even then only a few sips, to be polite. He took a swig of his sweet drink and darted back into the living room in time to see a conference of referees. They discussed whether a receiver's foot had crossed the white sideline marker when he had caught a pass.

Sherice came to mind again. She had been one of his mistakes, born out of grief from the sudden collapse of his wedding plans. Comparing the two,

Thomas recognized that Sherice was nothing like Laura. Years of eating right and pampering had produced Laura's refined, sculpted features. Sherice's beauty—including her large bosom—was purely an accident of nature. Laura enjoyed the theater, elegant restaurants and art galleries—the finer things. Sherice read romance novels and could stay on the dance floor for hours. While Laura was careful and reserved, Sherice was spontaneous and ebullient. Laura came from upper-class money and attended only the best schools, but Sherice seemed comfortable with her working-class background and state college education.

They had met only a month ago at a mutual friend's birthday party. The evening had been warm and humid with nearly a full moon upstaging the scattered stars. Guests spoke loudly to drown out the hum of the air-conditioner, on full blast. Sherice arrived as the friend of the birthday boy's girlfriend. He remembered that the dark-brown, lovely woman was easy to talk to and flashed a beautiful broad smile. Unlike Laura, whose obsession with making the right impression produced such caution when meeting people for the first time, Sherice was unguarded and forthcoming with information about herself and her family. She was a psychology major at the University of Massachusetts, entering her senior year. Thomas's eyes had zoomed in on the navy-blue top she wore, showing her ample cleavage. He couldn't remember who had initiated contact. No, come to think of it, he had asked her to dance. She had put on quite a show, twisting and twirling that wonderful body around. A few hours later, he offered to give her a ride home.

A half-hour after he parked the car in front of her apartment, they landed in bed. As safe sex between two virtual strangers went, it was pretty good, Thomas recalled. He remembered feeling a little guilty at first, like he would be cheating on Laura, but those thoughts lasted only a few minutes. Unlike Laura, Sherice was highly passionate and even a little loud. In the morning she offered to cook breakfast for him, but he declined, saying he had a busy day. She didn't put up a fuss or ask a second time but escorted him to the door and kissed him good-bye. Thomas promised to call her and did, once, about three weeks ago. He didn't leave a message.

She had been the first sexual encounter he had pursued "A.L." (after Laura) but she had not been the last. There had been another, but he didn't want to relive that one. Both were decent, intelligent women who, had he met them at a different time in his life, might have become more than just a one-nighter. According to one of his male friends, in time Thomas would adjust to being without Laura. But as a young, healthy man, he could not be expected to live like a monk while in recovery. According to this friend, a grieving, formerly engaged man could partake of a few transitional fucks as long as he took the proper precautions.

The next day at the Adams proved to be an eventful one. On a cool morning with the sun hiding behind large patches of clouds, Thomas served his first rotation of morning schoolyard duty. Although jacket weather, he noticed that a few kids, whose parents could not afford gradually thickening protection from the elements, already sported winter coats. The response his presence generated from the kindergarten, first- and second-grade children surprised him. Most knew his name. Several ran and hugged him. They spoke to him with affectionate familiarity. One little boy simply held on for dear life and pleaded, "Mr. Payne, will you be my daddy?"

Although three teachers were scheduled to provide morning yard oversight, Thomas supervised the area virtually without adult support, except for a few parents who stayed with their children until the bell rang. The tall man walked around the lot telling children to get off that fence, put that stick down, stop throwing that ball against the school wall, leave him/her alone, be nice, play fair, give him back his lunch box and stay inside the fence.

When the second bell rang, Thomas tried to shepherd over three hundred students into their class lines as best he could. He chose three of his pupils to assist him in the endeavor, a responsibility they performed well. Eventually, teachers slowly appeared to gather their own broods. A few seemed visibly impressed and commented on the orderly behavior of all the classes.

"For a change," Thomas thought to himself.

All of the inhabitants of Room 217 quietly climbed the stairs to the second floor and entered the classroom. A bottleneck formed in the line as students stopped at the door to confirm their inclusion on the All-Star List. The eleven who had earned a checkmark for all five days the previous week pointed and smiled. While continuing their journey to the closet and pencil sharpener, the fifth-graders showed open fascination for the various Halloween displays hanging from the walls and doors. A sample of the adult role models' pictures and quotes remained. Others had been replaced by pictures and posters of Frankenstein, Dracula and an assortment of ghosts, pumpkins, witches and other sights. Students pointed and commented on their favorite horror character.

As Thomas and the class prepared for the day, Mr. Dorn appeared. The man wore a dark suit and a blank expression on his face, as always. Thomas felt himself become self-conscious and tense. He turned to the Student of the Week and directed him to take care of the class, then stepped into the hall with the principal. After a perfunctory exchange of greetings, Mr. Dorn requested an after-school meeting, to which the provisional teacher immediately agreed. No further conversation ensued, but Thomas spent the remainder of the day worrying why the principal wanted to meet.

His concern was not assuaged by the performance of his pupils that morning. They showcased another poor Monday morning start. Apparently, the year before, Ms. Patterson gave far less homework than he and no assignments over the weekend. The students had not yet adjusted to being assigned homework every day, including Fridays. Individuals feebly offered explanations about weekend visits with their fathers, elongated church services and road trips, but Thomas accepted no excuses. A third of the class found themselves grounded for the day, including one former Student of the Week. The day dragged on from there until the last bell mercifully rang, providing much needed permission for everyone to go home.

That afternoon Thomas hung around the office trying to stay out of the way and not look concerned. A few after-school matters required the attention of the principal and assistant principal, including a late bus and three pupils who had missed their bus. A frightened Spanish-only-speaking first-grader waited nervously for her mother, who failed to pick her up on time due to car problems, she later claimed. Teachers barged into the office for one reason or another, their issues demanding immediate action, they insisted. Two fourth-grade students in Ms. Patterson's class waited for their parents to pick them up, following a fight during recess.

Finally, the two men sat down alone. Thomas privately acknowledged to himself that his boss had the home-field advantage. Judging from the shape of the office, the nervous teacher assessed that the principal was not much of a housekeeper. Books and papers were scattered everywhere. Thomas had to remove a pile from a chair in order to sit. Two computers performed low-pitched arias from opposite corners of the room, their monitors black except for dozens of shooting stars. The wires of Mr. Dorn's portable computer spread across his desk like spider webs. One desktop computer peeked out behind a stack of reports. Ten feet from the two men, boxes of new textbooks had been stacked haphazardly, blocking a side door—a clear safety hazard.

Mr. Dorn slid his five-feet, eight-inch frame behind his desk to confirm his power over his taller, statuesque rookie teacher. He spoke without emotion, as he almost always did at first when alone or nearly alone with someone. "Mr. Payne, first of all, I want to let you know that I think you're doing a fine job with that class."

"Thank you, sir," Thomas replied, waiting for the rest. Tired and anxious, he had no desire to suck up to his supervisor at the moment.

The principal continued. "It's my job to protect my teachers, especially in their first year." He raised his hands slowly. "Now there's nothing to be alarmed about, but I want you to know that there's been a few minor complaints from parents about you."

Thomas stiffened his posture. The announcement did not totally surprise him. His mother had warned him to be ready for such an event. Still, being prepared did not lessen the hurt. Wisely, he had spoken to Glen earlier in the day, informing his mentor about the upcoming meeting. The veteran teacher provided simple advice:

Don't explain yourself or what you do unless asked. Answer only questions you have been asked. Don't volunteer any information. If you're blind-sided by a parent complaint, simply say that you'll call the parent later and say nothing more. Don't give Dorn ammunition to use against you. Let information flow one way, from Dorn to you.

This seemed like strange advice but Glen had explained that Mr. Dorn received private castigation from the staff because he didn't always say the same thing to the parents as he did to his teachers.

Thomas raised his eyebrows to indicate that he would like to hear more.

After an uncomfortable silence, Mr. Dorn continued. "Yes, Ms. Walker called yesterday. She's upset that you sent in absent reports about LaShonda without calling her first."

"I simply followed the procedures you laid out for us at the beginning of the year," Thomas replied, trying not to sound too defensive. "I've sent notes home about LaShonda's absences. She missed over forty days of school last year. She lives only three blocks away. She walks to school. The girl has a history of missing school dating back to first grade. She's already missed four days of school!" Noticing the decibel rise in his voice, he remembered Glen's advice and finished with The Mantra. "I'll call Ms. Walker this evening."

"Fine," Mr. Dorn said. "I told her that we weren't going to allow LaShonda to pick up where she left off last year. But I also mentioned that we'd do all that we could to help the family." He paused and cleared his throat. "Something else: Another parent called yesterday. I spoke to Tyshaun Lincoln's mother. She said that Tyshaun told her that you called him 'dumb' last week."

Thomas's blood began to boil but he controlled himself. "Absolutely not! That's not what happened." He took a deep breath and paused. "I'll call her tonight."

"Good," Mr. Dorn replied. "I know what trouble Tyshaun can be. He'll tell his mother a lie just to keep in practice, and she always believes him. The boy practically lived in my office last year." The middle-aged man reached for a few papers on his desk and started reading them.

Thomas found his behavior quite rude but said nothing. He had hoped that it was a sign that the meeting had reached a conclusion, but Mr. Dorn looked up with more to say.

"One last thing: I just got off the phone with Deborah Anderson's mom a few minutes ago. She said Deb came home in tears."

"I'm not surprised," the slightly agitated guest calmly admitted. "She's a good girl and a good student. I made her Student of the Week a couple of weeks ago. But she had her first no-point day today for some missing homework, and she took it rather hard. I'd planned to call her mom tonight anyway."

The principal seemed satisfied and went on for a few minutes about how he supported his teachers and would do anything for them as long as they were straight with him. He gave Thomas the usual spiel that if the need arose, come to his office because the door was always open. He told a story about his own days as a fifth-grade teacher. Thomas laughed at all the right places. Then Mr. Dorn stood, announced that he was finished and told his first-year instructor to keep up the good work. Thomas took his cue and walked to the door. The headmaster put on a pair of reading glasses. Thomas turned back and approached the desk.

"Mr. Dorn, I just remembered something I need to bring up."

"Yes?" the principal called without raising his head. He fiercely punched the buttons of a cheap calculator, attempting for the third time to make some figures balance.

"I have a student in my class who can't read. I mean can't read at all. It's no secret to him or to the class. In fact, he's stoically told me 'Now Mr. Payne, everyone knows I can't read.' His math is pretty low too but not as low as his reading. I can't see sending him to middle school next year. I'm not sure what to do."

Mr. Dorn suddenly became interested. He took off his glasses and made eye contact with Thomas. "Who is it?"

"Doug. Douglas Berry."

"Shit. That's all I need, for word to get out about this," the principal grumbled while nervously tapping his fingers on his desk. "Tell you what. Get a hold of Ms. Cooke. Get the boy in the Reading One-On-One program ASAP, got that?" He pointed his finger. "And let's keep this under our hats— so as not to embarrass the boy."

Thomas opened his mouth to ask another question, but the telephone rang and the principal picked it up and started speaking, so the young teacher left and went straight to his mentor's room. Glen had just turned off the lights and stepped into the hall, tote bags in hand. As usual, from what his mentee could see before the room went black, the guy's Halloween displays were dazzling.

The two climbed the stairs back to Room 217. At the beginning of the year they had agreed not to discuss sensitive issues in Glen's room, located across the hall from the office. Once in his own room, Thomas told Glen the whole story.

The first-grade teacher shook his head. "That's what's fucked up about this place. Every year I recommend students to be retained in the first grade. The best time to do it's when they're young. But I'm almost always over-ruled by the parent. And Dorn? He just goes right along with the program. Ms. Knowles, when she was here, never tried to keep a kid back no matter how much the child needed it. Thought it was racist to give a Black kid a bad grade, even if it was deserved." He took a breath then changed gears. "What did Ms. Patterson say happened last year? Have you talked to her? She been any help?"

Thomas frowned and gave his friend a forceful wave of his hand. "We just don't speak the same language! Whenever I talk to her, all she gives me are soap opera stories about the kids' lives. She knows all the details. I ask her, 'Did this kid have trouble with math last year?' and she gives me a short answer, then proceeds to explain that the kid can't fucking add because he's worried that his dad is going to move to Georgia or some other tale."

Thomas strolled to a counter-shelf drawer and reached inside. He struggled to balance a stack of cumulative record folders, one for each child in his room. They contained the student's history with the Boston Public School Department. He motioned for Glen to approach the bench. "And look at these," he screeched, opening one. "These grades that Ms. Patterson gave the kids last year are way too high! It's gonna make me look like the Grinch when I do my report cards. You know how parents like to shoot the messenger." He raised his eyebrows. "You think Dorn got phone calls about me before? Wait until November 15 on Open House."

While listening, Glen opened a folder. He read it for a few seconds and whistled. Thomas raced on. "Look at this one." He handed it to his friend. "This is the boy I told you about who can't read. Look at his reading grade."

Glen's eyes widened. "Holy Mother of God! A fucking C–." He gave the bulk of paper back to Thomas and wiped his hands on his shirt as though his fingers had gotten dirty.

Ten minutes later the two men gathered their things and sneaked out the back door. They strolled around the building to their cars, parked on the street in front of the school. Thomas wondered why his new friend acted so cautiously. Glen had told him that he didn't like people to know his comings and goings. The Cincinnati native resolved to accept that his colleague, who was originally from New York City, had his reasons. They said good-bye and agreed to meet at Anthony's for a workout. Thomas had secured a membership for Glen at half the annual fee.

The next morning Thomas found himself in a strange and distant land—the John Adams teachers' room. He had generally come to regard it as an unpleasant place. Teachers did not seem to be the most content of professionals, he observed. They complained about almost everything. The new kid chortled at how much time his colleagues invested grumbling, especially since the most frequent complaints included how overworked they were. Thomas avoided the room. The area was often left unclean. Mice and roaches still sent occasional spies with the hope of one day recapturing their treasured feeding ground. Thomas ran in only to use the bathroom, get his lunch, obtain supplies or make copies. The alacrity of his visits led to word surfacing that Mr. Payne was "standoffish." Also, because he avoided contact with the single female teachers and paraprofessionals, and because he spent so much time with Mr. Bennett, word also surfaced that Mr. Payne must be gay.

Still, that morning Thomas had a mission to fulfill, and for the good of his nonreading boy, proceeded into the teachers' *sanctum sanctorum* with temerity. The smell of fresh-brewed coffee hung in the air, stirring the taste buds of the room's occupants. The old, ailing copy machine churned out another batch of uneven products. Two teachers stood at the opposite corner of the room, laughing and chatting in Spanish. One of the lights overhead, determined not to die without a fight, flickered in a hypnotic Morse code-like pattern. The room was chilly as usual because the windows had to be kept open to let the fumes from the copy machine escape.

Thomas entered and spotted Ms. Caine, a stoic, middle-aged woman and one of the senior teachers on the staff, waiting her turn at the copy machine. A veteran third-grade teacher, she had the 411 on just about everything that went on at the Adams, according to Glen. Thomas politely approached her and inquired about the mechanics of the Reading One-On-One program. While they conversed, a very attractive young Hispanic woman with tanned skin and a very faint mustache overheard them talking about Ms. Cooke and the "R Triple-O" program. The tallest female teacher in the building, she wore a short beige skirt showing her long, shapely legs, which she used to practically gallop over to them.

"Hi, you might not remember me," she offered, smiling at both of them while pointing at Thomas and back to herself, "but I'm Heléna Gutiérrez. I teach Reading One-On-One—bilingual. We started together. I'm new here too!" Her faced bubbled with energy, which warmed the chilly room.

"I leave you in good hands," Ms. Caine said. Her opportunity to try her luck at the copy machine had arrived.

"Thanks, um, Mona," Thomas replied, trying out his resolution to break the ice with some of the teachers. Somehow it didn't sound quite right. He turned back to the early twentysomething teacher. "You were saying, Ms. Gutiérrez?"

First, she insisted that he call her Heléna, then she launched into an enthusiastic account of her program's purpose. She explained that the program technically did not extend to students past the second grade but exceptions could be made in rare cases. The young woman of Venezuelan ancestry assessed that the fifth-grade student Thomas had described sounded like one of those cases. She further advised her fellow "newbee" to see Ms. Cooke right away because Cooke did English. Her job was to help Hispanic kids with their Spanish.

Her last words jolted the tall man's brain, and he did not adequately hide his shock. "What do you mean, 'I help kids with their Spanish?' " he inquired.

"Yes, well, I mean, I tutor my students to help them read in Spanish," Heléna replied.

Thomas interpreted her response as defensive. The pitch in his voice rose as he spoke. "You mean to tell me that first- and second-grade kids who obviously don't speak English sit down with you for forty-five minutes every day to learn how to read *in Spanish*? Please tell me that we're not spending tax dollars on such a thing!"

The whites of the young man's eyes could be seen from several feet away as he shook his head in disbelief. However, he abruptly remembered Glen's warning about revealing his feelings or thoughts too openly. Thomas suspected that he had made a serious mistake. He could feel the disapprobating stares of the two Hispanic women on the other side of the table. He waited for his fellow first-year teacher to speak, thus unanimously affirming his obvious sin.

"I know. Isn't that dumb?" she replied, giggling and shaking her head. "You'd think that we'd be doing everything we could to help Spanish-speaking kids learn English. I could teach them English just as well, and it would be better for them. But that's not how the bilingual side of the program is set up."

Thomas exhaled with relief that his new friend agreed but he grew uncomfortable because of the openness of their conversation. Apparently this young, sincere and very pretty woman had no mentor like Glen to caution her about the Adams and its ways. He looked at his watch and decided to attempt a circuitous rescue. "I better get outside. I've got morning duty. Thanks for—"

"And you know what else?" she added earnestly.

Thomas leaned against the refrigerator, helpless. He had tried. "You've got the ball," he answered. "Go ahead and run with it."

The young woman went on, oblivious to everything and everyone else surrounding them. She revealed that all the bilingual students at the Adams used Spanish-language textbooks for math and their other subjects. She also disclosed that all the bilingual classes were required to teach one course of *Spanish* grammar to their Spanish-speaking students. Heléna spoke with conviction and concern, obviously unaware of any contrary opinions in the vicinity. Thomas admired her courage—even if she did not appreciate that she had indeed displayed courage. He resolved to be a little less careful himself from now on and to be a friend to Heléna, if she would accept his friendship. He thanked her and excused himself, lest he be late for duty.

The dark-haired, dark-eyed woman seized his wrists and told him how wonderful it was to officially meet him. With youthful enthusiasm, she danced a half-jig as she shook his hands. Her sincere smile sent Thomas on his way with a positive attitude about the day. With her warmth encompassing the usually depressing room, the vacillating light overhead seemed to take its cue. It ceased to flicker and instead delivered constant brightness.

Outside that morning Thomas gladly accepted the hugs and attention of the primary students at the Adams. The five-, six- and seven-year-olds swarmed on him as if he were Santa Claus distributing presents. Playing the part to a certain extent, the fifth-grade instructor asked their names and the names of their teachers, then inquired if they had been good or bad. Each child smiled and insisted that he or she had been very good. Thomas lingered on the primary side of the field as long as he could, but eventually had to pry away from his admirers and supervise the older students. After a few minutes, he announced that time had arrived for everyone to line up.

Seeing again no evidence of adult assistance, he deputized three students, one from each fifth-grade class, to round up the primary students. A few of the more recent arrivals from the primary side of the playground ran over to him for a hug. He gave them each a quick one and told them to line up. One little girl in pigtails, the child Thomas recognized from across the street, offered him a picture she had drawn yesterday especially for him. He could not ascertain what the scene represented, but the people on the paper all smiled, so he thanked the girl profusely and picked her up as high as he could. She laughed and clapped her hands before he put her down and sent her on her way. When Thomas turned around, he was greeted by one of his own.

Maria smiled and embraced him as if they had always greeted each other in such a fashion. He hugged her back and they walked arm in arm to the class line. Several of his other girls approached him and similarly reached for a hug. Thomas gladly responded to their overtures of affection. As he passed several of his boys, he touched their shoulders or the top of their heads to greet them.

He turned to the current Student of the Week. "Alright," Thomas said, clapping his hands and rubbing them together. "Let's enter the building like the number one senior class."

That day, they produced their best work of the year.

That evening at home Thomas watched the news when, to his disappoint-ment, the telephone rang right as the sports segment began. He recognized the number and then the voice of his older sister. Obviously very excited, she talked so fast he could not understand her. He excused himself, muted the sound of the television and asked Vanessa to try again. She started over slowly.

"Thomas, we argued over which one of us would get to call you with the news, and praise the Lord, I won. Mama and Daddy are here with me," she blurted out breathlessly, then proclaimed: "Praise God, my dear brother! Edward's appeal was granted by the Ohio Supreme Court. He should be home in a few days!"

Thomas could hear yelling and cheering in the background. He reached for the remote control, turned the television off and sat down. "You're kid-ding!" he shouted, not willing to believe the news.

"No, Thomas. It's true. Edward is coming home by the end of next week—two weeks at the latest. Isn't it wonderful? God has answered our prayers!" She began to cry.

Thomas talked to his mother, then his father, then Vanessa's husband Jerry, then to his grandmother on his mother's side, then to his sister again. He was able to piece together the events from their varied accounts. Twenty minutes later they all said good-bye—after Thomas promised Vanessa that he would say a special prayer of thanks to God for freeing his brother from Satan's den of iniquity. Thomas staggered into the kitchen and poured him-self a stiff glass of orange juice, no ice. Its taste invigorated him. He reached for a napkin and wiped his eyes while mentally recapitulating his brother's bizarre odyssey.

It had been launched twelve years ago. Edward, the oldest of the three, after graduating from Ohio State with a degree in criminal justice, had opted to return to Cincinnati, marry his high school sweetheart and take the police exam. He breezed through the Academy and enjoyed a rapid rise through the ranks with the Cincinnati Police Department, loving every minute of it. After only four years he shed his uniform and became a detective. He ex-pected to swiftly be promoted again to sergeant, then lieutenant; it was only a matter of time. Edward even had ambitions of becoming commissioner.

However, allegedly, after two years of solid police work as a detective, he and five others from his team—one African American and four Whites—began siphoning off a "finder's fee" of up to fifty percent from their collars. Supposedly, this corruption expanded into wholesale avarice lasting several years. Drugs, household furnishings, cash and sex were theirs for the asking—or taking, depending on who told the story.

These alleged nefarious activities would have gone on indefinitely had it not been for the last vice. The mistress of one married officer became pregnant. She was a gorgeous, blue-eyed former exotic dancer from Amsterdam, who sometimes posed nude for "artistic" magazines. A year into their relationship, upon informing the officer of her condition, she was bestowed with five thousand dollars and told to get out of town—permanently. She did, but after giving birth she returned, got a lawyer, filed a paternity suit, went to Internal Affairs and told them everything she knew. Her account indicated a head for details and an insider's knowledge of police work. An investigation ensued, with piquant tidbits discreetly leaked to the press. Soon the sharks began circling.

The story broke and the woman's pictures occupied the front page of the *Cincinnati Inquirer*. The story included a photo of the dancer "in character" while working at her past vocation, her long blond tresses strategically placed. Adjacent to that image was a more current picture of her, clad in carefully cropped short hair and a conservative navy-blue suit. She stood with her lawyer holding a light-brown baby girl. The misty-eyed beauty presented herself as a repentant mother, just wanting to do the right thing. The *Inquirer* outlined a sordid and gripping saga, penned by two of its senior award-winning journalists. In it, the former dancer claimed that corruption existed in the Cincinnati Police Department and that Detective Edward T. Payne had fathered her child. The fact that she was White and an illegal immigrant from the Netherlands made for irresistibly juicy gossip. Women's groups flocked in droves to City Hall, brandishing signs in defense of the poor, abandoned woman and her baby. Eventually, the six officers faced indictments on charges of racketeering, income-tax evasion, et cetera, et cetera.

Of course Edward denied everything. He explained that several White police officers were jealous of him and had manufactured false charges to derail his career. Eventually, the women's groups stood opposite scores of angry African American citizens, brown flesh tightly clutching signs that expressed outrage against "modern-day lynching." Edward stuck to his story while on paid suspension. His wife, April, a reserved, dignified woman of substance, stood by her man every step of the way. She maintained that her husband and the father of her two children had been framed.

Then the result of the court-ordered blood test arrived. The proof of Edward being the father of the child in question was incontrovertible. Thomas still shuddered to this day when recalling the pain the news brought everyone in the family, especially his sister-in law. In public she maintained the same supportive appearance. She walked hand-in-hand with her husband, chauffeured the children to and from school and later sat right behind Edward during the trial. But in private she was quiet and pensive. Once Thomas stumbled onto a tragic scene in the kitchen of his brother reaching for his wife, only to be silently rebuffed.

The district attorney of Cincinnati offered deals of guilty pleas with reduced prison time to each officer in exchange for testifying against the others. Initially, they all declined, having collectively agreed to honor the infamous blue Code of Silence. However, right before the trial, like clockwork, the four White detectives agreed to testify against the two African American co-defendants. Edward was found guilty of eight felony offenses and sentenced to fifteen years in prison. His younger co-defendant received eleven years. Because they had cooperated and pleaded guilty to lesser charges, the White officers all received heavy fines and light prison sentences. One of them signed a book and movie deal, complete with final approval on the actor who would portray him on screen.

Thomas grieved for his brother and for the heavy toll the entire ordeal took on the Payne family. During the trial he frequently had to drive from Columbus to Cincinnati and back. Mom, who had always insisted on her son's innocence, developed a heart condition; once she had to be hospitalized. Dad became even more withdrawn. Right around then his sister and her husband got involved in that evangelical church.

In the middle of all the turmoil, Edward confided to Thomas that he had a few bucks stashed somewhere for a rainy day, something like 150,000 dollars. Also, he shared with his younger brother the fact that his legal bills were being secretly paid for by an "anonymous donor." At three o'clock one morning after consuming his fifth beer, Edward had whispered to Thomas that a drug dealer had fronted the money in exchange for Edward's closed mouth. Eventually, Edward went to jail. His wife divorced him and refused to speak to him or anyone in the family. The European-born dancer and the baby were deported. Edward never held the child in his arms or ever acknowledged that he had a daughter in Europe.

But, according to Vanessa, the Ohio Supreme Court had ruled that the jury should have been informed about *all* details of the deal the White detectives had made with the D.A. Edward and the other detective were ordered to be given new trials. However, a new D.A. decided not to retry the cases. His brother soon would be home.

Sitting on his living room sofa, holding a half-empty glass of cold orange juice, Thomas found his thoughts drifting back again to Laura. They had met in Boston, so at first she knew nothing about his brother. As they became closer, Thomas disclosed that ignominious part of his family history. Laura had insisted that Thomas never divulge the information to anyone she knew, especially to members of her family. But it continued to be a sore spot in their relationship. Eventually, they announced their engagement and flew home to meet his family, but Laura had exhibited such trepidation about visiting his brother that he ended up seeing Edward alone. His fiancée stayed behind with a "terrible migraine headache." To this day, Thomas suspected that his brother's detention had been the real reason she had broken their engagement. Laura harbored lofty ambitions, aspiring to become a prominent, rich corporate lawyer. What would the partners at the firm think?

The week at work did not progress as well as Thomas would have liked. He was surprised, then annoyed at the brick wall he encountered in trying to enroll Doug in the Reading One-On-One program. His very first conversation with Ms. Cooke was not promising. For most of her nineteen-year teaching career, she had taught reading only to very young children. A woman in her early forties with skin the color and texture of creamy peanut butter, she had an old-fashioned schoolmarm's look; wool sweater draped over the shoulders, black "halfees" reading glasses and hair tied in a tight bun every day. Thomas privately speculated that she would look quite sexy if she fixed herself up a little.

It became immediately apparent that she was opposed to sitting down regularly with an almost eleven-year-old boy who, by her way of thinking, had frittered away the opportunity her tax dollars had provided him. In what Thomas interpreted as an obvious passive-aggressive move, she announced that first he had to fill out the appropriate referral forms for the boy, get a parent to do the same and wait for a reply from Court Street (the Boston Public School central office) on the matter. Thomas accepted the forms, thanked Ms. Cooke and departed from her half-sized room, seething with anger.

The remainder of the week provided insightful, even alarming information about his class. Thomas frequently expressed shock at the poor academic skills demonstrated by so many of his students. A few had trouble adding and subtracting large, double-digit numbers. Most could not tell time from a clock with a face and hands. Less than a third could accurately write their own mailing addresses. Because of their low reading skills, they had significant trouble answering word problems in any subject. They made progress but at a snail's pace, as far as Thomas was concerned. Once, he had entered Mrs. Chang's room to borrow a textbook and paused to observe the lesson. The students raised their hands as they eagerly learned to divide fractions. Thomas returned to Room 217 and fought off the temptation to become angry at his students. After all, they were not completely responsible. The adults in their lives had failed them. He vowed not to be one who likewise failed them.

Another Friday finally arrived, and Thomas decided who would be the new Student of the Week. That afternoon, the members of Room 217 returned from recess—those who had been allowed to go. Thomas had devised a ruse with Glen. A student would be sent to Glen's room with the cover story that Mr. Bennett needed help distributing some new first-grade textbooks. With the chosen helper gone, Thomas addressed his class.

"The student currently in Mr. Bennett's room is my choice for Student of the Week today," he announced, and put his index finger to his lips. "I want this to be a secret, okay?" He observed heads nodding and explained the rationale for his plans. "In the past five weeks you've improved your behavior to the point where it's time to advance to the next stage—doing projects together as a team."

A volunteer was chosen as a model, and Thomas took fifteen minutes to rehearse how the Student of the Week ceremony would be performed. Then he sent the current captain to Glen's room to return with the unsuspecting nominee.

Instead of launching right into the ceremony, Thomas administered a two-minute multiplication quiz. He wanted to shift their attention to another topic. After collecting the quizzes, he put them aside and suggested that they hold the Student of the Week ceremony before correcting them. As usual by then, the class divided itself into two neat lines five feet apart down the center pathway of the room.

Thomas positioned himself in their midst. "How does one get to be Student of the Week?" he asked. Seven times he called on a student to name one of the criteria, using an "I" statement.

"In order to be Student of the Week, I must have my homework in every day … In order to be Student of the Week, I must play to win … In order to be Student of the Week, I must have good attendance … In order to be Student of the Week…." continued until the list was completed.

"Please turn around," the calm instructor requested.

After doing so, the two groups no longer faced each other but had their backs to each other. Thomas turned off all the classroom lights, tiptoed to his portable music box and pressed the button. The piano introduction, familiar to the children now, filtered into the room, then George Benson sang:

I believe the children are our future.
Teach them well and let them lead the way….

Thomas crouched behind each student one by one and whispered The Question, chosen especially for that day. "Are you a leader or a follower?" he asked. One by one, each student responded with the same answer. "I am a leader." He finished with the entire class and quietly stepped behind the newly-chosen Student of the Week. He placed his hands gently on the shoulders of the Captain-elect and the two of them slowly walked together to one end of the line.

"It's time. You're ready," he whispered, then assumed a spot on the opposite end of the line twenty feet away, facing his nominee. "Turn around and acknowledge your new Student of the Week," Thomas declared. The class applauded with enthusiasm. Maria Colón stood smiling at her peers, beaming with pride. Thomas spoke glowingly for a few seconds about the outgoing and incoming honorees and their chosen buddies, then asked the class, still in their two-line formation, to hold their arms straight out in front of them.

"Maria, I want you to walk down the center of this group and touch everyone's hand," he requested, looking her in the eye. "By touching everyone's hand you are saying that you accept the responsibility of setting the example and being the Student of the Week." He directed his remarks to everyone else. "And all of you with your hands open to her are saying that you accept her leadership as the Student of the Week." He looked back at Maria. Her expression conveyed respect for her new office and admiration for her teacher. "Captain, walk down the line, please."

The girl slowly paraded down the receiving line and touched everyone's hand. When she got to her buddy, Carmelita, she whispered something to her. Carmelita smiled and nodded in agreement. Maria continued her journey until she reached Thomas at the very end, who had joined a student line, his hands extended. They touched hands and she hugged him. He resumed his role as master of ceremonies.

"Captain, the class would like to show you their appreciation in a special way. Will you trust them and me and allow this display of admiration and respect?"

Maria looked confused. Such a request had never been made before during the ceremony. She felt nervous but trusted her teacher completely.

"Yes ... Okay," she answered somewhat diffidently.

On cue, the class encircled her. Maria switched her head from side to side. Everyone smiled. Thomas instructed Carmelita to stand directly behind her buddy as part of her special assignment. He sent Deborah to change the music selection, chosen especially for the occasion. Thomas explained that each person selected as Student of the Week would have his/her own "cradle" song. Maria's was "A Whole New World," song by Peabo Bryson and Regina Bell, from the Disney movie, "Aladdin."

Thomas nodded to Deborah and the music began to play.

"Please," he whispered to Maria. "Trust us." He put his hand behind her back. "Close your eyes."

She did as instructed, and several students slowly, delicately, laid her backwards and lifted her feet so that she stretched out horizontally above the floor, sustained by a mattress of almost exclusively ten- and eleven-year-old arms. Carmelita supported her head. Thomas smiled at the students and waited. At the right moment, he nodded for the next phase. Maria, arms extended and supported by the entire class, slowly floated straight up like a balloon.

They lifted her to a height of about six feet. Thomas directed the class, not with words but with dedication and determination. Every eye focused on the ten-year-old girl with her arms extended like an angel. The new teacher, who had assisted in the cradle, began to slowly lower her. The team followed as if of one mind. She descended until she was waist high, about one yard above the ground. For a few precious seconds Maria lay still, suspended, motionless. Then, just as they had rehearsed, Thomas moved his head upward, and she slowly floated up again, up into the heavens.

Maria could control herself no longer. Her body gently shook as tears flowed freely down her face onto the fingers of her buddy and best friend. She drank deeply from the respect that had been bestowed on her and silently vowed to serve with honor and distinction. Mr. Payne would be glad that he had chosen her. She would see to it that he chose her again in the future. Then without warning, she felt herself slowly returning to earth. After another few seconds, her feet touched the ground and she gradually awakened from her trance. As the cloud lifted, she saw her teacher and her classmates applauding her. Maria acknowledged their homage with a broad smile and wiped her face with her hands. She turned and embraced her buddy.

The outgoing captain hung the Student of the Week sign around Maria's neck. Thomas held out the now-familiar and coveted box for Maria to choose her gift. She picked a three-piece set of multicolored pencils. Several students admired the gift box and silently resolved that next Friday would be their day. Thomas held his hands open, an indication that he wanted to speak again.

The beauty and grace of the ceremony reminded him of his own cradle two years before. Toward the end of Revelations' Phase II program, he had been given a difficult personal assignment to complete with the help of a partner. For his successful effort, he had been rewarded with a cradle. His then two-hundred-pound frame presented no obstacle to the caring group of participants. He had risen into the air as easily as steam from a kettle. The memory of the experience at times still touched him, especially when he heard his cradle song on the radio.

"Class, you have made me very proud today with what you have just done," Thomas declared. "You all concentrated on one goal and played together like a team. You were able to do this because you decided to be givers instead of takers." His expression turned slightly serious. "This is the first thing I have asked you to do together, but it isn't the last. There will be more. I know you will accept each challenge put before you and pass with flying colors, as you did today."

The class responded with wild, self-congratulatory applause. A spirit of celebration and exuberance swept through the room. Thomas turned to

Maria. "Captain, please return the class to their seats," he instructed.

She nodded and ordered clearly and loudly: "Okay, everyone please take your seats quietly."

After an uneventful weekend of correcting papers, writing lesson plans and folding laundry, Thomas drove to the Adams with an uneasy feeling. Normally, he enjoyed the short drive past a local park. The fiery hues acquired by leaves on the trees provided him with a pleasant distraction. He paused at a stop sign, and a brown squirrel scampered across his path, carrying a mouthful of nuts, claiming the right of way. The air was crisp and cool, and the sky was clear.

Still, Thomas had come to dislike Monday mornings. The class had shown steady but meager improvements in their behavior in the past five weeks but were nowhere near where he wanted. Also, although he was pleased that most of them completed their homework every day, the existence of a small, stubborn core of chronic nonhomework-doers bothered him.

Thomas parked on the street behind the school so that he could walk through the schoolyard. The brisk wind in his face caused him to squint, but he spotted Maria. She had arrived earlier than usual.

"Hi, Mr. Payne," she called joyfully, running over to him for a hug. It had become their usual morning ritual.

"Good morning, Captain. Are you ready to assume your responsibility on this, your first term as Student of the Week?"

"Yes, Mr. Payne," she answered solemnly.

"I know you are, honey." Thomas replied. He surveyed the lot and motioned for her to come closer. "Captain, I want you to do something for me, first thing," he requested, pointing at no one in particular. "Make sure everyone, I mean everyone in my class has his or her homework. They must show it to their buddy or to you, *entiende?*"

"I'll make sure," she answered, reaching to carry his tote bag.

Instead, he patted her on the shoulder and went inside alone.

Thirty minutes later, after the last student had entered the room, Thomas approached Maria. After hearing the report, the tall man searched the room until he found two boys. "Gary. Asa. Would you two come over here please?" Gary, who was at his desk, stood and took twelve paces straight to Thomas and Maria. Asa, next in line at the pencil sharpener and only a few feet away, pointed to himself as if he were not sure he had just been addressed.

"Me?" he asked, with an innocent look on his face.

"Get over here, now!" Thomas ordered.

Asa bounded over to the caucus in three seconds flat, his rapid footsteps creating a thud-thud-thud sound.

"I'm not even going to play games with you this morning, young man," Thomas warned loud enough for the class to hear. "Did the Captain and your buddy ask to see your homework this morning?"

"She just asked me if I had it. She didn't ask to see it," Asa replied, still maintaining his innocent face.

Maria shook her head from side to side but said nothing. Gary spoke slowly and deliberately, as he always did.

"I asked my buddy to show me his homework but he said no, he had it done." Several of the spectators loudly confirmed his story.

"Quiet," Thomas commanded. "I didn't ask anyone out there anything. Take care of your own business."

The room grew quiet except for some half-hearted rustling of papers as students prepared for the day.

Thomas returned his attention to the three children. "Asa, I'm going to give you just one more chance to tell me the truth. I've told you and everybody in this room that I won't have my students look me in the eye and lie to me." He took a deep breath. "Now, I'm going to forget that you just said what you said." He looked at Maria. "To the board, Captain, if you please."

She did as she was told. A few voices could be heard exclaiming "Uh-oh!" Everyone knew what could happen next.

Thomas stood face-to-face with Asa, who had clearly become uncomfortable. "I'm going to ask you two questions, both easy to prove. Each time you lie to me I'm going to ground you for a week. And if you don't think I'll do it, ask around." Everyone immediately stared at Cleopatra, confined to her seat with three days left on her two-week grounding. "You understand what I've just said?"

Asa took his eyes off Cleo, and nodded, "Yes, Mr. Payne."

Thomas spoke solemnly. "Now don't get yourself in a whole lot of trouble holding onto something that has no value in my class. And lies have no value here—or in life. You know that. You've got a chance to recover your own fumble." He faced the side board where each student's name appeared written in fresh chalk. Maria stood like a sentry, chalk in hand, awaiting her orders. "One week for each lie, *capisci?*"

"Yes, Mr. Payne," she replied.

Thomas gestured towards Gary, faithfully standing alongside Asa. He had just whispered something to his friend. "Asa, did you refuse to show your homework to the Captain and your buddy when they asked to see it?"

Asa's cast his eyes down at his shoes. "Yes, Mr. Payne."

"Okay," Thomas said. "You're doing fine. Now keep it going." One eyebrow inched upwards as he posed the next question. "Do you have all of your homework, yes or no?"

"I left my math paper in my desk, and the Captain wouldn't—"

"That's not what I asked you!" Thomas snapped. "I asked you a simple yes or no question. Do you have all of your homework?"

"No, Mr. Payne," Asa answered clearly.

Thomas nodded. "Okay. You did the right thing, Asa, at least by telling me the truth." He turned to Maria again. "It's going to be two days grounding instead of two weeks." Then he pointed to the other side of the room. "Go to your seat, Asa." Finally, he laid a hand on Gary's shoulder. "Help him get ready."

Thomas went back to business. "Now, let's get to work." The sounds of banging books and shuffling papers echoed throughout the room. He eased his way to the student closet, where Gary had just finished putting away both his and his buddy's things. Besides not going out for recess that day, a student on grounding could only get out of his or her seat during bathroom breaks and "if a fire broke out."

The man whispered to Gary. "What did you say to your buddy?"

Gary replied without looking up. "I just told him that I was his friend. To just tell the truth and you wouldn't be too hard on him."

Thomas placed his hand on the boy's shoulder. "Thank you, Gary. You helped your buddy and the class—and me."

The following week the trees of New England laid out all of their brilliance in breathtaking glory for everyone to see. The local news stations boasted that this season produced one of the best displays of fall colors ever. This claim, of course, would attract hordes of camera-toting, money-spending tourists to the area. Thomas deliberately drove various routes to familiar places, just to bask in nature's annual kaleidoscope of colors. He had to admit that Cincinnati could not match nature's fashion show inside any Boston backyard. Thomas marveled every morning during his drive to work. He fancied himself perceptive enough to notice subtle differences in a specific tree or trees from a day or days before. He made frequent remarks to his children about the dazzling outdoor stage. The students, for the most part all born or reared in Boston, appeared much more subdued in their appreciation.

Thomas had mentally prepared for a backlash due to the warning notices he had recently sent to the homes of twenty-one students in danger of failing at least one course. He had included a letter explaining the purpose of the notices. That week, he received four phone calls, all from the caretakers of generally conscientious students who had been careless during a recent exam in one subject or another. He also received four handwritten notes from various parents. Two contained requests to call and provide suggestions on how the student in question could improve. The other two complained that Thomas's grading system was unfair or in error. Mr. Dorn also received two angry phone calls about the warning notices. He informed Thomas, who promised to call the parents. Unable to speak to them personally, he left messages but heard from neither of them. The remaining eleven students either returned the original warning notice signed without further ado or produced a signed second notice after being kept in for recess.

Thomas had little trouble getting his students to return the permission slips for their first field trip. Through Ms. Flores's efforts, 150 free tickets to the Ringling Brothers/Barnum and Bailey Circus at the Fleet Center downtown had been donated to the Adams, enough for every fourth- and fifth-grade student at the school. Because no money existed for school buses, the teachers and administrators agreed that everyone would use public transportation. The students would simply take the subway downtown.

Thomas thought it too soon to embark on a field trip. Certainly, his class exhibited generally good behavior—in his presence. But he still received too many complaints about misbehaving pupils when they strayed outside his field of vision. He kept an average of six students in for recess every day for homework or behavior issues. He believed that in another month the former "Wild Bunch" would be ready. However, not one to miss an opportunity, he declared that a trip to the circus required more than parent permission, a relatively easy feat. Payne's permission would also be required, a much more difficult accomplishment.

Circus Day finally arrived and the school bustled with anticipation and last-minute arrangements. Thomas welcomed Melvin's father and Connie's mother, invited as additional chaperones. He double-checked every permission slip to ensure that it contained legible home and emergency telephone numbers. Having faithfully monitored the weather forecasts for several days prior to the journey, Thomas had instructed the class to dress for rain. Fortunately, virtually every student heeded the warning. A light drizzle accompanied the subdued daylight of the big day.

Thomas had spoken to Glen a few days before, so both were prepared for last-minute changes. First, the Room 217 teacher checked his students' homework carefully. He had made it clear: no homework checkmark next to your name on the board, no circus. No exceptions. Asa produced a note from his mother explaining that her son had misplaced his math and reading assignments.

"No serious problem, my brother," Thomas assured the boy. "You can do the work downstairs in Mr. Bennett's room while the rest of us are at the circus."

Asa pouted and sulked but, escorted by Maria, left quietly. When she returned, Thomas felt his heart beat faster as he walked to the back of the room and stopped at Tyshaun's desk. He had made a decision but had informed no one but his colleague downstairs.

"Captain, would you open the Operations Folder and read item number twenty-five in the ground rules, please."

Maria reached into her desk and produced the folder containing the "black box" of Student of the Week items. Mr. Payne filled it with special forms created just for his class. She thumbed past the blue booklet serving as the official daily homework log. She had already dutifully copied the day's assignments from the chalkboard onto the log. She privately snickered about Melvin, the first Student of the Week, and his messy handwriting. Alongside the booklet were a half-dozen late-slip forms, for any tardy student to take home and return the next day with an adult signature. No need for them today, Maria thought, since everyone had arrived on time. She straightened out a dozen absentee notices. One would be sent home with a student who had returned from an absence without a note from a parent.

The small girl inspected, then returned a set of half-sheets containing a list of academic subjects. They served as one-day student homework logs, filled out by the buddy of an absent pupil and placed on the missing child's desk. Poor Lakeisha had filled out a bunch of those so far for her buddy, LaShonda. Maria picked up the blank behavior-report forms, used to detail some breach in behavior, which, of course, required a parent signature. She shuddered to think how her Mami would respond if she ever brought home one of those. Finally, she retrieved a wrinkled copy of the ground rules. She cleared her throat and prepared to promulgate number twenty-five, but the next voice everyone heard was Mr. Payne's.

"You want to mail it to me, Captain? I'd get it faster," he teased.

"I have it right here," she replied, holding it in the air. He could be so impatient sometimes, she thought. The girl flipped the page over and found the item. " 'Refusal to obey order from teacher: Left behind for next field trip, possibly all future field trips.' " Maria put the paper back in the folder and awaited further instructions.

Thomas faced the back of the room. "Tyshaun, gather up some things to take with you to Mr. Bennett's room. You're not going with us," he casually announced.

Tyshaun's mouth dropped wide open. He struggled for appropriate words to muster an effective appeal. His chosen buddy, Doug, put his hands on his temples and shook his head from left to right. The class began to murmur. Melvin looked at his father, who sat in the back of the room without emotion. But an almost imperceptible smile formed on the face of Connie's mother. Last year, Tyshaun had teased her daughter without mercy about the gap between the girl's two front teeth in spite of pleas and threats from Connie, Ms. Patterson, Mr. Dorn and herself.

"Wh-Why, Mr. Payne. I had my homework?" Tyshaun whined.

"I know you did, Tyshaun, and I'm very happy about that. But think back," Thomas replied calmly. "Two weeks ago at the end of recess you kept bouncing your basketball in line. Mrs. Chang told you to stop bouncing the ball, and you bounced it twice more, according to her and the Student of the Week then. Mrs. Chang told you to give her the ball and you refused. Do you remember?"

Tyshaun winced. "Yes," he whispered meekly.

"By the time I arrived I heard Mrs. Chang and the Captain tell you to give Mrs. Chang the ball. I told you to give Mrs. Chang the ball like she told you, and do you remember what you did?"

Tyshaun shook his head. The whole spellbound class did likewise. Almost all of them were there and remembered the incident clearly.

Thomas continued. "You slammed the ball towards her on the ground and pouted. I asked you twice to pick up the ball and give it to Mrs. Chang, but you stood in line copping an attitude. I had to bend down and pick it up myself in front of every teacher outside and their students. At the end of the day I even gave you back your basketball, but I told you then that I've got a long memory and you would have to pay for your defiance, didn't I?"

Tyshaun slumped down in his desk, his hands on his face.

"Didn't I?" the first-year instructor repeated more forcefully.

"Yes, Mr. Payne," came the muffled sound seeping from between the tall boy's hands.

Thomas felt some sympathy and compassion for his pupil but pressed on. "I'm sorry I have to do this, son. I really am. But you embarrassed me in public. You brought dishonor on yourself and me and on the class. I can't take the chance that I or Mr. Dilettante or Ms. Malone will tell you to do something and you'll refuse."

Tyshaun perceived the opening and seized it in desperation. "But I learned my lesson. I won't do it again, honest," he pleaded.

Thomas shoved his right hand in his pocket and walked to his desk. "I know you won't," he paused, "because you're not going with us. Go get your things, please. I can't spend any more time on this. My mind's made up." He spoke with his head lowered while recounting the permission slips. "If your behavior changes, maybe, just maybe I'll allow you to come with us in December when we go out for Christmas. Now go on." He pointed to the door.

Tyshaun reached in his desk and slowly removed a few items. Almost everyone in the room found it difficult to witness the look of agony on his face. Maria claimed the condemned student and took him to his destination.

Thomas surveyed the class and opened his hands. "Anyone else want to show me who's boss in my classroom? Huh?"

The only reply was the creaking of the heating system, pouring lukewarm air into the chilly room.

The group gathered their belongings and stood by the door, paired up like Noah's animals. Thomas delivered the final words of caution.

"First of all, I don't want to hear that any of you were teasing Tyshaun or Asa about being left behind. Do I make myself clear?" Upon observing head nods and hearing soft affirmations, he continued. "We're leaving but we're *not* complete, and I don't like it." He walked down the long line of youths and examined their faces. "Any one's failure here represents everyone's failure—especially mine because I'm the teacher." Thomas glanced at his adult chaperones, who watched him with curiosity and admiration. He pointed at the door. "I want you to be especially supportive of those two boys for the rest of the week. Hear?"

"Yes, Mr. Payne," the children replied.

Thomas scratched his smooth face and changed the subject. "Now, about our little venture downtown today: I don't care what the other classes do or don't do, but Room 217 is going out there and acting like the senior class of the Adams. You are to conduct yourselves with dignity and honor and set a good example at all times. Understand?"

"Yes, Mr. Payne."

After everyone signed a card thanking Ms. Flores for her efforts, they left the building in a confident mood. The class thoroughly enjoyed the day at the circus and returned without incident.

That evening Thomas plopped on the living room sofa and read his mail. He opened a telephone bill, three pleas for donations from charities and two sweepstakes notifications that he would soon be a millionaire if he acted quickly. Finally, his eyes fell on a letter from the Montgomery Education and Pre-Release Center, part of the Ohio Department of Rehabilitation and Correction. A notice that the letter had been opened and read before reaching the Post Office had been stamped on the back. Thomas eagerly opened the envelope, impressed that it had been resealed so adroitly. He read slowly.

Dear Little Brother,

Things are moving along a little slower than I would like. I was moved here recently to prepare for my release. As you can imagine, I'm a little impatient about leaving this place and seeing my family again. I hope that yours is one of the first faces I see when I get out. I don't know exactly what day that will be. But it might be around Halloween. Maybe I'll get to take my daughters trick-or-treating after all.

Mom told me that April has not been returning her calls about me seeing Ebony and Erika as soon as possible. She's even hinted about moving out of the state and starting over to get away from all of the confusion. I hate to ask you for anything, Thomas, but April always liked you the most out of all of us, sometimes even me. Perhaps you could call her and ask her to just let me see my babies. That's all I want, just to have a second chance to be a good father. I know that if you talk to her she'll be reasonable. Thanks.

Well, I better close now. It's hurry up and wait time for me. See you on Thanksgiving Day, I hope. I think the Cowboys are playing the 49ers that day. We'll watch the game over at the house. The 49ers don't stand a chance. Take care.

Love,

Edward

Thomas folded the paper and placed it back in the envelope. He scoffed at the idea of getting mixed up in his brother's personal life. Sending him a few books was one thing. Talking to his ex-wife for him would be quite another. No doubt existed in his mind concerning his brother's request. None. He would not call April. Also, the 49ers were going to murder the Cowboys.

The next morning Thomas drove to work taking an unfamiliar route, got lost and barely made it to work on time. When he entered the office he was greeted by Mr. Dorn. The principal was accompanied by a pear-shaped, bronze-skinned woman and a thin boy with short wavy hair who looked like her; obviously her son. Mr. Dorn introduced them. Thomas shook hands with both, welcomed Jonathan to his class and took the two upstairs. The mother praised the sight of the classroom, especially the large Halloween pictures the students had drawn. Thomas thanked her, looked at his watch and produced several forms for the mother to complete and send back. He distributed the ground rules and went over the important ones. The mother admitted that Jonathan had been attending a Catholic school nearby but couldn't stay because she had recently been laid off from her job and could no longer pay his tuition. Also, there had been some discipline problems at the school. She further explained that she was raising her boy and his two brothers alone because...

A few minutes later Thomas introduced Jonathan to the class and seized a desk from next door. Mrs. Chang protested that she would be left with no spares, but he counted her fourteen students and felt little sympathy for her. Playground intelligence sources reported that the newest member of Room 217 possessed talent as a basketball player. He possessed talent as a student also—above grade level in reading and math. Ten minutes before dismissal, Thomas asked the only triad buddy group to come to the front of the room. He always called them Diana Ross and the Supremes. They didn't know why. The three girls complied nervously.

"Now son, I want you to choose one of these girls as your buddy," Thomas said. He explained how buddies helped each other by checking each other's homework in the morning, making sure each had all necessary school materials (pencils, paper, rulers, etc.) and generally looking after each other. Jonathan clearly felt uncomfortable with the show he and the girls were providing. Nearly everyone in the room giggled and snickered and pointed at them. After an exorbitantly long search, Jonathan reluctantly chose Janet, a small, painfully shy girl. The class responded with howls, whistles and some very inventive renditions of "Here Comes the Bride."

During dismissal prep, a student asked if there would be a Halloween party at the end of the month, a question asked by a student every day for the past three weeks. Finally they received an answer. With only a week to go before October 31, Thomas announced that there would be no Halloween party. Instead, the class would have its regular Movie Day with a Halloween theme only for those who had earned enough points to participate. Eighteen points guaranteed admission for M-Day. Unfortunately, several students had already disqualified themselves from next week's festivities. The calendar, October Omar, doesn't lie, Thomas reminded the class.

On Friday Carmelita became the new Student of the Week. She was a bright student, the youngest child with six brothers and a mother in poor health. (To date, Thomas had not met her mother face-to-face.) She displayed more of an edge to her personality than her buddy, Maria. Carmelita raised her hand more than anyone to answer questions and already displayed obvious pleasure in the presence of boys.

Thomas had waited to anoint her because of her tendency to be petty with her classmates and to see the world in terms of "win-lose" instead of "win-win." Earlier in the year she would hold grudges about small slights and insisted on having the last word in arguments with her peers. The day before the announcement, Thomas consulted with Ms. Valdez, her teacher during the previous year, about Carmelita's impending selection. It did not surprise him to hear that the girl had stood out for her bad attitude and "fresh mouth." But as Thomas had expected, Carmelita had become more giving because of her association with Maria. Thomas and Maria invited Ms. Valdez to participate in the ceremony.

That afternoon during the ceremony, Thomas whispered to each student, "How are you playing?"

"I'm playing to win," came the invariant reply.

Ms. Valdez asked a different question. "Are you a giver or a taker?" she inquired.

"A giver," each fifth-grader answered.

A few minutes later, when Thomas asked Carmelita's permission to perform the cradle, she agreed, with obvious reluctance. As the class lifted her, Gloria Estefan's ballad, "Coming Out of the Dark," played in the background.

The young girl, taller and a few pounds heavier than Maria, appeared gracious and dignified during the activity. After the second elevation, her friends returned her feet to the ground. The lights remained off and the class acknowledged their new Student of the Week with applause. Carmelita's face displayed tension as she struggled to accept her classmates' accolades. She spun around, hugged Maria tightly and began whispering to her buddy in Spanish. Maria held her and answered in their first language. Then to everyone's surprise, Carmelita rested her head on her best friend's shoulder and closed her eyes as if she were about to take a nap.

Few understood their exchange but the class responded with additional applause. Thomas put his arms around both of them. Impulsively, Angelica joined them, then Jessica, then Christine. Eventually, the whole class found itself in a massive group hug. The mound of embracing students broke up and began laughing and applauding again. Thomas raised his hand to speak. Deborah turned down the music. He spoke directly to his new captain.

"Carmelita, you thought that you had to be tough. I saw it at the beginning of the year." He paused and smiled. "I kept saying to myself, 'Who does this wonderful, sweet child think she's fooling? She's got a heart of gold.' " He touched her cheek. "I knew it. Your buddy knew it. We all knew it. We were just waiting for you to open your eyes and see what we've seen all along. It just took someone like Maria to hold up that mirror so that you could recognize the giving spirit you have *always* had inside of you." He looked at her buddy. "Maria, keep holding that mirror for her and don't let her try to turn her head. She's doing fine with what she sees right now."

After everyone returned to his or her seat, Thomas turned to Ms. Valdez. "You are the first guest ever at one of our ceremonies," he informed her with a smile. "We are honored by your presence—but now you are no longer a guest but one of us."

The class applauded, welcoming her into its membership. Ms. Valdez, clearly dumbfounded by what she had just witnessed in Mr. Payne's room, struggled for an adequate reply. Was this the same girl who last year had slapped a classmate in the face for skipping past her in the lunch line? Was this the same class that had reduced Ms. Patterson to tears last May?

"Thank you for inviting me. I'm very pleased to be a part of this ceremony," Ms. Valdez gasped, placing her hand on her chest to catch her breath. Then she smiled sincerely at her former student. "Carmelita, I am very proud of you for what you have done."

Over the next few school days, various Adams teachers approached their junior colleague with polite inquiries about his Student of the Week ceremony. Apparently, Ms. Valdez had spoken so effusively about the event that several staff members expressed eagerness to see it for themselves. Thomas decided to have a different Adams employee as a guest participant every Friday. His next scheduled guest would be Glen Bennett.

A few days before Halloween Thomas drove to a local mall to purchase special napkins, plates and so forth for Movie Day. Inside one local discount store, he had to wade through yards and yards of floor space already dedicated to Christmas items. He saw brightly adorned trees of all sizes, material and prices; lights and ornaments of every color; and music selections for every taste. Thomas mentally cursed the store owners for their unmitigated avarice. He vowed not to be a victim of the over-commercialization of the December holiday when it arrived. He finally located the objects he wanted, paid for them and left the store, unaware that for the past fifteen minutes he had been humming Christmas carols.

On the last day of October, Adams primary-grade children paraded around the halls showing off their Halloween costumes. Even Thomas regaled at the sight of the little children in their outfits. He found every one of them to be absolutely adorable. Privately, he speculated about what kind of parents he and Laura would have been.

That afternoon Thomas dismissed nine students who had not accumulated enough points to participate in the day's activities. (It would have been ten but LaShonda was absent.) Most fell only one point short. Several had burned up points by not returning their warning notices promptly. Finding a place for them proved difficult because virtually every room hosted a Halloween party. Thomas called on the special class teachers who had classes during the last period, so the art, music, physical education instructors and the school librarian found seats for their temporary, stony-faced guests.

Meanwhile, Thomas and the rest of the class thoroughly enjoyed the remainder of the day. Jonathan, the new boy, joined the "in" group. The tall teacher showed a short, animated film based on the classic tale, "The Legend of Sleepy Hollow." The children were glued to their seats during the entire show. Ignoring a host of pleas during the show, he did not allow his students to overindulge in the sweetened snacks but insisted that they take most of them home. At the end of the day, with the class complete again and the room cleaned up, he bade them a safe evening, and Carmelita dismissed the group with her usual aplomb.

Thomas gathered his things and left the building after spending only an hour more in his room. The wind had gathered strength as it stripped trees of their former glory. Millions of leaves carpeted the streets, and the threat of rain hung in the air. Thomas admired the sight of miniature ballerinas, vampires, superheroes, ghosts and the like as he carefully drove through the streets of Boston. He stopped at the gym and worked off some of the junk food he had eaten—just to be sociable. He and Glen passed each other at Anthony's driveway; he leaving and Glen entering. They honked horns and the confident former college athlete cruised down Washington Street with George Benson plucking his guitar for him all the way home. It had been a good day.

November

Thomas held the envelope up to the desk lamp to see if anyone could read it from the outside. No, its secrets could not be breached. It was quite small, probably more of a note inside than a letter, he guessed. The return address read, "Laura Newman."

"Just open the damn letter," he blurted out. Having searched unsuccessfully for his letter opener, he reached for a pair of orange sewing scissors he had left on the center table, then carefully pried the top of the envelope apart. He could feel his breathing becoming ponderous as his eyes moved from left to right.

Dear Thomas,

I was so glad to hear about your brother. Thank you for writing to me about his impending release. I'm happy for both of you, but I'm especially pleased for your parents, who never lost hope. Tell them I said hello and tell your brother that although we did not have the chance to meet, he has remained in my heart and prayers.

I hope that you are well, Thomas, and taking good care of yourself. No doubt you have things at your school well under control. I always thought that you'd be a wonderful teacher.

As for me, I'm fine. A little frazzled from time to time as I do all that is necessary to finish this last year at BC. My dad has lined up several contacts for me. I should be ready to step into the real world by the end of the summer.

Well, that's it for now. God bless you and your family.

Love,

Laura

Thomas sat down and perused the letter a second time, then a third. He examined the handwriting. His former betrothed always did write with such beautiful script, showing off beautiful, flowing swirls on her T's and L's. This missive revealed nothing about her personal life, although she did close with the L-word. Thomas wondered what she meant. The ringing telephone slapped the contemplative man back into the real world.

A minute later, after declining an offer from some credit card company, Thomas inspected his surroundings. He had tracked a dozen wet leaves onto the carpet. The curtains still snuggled together, so the living room appeared dark and uninviting. Only the light of his desk lamp illuminated the area. (It would take time to adjust to limited sunshine. Daylight Savings Time had ended only a week ago.) The apartment was cold. The temperature never rose above fifty, but he had left a window open. Two plants Laura had given him needed watering and now languished lethargically, half-covered with brown spots. Leaves from each drooping plant lay on the floor, irrefutable evidence of his neglect.

Thomas took off his jacket and forced himself to hang it up right away in the hall closet. He twisted the dial on his halogen lamp, bringing some cheerfulness to the living room, then went back to Laura's letter and read it again.

Did not have *the chance* to meet, she wrote? Bullshit. There had been a chance, but Little Miss Stuck-up didn't want to go to a prison. And if she thought he'd be such a wonderful teacher, how come she wasn't more enthusiastic about his choice to work at a public inner-city school? Thomas tossed the letter on the dining table without putting it back in the envelope. It lay next to his new *Sports Illustrated* magazine, a sweepstakes offer and an appeal for funds on behalf of some worthwhile charity. He switched on the television and watched pieces of the local news, turning the volume up considerably louder than usual.

A few days later the rookie teacher explained to his class that they would try out a new activity and asked for their cooperation. He added that the class ground rule about talking without raising one's hand would be suspended for the time being.

"Does anyone know what a contract is?" he inquired.

Six students raised their hands. Habit.

"No, go ahead, just tell me," Thomas instructed with a laugh. He heard several responses. "That's right. A contract is an agreement between two or more people. Today, each of you is going to make a contract between yourself and the rest of the class about who you are." He strolled to the back of the room so he could see the entire board and looked to his right. "Connie, would you go erase everything off the board please?"

"I'm over here, Mr. Payne."

The teacher twisted his neck to the left. He and the whole class responded with snickers. It had happened again. At the beginning of each month he changed the position of almost everyone's desk. He hoped the relocations would stimulate the classroom. It would take a few days for everyone, including himself, to get used to the new positions.

"Oops, sorry. Please erase the board—wherever you are." He turned to his right again. "Melvin, start on the other end and help Connie, please." A few laughs and "Here Comes the Bride" choruses surfaced. Thomas allowed the activity to fade on its own.

When the main board became blank, Thomas spoke. "We're going to fill this space up with adjectives. What do adjectives do?" Hands went up. They couldn't shake the habit after two months. "It's okay, just tell me," he requested. Softly at first, then louder and with more frequency, he heard several similar, correct replies. Fortunately, they had recently covered adjectives during composition class. "That's correct," he said. "Adjectives describe things. I want you to tell me as many adjectives that describe a person as you can think of. But only positive words. Nothing negative. We'll write all of them down until we can't think of any more. You're going to choose three of them for your personal contract between you and this class." Thomas raised his eyebrows and shook his index finger in the air. "Choose wisely. Then we'll write the contracts down and post them up on that wall over there." He pointed to the wall near his cluttered desk. "And remember, once you make a contract you have to keep it, okay?"

"Yes, Mr. Payne," several students replied in unison. Another habit.

"Okay, I'll get you started." He took a piece of chalk and wrote three words on the board: Caring, Kind and Friendly.

After a slow start, for the next thirty minutes Thomas frantically scribbled words on the board shouted to him by his twenty-eight fifth-graders. Eventually exhausted from writing, the former athlete stepped back and admired their work. The board had become a virtual dictionary of words that conveyed humankind's potential: Loving, Helping, Warm, Giving, Productive, Truthful, Forgiving, Marvelous, Happy, Amazing, Creative and many others decorated the cold, dark thirty-feet space in full view of the entire class. Thomas and his students obviously enjoyed the activity. Overall, he was very pleased with the results.

He instructed that a small piece of paper be delivered to each student. Afterwards, Thomas stepped to the middle of the room again. "Choose three of those adjectives for yourself and only three. Print them on this paper and write your name. I'm going to collect them and copy each one onto one of these." He held up a multicolored set of nine-by-twelve-inch art construction paper. "Later, you'll sign it and we'll hang it up for everyone to see."

Thomas looked his students in the eyes, as he did when he was trying to inspire them. "Don't be afraid to choose the ones you fear. The ones you've been struggling with." He tilted his head and arched his eyebrows. "If you've been having trouble telling the truth, write 'Truthful' on that paper and from this day on, be a truthful person. The class and I will help you stick to your contract." He paused and stared at the board then back at the class. They sat at full attention, clearly enthralled by their teacher's words. "Been in a few arguments and fights in the past? Having trouble controlling your temper?" Thomas held up one of the slips of paper. "Put down 'Joyful' on that paper and from now on in our class, at this school, be joyful. We'll help you." He gazed upward at the clock, an hour slow. "Okay, you've got five minutes."

That evening Thomas brought home a stack of construction paper and two brand-new, black magic markers. In large letters he printed each contract as an "I" statement. After completing the task, he found himself impressed with the students' choices.

The following day the rookie teacher presented the contracts to his children and slowly, methodically explained where and how to sign. Some saw their choices printed on blue construction paper, some red, some white, some yellow while a few read the words on light-brown paper. Twenty-seven students shared five markers (LaShonda was absent). Thomas insisted that each student sign his or her name in cursive, a challenging task for many.

The next morning the students entered the room and saw the usual sights. The large bulletin board showcased the name of the Student of the Week,

Melvin Dilettante, the first chosen for a second term. Photographs Thomas had taken of each student hung above the main chalkboard with the pupil's name underneath. Above the photos loomed a large sign in capital letters that read: THE PLAYERS. On the opposite wall above the student closets clung two dozen photographs of adults who served the students of Room 217 in some capacity. The principals, the special class (art, music, etc.) teachers, the custodial staff, the volunteer lunch monitors, the crossing guards, Thomas himself and others vigilantly and silently stood watch over the fifth-grade class. Above them, a sign stating their rank: THE COACHES.

Several posters of influential role models remained; an athlete, a figure skater, a state supreme court justice and others. Also on display were several seasonal Thanksgiving posters the students had constructed featuring turkeys, cornucopias and personal reflections of "Why I am Thankful." Fourteen turkey pictures scattered themselves across the student-closet doors in the back of the room, with the names of a different buddy pair written on the protruding stomach of each one. Above the all but unusable sink: a display of birthday cakes for every month in the year and each student's birthday listed inside the cake for the appropriate month. On the wall near the teacher's desk, the calendar, now called November Nancy, revealed the point count for the first week.

Right above the teacher's chalkboard hovered huge new objects. An elongated banner asking, WHAT'S YOUR CONTRACT? dangled two feet below the ceiling. Underneath loomed the answers: a rainbow of construction paper containing the contract of each student. (That morning Thomas had caught LaShonda before the first bell and watched her sign the last one.) "I am a Friendly, Hardworking and Creative young woman" declared Connie. "I am an Intelligent, Strong and Happy young man" asserted Melvin. "I am a Wise, Successful and Trustworthy young man" decreed Gary. The declarations virtually covered the upper portion of the wall.

After the morning routine of checking for homework, Thomas distributed to each student a personal colored replica of his or her own contract. He spoke to Doug (the boy who could not read) privately outside the room. He read his contract to him and listened as the boy repeated it four times. After returning, he asked the entire class to stand while holding their contracts. Always one to seize a potentially dramatic moment, Thomas played a special musical number, Aaron Copeland's "Fanfare for the Common Man," while calling on a student and asking loudly, "What's your contract?" With trumpets blowing behind their declarations, one by one, each student announced his or her contract proudly to the entire class. It was another uplifting event for Room 217.

After lunch Melvin asked his teacher a personal question. "Do you have a contract too, Mr. Payne?" he inquired.

Thomas admitted that he did. "Yes, my brother," he replied. "I am an open, giving and respectful young man."

Later, while alone in the classroom, the Ohio native reflected on his life before his personal reconstruction two years before. Until then, during his late high school years and throughout most of his college career, he had fancied himself a real ladies man. Partly due to his choice of friends (almost all fellow jocks) and partly due to his older brother's influence, the handsome athlete had grown to view women as commodities to be solely judged on their attractiveness. It took little time for the much sought-after young man to become indifferent to the pain and heartbreak he caused. Recalling that period of his life still caused Thomas's face muscles to tighten as he grimaced in shame.

That evening Thomas relaxed at home, seated at his dining table surrounded by report cards. A string quartet playing Mozart and a hot cup of chamomile tea had been enlisted to soothe his nerves after a messy drive home. He had left the Adams at around 5 o'clock and found the canopy of darkness overhead to be depressing. The first ten weeks of school had faded into history, and the marking period was officially over. His first Open House would be held the following week. He wanted to double-check every grade decision. Glen had warned that it was not uncommon for Adams parents to object to a teacher's grade. A teacher had to be ready to prove a mark beyond a reasonable doubt.

To be fair and preclude any claims of favoritism, Thomas chose to let the calculator determine the academic component of each student's report card. However, with the Juilliard Quartet finishing an especially delicate largo, he had just discovered, to his dismay, that he had made a common rookie teacher's error—he had inadvertently overlooked the mediocre work submitted by some of his more reticent, best-behaved students. Especially troubled by one grade in particular, he punched the numbers again, remembering that the student spoke Spanish at home. It explained the child's average writing skills. Thomas took off his glasses and rubbed his forehead.

Agitated, the young man stood and stared at his grade book and the numbers one last time before writing the grade on the office copy in erasable ink. In composition, Maria Colón had earned a C+. She would not make the Honor Roll.

Just then the telephone rang and Thomas rushed to answer it. He would be spared further guilt for a few minutes. A long distance operator asked if he would accept the charges from an Edward Payne. The Boston resident gladly agreed.

"Go ahead," the operator said and thanked them both for using his employer's long distance company.

"Thomas? Thomas? Are you there?" the clear voice on the other line asked.

"Yeah, I'm here. How are you, my big brother?" he replied.

"Oh, good. I can't talk long. The maid is coming soon to turn down the bed," Edward joked.

Thomas laughed. "Okay, Edward. So when's the big day?"

"A fucking week before Thanksgiving!"

Thomas gasped. "Why so long? Did you forget to pay your bill at the last place?"

This time Edward laughed. "Yeah, the service was so lousy."

Thomas chuckled, then there was an uncomfortable silence. The two brothers started to talk at the same time and stopped at the same time. The silence returned. Each told the other to go ahead. Thomas started over. "Is there anything you want me to do for you?" It seemed like the thing to say.

"Not really. Well, maybe you could call April and ask her to let me see the kids when I'm out. I got a right to see my own daughters, don't I?" Edward didn't wait for an answer. "Lord knows, I didn't do right by April. I'd make it up to her if I could. Swear to God. Look, if we're through, we're through, you know what I'm saying? But you know how I love those girls? I just wanna get to see them. Can you help me out?"

The youngest Payne fought his brain and heart to formulate a coherent reply. He resented his brother for asking him to do such a thing. Their dad had admonished his children to never get in the middle of other people's marriage problems—even a member of your own family. Once, when Thomas had hinted to his brother that perhaps he was being a bit selfish regarding April, Edward had told him that it was none of his goddamn business. Now he was practically begging for help to get out of the corner into which he had painted himself. Thomas stuttered as he tried to form words to convey his dilemma but paused as he heard voices in the background. Edward spoke rapidly.

"Look, Thomas, if you don't feel comfortable doing it, I understand. I wouldn't ask but—" His voice trailed off as he angrily addressed someone nearby. He returned. "Look, I gotta go. They say my time is up. Don't worry about coming out to greet me when I get out. Mom, Dad, Sis and Grandma are all gonna be there. And they still might change the day. Will you be home for Thanksgiving?"

"Yeah, I'll be there."

"I'll see you then. Don't forget. The Cowboys by a touchdown."

Thomas's mood shifted. His eyes widened and he laughed. "You kidding? The 49ers by ten big ones!"

"We'll see. I'll see you in about two weeks. Love you, man."

"I love you, too, Edward. Bye." He heard a click. Then the strings of the quartet gently brought him back to Boston. Thomas lowered the receiver, dropped it on a pile of papers and returned to his work. He caressed his half-empty cup of tea, now too cold to drink.

The following day at school Thomas drove to work in a bit of a funk. Dark clouds hovered in the sky threatening to rain, as they had done on the way home the day before. Most of the once beautiful leaves had fallen from the trees, leaving half-naked, black skeletons silently shivering in an occasional brisk wind. An accident on the other side of the street managed to slow the lane Thomas occupied. (Boston drivers just had to satisfy their morbid curiosity.) He had worked sedulously late and had finished his report cards but hadn't slept well.

Not one of his students had earned an A or B in every subject, so no one had made the Honor Roll. The first-year teacher blamed himself. Maybe a couple would and should have made the list if he had been monitoring their progress a little closer. Apparently, the sure-bets from last year had been assigned to Mrs. Chang's Advanced Work Class. To make matters worse, everyone's attendance was required at an assembly, planned to announce the first-quarter award-winners. Thomas would have to endure the embarrassment of being the only teacher to present just a few Perfect Attendance and School Spirit awards, and one Merit Award winner (*nearly* all A's and B's, to Melvin). As he played with the radio station in his car, he felt the infrequent but disquieting pain of uncertainty in his own abilities.

The students did not seem to notice their teacher's blue mood. In fact, they seemed to be quite convivial and pleasant from the very beginning of the day. It was Francine's birthday, so she brought cupcakes for the entire class. Thomas whipped out an old acoustic guitar he kept in the closet, and the entire class struggled to sing "Happy Birthday" to her. He felt his spirits lift.

Later that same morning he was very pleased to witness the cooperative and competitive atmosphere of the morning's math class. The fifth-graders of Room 217 repeatedly tried to solve word problems employing multiple operations (first add, then subtract or first multiply, then add, etc.). The class had been grouped into their Working Partner pairs. Two weeks before, Thomas had rearranged his students into pairs for math. Unlike buddies, the teacher had chosen these pairs and purposely selected a student struggling in math to work alongside one more successful. When they had initially been formed, the first item of business for each pair had been to select a special name. Subsequently, for the past two weeks during math Thomas instructed them as a group only for the first half of class, then insisted that each student sit next to his or her Working Partner as they tried to solve problems together.

Now, as each group struggled, Thomas observed the patient and helpful "upper" math pupil with his or her "slower" partner. Connie explained to Cleopatra how to look for clue words like "in all" or "left" or "each" when solving word problems. Angel, who had nearly come to blows with Tyshaun three weeks before for sitting in "his" chair during lunch, now calmly drew a diagram so that his partner could comprehend why they should add, not subtract for the last problem. Thomas clapped his hands and employed his master-of-ceremonies voice.

"All right, who knows the answer to number one?" Hands shot up all over the room, and voices squealed with confident requests for acknowledgment. Thomas looked around and pointed to two girls seating in the back. "Sugar and Spice, would you two please go to the board and show the class how it's done?"

Playful boos and hisses filled the air. Undaunted, Deborah calmly stood, carefully ironed out the front of her blouse, then walked with Jessica, who bounded right behind her, swinging a head full of guaranteed one hundred percent real human hair.

Thomas grabbed another piece of chalk and hypnotically waved it in the air. "How about number two?" Hands sprang up again as several students pleaded for a chance. "Calm down. Calm down, now. There's enough for everybody," he cautioned, searching the room. "How about you, Road Racers? Are you ready?"

Melvin jumped out of his seat and reached for the chalk. That kid sure loved math, everyone acknowledged. Akeem, a quiet but hardworking boy with sparkling eyes, stood also. Thomas gave the chalk to the latter. Groans poured out from passed-over students. The two boys raced to the board to showcase their math erudition.

Thomas handed another piece of chalk to Carmelita. "Pretty Math Girls, you said number three was yours, right?" Carmelita agreed and gave a signal for her partner to join her. LaShonda looked around the room and stuck her tongue out at Asa, then giggled and fled to the safety of the chalkboard on the other side of her teacher. Asa dismissed her with a wave of his hand, announcing that he and Vince, aka Handsome Math Hunks, had deciphered the answer before anyone else anyway. Several classmates begged to differ.

That afternoon after dismissal Thomas approached Ms. Cooke and inquired about Doug's chances of receiving help. Ms. Cooke stoically replied that she had heard nothing yet. Who could he call to follow up on his request, the young man asked. He was forced to ask Ms. Cooke twice more because she insisted that calling would not hasten a reply. Eventually, she told him the name of a woman to call. No, she didn't have the number. He would have to call Court Street and please, don't divulge that she had helped him in any way. Thomas exited the room, coldly assuring her that she had nothing to fear.

That weekend he spent hours calling every student's home to personally invite each parent or guardian to the upcoming John Adams School Open House. All twenty-five adults to whom he spoke agreed to come. He sent handwritten letters to the homes of three students who had no working telephones.

The following week Thomas stood in his underwear examining the contents of his closet. The young teacher had read somewhere that men in dark suits were taken more seriously. He seldom wore a suit to work anymore but always a long sleeve shirt and tie. The previous night the loquacious meteorologist with the hair piece predicted that parts of Massachu-setts would see frost. After holding and inspecting several choices, he fi-nally lifted the wooden hanger holding his black suit and freed it from the crowded confines of his closet. He would look very professional at his first Open House.

In the last segment of the school day, Thomas informed the class that they would not hold their regularly scheduled fifteen minute DEAR time (a school-wide silent reading block, Drop Everything And Read). His students looked at each other, then at their teacher with uneasy anticipation. They recognized early on that Mr. Payne regarded DEAR time as almost sacred. At the end of every day, at 2:20 on the dot, Mr. Payne took out a book, pulled out a chair from his table and planted himself somewhere in the midst of their "student space," as he liked to call it, and read. He placed a "Do Not Disturb" sign on the door and tolerated no interruptions. Today was obviously a special day.

Thomas requested that each student sit with his or her buddy, then produced a small stack of folded papers and distributed them. "I'm going to give you a peek at your first report card," he announced. "You can't take them home yet, but I don't think it's unreasonable to show you the results of your hard work—or lack thereof—so far."

His jaw became tight and his footsteps heavy as he made his appointed rounds to each student. He appeared noticeably disappointed by the re-sults, as were most of the class. Exclamations of "Oh my God!" and "Oh no!" surfaced frequently, mired with trepidation. Thomas did not want to end the day on a sour note. He would have to instill some hope in the class, so he spoke solemnly and with compassion.

"Class, I know that many of you are disappointed by your report cards. You may have noticed that you got lower grades than you've received in the past. To be perfectly honest, I'm disappointed too." He stopped and cleared his throat. "But this is only the first quarter. There are three more to go, and I know that all of us are going to work harder next quarter to bring these marks up," he exclaimed, pointing to the ceiling, then at them. "I know you can do it."

He heard a whimpering sound to his right and turned to investigate. Maria had burst into tears, and her best friend sought to comfort her. Carmelita put both arms around her buddy and struggled to lift her out of her seat, apparently to walk her to the girls' bathroom. Thomas was deeply hurt at seeing the pain of one of his favorite pupils. Nevertheless, he made the decision to deal with Maria differently than expected.

"No, let go of her!" he demanded. "Both of you, sit down!"

The class was absolutely shocked at their teacher's tone. They had never heard him speak in such a way to Maria—ever!

His eyes burned with fire. "What? You don't think I'm disappointed about this? Of course I am. But crying won't get the job done." He glared at his melancholy angel. "Maria, *mira, escucha, por favor!*"

She sobbed twice more, then lifted her heavy head and stared at him.

"Are the grades I've given you fair? I mean, didn't you receive several composition papers from me with C's on 'em? Yes or no?"

"Yes," she answered meekly.

Thomas continued his interrogation. "That day after school when you came to see me because I hadn't selected you Student of the Week, did you come in crying?" he asked, folding his arms across his massive chest and waiting.

"No." She answered in a stronger tone.

"You became Student of the Week because you did what you had to do to improve yourself, yes?"

She shook her head, then answered calmly. "Yes."

"Can you change that C+ to a B or even an A next quarter?"

"Yes."

Thomas moved in closer for the kill. "Then who will it be up to for that to happen? Me? You? Your mom?"

Maria cleared her throat and pointed to herself. "Me."

Thomas smiled and gave her the thumbs-up sign. "I believe you, honey. You just have to believe in yourself." He turned back to his transfixed students. "And that goes for the rest of you. Before you go home whining about how Mr. Payne gave you this grade or that grade, remember, I didn't give you anything you didn't give yourselves. You can cry about it, or like Maria just discovered, you can get your head on, pick yourself up and declare that next quarter is going to be different. It's up to you."

It wasn't Friday, but Thomas huddled the class in the center of the room, and they proclaimed themselves ready for the second quarter. The coach then introduced a competitive element into the evening's turnout: since they could not match the Advanced Classes on Honor Roll awardees this quarter, how about beating them by bringing in more parents for the

Open House, just to show them who's boss? Thomas promised that he would perform a special feat just for them if they pulled it off. The class readily agreed. They ended the day with the room number cheer and were dismissed to go out and do battle.

The entire staff at the Adams busied themselves preparing for the 5 o'clock event. Mr. Dorn personally inspected each classroom and held a special impromptu after-school meeting. He presented the big picture of the day's activities, then left Ms. Flores to discuss details. She reminded the staff to make sure that every parent signed the guest sheet distributed to each teacher. The Adams crew, dressed more professionally in Thomas's opinion, spied on their watches as Ms. Flores's soft voice trickled across the room. Finally, she looked at her watch and abruptly brought the meeting to an end.

As they were leaving the library, Thomas overheard two teachers complain that they had never seen more than a third of their parents at a school Open House. Most teachers were happy to get half. According to the building grapevine, the two Advance Classes usually pulled in seventy-five percent or so. Ms. Paterson informed Thomas that she had seen only nine parents or caretakers last year and, given the bad news they received year after year, advised him not to expect too much. If he got ten, he should count his blessings.

Since Open House did not officially begin for another two hours, Thomas worked in his room with the door closed, a sign at the Adams that a teacher did not wish to be disturbed. He felt nervous and even slightly apprehensive about the upcoming visits. The week's earlier events did not help: Two days earlier, Mr. Dorn had asked to see his report cards and grade book (checking up on the "new kid," Thomas speculated). That morning Ms. Flores returned the items. She only reported that Mr. Dorn expressed concern about what he had seen but found no obvious fault in the young man's system. However, she admonished, the principal did send word that his new teacher "had better be very sure" about the grades he had assigned.

Thomas returned to the present and placed a folder containing past student work on each desk. He heard a knock on the door and fought the urge to be annoyed. Receiving a visitor was probably better that torturing himself alone in his classroom. Besides, with the door closed, it could only be Mr. Dorn, Ms. Flores, Glen or ...

"Hi, Heléna," Thomas said, with a genuine smile.

"*Buenes tardes*, Tomaso," Heléna Gutiérrez replied with her ever-present smile. She entered his territory unabashedly, as she did everywhere she went; not out of arrogance, but because of her unflappable belief that all human interaction had profound, intrinsic value. She wore a white silk blouse and black pants. Her black hair fell down past her shoulders. Large, gold hoop earrings dangled from her ears. Thomas took in a whiff of strawberries from her perfume. Her presence immediately improved his mood.

She stared out the window and made a face. "Don't you just hate how dark it is already?" Before her host had a chance to answer, she changed the subject. "Whatcha doing?" Thomas shook his head but said nothing. A distant flash of lightning briefly illuminated the vast darkness outside of the classroom windows. Thomas turned his head toward the windows and frowned. Like a honey bee, Heléna buzzed from desk to desk, peeking in students' folders until she found one with welcome news. "Now that's more like it," she declared.

Thomas glanced at the name card taped to the front of the desk. Next to it were two Student of the Week stars. "Oh, yeah," he said. "That's Melvin. He's my only top student—so far."

She shook her head and returned the folder to its rightful owner. The cheerful woman continued her meandering journey. She had been in the room recently so nothing new appeared on the walls. Still, she re-examined the student contracts and Thanksgiving posters, then wandered over to Thomas's desk. He joined her and sat down in his chair. Heléna sprang backwards, landing on the table next to him and playfully kicked her long legs while humming a song with an obvious Spanish flavor. She and Glen were the only real friends Thomas had made at the Adams. The more time he spent with her, the less he noticed her mustache. In fact, now he didn't notice it at all. She was a very attractive woman anyway, and her zest for life made her even more so.

"Well," Heléna purred. "Are you ready?"

"Sure," Thomas replied without making eye contact. "And you?"

She shrugged her shoulders wistfully. "Me? Of course. After all, what do I have to do? I only have twelve students." She inspected the table on which she was sitting and picked up a book about the game of chess and flipped through it. "What's this?"

Thomas recognized the book. "Oh, it's an idea I have."

Heléna suddenly remembered the reason for her visit. "Whatever happened with your student? The one who can't read?"

Thomas frowned. He told his friend about the lack of progress in getting help for Doug.

The Venezuelan native grew earnest and her eyes widened. "Listen, Tomaso. I can work with him a couple of times a week if you want me to. I mean, maybe I could even see him every day. Let's not wait for somebody else to help. It'll be our secret."

Thomas perked up and sat upright in his char. "Would you? I mean, it wouldn't be too much work or get you in any trouble?"

Heléna smiled again and waved her hand. "Oh no. Besides, if anyone makes a fuss, we can always claim that because we're new, we didn't know any better." The two co-conspirators spent several minutes formulating a plan to send Doug downstairs to Heléna almost every day. Her room had formerly been a storage closet and was out of the way in the basement of the school, so few would notice the boy's presence. They hashed out a scheme for their clandestine operation. Thomas thanked his friend for her generosity.

She looked at her watch. "I better get going. Parents will start coming in soon." The man thanked her again for her kindness. She jumped off the table and put her face close to his. Thinking she wanted to whisper some further secret in his ear, Thomas leaned closer. To his surprise, Heléna touched the side of his face with her fingers, which glistened with ruby-red nail polish. She gracefully turned his face to hers, then softly and tenderly kissed him on the lips. "You're welcome," she whispered. She took to her feet and walked out the door without turning around.

Thomas put his hand to his mouth and picked up his pen as if he were about to commit some matter to paper. Exactly what, he could no longer remember. He felt confused and slightly upset about what had just occurred. He could still feel the impression on his lips. He could still hear the soft smacking sound. But he wondered if he was making much out of nothing. Heléna was a vivacious and spontaneous woman. He recalled seeing some of the other Hispanic teachers in the primary wing kissing some of their children goodbye, especially their girls. Perhaps some cultural explanation existed for Heléna's impetuous overture. No need getting a woody in his pants because his new friend offered what she thought was akin to a handshake. He could not dwell on such matters any further; his first parent had arrived.

A large-framed, tall woman wearing an olive-colored suit entered the room. "Hello, Mr. Payne. Am I too early?"

Thomas stood and stared at the women's face. Earlier he had cautioned his students to make sure that they accompanied their visitors, so that he would not be embarrassed trying to associate a face with a name. The woman held her coat in her arms and extended it to her host, who accepted it and laid it on his chair. She took some time to carefully hand-iron her suit. The light of recognition flashed in the Thomas's head.

"Ms. Anderson, how nice to see you again," he exclaimed, then searched the room with histrionics. "Where's my girl?"

Almost on cue, Deborah appeared in the doorway demure and shy, as though she had arrived for the first day at a new school. When she and her teacher made eye contact, she dropped her smile and looked away. Thomas chose not to say anything about her not entering the room with her mother. He did not have to. He would simply keep it in mind when selecting Student of the Week for the rest of the month. He gave Ms. Anderson the ledger to sign and directed her to Deborah's desk. She picked up her granddaughter's report card and folder containing past work. Thomas remained silent while she flipped through the material. It didn't take long before Deborah was hanging her head, enduring a forceful scolding from her grandmother. The well-dressed woman returned to her child's teacher.

"Believe me, Mr. Payne, you'll see an improvement. We're going to cut down on that TV and that talking on the telephone to ... " She stopped and made a face. "What's that girl's name?"

Deborah flashed an embarrassed grin and answered softly.

Thomas arched his eyebrows in surprise. "Cleopatra?" He frowned and put his hand on his forehead in an exaggerated manner. "No wonder her work's been falling off lately."

"Well, Mr. Payne, I'm putting a stop to that starting *today*." Again, she stared at her granddaughter. "Do you hear me, child?"

"Yes, ma'am."

Just then, Pedro, a dependable student with a touch of gray hair entered the room with his grandmother, judging from the lines on her face and her snow-white hair. Everyone turned to face them. Deborah, recognizing her opportunity to escape further chastisement, raced over to greet them as if they were long-lost relatives. Her teacher and grandmother chatted for a few seconds about the latter's job as a legal secretary. After the Andersons left, Pedro introduced Thomas to his grandmother.

"*Mucho gusto*," Thomas said, hoping he had not unknowingly uttered a Spanish obscenity. He launched right into discussing Pedro's progress.

At the beginning of the year, he explained, Pedro did not raise his hand much to participate in class—probably had just gotten used to withdrawing from the classroom craziness over the years. Thomas went to his desk, retrieved his grade book and showed her how Pedro had started out with low grades, then for the past three weeks had gotten B's in just about everything. Finally, he added that Pedro was also one of the best behaved kids in the class—a boy with excellent manners.

The boy's instructor stopped talking and finally noticed the puzzled look on the elderly woman's face. He recalled that he had heard Pedro and his grandmother conversing in Spanish. The rookie teacher mentally kicked himself. Just because Pedro had never been in the school's bilingual program didn't mean that his *abuelita* from Puerto Rico understood English. Thomas suspected that she had been attentive just to be polite and not embarrass him, he being so effusive about her grandson and all. He thought the best thing to do was to shut up, listen and trust Pedro to translate accurately. The matriarch spoke with a noticeable accent but could be clearly understood.

"Theez eez the first year I no have trouble with Pedro," she announced, pointing at her grandson.

"Who? You mean Pedro was trouble?" Thomas exclaimed, turning to his student. "Really?"

The lad flashed an embarrassed smile and looked away. The tickled teacher leaned backwards and burst into laughter. Several parents paraded into the room together, so Thomas escorted the woman to the door. She smiled and placed her small, wizened hand on top of his. The old lady looked the young man in the eyes.

"Tank you and God bless you for what you done for me Pedro." She paused for a moment and cast her proud gaze on her grandson, who smiled back. "One day he be a doctor, no?"

"*Sí*, Abuelita Alverrado. I am sure that he will." Thomas concurred proudly.

The woman nodded and slowly trudged down the corridor, with Pedro faithfully lending his arm for support. Thomas admired this devoted boy, who displayed not the slightest embarrassment about her presence or impatience about her slow pace. The Cincinnati native found himself missing his own grandmother on his father's side. She had passed away a month after his eleventh birthday. He sniffed the air, enjoying the aroma of her delicious apple pie when voices from his classroom nudged him back to the present.

Thomas tried his best to manage all of the visitors in his room. Melvin's entire family came. They were dissatisfied with his first-quarter results and warned him that the next quarter must be better. Thomas had to assure Maria's mother that her daughter could handle a monolingual class. A small woman with long, braided hair who did not seem to fully comprehend English, she agreed to give it one more quarter. Maria was visibly disturbed at the idea of leaving this man who had become like a father to her. Later, Thomas broke up a civil but earnest argument between a noncustodial father and custodial mother about the former being at the Open House.

Thomas was very pleased about the turnout. Glen had warned him about how argumentative some parents could be. Of course, several parents displayed irritation or suggested that the young man had been too harsh in his grading. They limited their complaints to a few obligatory comments, nothing he couldn't deflect. No one had gotten loud or rude— until Cleopatra's mother arrived.

She was tall, fair and, like her daughter, possessed a pretty face made less so by a near-constant scowl. She stepped up to Thomas, bypassing the other parents who had been there waiting before her.

"How come you gave Cleo a D+ in Reading, Mr. Payne? Cleo's an excellent reader. She's been reading since she was in the first grade!" The woman stood arms akimbo waiting for an answer. Her thick hair had become soggy from the light drizzle.

Thomas stared at his agitated guest. He remembered when he played ball. The opponent's cornerback would snort and grunt at him, trying *unsuccessfully* to put him off his game. He could also feel the hungry eyes of his guests. Various family members of several students watched with a mixture of curiosity and fascination. They wanted to see whether the new kid on the block could hold his own against the perennially disagreeable parent.

Thomas paused for a moment, then spoke softly. "I'm glad you made it, Ms. Atkins, and I'm anxious to talk to you about Cleopatra. However, I must see to a couple of parents who've been waiting patiently for—"

"That's all right. You go ahead, Mr. Payne." He heard an adult reply, followed by a chorus of similar sentiments. Cleo's mother, given half a chance, sure could make the damnedest fool out of herself, they whispered to each other. Remember that scene she made last year with the bus driver? All because Cleo got caught throwing rocks off the bus. And remember before that when....

Thomas turned back to his challenger. Cleopatra (he always called her by her full first name) stood behind her mother grinning from ear to ear. He decided to start off congenially, nodding his head in agreement. "You're right, Ms. Atkins. Cleopatra reads aloud about as well as any student in the class—maybe even better."

"Then how come she got this D in reading? That's what I want to know," the impatient woman snapped. "The girl got nothing but A's and B's in reading last year."

I'm sure she did, the first-year teacher thought to himself. Damn. Ms. Patterson's generous grades would surely haunt him for months to come. He delivered the news dispassionately. "Cleopatra reads as smoothly as a reporter on the national news. Unfortunately, she doesn't appear to under-stand—or comprehend—what she's reading." In one swoop he reached be-hind his irate guest to his desk and produced his bible (grade book). "She's taken six short comprehension quizzes this quarter and hasn't passed a one, see?" He pointed to the evidence in black and white.

The perturbed woman hovered over the battered book. Her face be-gan to untighten but she tried one more protest. "Well, if she's so bad, why didn't you tell me? That's your job—to let me know 'bout these things. You're the teacher 'round here."

Thomas tried to hide his smug satisfaction. A protest made after the ref had made a call always proved to be an exercise in futility. Also, in this setting the teacher had the home-field advantage. He excused himself and quickly stutter-stepped around two small children (somebody's little brother and sister) and returned with Cleo's folder. He removed a white piece of paper and examined it.

"Why, I did, ma'am," he stated, putting on his sincere face. "I sent a warning notice home, and you signed it, see?" Thomas raised it into the air like a shrewd litigator.

Ms. Atkins took the slightly crumpled paper out of his hand and read it, then turned around, her blood-shot eyes glaring at her daughter. Cleo im-mediately started to cry. "Who signed this paper, girl!" she shouted. At this point, no one in the room even pretended to do anything other than watch the spectacle.

Cleo put her hand over her face and sobbed. "Neffie," She feebly admitted.

The woman grabbed her daughter by the shoulder and shook her. "Your sister Nefertiti signed my name! Girl, you in so much trouble *I'm* even scared for you!" She turned to Thomas, whose enjoyment had turned to compassion for the mother and daughter. She could not meet his gaze. The beaten woman stared at his chest and sighed. Her own eyes seemed to fill with frustration.

Thomas sought to salvage her dignity. "Thank you for coming," he said sincerely. "I know right now this is disappointing, but I've been telling Cleopatra, for I don't know how long, to settle down, get to work and take responsibility for her actions. I think now that we're all on the same page, she'll do better."

Ms. Atkins buttoned her coat. "I know she will, Mr. Payne. But right now let me get this girl home, get her and her sister in the same room and get me some exercise." Cleo whimpered as several children put their hands over their mouths. The angry mother still had her child by the shoulder when they marched out of the room.

The rest of the evening, although frantic at times, seemed tamed by comparison. At 6:50 Mr. Dorn announced over the loudspeaker that everyone had to be out of the building in ten minutes. Thomas checked his list to see how many parents had arrived. He was pleased at the results. As he arranged items in his briefcase, he jumped at the unexpected sound of a girl's voice.

"Mr. Payne, am I too late?"

Thomas faced the door and saw LaShonda and another woman, who strongly resembled the girl's mother, standing in the doorway. LaShonda's mother was a heavy-set woman who possessed sad, listless, life-defeated eyes. This visitor, slightly younger and thinner, did not have the same vanquished look. At the moment, the woman's primary concern involved a spirited engagement with an old umbrella, trying to get it closed properly. LaShonda took the item from her companion and continued the struggle.

"No," he muttered, resettling his briefcase on the floor. He glanced at the girl and shamelessly resorted to old-fashioned flattery. "LaShonda, I don't believe I've had the pleasure of meeting your sister," he said, extending his hand.

The mother look-a-like broke into a wide grin as they shook hands. LaShonda flashed a bewildered look on her face, then giggled and stomped her feet impishly. "This ain't my sister, Mr. Payne. This is my aunt."

"Oh, forgive me," Thomas exclaimed. "Well, that sure explains the strong family resemblance." He glanced at his watch. "We won't have much time to talk. I'm sorry that Ms. Walker—LaShonda's mother—couldn't make it but thank you for coming.

The Other Ms. Walker nodded. "We—you know, her mother and me, she's my sister—we don't have a car. I live with 'em too—me and my son. My sister ain't feeling good so I told 'Shonda that I'd come down here. Some girl named Lakeisha called and said that everybody been here but us. Said they was going to miss out on the teacher doin' fifty pushups in the middle of the classroom 'causa us. Then the girl's father got on the phone and offered to pick us up. He's waiting for us out back. So I sez yes, just to get me some peace." She leaned against the wall and took several deep breaths.

A mixture of pride and discomfort filled the young man's heart. Although grateful that the Walkers had invested the time to attend the Open House, he did not have a good report for them. He struggled for something positive to say but was interrupted by a second order over the intercom for everyone to leave the building. Thomas ran over to LaShonda's desk and retrieved her report card.

"I wish I had good news for you but I don't. LaShonda could be a successful student, but she's missed *twelve* days of school already." He shrugged his shoulder's and handed the Other Ms. Walker the folded paper. "Boston Public School policy states that a child has to attend school at least eighty-five percent of the quarter or get all F's. LaShonda's attendance was only seventy-four percent. I had to fail her. I'm sorry." He waited for the inevitable argument, prepared to inform LaShonda and the Other Ms. Walker that, according to procedure, he had submitted a report to Mr. Dorn for a possible waiver. Mr. Dorn had declared that he had granted the family waivers in the past, which only seemed to encourage additional absences, and had declined.

To his surprise, the Other Ms. Walker surveyed the paper for only a few seconds before handing it to her niece. LaShonda took her thumb out of her mouth and moved her eyes for a few seconds before closing the card and placing it back in the brown envelope.

"Oh, 'Shonda always fails the first quarter," the aunt calmly revealed. She turned to her niece. "Come on, girl, we'd better get going." She glanced back at Thomas. "She'll do better next time, Mr. Wayne."

Thomas had no time to be shocked by the response he had just witnessed. He gathered his things and walked his guests halfway downstairs. He admonished the Other Ms. Walker that "Shonda's" attendance had improved recently but she had to be in school no matter what. She could get caught up if she came to school and worked hard. The aunt promised that she would do her part.

By 7:05 Thomas entered the office and turned in his sign-in sheet. The large, black windows and peeling, dirty, white paint on the walls made the depressing area look even more dreary. He was forced to endure the voices of his colleagues as they complained about the lack of cooperation from the parents. Their griping quieted considerably when Mrs. Chang waltzed in. She commented about how much she always enjoyed the first Open House. Thomas observed three teachers exchange glances and furtively roll their eyes.

"How'd you do, neighbor?" Mrs. Chang asked him slyly.

"Oh, pretty good. How about you?"

She pounced on the opportunity. "Not bad. Eleven of my fourteen parents came in today. That's..." She paused, pretending to do the math in her head. "Seventy-six percent!" Further unnoticed eye-rolling followed.

Thomas whistled. "That's terrific!" He stepped over to his mailbox to see if anything had been placed in there since the last time he checked seconds ago, then turned around and walked towards the door. He knew that the staff would sneak a peek at his parent sign-in sheet. They secretly examined each one at the earliest opportunity. Thomas turned left and counted softly: "Three, two, one..."

"A hundred percent! Mr. Payne got all of his parents in today!"

"What?"

"You're kidding!"

"Let me see that!"

The proud man strolled casually down the hallway, ignoring the throng of voices in the background. He pulled up the collar to his coat for protection against the freezing rain and trotted to his car. Once inside, he located an oldies station on the radio and slowly drove home.

The flight to Cincinnati quickly became tiresome. Holiday traveling could be such a pain, Thomas lamented. Scores of noisy travelers squeezed together on the plane, all anxious to arrive home in time for Thanksgiving.

Two rows in front of him, a baby cried as her father tried to comfort her. In the coach section, amidst 139 warm bodies, the weary passenger adjusted his long legs and tried to relax. His window-seat view hardly provoked intrigue, given that the glass revealed only darkness. He opened his book, some murder mystery about a man with amnesia, and declined an offer of earphones from an attractive Asian flight attendant with a wide, toothy smile. The Ohio-bound traveler decided that if presented with the opportunity, he would strike up a conversation with the woman. Lately, he noticed, he had been thinking a great deal about sex.

He stretched his neck to survey the space of the plane. There seemed to be a lot of college students aboard. They were a little noisy, finding humor and mirth in just about everything. Thomas fondly remembered those days. He closed his eyes and took in a few deep breaths of recycled air. Like everyone aboard, he could hardly wait to get home and see his family. For some reason, his anxiety rose at the thought of seeing his brother unencumbered by a glass screen for the first time in four years. He settled in to take a nap. Already he missed his kids and wondered what they were doing and if any of them missed him. After a half-hour of speculation about them, his brother, his former fiancée and the unnamed flight attendant, he closed his book, set it in his lap and drifted off to sleep.

Three hours and forty minutes later, Thomas rubbed his forehead, trying not to become impatient. Exiting the plane was taking forever. He stayed in his spot at the back of the plane and waited for the horde to clear out. He would be just about last anyway. After an excruciatingly long wait, the tired passenger could finally see the bright lights of the airport entrance. He paused at the door. The lovely flight attendant who had been the object of his fantasies wished him a Happy Thanksgiving. He tried to conjure up some sexy and witty reply.

"Thank you. You too," was all that came out of his mouth.

In the airport waiting area, people gathered everywhere. Old ladies greeted grandchildren. Young, reunited couples kissed. Security guards placed a watchful eye on the patrons and their packages. A sleepy young girl in blond hair and pigtails shook her doll gently to wake her up. Excited voices filled the air. The Greater Cincinnati Airport, technically across the border in Kentucky, was home-sweet-home to Thomas. It wasn't large and sprawling like Boston's Logan Airport, or LaGuardia in New York or O'Hare in Chicago. You could still pretty much park your car and walk where you wanted to go. Thomas looked around for familiar faces. No one yet. He felt a slight feeling of panic in his chest. What if they got delayed in traffic? What if on the way to the airport, Edward got stopped for speeding and, because of some bureaucratic mix-up, was arrested for escaping from prison? What if—

His irrational thoughts were interrupted by the comforting sight of his waving mother and father. A streak of very thick but mostly gray hair covered Mom's head. Thomas's late grandfather on his mother's side had a thick mane, too. She still had that fire in her eyes and appeared as thin as ever. And she wore new glasses. Dad looked the same. Tall and strong, with virtually no hair at all. (Hopefully, it was true what they say about baldness coming from the grandfather on the *mother's* side.) However, they appeared to be Edwardless.

Thomas waved back to his parents. Their eyes met and the middle-aged couple slowly fought through the crowd toward their son. Thomas searched for his brother but could not pick him out amongst the hundreds of people clamoring about. Then, out of the corner of his right eye, he spotted a tall man attempting to surreptitiously creep towards him. The figure tried to hide under a black hat, deliberately pulled over his eyes. Thomas allowed the man to close in within three feet, then whipped around and declared, "Hey, dude, seen any good movies lately?"

His brother took off his hat and beamed at his younger brother. Thomas noticed that he looked about the same. Maybe he had acquired just a bit of weight around the middle. Mom probably had spent the past week upset about how skinny her oldest child had become and how he needed to be fattened up. Thomas hugged his brother, squeezing him hard and fighting back tears. Edward responded in kind. They held on to each other as if only the two of them lived on earth. Their parents had reached them by then but waited patiently, understanding how important it was to let them have the time together. Mom reached in her purse and took out a purple silk handkerchief. Dad simply nodded with approval.

"Everything's all right now," he officially declared.

At their parents' house, the telephone constantly rang throughout the evening. Family members and friends called day and night to wish Edward well and pay their respects. Edward talked to them as if they were old army buddies for as long as they wanted. Frequently though, after hanging up, he would scowl and curse the caller for abandoning him. Thomas noticed a bitterness in his brother's voice that had not been there before.

Thomas and Edward stayed up all night, talking in the family recreation room, comfortably furnished with a large television, a pool table and a stereo, the latter fenced in by dozens of old music selections. The newer material was kept upstairs in the living room. The furniture of Thomas's adolescence had been transferred to the basement after Mom got her new living room suite. Now no one could sit in the living room. Pictures of various family members graced the fireplace mantle that Dad had recently rebuilt. A picture of Edward's now ex-wife had been removed.

The brothers exchanged childhood stories and argued over whose version was more accurate. They feasted on their mother's pot roast and apple pie. Thomas teased his brother about how soft he had become, to which Edward replied that he could still take his little brother in whatever sport he chose. The challenge having been duly noted and accepted, Edward ran upstairs and returned with a football. Thomas recognized it as the gift his brother had given him for his fifteenth birthday. They spent hours throwing the ball, shouting, rolling on the floor, laughing and swearing. Twice Mom called out, "Who's that?" Mom didn't like profanity—and Edward had acquired a new vocabulary after four years on the inside.

Thanksgiving Day was wonderful but hectic, with a dozen people coming and going from morning until night. The Payne boys had not gotten the chance to speak much that day; several sporting events dominated the television airways and their attention. Thomas, who hated to lose even a gentlemen's wager, actually felt good for his brother when the Dallas Cowboys walked all over the San Francisco 49ers 27-13.

The following day the two brothers sat in the rec room chatting and playing as they had two days before. Mom and Dad had gone to bed hours ago, exhausted from getting an early start (if you asked Dad) or a late start (if you asked Mom) on their Christmas shopping. Thomas and Edward picked right up where they had left off. They discussed the usual array of favorite subjects among African American men; sports, racism, women, etc. Thomas had decided on the plane not to broach the subject of his brother's stay in prison but to wait until Edward brought it up. Two nights ago Edward had said very little about his four-year ordeal. Tonight he was philosophical about his past predicament.

"Man, I saw brothers who had been in the can for decades and hadn't seen a visitor in years—except for the volunteer do-gooders who visit unfortunate souls like us." He put his hand on his heart. Thomas chuckled nervously. Edward resumed his observations. "I felt sorry for them." He scratched his head and kicked his slippers on and off. "I'm tellin' you, it ain't right not to have nobody."

"Man, you know I'm on your team," Thomas offered. "Me, Mom, Dad, Sis and a whole lot more." He hated to see the look of hurt on his brother's face. He didn't quite know what to say.

Edward nodded in agreement. "Man, you don't know how much it meant that you all were with me and never gave up." He picked up his beer, took another swig and put it back on the end table. The can produced no sound as it landed on the soft coaster. Edward got up and grabbed a picture of his daughters when the oldest was about five years old. He spoke slowly. "Thomas, I didn't want to ask you before, but I'm desperate, you know?" He kept staring at the picture. "Have you given some thought about, you know, talking to April?" He turned around to face his brother. "I'm not saying bother her or anything."

Thomas felt uneasy. He knew that Edward hated not getting his way and took it very personally whenever anyone said no to him. "Edward, that's just about all I've thought about since you asked me. You know how as a family, we get along because we don't interfere in each other's lives. I can't go butting into your personal business." Edward said nothing, so he continued. "Besides, that's what lawyers are for." Thomas decided to slightly change the subject. "What'd your lawyer say?"

"He said he's working on it. She took my babies and moved to Pittsburgh, close to her sister. You know, that bitch never liked me." Edward's voice grew louder with each sentence, and he started to sweat. "Man, shit. I know that I did wrong. I'd go back and change it if I could. I don't blame her for hating me but don't take it out on the kids, you know?"

Thomas wanted to show Edward that he understood. He joined his brother in front of the mantle and gazed at the picture of his beautiful nieces. "I agree with you, man. I'm on your side. I miss them, too. She should let you see the kids. I'm sure that—"

"Then why don't you help?" Edward barked. "I'm not asking you to do anything illegal or anything. Just make a fucking phone call!" His eyes glowed incandescently as he became more agitated.

Thomas opened his arms and sighed. "I want to help, Edward, but come on, man. How do you know that my calling won't make things worse?

You told me that April's real spooked these days. Maybe she just needs to—"

"Fuck it then!" Edward yelled. He grabbed the picture out of Thomas's hand and slammed it back on the mantle. "You always had it easy! Mom and Dad were doing pretty well financially by the time you came along." He stomped back to his seat and threw himself onto the sofa. The irate man frowned, made a face and exaggerated a whine. "Whatever little Thomas wanted, little Thomas got."

Little Thomas didn't appreciate that one at all. He stood in front of the television, knowing that it would annoy his brother, even though they hadn't been watching anything in particular. "What you talking about? I don't remember you going without clothes or shoes—or a car to drive when you turned eighteen—which you wrecked, by the way!"

"Just wait 'til you get in trouble and you need something. Then you'll understand," Edward shouted, attempting to rise. He had more to say and so did Thomas, but their argument was interrupted by a more pressing emergency.

While reaching for his can of beer, Edward accidentally knocked it off the table and its contents spilled on the carpet. The smell of beer rose from the postcard-size wet spot.

"Oh-oh." Edward gasped. His eyes grew wide and fearful. He ran to the entrance of the rec room and parted the door. Thankfully, their loud words had not awakened their mother. He turned back towards his very anxious brother. "Nope. She's still asleep."

Thomas ran into the adjoining kitchenette. "I'll get some paper towels," he announced in his "take-charge" voice. "See if you can find the carpet spray cleaner. It's upstairs under the kitchen sink."

"I'll get it," Edward replied, agitated.

"Hurry," Thomas ordered. "You know Mom'll have you shampooing the whole room if she detects beer on that carpet, AND she'll stand there while you do it."

"Man, you don't know the half of it," Edward declared.

The next night the two brothers went out for the evening. While in Edward's car—a recent gift from their Dad—they joked about the previous night's "close-call carpet caper." Neither brought up their argument about Edward's daughters. The Payne men drove to a huge nightclub in Kentucky and enjoyed the sound of dance music and the sight of beautiful women. Thomas wasn't in the mood to "hunt," as his brother like to put it, but after four years in prison, Edward could barely contain his obvious delight. An hour after they had arrived, Edward said goodnight to his brother as he accompanied a very young Spanish-looking woman with reddish hair to the door. Thomas thought he had heard her call his brother "Michael." He shook his head and worried about his brother's tendency to live life on the edge. Preoccupied with concern about Edward's well-being, within fifteen minutes, he drove home alone.

Thomas was enjoying a wonderful dream about receiving an award of some kind from the President or someone important like that. He appeared older and obviously had married Laura, who stood next to him smiling broadly, while he lowered his head to accept the honor. Everyone sported very expensive formal attire. Television cameras and photographers roamed everywhere. Thomas proceeded to dance with the First Lady—the woman who seemed to be the important man's wife. She smiled slyly and whispered something to him, then started to undress right there in the middle of the dance floor—when she was interrupted by the sound of the local news on the radio.

Thomas rolled over, hit the snooze button and rolled back into the warm spot of his king-sized bed. The basketball-shaped clock had just informed him of the time: 6 o'clock in the morning. At 6:10 he was reawakened by the sound of an important-sounding man describing the weather. He heard the word "snow" and jumped out of bed and peeked out the window. Indeed, a few snow flurries chased about, driven by a significant gust of northwesterly wind. According to the authority on the radio, the temperature had only reached twenty-nine degrees. Thomas did not like the way the first day back from Thanksgiving break had begun.

Later that morning he collected his students from the downstairs hall (it was too cold to let them roam outside) and brought them to the classroom. Within a few minutes he was approached by the fourth student offering to explain why the homework had not been completed. Thomas waved her off with his right hand and growled.

"You know the rules," he bellowed. If you don't have your homework, don't come to me with a fairy story. Sit in your seat and wait for someone to take your things and put them in the closet. In the meantime, get to work!" His crescendoing voice punctuated the last three words. "I'm running school.

Not frickin' daycare!" He looked around. Although no one dared meet his gaze, he had plenty more to say. "I gave you a simple, straightforward assignment, and if it's not done, keep your butts in your seats."

One by one Thomas approached each student with his hand out. Six did not have the assignment at all—a twenty-page story with six essay questions *answered*. None of them would enjoy recess for the next three days. He ordered another six confined to their seats for a week for writing "junk answers"—as if they had read the story when in fact, they had not. He considered it the same as lying to him, he angrily explained as he crumpled Asa's, then Cleopatra's papers into a ball and threw them in the garbage.

However, the fussy instructor was very pleased with the quality of the work submitted by ten of his most trustworthy pupils. The remaining students' work amounted to, as Thomas put it, "just barely good enough to stay out of trouble."

By lunch some sembalnce of order had returned to the classroom. Thomas had calmed down. He stood by the door and prepared to send the class downstairs to eat, but separated them into two groups: "Yes Homework" and "No Homework." The former sat together and could talk during lunch. The latter sat together but could not. Thomas was further pacified by Maria, who gave her teacher several pieces of coconut candy favored by Spanish families called *dulce de coco*. He found them to be absolutely delicious.

The work day dragged on but finally ended. Thomas sent notes home along with a clenched-teeth, squinted-eyes, finger-pointing verbal warning to bring back all homework—past and present—or there would be dire consequences. That evening he spent an hour on parent telephone calls.

The following day brought a marked improvement in the class's productivity. The children received praise for being back on their game. Christine raised her hand and Thomas called on her.

"Mr. Payne, some of us would like to have a class meeting," she announced with just a hint of reservation in her voice. A few others nodded in agreement.

Thomas spied the faces of the students in his room. "What's this about, honey?" he asked.

The plump girl looked around at her classmates. She cleared her throat and answered. "Some of us would like to change buddies."

Whispering and murmuring circulated throughout the room. Thomas placed a paper he had in his hand back on his desk. "Okay," he said and motioned for Angelica, a small girl with a quiet voice, to approach him. She jumped out of her seat and headed towards the teacher's desk. "Captain, please close the door and hang the 'Do Not Disturb' sign—Everyone, clear your desk," he commanded loudly. "A class meeting has been requested and granted." Papers rustled and desks creaked opened and slammed shut. Thomas waited patiently, staring out the window at the sun, shining so brightly on such a chilly morning. He took his position at the center of the room. "Christine, would you care to present your case?"

The young girl blinked her green eyes and searched around the room for support. "Well," she opened. "It's like this: You said that we can't be Student of the Week unless our buddies do right too. But some of our buddies just don't do right, no matter what we do. They don't listen. They don't bring in their homework. They always be causing trouble or they always be in trouble, and it's almost Christmas now."

"You're right, honey," Thomas replied. "That is the rule here. I've done this for a reason. But I want to hear from others before I explain again." He scanned the faces of his class and called on Lakeisha, who had raised her hand earlier. "Lakeisha, you wanted to speak?"

The opinionated fifth-grader nodded slowly. She was a large girl and one of the few students being reared by a married father and mother, both of whom had attended some college. The latter though, always rubbed a lot of grease in her daughter's hair, causing it to shine. Lakeisha glanced at a few classmates, then spoke rapidly, as she always did. "Well, Mr. Payne. It's like Christine said. Some of us ain't never going to be Student of the Week if our buddies don't shape up and do right. You tell us all the time not to let personal feelings interfere with business. This is business."

Several more students raised their hands. Thomas understood that some-times it took a while for the meetings to heat up. He spoke to a boy seated near the window. "Akeem, go ahead, son."

Akeem adjusted his seat and stuck out his lower lip. "I agree with what the others said. It ain't fair that we get punished 'cause our buddy acts up or don't obey the rules."

"Wait a second, there, Akeem," Thomas interjected. "Please understand, as I've said several times, there is no 'right' to be Student of the Week. Not being chosen is not a punishment. Being chosen is an honor, okay?" He saw Carmelita's hand. "Carmelita, please."

She took off her glasses. "I don't think you should let them switch buddies, Mr. Payne," Carmelita offered solemnly. "You told us a bunch of times to be careful when picking a buddy 'cause if your buddy messed up, you couldn't be Student of the Week. Everybody knew that. Well, it's too late to change now."

Suddenly, a sea of voices mixed with the stale air of the poorly ventilated room as additional comments erupted from Carmelita's classmates. Thomas put his hands up to quiet them. He chose another student with an excellent arrangement: Angel, whose buddy happened to be Melvin.

"That's right, Mr. Payne," Angel stated with conviction. A short boy with a shrill voice whose family originally immigrated from the Dominican Republic, Thomas remembered that his mother was vivacious and stunningly beautiful. Angel was not only handsome but confident and pleasant. He paused, then calmly articulated his position. "That's what you told us. I like everybody here, but I chose Melvin 'cause I knew from last year that he plays to win."

Thomas looked at the clock, then his watch, then back at the class. After another visual sweep, he decided to try a different approach. "We're not here to hurt anyone's feelings, but I need to understand how many want to change buddies." His voice became softer but didactic. "Okay, instead of counting, let's do this. Let me explain why we have the rule again and see if it doesn't change any minds."

A few students nodded, allowing him to proceed.

He shook the index fingers of each hand in the air as he spoke slowly. "I believe that there are no real accidents in life. The buddy you have is the person you need to be with to teach you something about yourself. You guys remember how Hernando used to argue and fight. But after a couple of months with Pedro he's become much more gentle. Why, he's just a great big cuddly teddy bear now, who's just as cute as he can be."

The class offered fake cheers, animal sounds and groans. Hernando waved as if he were the President getting off Air Force One, which generated louder responses. Thomas opened his hands and the room became quiet.

"Anyway, if you can't take care of one, how you going to handle twenty-seven? I believe you've gotta go all out for your buddy and be willing to even lose the friendship if it means that your buddy'll move on to the sixth grade next year. I know it isn't an easy assignment—for some of you it seems like an impossible assignment—but I'd hoped that you wouldn't give up on your buddy, just like I would never give up on any of you." Thomas stopped and pointed to himself. "Like I always tell you, my job isn't to get you to like me. It's to get you ready for middle school next fall." He paused. "Now that I've explained the reasons for the rule, does anyone have anything to say?"

Hands sprung up like jacks-in-the-box. The tall man again studied his watch. "Okay, class, let's take a few more minutes on this." A new hand dangled in the air. Thomas called on Cleopatra's buddy and good friend, Melissa.

"Mr. Payne, I th-think you should let th-those who want to ch-change buddies ch-ch-change buddies." The class listened intently, startled. Everyone recognized that for years Cleo had treated Melissa like a servant. They were an odd couple. Cleopatra was tall and statuesque with a loquacious tongue while her buddy was short, overweight and stuttered.

Soft but firm student affirmations punctuated Melissa's comments. Cleopatra responded by slouching in her chair. Known to sulk and pout better than anyone in the class, she put on a tour-de-force performance of her greatest hits.

Thomas decided to try a different tactic. "It appears that some of you are happy with your buddies while others are not. I'm not trying to be mean, but those of you whose buddies want to leave; do you have anything to say before I make my decision? Anything at all?" His eyes shifted from Cleopatra to Francine, then to LaShonda. Slowly, LaShonda's hand inched upward.

"Please," Thomas said.

LaShonda freed her thumb from her mouth and called to her buddy. "I know that I haven't been a good buddy, Lakeisha. But I promise that I'll be better. I promise I will." She lowered her head. No further sounds circulated for a few seconds as the class watched the two girls.

"How are you gonna be better when you ain't never even here?" Lakeisha fumed.

"Perhaps that's my fault, too, Lakeisha," Thomas interjected. He thought for a few seconds. "I'll tell you what. From now on, right after homework check, anyone whose buddy is absent should be assigned a temporary buddy for that day. Would that help?"

Lakeisha nodded. "But I still say we should change buddies."

Hands remained extended into the air, but Thomas felt other pressures. "Look, class, I'm afraid that we just don't have any more time. We have to get to math, but listen. I'll think about what everyone said and let you know what I've decided tomorrow. I want to thank all of you for speaking out today, especially, you Christine. Apparently, this issue needed to be discussed." He took two steps forward and stood over Doug's desk. The boy sat directly in front of the chalkboard. "I hereby declare that our class meeting has ended." The acting magistrate slammed the palm of his hand on top of the desk, his last official act to bring the meeting to a close.

That same day was also the last day of November, which made it Movie Day. Of the twenty-six students who were in attendance, November Nancy revealed that nineteen "had a ticket." Thomas ushered out the remaining students to various classrooms and returned to his room. He showed a short film and lavished the attendees with snack food and praise. He especially applauded the "first-timers." After the tense emotional event of the class meeting that morning, he was relieved to lighten the mood.

Later that afternoon, as he wiped the point count from November Nancy clean, Thomas felt pride that his students had shown some improvement in their productivity. But his mood was pensive as he pondered whether he should allow some pupils to change buddies. He recognized the courage it took for a child to bring up the subject. He also knew that whatever he announced tomorrow, someone would be unhappy.

December

On the first morning of December the sun emerged slowly and could be sporadically seen. The yellow ball played hide-and-seek with patches of gray clouds that methodically revealed its hiding place. Overnight, frost had stuck to the windshields of every motor vehicle unprotected by a garage in the Boston area. Thomas, encased in a new winter coat his mother had given him a few days before, cursed as he scraped the stubborn frozen water off the windshield of his car. He still arrived at the Adams earlier than usual, determined to finish hanging the winter pictures the students had drawn.

Scanning the exhibits forged on the nine-by-twelve-inch white paper, Thomas assessed that some of his young artists possessed real talent. Melvin, Angelica and Connie had all produced wonderful winter scenes. Maria had drawn and colored a huge, beautifully decorated Christmas tree in what appeared to be her own living room. (She had told him that her family could only afford a small tree, when they had one at all.) Thomas examined each picture carefully.

He held one drawing at arm's length and admired it. He knew little about art—his sister, Vanessa, was the artist in the family—but he surmised that Gary had a gift. Deliberately using only his pencil, the boy had created a spectacular scene of an evening snowball fight between several friends. Gary had mastered the technique of showing perspective; he displayed characters in the foreground larger than those in the background. He utilized gradation, increasing the shading of figures in the background. His picture would be placed on the wall near the door.

Forty-five minutes later Thomas stood in the center of the classroom. After wrestling with the options, he would now disclose his decision about some being allowed to change buddies. His eyes roamed as he surveyed the room. Pictures of Santa Claus, Rudolf the Red-nosed Reindeer, Christmas trees and other yuletide images surrounded the students. A string of multi-colored lights stretched across the wall behind the teacher's desk, flashing at a steady pace. More than a score of winter pictures clung to the walls and doors. The students had shown considerable interest in the holiday trimmings that morning but currently focused on him, prepared to witness the wisdom of Solomon.

"Class, I've thought about your request for quite a while," he began. "Clearly, some of you are happy with your current situation, and some of you are not." He paused, scratched his head and observed his audience. Lakeisha and Christine crossed their fingers. LaShonda worked on her thumb. Cleopatra rested her head on her left hand, annoyed that because of the warning notice incident and the lack of Thanksgiving recess assignments, she still had considerable time left on her grounding.

Thomas took a deep breath and continued. "I'm just not yet convinced that we've gone all out for our buddies, making sure that they're a part of the team. I share in the blame. We all have to work harder. Me too. But for today, my answer is to *deny* any request to change buddies. Everyone will keep his or her own buddy."

Several students exclaimed, "Yes!" or clapped their hands. Others slammed their fists on their desks or angrily blurted out, "Shoot!"

"Listen, everyone," the fifth-grade instructor pleaded. "I know that some of you think you've been sent a bad play from the coach, but I want you to try harder for your buddy. Push a little more. I'm telling you, there's some talent in there you haven't seen yet. It's there, I promise you. Please, give of yourselves a little more. You might be surprised at what you discover about your buddy and about yourself.

"And let me say this to you do-nothing buddies!" he announced, his voice gradually booming. "You better shape up. I said we won't change buddies *now*. But I'm telling you, I'm not going to let my good students suffer for long. I might change my mind and grant their request at any time." He stared at Cleopatra, then at Asa, then LaShonda. "Some of you better get your acts together and soon. Get your selfish butts focused off yourselves and onto the team. Do you understand?"

A few voices replied, "Yes, Mr. Payne." Several hands raised.

"I'm sorry," Thomas said, motioning for hands to be lowered. "No questions or comments about this. My mind's made up." Christine put her hands over her face and wept. The man felt his anger melt. He put his hands in his pockets and approached her, treading so softly his footsteps were inaudible. The other students looked on with a mixture of curiosity and compassion.

"Sweetheart, I'm sorry," he offered, putting his hand on her arm. "Please give it a little more time. I know you can make a difference with that girl." Aware that Mr. Payne was referring to her, Francine raised her hand.

"What?" Thomas prompted coldly.

"Can I talk to my buddy outside the room?" she asked.

A student could request permission to speak to his or her buddy in the hall to admonish someone about inappropriate behavior or provide encouragement, a request Thomas frequently granted. Such impromptu sessions had proven to be amazingly effective.

"No. You've done enough harm," he scoffed. Recognizing the emotionally volatile atmosphere in the classroom, he turned to Angelica. "Captain, take the class to the bathroom. We'll go early today." The rookie teacher stood to his full height. "When you return, I want to see all of you ready for work. We all have our jobs to do." He clapped his hands twice. "Let's go! Multiplication drill in ten minutes."

He crept over to Angelica. "Captain," he whispered. "Make sure that Christine, Lakeisha and the others who wanted to change buddies get to serve as monitors during the bathroom breaks."

"Yes, Mr. Payne," the small girl obediently replied.

"And," he added, "see to it that they pass out papers for the rest of the day." Throughout the morning Thomas made sure to call on those particular students to answer questions or go to the board.

Shortly before lunch, holding half a sheet of paper in his hand, Thomas made an announcement. "Right after lunch I'd like to see these students back upstairs. I'm going to need you to do something for me. It'll take all of your recess time. I ask this as a favor."

The class listened intently. Mr. Payne had never done this before. He read the names of a dozen students. On the list were Carmelita, Melvin, Maria, Pedro, Deborah, Connie and others who had done comparatively well in the first quarter.

Within a few minutes, only Thomas and twenty-eight empty chairs remained.

He took out a large thermos and gulped several pints of orange juice while considering the possible ramifications of what he was about to do. The Whispers exercise could be a powerful agent for transformation. It presented an opportunity for successful students to be helpful to those less so. True, the exercise could be perceived as "spooky," but if done correctly, it might open the floodgates for some pupils to seriously commit themselves to change. Through the efforts of a selected group of giving students, the walls of isolation and self-imprisonment created by so many of their struggling classmates could be torn down.

Twenty minutes later Thomas sat on top of a student's desk addressing his chosen dozen. "I've asked to see you because you've been doing well in my class, and I'm very proud of you. I'm sure that your families are proud of you—and that you are proud of yourselves." He looked at each one of them. They beamed with self-satisfaction as his words touched their ears and hearts. "Well, today I'm going to ask you to help some of your classmates who are struggling." He opened his arms. "They're part of our family and they need our help. I'm asking you to do this because I trust you. Will you trust me and help them?"

The twelve chosen all readily nodded in agreement. Had he asked them to give him the shoes on their feet, they would have done so. Thomas stood and started to pace a bit. "Today we're going to do something called 'Whispers.' "

He took the remainder of the recess time to describe the production. He showed them where they were to position themselves during the ceremony. He explained how the words they whispered to their fellow classmates could only be positive words of encouragement. Thomas instructed his trusted group to make sure that they stood close to the person to whom they whispered and make sure that they got to everyone. There would be no order, he stated. "If someone gets to a student before you do, just go to another." They even did a short practice run. After some discussion, they decided that the ceremony would take place during the beginning of the last period. The students laughed when they each received a small individually-wrapped breath mint for the occasion. Finally, everyone agreed to maintain secrecy.

When the class had been reunited and were returning from the afternoon bathroom break, Thomas overheard some inquiries about the nature of the clandestine meeting. No one broke. The first-year teacher smiled to himself, even more certain that he had selected the right team.

At around 2 o'clock Thomas asked that everyone clear his or her desk, then sent the entire group out of the room for a drink of water. (Such consideration generally had been extended during the hot days of September or after munching a birthday treat.) He knew that their trip would take more time than usual because he had checked the water station downstairs. A custodian would have to be summoned to replace the empty six-gallon water jug. (The John Adams was one of a few dozen buildings in the Boston Public School system with tap water judged to be undrinkable by the Water Department.)

Alone, Thomas quickly pushed all of the desks to the far corners of the room, leaving a huge empty space in the center. When his students returned, he separated the chosen ones and told them to wait, then escorted the remaining sixteen into the classroom. When they saw the position of the furniture, and that the shades had been pulled down, they expressed surprise and curiosity. They heard soft music playing in the background. Their teacher spoke clearly, in an inviting, almost aristocratic tone.

"Please form a circle in the center of the room," the man kindly requested with a genteel sweep of his right arm. Their eyes grazed each other, then they leisurely complied. Thomas stepped inside the circle and spent a few seconds rearranging them boy-girl-boy-girl. Next, he brought them closer together to form a tight circle. The host delivered his opening remarks.

"My dear students, you have been a part of this family for several weeks now. You have been blessed with talent and abilities that are useful to you and to this class. I want you to use those talents. I want your light to shine this year as brightly as it can." He wandered about inside the circle as he spoke, occasionally touching the face or shoulder of a student. "Some of your classmates would like to talk to you in a special way. They want you to know that they see the light that is within you waiting to shine. I'm going to bring them in so that you can hear not just my words, but theirs."

Thomas squeezed past two students, stepping outside of the circle. He turned back towards the mystified group. "Please turn around so that you are facing out instead of in." Most did so. Confused by the request, three had to be physically spun around by a classmate, much to everyone's amusement. Their host walked over to the door and switched off the lights. "Now join hands so that our support circle is unbroken." The students responded slowly to melting their New England aversion to physical contact. Thomas reassured them. "Trust me," he said softly. He wandered over to a pair of students and joined their hands. "Please," he whispered. A few reluctantly obeyed. Eventually, they all did. He made a final request. "One more thing: I want you to close your eyes like we do during Student of the Week." Being somewhat comfortable with that petition, the sixteen students closed their eyes almost in unison.

Thomas changed the music to a slow, instrumental jazz-like piece, then opened the door and silently invited the Twelve Chosen to enter. He put his finger to his lips and motioned for them to form a wide circle around their classmates, who stood silently and nervously waiting, eyes closed and holding hands. He motioned again and the Chosen began slowly walking in a counter-clockwise direction, just as they had rehearsed. They held a moving circle position and watched for the signal. When they had moved about one complete revolution, Thomas motioned with his arms, and the Chosen descended on their classmates and began whispering in their ears. The students on the inside with their eyes closed could not tell who whispered to them. They clutched the hand of the person on the left and the right as they listened to softly spoken words of unequivocal encouragement.

"I'm you're friend, Maurice, and I'm on your team," Jonathan whispered and moved on to another student.

"If you need anything, just ask. I'll be here for you," Melvin told Akeem, then walked over to someone else.

"We're a family. You don't have to be afraid. Just do the best you can. That'll be enough," Carmelita said to Janet, who nodded.

The ceremony continued as Thomas, who had watched for a few minutes before participating as well, approached Melissa. He found her standing, gently shaking and in tears. One of the Chosen girls had whispered to her that she was sweet and special. Melissa's tears came gushing forth from deep inside of her. She wept from the first glimpse that she could be more than the fat girl in the class and the personal target of someone who disliked herself.

The soothing music in the background created an atmosphere of safety, allowing the children to freely express their emotions. Thomas heard the sounds and looked around. Janet cried. So did LaShonda. And Akeem. And Asa. Francine, her eyes welded shut, sobbed and tightly squeezed Doug's hand, unaware of anything other than the comforting words that had been delivered to her by her classmates. Carmelita spoke to Hernando in Spanish, and he struggled to control himself. Several of the Twelve Chosen wiped their own eyes. Thomas had one more student to reach. Choking back his own emotions, he put his arms around LaShonda and whispered to her. She laughed and cried as she listened.

After he finished, Thomas slowly retreated, then tiptoed about, tapping the shoulders of his Chosen and motioning for them to stop. Jonathan finished the last of his words to Doug, who, eyes closed, smiled and shook his whole body in agreement. The Chosen reformed a wide circle. Thomas pressed his fingers against the corners of his mouth and moved his lips without uttering a word, telling them to smile. They did. The Captain turned on one set of lights and the darkness became a schoolroom again.

"Release your hands," Thomas told the whisperees, "and open your eyes."

The sixteen students opened their eyes and saw twelve of their classmates standing before them smiling, some presenting the thumbs-up sign. Those on the inside wiped their eyes with their hands. Thomas pointed to the box of tissue on his desk, then at the weeping students. Angelica, herself in tears, made rounds distributing tissues. The music stopped momentarily, but another selection began. Its mellow arrangement mixed smoothly with the sounds of crying children. Thomas raised his hands to speak. By then, the sobs had grown louder.

"Those of you on the inside, do not forget what you've been told today," he requested. "What you've heard is from the hearts of your own friends. Take their words with you. Serve your buddy, serve this class and this school and your families with this newly discovered power." Thomas faced the Twelve Chosen. "Those of you on the outside, acknowledge those on the inside." He extended his hands and applauded the inside students, some still trying to recover from their experience. The Chosen applauded. "Those of you on the inside, acknowledge those on the outside." Thomas clapped his hands several times and was joined by the sixteen students, who cheered and whistled.

The teacher glanced at his watch. "Okay, people. Let's put the room back together and get ready for DEAR."

Several female students held each other, then joined in the group effort of moving chairs and desks. Thomas walked around and embraced a few of those who had been on the inside and outside circles. He went to his desk and stood face-to-face with Angelica. She applied a tattered tissue to a steady stream of tears. A small, plain-looking, brown-skinned girl with short hair and a generous heart, she tended to be very emotional. Her mother had shamefully neglected her for the first six years of her life, but she had been rescued by her grandmother and would soon be formally adopted by her. She and her teacher hugged.

Thomas took her face in his hands. "I'm proud of you," he told her.

"I love you, Mr. Payne," she whispered without reservation.

"Thank you, sweetheart. I love you, too," he replied sincerely.

After school that same day, he retold the day's events to Glen, who appeared genuinely fascinated by the whole account. Glen obviously loved teaching first grade, but occasionally envied his junior colleague for the stimulating environment on the second floor. Thomas recounted the day's activities to Heléna Gutiérrez also. She found the tale to be "just peachy" and insisted that her friend invite her to the next such ceremony.

On Saturday morning Thomas settled down to complete one of the more jejune tasks of being a teacher—correcting papers. He sat, pen and pencil in hand, punching numbers into a small calculator. The apartment was comfortable and warm. He kicked one of his overpriced sneakers off his right foot, then fitted back into it, an unusual game he had been unconsciously playing for the past fifteen minutes. The shades were open, although sunshine appeared only intermittently. About a mile away, a squadron of squawking birds could be observed practicing a flight drill, swooping back and forth in a figure-eight-like pattern. Near the picture window, a four feet high artificial Christmas tree, enveloped by a host of flashing lights and sparkling ornaments, perched on top of an end table. Thomas listened to Tchaikovsky's *The Nutcracker* ballet on his stereo. During the "Waltz of the Flowers" he volunteered to break from his chores and direct the talented musicians. After a few minutes of pantomiming, he bowed gracefully then sat down amidst deafening applause to return to his paid duties.

With twenty-eight students—the limit under the contract—he always had a pile of work to correct. He assigned large amounts of homework, about which his students constantly complained. They were given so much homework because they needed so much practice. The rookie teacher noticed some small victories. The entire class had all but mastered their multiplication facts. The recent unit on division had proven to be a major challenge, but eventually the group managed to grasp the concepts and techniques involved. Their writing had even begun to improve, as did their spelling. He required that written assignments be drafted three times before being submitted for grading. These efforts produced positive results but took time. With the calendar year in its last month, Thomas already felt considerably behind schedule.

He had started on Friday evening and by late Saturday afternoon, the young man had finally finished the laundry and correcting the last of the social studies tests; mostly D's, a few C's, four B's, a couple of A's and some dismal works on which he wrote "HN" for Help Needed. (He refused to place an "F" on tests or homework.) Actually, it was a stark improvement over the previous test. The two-week unit had taken nearly three and a half. Thomas took a deep breath, threw his pen down and rose from his dining room table. Suddenly, he felt trapped in his apartment. Lately, he had been withdrawing from his friends somewhat as the pressure to stay on top of his duties mounted. He hadn't watched a college football game in two weeks. A thought popped into his head and he turned on the TV. Unfortunately, he had missed the first half-hour of a movie he had been waiting all week to see.

Frustrated, he picked up the telephone and called Glen. They usually spoke on the phone at least once over the weekend. Apparently, his new best friend had gone out. Thomas imagined that maybe Glen had whizzed through correcting his work—subtracting single digit numbers, printing last names, coloring circles or whatever kids did in first grade—and now waltzed around the mall enjoying Christmas shopping with his attractive girlfriend Jean. Or was it Jane? (They had never actually met. Glen had only shown him a picture of her once.)

Thomas considered going out to a mall for his own shopping but didn't feel like fighting the weekend holiday crowds. He didn't feel like hitting the gym either so again he played with the remote control to the television. A commercial for make-up featuring several beautiful women stirred and disturbed him. After turning off the TV, he guessed the nature of his problem. He hated to admit it, but he was lonely.

Thomas suddenly thought about Laura. He wondered what she was doing right now. Had she settled into a new routine with her expensive-suit-wearing boyfriend? Last Christmas, she and Thomas had gone shopping together. She charged thousands of dollars worth of merchandise without batting her beautiful brown eyes. He remembered how awkward he felt when they exchanged gifts. She must have outspent him four-to-one. She said that it didn't matter. Of course it did—to him.

The bachelor bolted into the bedroom and returned to the living room with his personal phone book. He searched for the telephone and called a female friend who lived about an hour west of Boston—Marlene, from Selma, Alabama. She was a petite woman with smooth, olive-colored skin who visited a hairdresser to have her hair straightened every four weeks. They had gone to college together at OSU. She had majored in some type of design discipline and had gotten a good job working for some college in Worcester, Massachusetts, of all places. Because of her thick Southern accent, she had endured endless teasing from her college mates, who also found it amusing that she had decided to move out east and live in a city spelled Worcester but pronounced "Wustah."

She and Thomas had slept together on and off a few times in college, nothing serious. When he moved out east to attend Boston College, he knew almost no one at first so he called Marlene. She reported how much she loved her job but hated the city, lamenting about being lonely due to the "lack of eligible Black men in town." Subsequently, she and Thomas visited each other a couple more times in order to have company and sex. When he became involved with Laura, he discontinued their "relationship."

He listened for the phone to ring.

"Hello?" the female voice answered.

The nervous man felt relieved. He wouldn't be faced with the dilemma of whether or not to leave a message on her voice mail. "Hi, Marlene. It's Thomas. How are you?" He felt his pulse rise but wasn't sure why. "Have I caught you at a bad time?"

"No," she answered. "I'm fine. I'm glad you called. I was just thinking about you. You know, wondering what you've been up to and all." She paused. "Come to think of it, I never got a wedding invitation, my friend. What happened?"

He winced. "It's a long story. I'll tell you about it some day. Suffice it to say there wasn't anything to invite you to," he declared, his teeth grinding. "Anyway, I wanted to, well, perhaps drive out there and see a friendly face. Maybe even tonight. Um, maybe I could take you to dinner." He thought about what more he could say. "That is, if you don't have other plans this evening."

"No, I don't have any plans. I'd like that. It'd be nice to see you."

They negotiated the time for his arrival and said good-bye. Thomas turned off a lamp and immediately went to the closet. Resolving to finish recording his grades the next day, he put on his hat and coat, grabbed his keys, and headed out the door. Ten seconds later he returned to the apartment and re-entered his bedroom. He opened the drawer to the nightstand next to his bed and withdrew a small package. On the cover, a man and woman smiled lovingly at each other. On the way back to his main doorway Thomas noticed the two plants next to the window, the ones Laura had given him. Their situation appeared hopeless. He vowed to attend to them properly upon his return.

On Sunday, Boston welcomed its first accumulated snow of the season, a weak system, dropping barely an inch on the ground. The sporadic evergreen trees stood tall, showing off their new white trimmings with pride. Lawns looked more like cotton fields. The streets glimmered, shiny and wet but generally safe. Still, the local news made quite a deal out of the event. Forecaster's huddled around computer-generated images of weather patterns, explaining the phenomenon. One TV station produced a segment questioning whether Boston was adequately prepared for the winter in terms of salt and sand tonnage. Its reporter, a dark-haired, dark-eyed man with a low voice, sternly faced the camera and promised to pursue the story until answers were obtained.

On Monday, Thomas and the class entered the incipient stages of preparing for the holiday season. They had decided to produce a theatrical version of the Charles Dickens classic, *A Christmas Carol*. Thomas had purloined an adaptation of the story from the school library and had made copies of it, a move he suspected might have technically violated copyright laws. He insisted that the whole class read one-half of the story one day and the other half the next. They also watched a film version of the tale he brought from a library. At first, when he had announced that they would perform the play for another class, the students moaned and groaned about being involved in such "old-fashioned stuff." But after reading the story and seeing it performed, they became excited and enthusiastic.

That excitement and enthusiasm turned to horror when Thomas declared that the Room 217 Players would perform the play for Ms. Patterson's fourth-grade class. Mr. Payne's class immediately and vehemently protested. Every day "those kids" made noise in the hallway, threw food in the cafeteria or did their best to start trouble. "Those kids" would steal anything that wasn't nailed down. And they could erupt into a pugilistic battle almost anywhere. During a recent fourth-grade field trip, Mr. Dorn was summoned by the security director at the Children's Museum to personally drive to the museum and return with four of Ms. Patterson's students; two for fighting and two for stealing.

About once a month, in the middle of class, Mr. Payne would be interrupted by frantic girls from down the hall screaming to come to Room 214 right away. During last month's emergency Thomas returned to his own room, holding onto the arms of a boy hurling profanities at him nonstop. After the boy reached the limit of his scatological vocabulary, he made the unfortunate decision to hurl physical blows at Mr. Payne instead and was immediately sent careening into a wall.

Thomas listened with some amusement as his students whined and complained about his choice of audience. They supplied him with a myriad of anecdotal and eyewitness reports to support their predictions about the tragic consequences that would befall their sacred space if Ms. Patterson's twenty-three students entered without gags and handcuffs. But their exhortations fell on deaf ears. Their audience had been chosen and the matter decided.

On the first day of rehearsal, Thomas chose to cast the play conservatively. He explained the process of auditioning for parts. No real script had been written, so he fed the actors their lines for them to repeat. Eventually, several roles were filled. Melvin won the part of Scrooge, and Jonathan would play his nephew. Maria, with her small frame and soft voice, would be perfect as the Ghost of Christmas Past. Christine's ebullient nature would serve well as the Ghost of Christmas Present, while Asa's tall, dark ghostly presence was perfect for the Ghost of Christmas Yet to Come. (Thomas warned that he could keep the job as long as he brought in his homework.)

Everyone had a part or a job to do. Gary and Angelica headed the set-design brigade, gathering materials and constructing costumes. Akeem, who did not celebrate Christmas because he and his family ardently followed the teachings of Islam, volunteered to be in charge of playing the background musical selections. Melissa, reserved but extremely focused, proved to be better than anyone at turning the classroom's three light switches on and off on cue. (She and her family practiced the Jehovah's Witness faith and also did not celebrate Christmas.)

Unfortunately, the first two days of rehearsal turned out to be frustrating for everyone, especially Thomas. In spite of the joyous theme of the material, he found himself scolding his students constantly. The usual structure had to be relaxed so that groups could simultaneously perform various tasks, such as creating costumes, rearranging furniture and the like. This new freedom brought disappointing results. Thomas could barely spend five minutes with one group before someone from another would approach him to complain about a classmate.

The unwieldy behavior of his class did not sit well with the first-year teacher, who lost his temper several times, yelling at the top of his lungs in genuine fits of rage. He banished students to isolated chairs in various corners of the room and removed two students from the production altogether. Once, he stopped the rehearsal early and called for DEAR time, only to resume practice fifteen minutes later. He interrupted actors in the middle of their exclamations to deliver stinging criticisms of their poor acting or line mistakes. This even included Maria, who for some inexplicable reason on the second day announced, "I am the Ghost of *your* Christmas past" instead of "I am the Ghost of Christmas Past" five times straight. The severity of the rebuke she received shocked everyone in the room.

Thomas couldn't admit it openly but he was afraid. He had already invited Mr. Dorn and Ms. Flores to the performance. With less than a week before the opening, he knew that unless his class made substantial improvements, he would have to suffer the humiliation of canceling the show. Either that or risk a shaky exhibition, guaranteed to produce disruptive antics from Room 214, otherwise known as the "Dog Pound." The possible damage to his reputation as the Miracle Man brought panic to his heart.

Uncharacteristically, while at the gym working off the frustration of the second day's rehearsal, he complained bitterly about his class to Glen, who as always, listened patiently. Over one hundred people exercised in the various rooms of the brightly-lit building. For their own personal reasons, the patrons clanged, banged, grunted and counted simultaneously in the background. In spite of the noise and the constant movement of human flesh in all of its splendor and disappointment—and a loudspeaker spewing out fast-paced dance tunes for the proper workout atmosphere—Glen hung onto every whining word. After ascertaining that his colleague had thoroughly spun his wheels in one place, Glen asked a simple question. He did not look at Thomas but instead checked the amount of weight on the lat machine; he wanted to improve the width of his back.

"Can you recall why you wanted to do this play in the first place?"

"What do you mean, dude?" Thomas inquired with a puzzled expression on his face.

Glen shook a canister of powder on his hands, rubbed them together and sat down on the machine. "Can you tell me why you wanted your class to do this play in the first place?" He turned towards his tall friend and tilted his head slightly upward, then arched his eyebrows to accentuate his question even more. His eyes shone with vitality.

Thomas sat down on a wooden bench and rubbed his hands together. "Well …" he pondered the question for a few seconds. "I wanted the kids to really get deeply into the material. You know, to make it come alive." His voice became more rapid. "Hell, the story's not even in the book. I got it from the school library. It's a great story. One of the greatest ever told. That's why it's still a favorite today." He shrugged his broad shoulders. "Also, I thought they'd get a kick out of performing the piece, you know, working on something together. To tell you the truth, I thought they'd have— we'd have fun with it."

Glen blinked his eyes and produced a half-smile. "Have you?"

"Hell no!" Thomas said, returning the smile.

"It sounds to me like you started off wanting your kids to learn something and have fun while doing it. That's a good goal. That's about them." Glen paused and scratched his nose with his thumb, unaware that he had left a residue of white powder on it. "But once it became about you, making sure you looked good, everything fell apart. Like we always say, we can't lose track of the goal. We're here for them. They're not here for us."

Thomas walked closer and laid his elbow on his friend's shoulder. "How the hell did you get so smart? You're not even that much older than me!"

Glen smiled to acknowledge the compliment. "I didn't tell you anything you didn't already know." He shifted his weight and placed both hands on the bars of the machine. "Now, are you gonna help me count here or what?"

Thomas began the following school day by apologizing to the class. He told them to forget about the past because they would start over, and reminded them that they had only four more days to get the play ready. He wanted them to learn but most of all, he just wanted them to enjoy the experience. Everyone agreed and aligned with the goal of pulling together and putting on a terrific performance.

That morning's rehearsal went much better. Two events greatly aided in that endeavor. First, Christine, in her role as the giant Ghost of Christmas Present exclaimed her opening line with her usual inimitable zeal, but also with a slight twist.

"I am the Ghost of Christmas Present," she boomed. "Come. Come in and know me better, *MON!*"

"Cut!" Thomas commanded. He strolled casually over to Christine, who wore a paper crown wrapped in gold foil, and Melvin, sporting an old bath robe. Everyone in the room stopped and stared at their director. Already he was about to embark on another terrorizing rampage, they thought. Christine closed her eyes and prepared for the onslaught. Melvin began to unobtrusively creep out of harm's way. But Thomas only put his hand on the Ghost's shoulder and chuckled.

"Come and know me better, *mon?* Mon? Honey, he ain't a Jamaican," he revealed. He repeated the line with a Jamaican cadence. Much to the amusement of the entire class, Thomas kicked up his legs and added a jig. The class roared with laughter. Several students joined their tall teacher on the dance floor, jamming and chanting "Come and know me better, mon" over and over. Christine flashed an embarrassed smile.

The second event occurred later, during the party scene involving Scrooge and Maria—who effortlessly breezed through her lines—and more than a dozen other performers. Cleopatra, who already stood a lanky five-feet, eight-inches tall, displayed tremendous gifts as a dancer. She danced with Tyshaun, the only tall boy in the class other than Asa and Maurice, as one of six waltzing couples in the scene. It called for precise timing, requiring Melissa to turn the lights on over Maria's and Melvin's heads when they spoke, but to keep the rest of the room dark. Then on cue, the lighting had to be reversed, so that Maria and Melvin stood in the dark while the waltzing six couples, including Young Scrooge and Young Marley, received illumination.

Over the past few days, the dance scene had begun to improve. Each boy-girl couple had been assigned to each other permanently, so they had begun to shed their diffidence about touching a member of the opposite sex and acclimate to each other's movements—except Cleo and Tyshaun. Besides the fact that they genuinely detested each other, Tyshaun was a horrible dancer.

Several times Thomas took hold of Cleo and, facing Tyshaun, demonstrated to the central dance couple how they should move. But Cleo wanted to lead and Tyshaun couldn't follow her fluid and blithe movements even for a few precious seconds, let alone for two minutes. Thomas stepped back onto the stage and danced with Cleopatra while speaking to all of his dancers. The two glided through the air as if they had been dancing together for years. When Thomas took to the stage, the scene went well. Without him, it almost immediately fell apart.

Carmelita, always outspoken, exclaimed the obvious. "Why don't you just dance with Cleo yourself, Mr. Payne?" she asked.

Everyone, including Tyshaun, chimed in with similar sentiments. Thomas shrugged his shoulders and looked uncomfortable.

"I don't know, guys. This is your play, not mine," he protested.

"But Mr. Payne," Hernando said. "We don't have much more time. And you and Cleo dance perfectly together."

Everyone insisted—especially Cleopatra—so he agreed.

That evening Thomas raced home to shower and change clothes. The annual John Adams Elementary School Christmas party would be held away from school. Attendance required paying a fee for the catered food and drawing a name for the exchange of gifts. Each person wrote his or her name on a piece of paper, along with the suggestion of three inexpensive items, and dropped it into the gift box. The "Secret Santa" giver could choose one. Thomas had chosen to receive a calendar with a sports theme, a pair of gloves or a music selection. He had reached into the box and retrieved the name of the school secretary, Marilyn Walker. She had expressed an interest in only one thing—lottery tickets!

Thomas drove to a restaurant in the affluent city of Newton, with the sky and traffic both very clear. A half-moon and gospel-style Christmas music kept him company during the journey. He finally arrived after searching around the clean streets of Newton Centre for a few minutes. He recognized the cars parked in the well-lit lot of a restaurant tucked between a bakery and a movie rental store. Most of the guests from the school had already arrived. Most.

Earlier that afternoon mentor and mentee had endured their first argument. Glen had waited until then to inform his friend that although he had purchased a ticket and drawn a name, he had decided not to attend the party. Still, he had asked Thomas to take his gift to the affair. Thomas had agreed but also expressed displeasure that Glen had left him out in the cold—literally.

Thomas looked at his watch. It was nearly 8 o'clock and the party had begun an hour earlier. He checked his coat pocket again for Marilyn's gift, wrapped in a small box stuffed with newspaper. On the passenger's seat rested a foot-long rectangular box. It was covered by blue paper spotted with Santa Clauses. Thomas grabbed the box, containing Glen's gift, tucked it under his arm and opened the car door only to receive a slap in the face by the cold, brisk wind. He could hear the faint sound of music playing, music that seemed out of place.

Much warmer air greeted him as he quickly stepped inside. A short man with gray hair and a well-trimmed beard stoically pointed to the room in the back, the location of the soiree. Thomas walked past several older, White patrons who glanced at him, then quickly shifted their eyes away but continued to observe him.

He opened a door, closed it behind him and walked about ten feet down a corridor, approaching a set of double doors. He opened them and recognized several workmates draped in classy evening clothes. They generally sat Hispanics on one side, Blacks on one side and Whites on another, just like at school. The room itself was small, maybe twice the size of a classroom but it stretched fourteen feet to the ceiling; its walls painted a cheerful white and orange color. The floor, half carpeted and half parquet, absorbed the noise coming from the disc jockey's area, a slightly raised platform on the other side of the room. A few feet away behind a large portable bar stood a young, pretty woman in uniform with long blond hair tied in a pony tail. She bobbed and swayed with the music while pouring drinks for several guests.

Everyone looked so different. Ms. Bishop, who like Thomas was new to the Adams and had come overdressed on the first day of school, wore her hair down and had wiggled into a skimpy, dark-blue dress covering a padded bra. Ms. Mustafa, always lovely but usually in dark colors, sported a long pink dress with a split up the side. Ms. Flores's face bore more makeup than usual. But the biggest surprised was Ms. Cooke. With a form-fitting black, backless dress, high heel shoes and contact lenses, she was absolutely stunning! She moved frantically on the dance floor among two dozen bodies.

Thomas was approached by Ms. Patterson, the coordinator of the evening's activities. She escorted him to the coatroom, then led him to a large table where he unloaded his gifts. She also introduced him to her very handsome husband (who happened to be *Black)* and the husbands and boyfriends of the staff. Thomas shook hands, then finally sat down at a small table that wobbled when he leaned on it. He felt a bit uncomfortable until Heléna strutted straight towards him and planted herself in the chair next to his. She had raised her long hair up off her neck and wore a shiny, red one-piece jumpsuit. It made her look very sexy, although Thomas tried not to notice. There had been no further kissing incidents, so he had resolved to put the matter out of his mind.

"*Buenes noches,* Tomaso," she said, raising her voice to be heard over the music.

"Hi, Heléna. Boy, am I glad to see you," he replied. He widened his eyes and looked his friend over from top to bottom. "You look very lovely. When did you get here?"

"Are you kidding?" she said. "Me and the paras have been here for hours. Who do you think set up everything and did the decorations?"

Thomas rolled his eyes up, down, left and right. He hadn't noticed it when he entered, but the room was garnished with red and green balloons and ribbons, adding to the festive mood of the evening. "It looks very nice, Heléna. You guys did a great job."

She flashed a broad smile, then abruptly changed the subject, as she frequently did in conversations. "Hey, Tomaso. What about that ol' party-pooper Glen? Is he coming?" Her eyebrows grew closer together as she tried to look angry. Thomas smiled at her, and she softened and did likewise. "I think Glen's very sweet, but you know what? For some reason, I don't think he's happy. Maybe it's the holidays. Some people get like that during this time of year."

Thomas nodded. "I agree. He told me once that he and his dad weren't close. I know it bothers him. Maybe that's it."

"Yeah," Heléna concurred. "Maybe he needs a nice girlfriend. I know a few friends I could introduce him to. They're nice. Maybe—"

"He has a girlfriend. He showed me a picture of her. She's pretty."

Helena raised her glass of wine. "Let's drink a toast to our friend."

Thomas lifted his full glass of orange juice. "To Glen."

A half-hour later Thomas joined the merrymakers on the dance floor. The DJ, a real pro and the brother of one of the paras, played a mixture of tunes, old and new, English and Spanish. Behind those dark sunglasses, he could size up an audience and play songs he knew they would enjoy. Thomas danced with several of the women, but mostly with Heléna and Marilyn Walker, who had unabashedly slid into a satiny burgundy dress designed to push up and show off half of her mammary glands. Her date, who looked barely old enough to have graduated from college, spent much of the evening posing by the bar, drinking champagne.

Throughout the evening, a few more "guests" arrived. Mrs. Chang entered with her husband. After meeting him, Thomas became secretly annoyed at himself. He had assumed that they would not come because of the racial makeup of the school staff. By assuming they might be racists, he discovered his own racism instead. He enjoyed conversing with Jeffery Chang, a very pleasant and down-to-earth man. Later still, Ms. Enriquez, the bilingual second-grade teacher, arrived with her husband. The scuttlebutt about their unhappy marriage appeared to be on target. They barely spoke a word to each other all evening.

At 9:30 several of the older members of the staff started to disperse. An hour later, the DJ slowed down the tempo of the music. As the paras strolled onto the dance floor with their dates, Thomas and Heléna looked at them, then at each other. He grinned and wiggled his eyebrows.

"Shall we, lass?" he asked with an exaggerated British accent.

"Oh, lovely," she replied similarly. Heléna took his hand and they casually strolled onto the dance floor to join the others.

The room had become quite warm from all the activity. Thomas put his arms around Heléna and studied her face. There was something different about her but he couldn't quite place it. Not just her hair... actually, it was her mustache. She didn't have it anymore. Thomas examined her mouth and tried to guess how she got rid of it. Heléna noticed her dance partner's attention. She gazed into his eyes and smiled.

"Heléna," Thomas said. "Thank you for being here and saving me from what would have been an unpleasant evening."

"*No problema, mi amigo,*" she answered, caressing his back and squeezing him as they continued dancing. After a few seconds she softly whispered, "Thomas, I don't have to stay to clean up. I rode with Margarita, but she wants to stay and help out anyway." She held him closer and purred into his ear. "Could you take me home?"

Thomas said that he would. Heléna, feeling quite mellow after three glasses of wine, rested her head on his chest and began to softly hum with the music.

Later that same week, the day of the show arrived. Before the start of the school day, Thomas and a few selected students busied themselves in the morning preparing for the event. Although only a small classroom show, Thomas felt nervous. In fact, he had not slept well the previous night, fretting over details of the morning. As he carried objects to the back of the room, he mentally reviewed last-minute details. To his surprise, he possessed the same feelings as he did before a big game in college.

At 8:25 Thomas brought in the rest of the class and checked for homework. He had dispensed only a small reading assignment and two pages of handwriting, plus a short math worksheet (telling time on a "face clock" still proved to be a difficult task for some). Everyone turned in his or her work. The reading confirmation slips had all been signed by a parent or guardian.

"We'll do one complete run-through with no director interruptions before they get here at 11 o'clock," Thomas explained. LaShonda was absent again. Fortunately, her role could be easily assumed by another girl. Thomas reached in his desk and retrieved a blue non-attendance report form and slammed it on his desk. Before leaving for the day, he would submit it to the Boston Public School attendance officer—again. He noticed Connie with her hand up and called on her.

"Mr. Payne, this morning I saw Mr. Dorn out in the playground. He rounded up a bunch of Ms. Patterson's kids and took them with him to the office."

Thomas raised his eyebrows. "Oh? Does anybody here know anything about this?" he asked, looking around. Hands went into the air. He acknowledged Jessica's.

She shook her new braids and blinked her eyes. "Ooooh, Mr. Payne, there was a big ol' fight after school where they're building that new McDonald's. Awholelotta Ms. Patterson's kids were there."

"None of ours?" Thomas inquired. "Yes, what is it, Maurice?"

"My brother wanted to go. He's in Ms. Patterson's class, the little flea.

But I dragged him home," the boy reported.

"Heads up work there, Maurice! You definitely called the right play," Thomas exclaimed, giving him the thumbs-up sign. The class broke into applause. Maurice smiled proudly. Thomas prepared to announce the day's lineup when Connie's hand went up again. He looked at his watch, took a deep breath and called on her.

"Mr. Payne, do we really have to do the play for them? Can't we do it for Mrs. Chang's class instead, pleeeeaaaassse?" she begged.

Apparently, the girl's request struck a sensitive nerve. Suddenly, a spontaneous combustion of noise erupted as virtually the entire class clamored and gestured, expressing similar sentiments. The display caught the first-year teacher off guard.

"Waitaminute! Wait a minute, class. Listen to me!" he replied waving his hands frantically. "If you can hold that group's attention, you're really doing something," Thomas declared. "Come on. Give it a try."

"But, Mr. Payne, they're so bad. They be acting up on the bus and everything," Connie whined. "They be calling the bus driver names and stuff."

"Mr. Payne?" Christine said, raising her hand.

"It's all right, Christine, just go ahead." Thomas said.

She swallowed. "Could we vote on this, just this once, please?"

Thomas couldn't help but snicker. The whole class did likewise, gradually erupting into broad guffaws.

"Honey," Thomas finally responded, still chuckling. "What teacher has his name on that Room 217 door?" The voting idea ended as quickly as it began.

Thomas balled both of his hands into fists. He became positive but serious. "I say not only will you hold that group's attention, but you'll put on a brilliant show." His voice abruptly shifted to that of a gentle-speaking philosopher. "Besides, who do they remind you of?" He tilted his head and waited.

Only two hands went up at first, then three more, then a half-dozen.

Thomas scanned the room and called on Melissa. Tyshaun covered his mouth with his hand, expecting a long fight before the stuttering girl would force out an answer.

"Us," she declared clearly.

Thomas nodded. "That's right. Not too long ago, they were you." He searched for another student. Recently, he had moved her seat so that she could see the board better and was still getting used to the change. "Carmelita, remember what you told me the other day? What did your class say about this group last year?"

Carmelita didn't hesitate. "We used to say they was bad. We used to laugh at them. Ms. Valdez told us not to play or even talk to anyone in that room. If one of us be bad, Ms. Valdez would say that she was going to have him transferred to Ms. Patterson's room. When she said that, we would beg her for another chance and say we would straighten up, mmm-hmm." Carmelita took her glasses off and sat erect in her chair, smug and superior.

Thomas thought he should end on a positive note. He opened his hands and gestured to the class. "But now what class is the number one class in this school?"

"Two-seventeen," they replied in unison.

He put his hand to his ear. "I'm sorry. What was that?"

"Two-seventeen!" they shot back. Just then a gust of wind blew, rattling the windows and confirming their acclamation.

At exactly 11:09 a.m. Thomas stood in a dark corner and held onto his pen-sized flashlight as he read aloud. "Christmas is a wonderful time of year. It is a time for people to be nice to each other, exchange gifts and spend time with their families. It is especially a time to be generous with those who are less fortunate than you. But a long time ago there was an old man named Ebeneezer Scrooge, who had forgotten the true meaning of Christmas. This is the story of how he found it again, with a little help." He paused and licked his lips. They were dry but he continued. "It was Christmas Eve, and people were busy getting ready for this important day."

He aimed his flashlight briefly at Melissa. When the beam hit her face, she turned on the lights at the front of the room. Ms. Patterson crossed her fingers. Nineteen of her students suppressed snickering (one was absent and three had been suspended). They had been scattered all over the classroom and rocked in their seats, whispering aloud to no one in particular. Heléna Gutiérrez widened her eyes in curiosity, trying to avoid staring at Thomas. Mr. Dorn reclined in the front row by the door, expressionless with his arms folded across his chest.

Next to him sat Ms. Flores. An art major in college, she inspected the makeshift stage. The board had been covered by tall sheets of paper. Across the paper, which stretched for twenty feet or so, she examined a wonderful street scene painted in an old English style. The slight smell of oil-based paint still hung in the air. The street design had been constructed in sections and aligned together with exquisite workmanship. Buildings with names painted across them such as "Ale House," "Butcher Shop," "Stable" and "Haber-dasher" filled the space. In the middle loomed a slightly larger structure with a large, prominent sign: "Scrooge and Marley." Two old-style street lamps stood on opposite ends of the street.

Thomas tapped Akeem on the arm and the boy pressed the button on the music player. As "Here We Come A Caroling" was sung by a children's choir in perfect harmony, several of Room 217's students marched to the front from "offstage." They made loud noises, greeted each other and spoke all at the same time. After a few seconds of milling about, they exited the area in different directions. With the music still playing, Melvin, playing Scrooge and wearing a pair of drugstore reading glasses and a tie, entered from the darkness. He came upon a little boy, played by Angel, who held out his hat. Scrooge dismissed the boy with a scowl and a wave of his hand, then wobbled, cane in hand, to his office. He came upon Vince, playing Bob Cratchit and chastised him for his Christmas spirit. A few minutes later Jonathan, as his nephew, received the same treatment.

Thomas proudly watched as the actors delivered their lines without the slightest outward hint of nervousness. They displayed poise and confidence. Three merchants entered and made their pitch to Scrooge for a contribution for the poor. Instead, they received a derisive rebuke. Scrooge and Cratchit finished their scene together, and Scrooge left to go home.

Melissa turned off all the lights and Thomas read aloud again. While he read, several students tiptoed onstage toting a bench on which Melvin would lie down when Scrooge retired for the night. Thomas resumed narrating but in a slightly more dramatic fashion.

"Scrooge arrived at his gloomy home, which had once belonged to his partner, Jacob Marley. Marley, now dead, had been as mean and stingy as Scrooge. When he was about to unlock the door, Scrooge thought he saw, on the door knocker, the face of his dead partner...."

The scene between Scrooge and Marley—the latter played by Pedro, the devoted grandson Thomas admired—was brilliant. Pedro proved to be a surprisingly macabre and scary Marley. Draped in paper chains, he shook them at all the right moments. Ms. Patterson's students stared, spellbound.

After Pedro faded out stage right, Maria appeared, wearing a white sheet draped around her small body and another covering her head. Thomas felt his pulse rise. Would she say her opening line correctly?

"Who are you?" Scrooge asked, frightened.

"I am the Ghost of Christmas Past. Your past, Ebeneezer Scrooge," Maria replied.

Thomas breathed a sigh of relief and relaxed to enjoyed Melvin and Maria's exchange.

Eventually, the dance scene arrived. By then Thomas had lost his nervousness. He stepped onto the stage with Cleopatra. The audience started to rumble from genuine amusement and involvement in the festivities. Ms. Flores and Ms. Patterson clapped their hands with delight. Mr. Dorn raised his eyebrows. Heléna put her hands over her mouth, regaled by the spectacle. Akeem worked the buttons on the music box, which emitted Johann Strauss' melodic "Skating Song" waltz (actually written about fifty years later than the story). Thomas smiled and danced with Cleopatra, who enjoyed herself immensely. He gave Melissa a barely perceptible head signal, and the lights over the dancers went dark. Scrooge and the Ghost of Christmas Past stood under the lights to say their lines.

"I remember that day!" Scrooge screamed, pointing and laughing. "It was a wonderful time. A wonderful time!" He kicked his heels and danced with an imaginary partner. The spectators laughed at his exaggerated movements, as intended.

Twice more the lights switched back and forth during the dance scene. Then Thomas, Cleo and the entire waltzing troupe gradually strolled off the floor. Thomas gave his dance partner the thumbs-up sign and half a hug, then returned to his spot in the corner.

The production continued virtually without a mistake. Christine injected even more energy into the play as the Ghost of Christmas Present. Thomas and his class all went into silent laughter at their private joke when Christine invited Melvin to "Come and know me better, man!" At the pivotal time, Melvin hammed up his big cemetery scene with the Ghost of Christmas Yet to Come. Doug had brought a black Halloween mask, which covered Asa's face completely—even his eyes—as he stood silently pointing, commanding Scrooge to view the tombstone bearing his name. A black hood, gloves and cape made the figure appear even more sinister.

Finally, Scrooge stood on stage with Bob Cratchit and his family. They all raised their plastic champagne glasses as the old man proposed a toast.

Brian, a.k.a. Tiny Tim, a quiet student with a baby face and the shortest boy in the room, delivered the classic last line.

"God bless us, every one!" he exclaimed, leaning on his modern-looking crutch.

"The end," Thomas announced. The room instantly became dark.

The audience immediately and loudly applauded. Melissa turned the lights back on only in the front, and all of the participants crowded on stage, except Thomas. Everyone bowed, and quickly exited except Melvin, who took one quick bow, then left. Thomas motioned again, and the room became completely dark for a few seconds, then completely bright again. The director stepped on stage and said a few closing words of thanks to bring the event to an end. A chorus of "We Wish You a Merry Christmas" entered the environment from where Akeem stood, and the room grew noisy as all the guests prepared to leave.

Mr. Dorn expressed his appreciation to his host and the class without fanfare and quickly left. His supervisor's perfunctory behavior puzzled Thomas. Ms. Flores stayed and provided much more effusive feedback before being summoned to the office over the loudspeaker. Thomas felt more gratified by her response. Heléna hugged and praised almost every Room 217 student. She stopped in front of her colleague and exclaimed, "You and your class did a wonderful job, Mr. Payne." He thanked her and escorted her to the door. They started to speak but became distracted by noises behind them. Heléna simply said that she would see him later and bounced down the hallway, humming "We Wish You a Merry Christmas." Thomas returned to his classroom where additional Christmas songs contributed to the festive atmosphere.

Watching Ms. Patterson's class struggling to leave the room produced painful feelings for Thomas and his students. Ms. Patterson tried to congratulate him and his young thespians for a job well done but was frequently interrupted by the noise and antics of her clashing students. Eventually, she managed to praise the production and thanked her colleague for inviting them. Thomas tightened his hands into a fist but said nothing as they filed out the door, even when a long-legged boy tore one of the background sheets as he was pushed out of line by another. Gary moved to protest but Thomas shook his head, stopping him.

The second he closed their door, Thomas and his troupe exploded into wild excitement over their successful debut performance. Everyone talked at the same time. Students shouted about an especially memorable moment. Each student received acknowledgment from the teacher. He had never seen a better Scrooge than Melvin. Tyshaun's chilling and effective presence made the final scene impressive. Maria delighted the audience with her innocence…. They were all big winners! The cast and crew glowed, basking in the recognition.

It took nearly a half-hour to put the room back together again. With the lunch period approaching, Thomas darkened the room and gently instructed his students to sit in their chairs with their eyes closed. Next, he asked them to listen to a soft, slow classical music selection. After playing about two minutes of music, he asked them to identify the instruments. Thomas presented the exercise as a listening activity but he actually employed it to soothe the class and calm them down. Hands sprang into the air, and individual pupils correctly named the violin, the piano and the oboe. They had done this exercise several times before. Also, for the past six weeks the music teacher had been expanding their knowledge of musical instruments used in classical productions. In fact, they had just finished a major unit on *The Nutcracker*.

After school Thomas trudged downstairs and knocked on Heléna's door. Her familiar voice permitted him to enter, so he slowly opened the door. The former storage closet had been made reasonably comfortable by Heléna's taste in decorating. Student artwork and stories covered half the wall space. She had also hung posters of Latino and American celebrities brandishing a book and extolling the joys of reading. A small space heater provided much-needed additional warmth, probably in violation of some building code. The tall woman stood over her small table-like desk, sorting through a half-inch stack of papers. Spotting some writing that apparently did not meet with her approval, she made a face and shook her head from side to side, causing her ever-present large, hand-made earrings to rattle and clang. She directed her attention to her guest.

"Hi, Tomaso. *Cómo esta?*"

"I'm fine, Heléna. How was your day?" he replied.

"Fine, fine. The kids are catching on," Heléna assured him. She resumed attending to the papers in her hand. "Doug's even showing a little improvement. It's still slow. I'll stay with him. Don't worry. We'll have that guy reading *War and Peace* in no time."

The words emanated from the same Heléna, but the insouciant spirit was absent. Thomas took two steps forward and took hold of her arm, gently turning her towards him. Now that they faced each other, he suddenly put his hands in his pockets and took a step back. His eyes briefly peered towards the door to ensure their privacy. He quietly recited his rehearsed speech. "Look, Heléna. I'm sorry about the other night. I mean, I'm sorry if I gave you the wrong idea."

Heléna frowned and started to reach for him but resisted. "You didn't do anything wrong, Thomas. It was me. I guess the wine and the atmosphere just went to my head. You did the right thing—stopping us, I mean. A few more minutes alone in my apartment and we might've done something we both would've regretted later." She clutched her papers in a tight grip. "I'm glad one of us came to his senses. Like your dad said: 'Don't shit where you eat.' "

Thomas had never heard Heléna speak profanely before. Her words stung his ears. Obviously, seeing him had upset her, perhaps due to embarrassment at their romantic foreplay the night before last. He thought it best to make a graceful exit, but at the same time he wanted to pull Heléna close to him and taste her mouth on his again. He decided to allow them both to save face.

"You're right, honey, um, Heléna," Thomas replied. "We're both adults. These things happen at office Christmas parties. You hear about it all the time. It's a good thing we stopped before we went too far. Let's consider the whole thing forgotten." He backed up and reached for the doorknob. He opened the door and felt the draft from the cool basement air. "Um, well. I wanted to tell you thanks for coming to see our play. It meant a lot to everyone."

Heléna met his eyes again. "Oh, I enjoyed every minute of it. You were all terrific! That girl you had playing that second ghost, she was great. And Melvin was pretty sharp, remembering all those lines. And your dance with that tall girl; I liked that part the best!" She bounced and gestured as she talked, more like her old self.

"Thanks again. Well, see you later," Thomas said, now on the other side of the threshold.

"*Hasta mañana,*" Heléna said, wiggling her fingers at him.

Thomas closed the door and proceeded up the two flights of stairs to his room. His thoughts compared the pleasurable Christmas party evening he had spent with Heléna with their recent encounter. His dad was right.

He mused about having stumbled upon another woman who might have been a good mate for him, had he met her at another time. He could not deny that he cared about Heléna. She was intelligent, attractive and enjoyed life. Not overly cautious at all like Laura. Thomas blinked his eyes to erase the thought and wondered how long he would continue comparing women he met to Laura.

That evening Thomas tossed and caught a small plastic football while talking to Glen on the telephone. It was not uncommon for the two of them to spend an hour or more on the phone like a couple of high school buddies. Thomas no longer harbored any ill feelings towards his friend about missing the party. His fears about being the only male there turned out to be unfounded. Besides, endangering one friendship over that event was enough. Although he and Glen discussed several issues, Thomas decided not to mention the near miss with their effervescent Venezuelan friend. He did, however, express profound distress upon hearing the main reason for his buddy's call.

"Tell me this is a bad joke, please," the younger man pleaded.

"I'm afraid I'm serious, m'man," Glen answered. "That's what Dorn said."

"Tell me again, slowly this time, what happened."

"Well, it's like this …" The veteran teacher paused as he tried to recall more details for the retelling. "I'm sitting at my desk minding my own business, and Dorn comes in. I thought he was coming to ask me about the new reading textbooks we're using, you know." He switched the phone to his other ear, so he could continue ironing his shirt. "But the man starts off talking about nothing, you know how the guy is."

"Yeah, I know," Thomas replied stiffly.

"Anyway, he starts talking about being up in your room earlier and seeing your play. I tell him that you told me how pleased you were that he and Flores had come. You know, that loyal-servant-happy-to-please crap. Then Dorn tells me that the kids were real good. That he couldn't believe it was the same group as last year. Then he says that it's not his place to interfere, but he didn't think it was a good idea for you to dance with Cleopatra. He goes on about how you're new here, and people might get the wrong idea."

"You're fucking kidding me!"

"I wish I was, brother. Finally, he tells me why don't I pass this information on to you, off the record. Not that you did anything wrong, he said, but just to be careful. You know, not everyone is as open-minded as he is." Glen turned off the iron and unplugged it, then held his shirt at arms-length to inspect the results.

Thomas fumed. "You know what? Fuck him! Fuck Dorn! Who cares what he thinks! Only his twisted mind could come up with something like that!" He paused and snorted. "You know what? First thing tomorrow, I'm gonna tell him what's what. The kids worked hard. They really did. I don't care about me but I'm not gonna let anyone besmirch their efforts. If Dorn doesn't like it, that's too bad." He stopped to catch his breath.

As always, Glen listened patiently to his very passionate but sometimes irascible comrade. The older, wiser member of the Adams staff calmly prodded his friend. "Listen, buddy, I want you to think about this. What would it accomplish if you stomped into Dorn's office and told him off?"

Thomas paused. "Well, it'll let Dorn know that he can't …" He stopped, then cleared his throat. "Well, I guess it wouldn't do much other than get it off my chest."

"And what else?"

A long silence ensued. "Not much else."

Glen felt immediate relief that his friend had arrived at a logical conclusion. He wanted to caution Thomas about letting his emotions take off on him, but he remembered that it wasn't that long ago when he sounded the same way. Now was not the time to dispense such wisdom. Instead, a bit of practical information would be more appropriate. He spoke slowly. "Dorn can be vindictive and petty," he admonished. "But he's the principal. If he wants to, he can make you permanent in your first year—or he can make you wait for the whole three years. I'm asking you, would it be worth it for you to spend the rest of the year in the doghouse just to get your cathartic rocks off?"

"Naw, I guess not." Thomas took a deep breath and a deep sigh. "Well, I guess I owe you again"

"You don't owe me nothing, man. In the morning you would've arrived at the same conclusion. But why waste a good night's sleep, huh?" Glen struggled internally but decided to take a risk. "You know, Thomas. I don't agree with Dorn but I'm telling you, you've got to be careful nowadays with touching the kids. Here in Boston, they're funny about it. It's sick. But be careful; you know what I'm saying?"

Thomas twisted his face from side to side and sighed again. "Yeah, I do. I swear, I just haven't gotten used to how distant people are here. It's not like Ohio at all." He didn't want to dwell on it any further, so he changed the subject. "I'm looking forward to going home for Christmas. How about you?"

"I'm going to spend time with my sister and her husband and the kids in New York, maybe stop by and see my dad." Glen's voice dropped at the last part. This time he changed the subject. "Well, I better get going. I've got to practice one last song for the Christmas Eve service at my church."

Thomas heard a cord of piano music emerging from the earpiece of his phone. "Okay, buddy. See you tomorrow—and thanks again."

The morning before the calendar year's last day of school, Thomas checked his students to ensure that they had dressed appropriately. The sun was not scheduled to make an appearance at all that day. Snow flurries fell from the sky, and the wind gusted noticeably. At 9 o'clock, after a ten-minute walk and another ten-minute wait, the inhabitants of Room 217 boarded a public bus to Boston's Theater District to see a production of *The Nutcracker*. It was the first live ballet any of them had ever seen. Tickets to the event were quite expensive; few parents could have afforded the steep price, but no one in the class had to pay for more than his or her own transportation plus three dollars. Gabriel and Alberta Payne, Thomas's parents, had donated the price of the tickets as a Christmas present to their son's students. (Thomas had decided to charge the three dollars to purchase a thank-you gift for his parents from the class.)

They had great seats; only a few yards from the orchestra. ("If you're going to do it, do it right," Mom had proclaimed.) All three fifth-grade classes at the Adams had studied the music of Clara and the Nutcracker Prince for the past few weeks. And Thomas's group had studied the story itself during reading class, when they weren't rehearsing for *A Christmas Carol*.

The crew of Room 217 found the ballet to be absolutely marvelous! Several of the boys had predicted that they wouldn't enjoy watching such a sissy spectacle for girls. But they soon changed their minds after witnessing the athletic prowess of the male dancers (and after Thomas revealed that football players sometimes took ballet lessons to improve their balance). Seeing *themselves* on stage, in a sense, especially surprised and pleased them. Thomas had chosen a first-class, multi-cultural, color-blind production. People of color filled many of the roles. An Asian woman portrayed Clara, while African American performers paraded on stage as her brother, Fritz, and the mysterious Herr Drosselmeyer. The Prince was played by an extremely talented and handsome dancer from Spain.

Before leaving the Adams, Thomas had expressed satisfaction that he could take every student on the trip, including his frequent homework no-shows. Everyone had come to school and with his or her homework at least minimally done, producing the first official "All Star Day" of the year. (Citing the ground rules, Thomas agreed to allow an additional recess period, further adding to the Payne largess.)

At the theater, there were no discipline problems. In fact, after escorting his students to the restrooms, two senior citizens who served as volunteer ushers informed Thomas that it had been many years since they had witnessed such a well-behaved group of youngsters. When they returned from the ballet, Cleopatra declared that she would study dance and eventually become a ballerina.

Accomplishing much academically the following day, the last day of school, proved to be challenging, but Thomas pressed on. Only twenty-four students attended class that day. He reminded them that it was still a school day, and their parents had sent them to school to learn, not partake of Christmas festivities. He angered Ms. Mustafa, the kindergarten teacher he found so attractive, when he would not allow Asa, who had a sister in her class, to go downstairs and see the child perform in a Christmas play.

"Sorry. He's grounded for one day. He's got to learn that when I say I don't want to hear another word from anybody, I mean it." Thomas informed her.

"But it's just for a few minutes," she explained.

"You do the crime, you do the time in Mr. Payne's class," Thomas recited smugly.

"Fine, I'll tell his sister that Mr. Payne won't let her brother come down," Ms. Mustafa said, heaving what Thomas considered to be her impressive chest.

"Yeah? Well, tell her why too," he replied curtly and closed the door in her face. He heard snickers and giggling behind him and felt immediate regret. Thomas knew better than to argue with a colleague, even slightly, in front of his students. He resolved to locate Ms. Mustafa after school and apologize.

That afternoon brought forth the fourth Movie Day of the year. Santa Claus knew who had been naughty and who had been nice—and so did December Diane and Mr. Payne, he announced. Christmas or not, he assured his class that the same rules still applied. If you had earned enough points, you could stay, and if you didn't, you could not. Had all twenty-eight pupils shown up, twenty-two of them would have been eligible to enjoy the movie and goodies; two more than last month, seven more than in September.

By prior arrangement, Cleopatra, Asa, Tyshaun, and Maurice were escorted to the library. They sat at separate tables while the library aide, Ms. Higgins, munched on Christmas cookies. Two of the "outies" had not come to school. Thomas gazed at Asa's despondent face and felt some sympathy. The boy had shown improvement over the month but unfortunately had burned up several points during its first week.

An hour later, after the class had been reassembled at the very end of the school day, Thomas gave each student a homework packet. "You'd be better off coming to school without your pants on than without this homework," he admonished. "I don't want tears or excuses in January. Don't bring me notes from mommy, grandma or the President of the United States. Got that?"

"Yes, Mr. Payne."

He pointed at their desks. "Have that cover letter signed only by a parent or guardian and dated for today or tomorrow, at the latest. No signature from a big brother or sister, as I let you do for other assignments." They nodded and he went on. "And just to be on the safe side, I'll be on the telephone this evening to inform every parent about your homework. And don't worry about your friends who missed school today," he playfully sneered. "I'm dropping their packets in the mail on the way home."

The class playfully booed and hissed, referring to their teacher as "the Grinch."

Finally, the coach gathered his team in a circle for the last time in the calendar year. He pursed his lips and nodded his head approvingly. "Not bad," he announced. "Not bad. It looks like most of you are starting to get the hang of what we're here for." He played with them, spying on his team like a cartoon character, rocking his head from side to side and cutting his eyes to the left and right. They responded with guarded laughter. "I've seen some improvements this year. For example, Melissa's coming around nicely."

Melissa blushed and showed all of her teeth.

"Asa had a small setback, but he's back where he belongs now and we're real proud of him," Thomas declared. "By the way, he told me that you guys better not drop him when he's selected Student of the Week, and you do his cradle." The class broke into their usual badinage, giggling and making animal sounds. Thomas laughed out loud.

"But I've got some students here who've been doing right, right from the beginning," he acknowledged. "They've been setting a good example for quite a while now. I'm talking about those who've already been chosen Student of the Week more than once, like Melvin, Maria, Carmelita and Pedro."

The four mentioned acknowledged his praise with wide grins.

Thomas shook his right index finger at no one in particular. "I'm telling you now: I want everybody in this room to be Student of the Week, but I'm not giving it away. Nope. You're going to do it the old-fashioned way." He lowered his voice so that it was barely audible. "You're going to earn it." He looked at Christine and Lakeisha. "And those of you who've had an extra burden on your backs, I'm not going to let you suffer much longer. I'm going to lift that burden off your shoulders soon, trust me."

Christine and Lakeisha nudged each other and smiled.

"We've got a long way to go. There's still six more months of school left," he cautioned, raising his eyebrows. Suddenly, his voice elevated. "You think I've been tough? Next year, you'll be looking back at this as the good old days when Payne was soft." He saw his students' eyes grow wide and scoffed. "That's right! I've been taking it easy on you."

The instructor suddenly felt a twinge of sadness at the prospect of not seeing his children for almost two weeks. His eyes displayed his feelings. He deliberately avoided the faces of Angelica, Melvin and Maria as he spoke. "I want to tell you that I'm very proud of every one of you." He looked up at the clock and decided to close. "Well, take good care of yourselves. Rest up for next year and be ready to kick some butt when you get back." He put his hand in their midst, and they joined in.

"Who's the best class at the Adams?" he called.

Ten minutes later Thomas stood by the door handing out small boxes of Swiss chocolates. A few students had given him gifts earlier during the day. Several girls stopped to give their teacher a hug. Angelica held him, groaning that she would miss him.

"My grandma said that God sent you to us, Mr. Payne."

Thomas's eyes widened and blinked several times. He didn't know how to respond. Public school staff were so obsessed with being careful not to offend anyone. Thomas had been taught in college that, in the classroom, avoid even acknowledging the possibility of God.

He put his large right hand on his little girl's head, almost as if to bless her. "I believe that your grandma may be right, honey," he whispered, and hugged her again. Just then, Mr. Dorn walked by in time to witness the contact but said nothing.

To save money, the Ohio native flew home to Cincinnati on Christmas morning. On the plane—less than half full—the fact that he missed his children so much and so soon surprised him. A slight depression surfaced during the lonely flight. While at the airport of his hometown he bought twenty-eight picture post cards of Cincinnati and enough stamps for each. The next day he mailed one to every student with a message to enjoy the time off.

Eventually, Thomas settled in to enjoy his vacation. He especially delighted in seeing his brother beam in the company of his two lovely daughters—and they had grown so!

Toward the end of his visit, Thomas declined an invitation from Edward to enjoy "a night on the prowl." Edward joked that his little brother didn't have a life anymore; he talked so much about *his* children. It was "Jonathan did this," or "Deborah said that." The young teacher had to admit that his brother spoke the truth. Later, while alone with his mother, he confided to her how much he had become attached to them. She understood.

"Have you been praying for them?" she asked her son.

"Every day, Mom." Thomas assured her.

January

"Give her a week too, Captain," he called to Jonathan.

The eleven-year-old scribbled "G5" next to the name on the small chalk-board behind the teacher's desk. He pinched the chalk in his left hand and observed the six-feet-four figure approaching each student. Those with a checkmark would be allowed to get out of their seats, enjoy recess and sit with the class during lunch, chatting with their friends. So far, four would not. The Student of the Week counted those who had earned five days grounding and the ire of Mr. Payne. Jonathan didn't understand how they could be so foolish. After all, they had been warned.

While waiting for a girl to produce her math, Thomas looked out the window. The sun, barely visible, fought for recognition through a shear layer of clouds. The school playground served as a parking lot. Snow had been pushed into what remained of the battered fence guarding the perim-eter. Only twenty minutes ago, small children slid down one particularly huge, formerly white mound. Snow from the storm two days before cov-ered the roofs of half the cars in the yard. Apparently, some drivers chose to brush off only their windshields, leaving several inches of thick snow on top of their vehicles. Thomas checked his red sportscar near the backdoor. It was clean and shiny.

While waiting his next instruction, Jonathan focused his attention on the interior environment. Several pictures and posters of Dr. Martin Luther King Jr., as well as the words to his "I Have a Dream" speech, were taped to the walls. The photographs of the student-players and the staff-coaches continued to reflect the dull light of the classroom. The contracts still hung proudly behind the teacher's desk. The winter pictures and student birth-day charts also remained. This month Maria would be eleven years old; four days later Tyshaun would turn twelve. Near the closet doors, on the bellies of fourteen snowmen or snowwomen flashed the names of buddy pairs. Near the main door, written on index cards, the name "Jonathan Franklin" appeared in the Student of the Week display. Attached to the door was the All-Star List for the previous week of school and the Superstar List for the entire month of December. Jonathan sighed, pleased that his name appeared on both. He was confident that he would earn a checkmark for every day on the new point calendar, January Jennifer, posted on the wall next to the teacher's desk.

Jonathan mused about the short welcome Mr. Payne had given the class. They had stood with raised plastic champagne glasses in hand, half-filled with chilled apple juice and had sung a song welcoming the new year. Mr. Payne explained the meaning of the lyrics to "Auld Lang Syne." The words still loomed in large letters on the front chalkboard. It had been so much fun.

Thomas strutted to the back row area designated for his most difficult students. He had declared that if they did not feel inclined to showcase the fruits of their labor, they could not play, talk, eat or sit with the class. A few—like Tyshaun, Francine and Cleopatra—had seen the same view of the room for virtually the entire school year. Their status became known as ISP, for In the Seat Plan. Someone reduced to ISP had to earn a point for five straight days before being allowed to return as a member in good standing. A class meeting preceded such a return, in which she or he stood in the center of the room and fielded sometimes grueling questions posed by skeptical classmates. Although the candidate may have met the minimum standards to be considered rehabilitated, Thomas insisted on a vote to determine if the former pariah had secured at least the minimum confidence of his or her peers. If over one-half of the students voted no, the outcast remained on ISP until another vote was taken two days later.

Thomas stared at Francine "You got *all* of your work or not?"

Francine looked at the floor. "Not all of it."

"G5 for her too, Captain," he announced.

"She's already at G2, Mr. Payne," Jonathan replied.

"Then add it to what she's got. You know the routine," he growled, a little irritated. Thomas wore a serious expression on his face by the time he reached another pupil and said, "Asa, you've been doing well for the past few weeks. Keep it going. Whatdoya have for me?" He accepted the boy's papers and examined them. "Where're the rest of the answers to the reading?" he inquired. A few students could be heard murmuring, "Uh-oh."

Asa's eyes grew wide with panic. His heartbeat accelerated, and in spite of the chilly temperature of the room, sweat beaded on his forehead. But he caught himself and tapped the other side of the paper. "On the back," he answered, his voice breaking.

Thomas turned the paper over. A few seconds passed. The heater began clanging as it attempted to push some warm air into the room. "Not bad. Could be neater," he assessed, placing the paper inside a manila folder and tucking it under his left arm.

The room broke into applause. Asa let out a deep sigh.

"Mr. Payne, Brian's here."

More uh-ohs.

Thomas walked down the gauntlet, then to the door and opened it. The cold air of the hall rushed in. A group of girls a few feet away laughed and conversed about something indecipherable. One girl with golden-brown skin and long, dark curly hair poked her friends and whispered. They tried to avoid looking at Mr. Payne.

"You ladies lost?" he asked calmly. "Perhaps I can help you find your classrooms," he suggested, taking a step in their direction.

"No, thank you, Mr. Payne," the girls answered as they dispersed.

Thomas smiled and returned his attention to his tardy student. Brian, a baby-faced boy who had played Tiny Tim during the Christmas play, coughed, reached in his bag and handed Thomas a note. He looked like he had just gotten out of bed.

"You're late." Thomas stated coldly after accepting the note but not reading it. The boy spoke quickly. The first-year teacher scowled. "You're a walker. What's this you're saying about snow?"

The small pupil took off his hat, revealing a recent haircut, and scratched his head. He started to reply but decided against it and shrugged his shoulders instead.

"Um-hum," Thomas muttered. "Listen to me, Brian, and listen good." His voice rose just slightly. "We went through this in September and October with you coming to my class late. We're not going through it again, *capisci?*"

"Yes, Mr Payne," Brian answered.

"I mean it. I'm not going to have it." He placed his hand on the boy's shoulder and lightened his tone. "Now we can always go back to you coming late and me checking your homework during recess—when I get around to it." Thomas raised his eyebrows as if to ask the boy's opinion. Hearing none, he retreated into the room and motioned for Brian to enter. "In other words," he added. "Get your butt to school on time. Got that?"

"Yes, Mr. Payne."

He clapped his hands twice. "Then what are you waiting for? Christmas? It's 350-something days off. Let's go!"

Brian and his buddy, Vince, one of the top math students in the class and only an inch taller, hurried to complete their tasks.

Thomas faced Jonathan. "Mark him late. No penalty—unless there's no homework." Fortunately for him, Brian produced all of the homework assigned over the vacation.

Finally, Thomas stood over Carmelita's desk. "What's the matter, honey?" he asked.

The girl shook her head in disbelief. She stuttered as the words escaped. "I can't find my reading question and answers."

A sea of voices could be heard in the classroom exclaiming surprise. Carmelita always brought in her homework. Always.

Thomas turned to the left and stared at Maria. "You know anything about this?"

Maria stood, horrified. "Maybe they're in her bag. I'll go see." She stepped towards the closet.

"No you won't," Thomas retorted. "No special privileges for special little boys and girls here. You know my rule: Once those closet doors close, they stay closed until lunch—unless there's an emergency." He turned back to Carmelita, who had put her head on her desk. "Sorry, honey," he said. "G5 for her, too, Captain," he announced. Jonathan obeyed. Carmelita sobbed.

The young man scanned the faces of his students. He had missed them terribly but didn't want to show any sentimentality. "The rest of you, clear your desks except for your math." The room became noisy with muffled voices, banging books and shuffling papers. Students fought to manage their broken-down equipment. The top of Akeem's desk came completely off its hinges, but he matter-of-factly returned it to its rightful place and closed it. Thomas looked at Jonathan, still at his post in front of the chalkboard, and flicked his head in the direction of the chatty class.

"I'm at the board," the boy declared loudly.

What little conversation lingering in the air immediately vanished. When the Student of the Week made such a declaration, all talking immediately ceased. Anyone who ignored the warning found a checkmark erased, and no one wanted to lose his or her recess over muttering a few words.

Jonathan spotted Tyshaun, whose face bore a mile-wide grin. He rocked in his chair and pantomimed clapping his hands in glee, no doubt at Carmelita's predicament. Cleopatra, who sat next to Tyshaun, nodded and covered her mouth to hide silent laughter. Tyshaun and Jonathan made eye contact, but the boy on ISP continued his theatrics. Initially, Jonathan had found Carmelita to be too opinionated and competitive, but lately he had noticed that she was very pretty. Tyshaun and Cleo had bought themselves a week of extra grounding just this morning and had a lot of nerve to make fun of Carmelita, he thought.

"Tyshaun, knock it off!" Jonathan called to him.

Tyshaun's hands immediately dropped to his desk as he groped for his math paper, pretending to review the document. He peeked at the teacher's chair, now occupied. The rest of the class whipped their heads to the back of the room but were too late to witness the infraction that had prompted such an outburst. Everyone then stared at Mr. Payne, writing something in his grade book, to see what would be his reaction to Jonathan's assertion of authority. He did not raise his head.

Later that same day Thomas sat at his desk arranging papers. He pondered the wisdom of having accepted a birthday party invitation from Maria. His mother had gone to countless such events over the course of her career. He often received invitations to sports events, recitals and the like—and attended when he could—but he had never been invited to a student's home. Perhaps, he thought, some families might be embarrassed about their meager domestic surroundings. Thomas eventually decided that no harm would occur if he made an appearance at a child's birthday party to bring a gift and eat some cake and ice cream. Reportedly, earlier during lunch Carmelita had tried to persuade Maria to invite some boys, especially Jonathan. Maria had declined, saying that her Mami didn't have enough money for a big party.

Thomas glanced at the schoolroom clock. Surrounded by peeling paint and falling plaster, it had been stuck on 10:47 for the past month. He pushed back his black sweater and white shirt to uncover his new watch, bestowed on him by his brother. The slim second hand slowly revolved inside a set of Roman numerals. It was nearly 4 o'clock. If he hurried he could make it to Anthony's Fitness Center before the after-work crowd arrived.

Later that evening Thomas and Glen sat in a Chinese restaurant, laughing and joking about their favorite subject—the Adams family. Thomas expressed surprise when Glen suggested they eat out after hitting a few weights at the gym, not that it was uncommon for them to grab a bite after a couple of hours at Anthony's. But this time, instead of the usual spots, Glen insisted that they try an eatery where neither had dined before. Also, the establishment wasn't in the neighborhood.

Glen and Thomas made up the total number of African Americans present. The predominantly Asian clientele paid them little attention. The place wasn't very busy, but the food tasted quite good—and the service was speedy. A young teenage girl waited on them. She wore just a touch of apple-colored lipstick and had skillfully braided her long hair down the middle of her back. Thomas found her modest ways to be very relaxing and refreshing. He agreed with his mother: today's teenagers were too "fast."

The restaurant, although somewhat darkly lit, seemed colorful and cheerful. Small red lanterns rested at the center of each table. A very large aquarium housed dozens of exquisite and exotic fish, flashing brilliant colors as they chased each other inside the tank, oblivious to the spectators. Thomas was smitten by the various aromas and the sight of delicious foods floating by, riding atop waitstaff trays, heading in the wrong direction, as far as he could tell. Each time someone cruised by carrying a dish, he wished he had ordered that particular item. The prices were a little more expensive than the gentlemen's usual fare, but it was Glen's turn to pay, and the payer always chose the restaurant.

Thomas played with his chopsticks for a few seconds, deciding whether or not to give them a try. He and Glen took turns auditioning voice impressions of various Adams staff. Eventually, their meals arrived and they moved to other subjects. They assured each other that all family members were healthy and well. Glen expressed relief to hear that his friend's brother was gradually adjusting to being free. The first-grade teacher did not talk much about his vacation. Thomas decided that they had become good enough friends to ask about it.

"Hey, buddy," he started, half-confidently. You haven't said one word about whether or not you visited your dad last month."

Glen shrugged his shoulders. "Sure, I went to see him," he answered, absent much emotion. "He *is* the only biological father I've got, you know." He scooped up another forkful of rice and slowly aimed for his mouth. "It was better than usual," he declared. "I don't know if I've ever mentioned this to you," he lied, then paused, waiting for three newly arrived patrons to pass out of possible earshot, "but my dad used to drink a lot." He saw his friend's shock and added, "He's off the stuff now but ..." True to form, he paused again and spied about to ensure their privacy, then continued. "See, my parents divorced when I was nine. My mom remarried a terrific guy who was a great stepfather to me and my younger sister. My dad didn't come around much or help out. I guess he spent his money on his first love—booze." He took a sip of tea. "I've forgiven him, but hey, I don't really know the man."

"I understand," Thomas said apologetically. "I guess sometimes I don't appreciate how lucky I am to—" He was about to add more, but the young waitress politely interrupted to ask how they were doing. After being assured that they were fine, she left.

Uncharacteristically, Glen did not ask Thomas to finish his thought but initiated his own. "Listen, Thomas," he said. "Another reason my dad and I aren't so close is what I wanted to talk to you about." He took a couple of deep breaths and forced courage into himself. The nervous man lowered his voice and spoke barely above a whisper.

Thomas gave up on his chopsticks and picked up his fork. He leaned in and listened to his friend describe his life and his secret.

Forty minutes later Thomas endured a disturbing drive home. Traffic was light but slow. The roads had narrowed due to the snow. Lanes had shrunk or offered noticeably slushy pockets. The streets shone from the melting snow. But it was not the condition of the roads that caused the Cincinnati native's discomfort. He could not believe what had transpired between one of his best friends and him less than an hour before. As impressed as he had been with his colleague's performance, he had been all the more disappointed with his own. Glen had chosen to reveal a very private matter, and he, Thomas Payne, who always complained that Boston-isn't-as-friendly-as-Cincinnati, had responded poorly. Why hadn't Glen told him sooner? He shifted into second, then third, then fourth gear and heard the words again.

"I'm gay."

He just couldn't believe it. He couldn't accept it. His best friend in Boston was a queer. His best friend in Boston fucks men. He shook his head, attempting to fling the thought from his mind.

As he waited for another light to change, Thomas recalled the look of apprehension on Glen's face as he disclosed his secret. He remembered his own days on the football team at Ohio State. The worst thing to happen to a teammate was to be suspected of being a homosexual. So that the rest of the team could assuage their own discomfort at having him around, a man could be subjected to endless harassment: pink panties and feminine napkins stuffed in his locker, anonymous letters, behind-the-back name-calling, pictures of nude women glued to the wall with the player's face pasted over the model's and more. The coaches didn't interfere. They preferred to see the guy banished, too. There were some simple, unwritten rules: Don't look at a man in the shower below the waist. Don't be seen with a known homosexual. Don't defend homosexual rights. And for God's sake, *get a girlfriend*, the prettier and sexier the better.

Thomas's thoughts leaped to the times he and Glen had been in the shower after a strenuous workout at the gym. Perhaps Glen had been hawking him, he feared. Thomas knew he had been a jerk, asking those stupid questions. What about the picture of Jane or Jean, his girlfriend? Didn't he find her attractive? The picture of a good friend, Glen confessed, also gay—and her name is Jena. How can a man be attracted to another man? What about his religious faith? Wasn't he afraid of God's judgment? Couldn't he get help, like go to a therapist or someone? How would he be a father someday without a woman in his life? The rookie teacher remembered his anger at his mentor for not telling him earlier. Glen explained that he was afraid that he would take it poorly—which he had.

Thomas was startled when a dark sedan swung in front of him from across the street, making a left turn. Asshole. Boston drivers are crazy, he fumed, as he finally reached the driveway to his apartment. By the time he pulled into his assigned space, his body ached with exhaustion.

He climbed the stairs to his apartment and entered. The place was cold and dark, so he turned on a light and twisted the thermostat dial near the door. He walked to the large balcony window on the other side of the room to close the drapes, but the view of snow on the roofs, mingled with house lights, provided such a lovely view. He decided to allow the sight to remain.

He picked up his telephone, dropped it back on the center table, then retrieved it again. He wanted to call Glen to let him know that it really didn't matter. That it wouldn't change their friendship. In fact, Thomas thought, he would inform his friend and mentor that he was honored to have been chosen as his confidant. He practiced a few lines and picked up the telephone again. The young man dialed the first three numbers, paused, then hung up. He clicked on the television, then went to the balcony window and closed the drapes.

Thomas carried the last box into Room 217 and set it on Doug's desk. The students were at lunch and would not be back for another five minutes. He was surrounded by half-page pictures the students had drawn relating to the theme of Dr. Martin Luther King's birthday. The bottom half of the papers contained a two-paragraph essay on each pupil's personal reflection about Dr. King's legacy. A few of the strictly winter scenes some students had drawn remained. Clearly excited, Thomas proceeded to carefully unpack one of the three boxes that had just arrived. Although alone, he spoke aloud, reading the title of the invoice: "From the American Federation of Chess Instructors." He pried open the smaller box containing instructional literature and thumbed through one of the books. "Chess for Beginners," he declared. While rummaging through the last box, he heard a gentle knock at the door and took a deep breath. He hoped that it was Glen—and hoped it wasn't. They had spoken very little since their dinner four days ago. He knew it couldn't be Heléna. She wouldn't have knocked. "Come in," he shouted, slight agitation creeping into his voice.

To his surprise, Ms. Flores entered. She held some papers in one hand and her glasses in the other. The woman, half a generation older than Thomas, wore a long, yellowish sweater over a brown dress. An oval-shaped white stone hung from a gold chain around her neck. Her unflashy flat shoes dwarfed her next to Thomas. She always walked softly. Although in her second year at the Adams, she had the manner of a newcomer. Nevertheless, she had gained the respect of Thomas and the staff. She listened well—more than anyone could say of the principal. Her attempts to raise the professionalism of the paraprofessional staff had initially met with some resistance from everyone: the teachers, Dorn, even the paras themselves, but after a year and a half of retraining, evidence of positive results had begun to show.

"Forgive me for interrupting your lunch Mr. Payne," she opened respectfully.

"No problem. I was just looking at my chess curriculum," Thomas answered, holding up an instruction book proudly, glad to have someone to whom he could show off.

"Oh my," she responded, genuinely impressed. "I'm sure that you'll produce more than a few chess champions by the end of the year, Mr. Payne. Maybe I'll learn the game myself." She took her eyes off the boxes and placed them on the young man. "Please let me know if I or Mr. Dorn can be of assistance."

"Thanks," Thomas replied and laid a bag of black chess pieces on top of another student's desk. "Now, how can I be of assistance?"

The short lady looked at the papers in her hands and frowned. "I don't know how you'll feel about this, Mr. Payne, but there's going to be a change." She took two steps closer and held the papers up so that Thomas could see them. "One of last year's students is to return to the Adams immediately. He will be in your class on Monday. Because you already have twenty-eight students, one of them will have to be transferred to Mrs. Chang's Advanced Work Class; needless to say, your best academic performer."

Thomas's mood changed. "What? You mean I've gotta give Nancy one of my best to make room for some kid who's been—" He stopped and grimaced. "Yeah, just where's he been all this time anyway?" Ms. Flores lowered her head and handed him a sheet of paper. He read it and looked up, visibly disturbed, exclaiming, "Freddy Wilson? Freddy the Firebug Wilson? The one sent away in August for setting fires? I gotta trade one of my all-stars—my boy Jonathan—my Student of the Week," he gestured towards the huge board bearing the boy's name, "for a kid who's been kicked off the team for breaking the law? This isn't right at all!" His breathing grew labored.

"I admit, Mr. Payne, that this isn't fair to you," Ms. Flores agreed calmly. "But you've done such a wonderful job with this class. Mr. Dorn and I are very relieved that we haven't had to come into this room to collect any of your students, like we did last year. But I—we believe that what you've done with twenty-eight you can do with one, yes?"

The rookie teacher said nothing. The woman had disarmed him by sympathizing with him. Ms. Flores had a point, he had to admit. It wasn't so much taking Freddy as it was losing Jonathan. Melvin and Maria showed promise, but that kid was head and shoulders above the entire class. Jonathan had attended a parochial school since grade one. Those nuns had pushed and prodded him into being a top-notched student with good work habits. He had been toying with the idea of talking to Dorn about placing the boy with Mrs. Chang anyway.

"Okay, okay," Thomas finally muttered. "Let me tell him and the class myself, okay?"

Just then, they heard footsteps clomping outside the door. Jonathan poked his head inside and waited. No voices could be heard behind him. Thomas held up his index finger, silently requesting additional time. Ms. Flores looked at her watch, mentioned something about the time and backpedaled to the door.

"Thank you for your understanding, Mr. Payne. As you would say, you're doing the best thing for the team."

Thomas mumbled some terse acknowledgment to the assistant principal, who had stepped out of sight. He could hear her compliment the students on how quiet they had been while waiting. Thomas respected Ms. Flores. She wasn't bad looking either, he noticed. Kept herself in good shape. Nice ass. She couldn't have been more than thirty-five. Besides, she really was in an awkward position, having to do Dorn's bidding. And Dorn was smart too: sending her to deliver the news instead of doing it himself. He knew Thomas would take it better from her.

As the last of Room 217's students hung up their coats and sat down, several commented on the boxes scattered about. With their inquiries setting up the opportunity, Thomas introduced the game of chess to his pupils. He explained that they would take one and sometimes two classes a week to learn how to play. With no outdoor recess for the foreseeable future, they had an additional opportunity to learn the fundamentals. A few claimed some familiarity with the game already. Jonathan had been on the chess team at his previous school. After several questions, the tense instructor broke up the normal routine further by calling for a class meeting.

Thomas sadly explained the change in the roster starting on Monday. The class immediately murmured and complained. Jonathan shook his head, indicating his profound disagreement. Carmelita became especially upset. "If one of those stuck-up girls in Mrs. Chang's room even looks at my man, I'm gonna break the bitch's clock but good," she whispered to Connie. Gradually, complaints surfaced about Freddy. Several members of the class volunteered that he had been the worst of all of them. But the real furor occurred when Thomas announced that because Jonathan was leaving, Janet would have to be Freddy's buddy.

Janet, a quiet and shy girl, closed her eyes in silent pain and said nothing, but others, mostly girls, took up her case pro bono. Everyone noticed the positive influence Jonathan had on her. For example, she raised her hand to answer questions much more often. And once, when Cleopatra teased her, she told the much taller girl to stop or she would tell Mr. Payne. She and Jonathan genuinely liked and respected each other. They were both Catholics and, with Angelica, shared the comfort of their faith together. With her careful, methodical ways, Janet had taught Jonathan, who was very talented but impulsive, the virtues of checking over his work before turning it in. Recently, Mr. Payne had hinted that she appeared ready to take on the next step—leadership. The laconic girl feared that now with the Buddy Rule, as it had come to be called, she would never be chosen Student of the Week. Still, it was her way to accept, without resistance, the decisions of the adults in her life. Father Tom at the Our Lady of Fatima parish had once explained that God expected children to obey their parents *and teachers*.

"Honey," Thomas said to her. "Try not to be too upset by this. You may be just the perfect buddy for our new boy. Perhaps what he needs is patience and peace, and Lord knows you've got plenty of both." He arched his eyebrows and continued. "Also, you're not alone in this. I'm going to do my job, and the class is going to be behind the two of you, I promise." He looked around, then pointed to a batch of photographs taped to the side of a file cabinet facing the students. "Remember last month when you first got on the floor to do the dance scene in *A Christmas Carol?* Remember?"

A few pupils started to chuckle. Some graduated to broad laughter. Janet smiled.

Thomas continued. "You were uncomfortable at first, then proved yourself to be a class act, just like I knew you would be." He folded, then opened his hands. "Will you trust me and yourself? You know I wouldn't give you this task if I didn't think you were up to it. You'll do fine, okay?" He waited for her reply.

Janet looked up for the first time and replied softly, "Okay."

The class applauded her. Thomas felt such pride in all of them.

Later that afternoon, after a short indoor recess, a science lesson and a spelling test, the Student of the Week ceremony was held. The class performed the cradle flawlessly. Next, the team met in the center of the room for the group circle and cheer. Later, as they prepared for dismissal, Thomas distributed the usual admonishments about weekend homework and sent them on their way.

Virtually everyone was saddened by the knowledge that on Monday, Jonathan would not be among them. Several boys patted him on the back and wished him good luck next door. Angelica surprised him with a hug, declaring that she would miss him. Jonathan told a couple of his friends that he would call them later. After gathering his things, he stopped in front of his soon-to-be-former teacher. Sadness appeared in both their eyes.

"Mr. Payne," Jonathan quizzed. "Why did it have to be me?"

Thomas put his hand on the boy's shoulder. "Because I had to sacrifice my best student—and that's you, son." He patted him on the shoulder, then winked at him. "You do a good job over there and make me proud, just like you did with me, hear?"

"Yes, Mr. Payne," he replied.

With that, Jonathan turned and marched down the hall for the last time as a member of Room 217. Carmelita caught up with him. "I've got friends in the Advanced Class next door who'll tell me everything," she warned the boy. He smiled at her and nodded. Thomas felt uncomfortable with such behavior from children, but it was his rule not to interfere in the personal lives of his students.

The teacher leaned against the door, continuing to wish his students an enjoyable weekend. Angelica embraced him. He smiled and hugged her back. As one particular student said good-bye, he noticed the new three-piece set of pencils with the words "Student of the Week" etched in gold trim on each. It stuck out of her book bag.

"You'll do a good job for me next week, won't you, Captain?" Thomas asked.

"Yes Mr. Payne," Janet answered with an uncharacteristically broad smile. "Bye," she said, waving as she whizzed by.

That evening Thomas made an appearance at Maria's apartment, a very modest place with modest furnishings. Against the wall opposite the living room entrance, a soft brown blanket covered a long sofa, no doubt to hide the ravages of time. The flowers on the wallpaper in the room had faded from the effects of age and sunlight. A Nativity Display rested in the corner by the window. It had not been that long since Three Kings Day on January 6, a holiday commemorating the Magi bringing gifts to the baby Jesus, observed primarily by Latin families.

Angelica saw Mr. Payne and screamed so loudly several guests came rushing from the kitchen with alarm. The girls looked so lovely, wearing dresses and jewelry. They had already grown so in four months, Thomas noticed. He was pleased that Maria had invited several non-Spanish girls from the class. They all nearly drove him crazy, talking at the same time. After presenting his gift and paying his respects to the mother of the hostess, he made a graceful exit.

Thomas was glad that he had visited. Glen had advised him not to attend. Sometimes, he thought, his mentor could be too cautious. Of course, now he understood his friend's reason.

That Saturday Thomas returned to his usual task of correcting papers and never left the apartment. It was cold and windy that day anyway. Snow flurries fell on and off.

The following day after church, he returned to his unfinished work and scribbled congratulatory words on Deborah's science homework, the last to be graded. The telephone rang and he became slightly uncomfortable. The prospect of receiving a telephone call from Glen usually pleased him. He missed their friendship. It turned out to be a wrong number. The receiver burned in his hand, so for the fourth time that weekend, he struggled to dial Glen's number. This time he did not hang up. He heard the familiar ring and felt his pulse rise. Then the click and broken ring as Glen's voicemail system took over. The recorded voice praised God and encouraged the caller to leave a message.

"H-Hey buddy, th-this is Thomas," he said, trying to sound as he usually did, which made him sound stranger. "Nothing earth-shattering. I just called to kick the ball around. Well, I'm going to be out for most of the day. I'll see you at work. Bye." After hanging up, for some inexplicable reason he felt immediately better.

A few hours later the young man fitted into his suit from church and drove to a small, recently renovated building a few blocks from the Adams. The roads were somewhat clearer after enduring an assault of salt and sand, and a few days' worth of rush hours. It was not just any Sunday. An important football play-off game brewed, but Thomas had promised a friend that he would visit the African American Museum of Greater Roxbury for the opening of some local artist's exhibit.

From the outside, the museum didn't look like much. The brown bricks looked worn from years of nature's onslaught. Several newly planted trees, not much taller than Thomas, offered a modest greeting as they stretched along the short walkway to the front door. The barren figures fought to remain erect against a cold north wind.

He had to admit that the interior was impressive. The glistening hardwood floors were obviously new. The walls were brightly painted white and yellow. Dozens of newly-acquired lamps directed the visitors' eyes to large and small paintings, drawings, sculptures and so forth. The selections had been carefully arranged on or near the thirteen-and-a-half-feet-high walls. Thomas longed for his sister's company. Vanessa would explain the nuances and meanings of the artwork—the brushstrokes and lighting and other matters that he did not fully appreciate. He admitted that such things had been Laura's strong suit. Her presence on his arm would have been welcomed. Among over three dozen patrons, he still felt alone.

Thomas met a few people and made polite conversation. The crowd consisted mostly of older patrons. A few bored children whined and fought sleep as their mothers desperately clutched their arms, ensuring against any expensive accidents. The bachelor eventually spotted three young, attractive African American women, who had arrived together. They dressed conservatively, as if just coming from church. He continued to marvel at the artwork but saw to it that he kept an eye on the three "sisters" as well. He spoke to the curator, a stately African American gentleman with a beautiful voice, no doubt seasoned from years of public speaking. Thomas could not help but wonder if the man was gay. Looking at his watch, he decided to forget about the women and head home. Just as he started for the coatroom, he heard a familiar voice call his name and turned slowly, with a forced smile on his lips.

"Thomas, I thought it was you," the woman said.

"Laura! What a surprise! How nice to see you," he fibbed. He could feel his breathing becoming short as he lightly hugged, then air-kissed her on both cheeks. (She would never forgive him if he disturbed her makeup.) Thomas was immediately subdued by the sweet smell of her perfume. Every bit as beautiful as he remembered, she wore a satiny purple dress. Both shoulders would have been exposed if not for a white silk shawl draped around them. Slightly overdressed, as usual.

They exchanged amenities. Laura expressed satisfaction about his brother being "home." With each passing minute, Thomas became more and more uncomfortable conversing with her. If she felt likewise, he could not discern it. Of course, she was an expert at hiding her feelings; one-tenth legal training, nine-tenths nature. He decided to make a hasty exit, citing an impending previous commitment when a well-dressed male invaded their space. Thomas had seen the man before, back in the fall—at the Boston College Law Library.

The intruder pointed at the other side of the room. "Laura, there's someone I'd like you to meet—Oh, excuse me, darling," he offered apologetically.

Laura and the gentleman leaned closely together. She spoke calmly. "Patrick, I'd like you to meet Thomas, a very dear friend of mine. Thomas, this is Patrick."

They shook hands. Thomas was clearly taller than his replacement. Taller and younger. Her new flame looked at least thirty years old. Both men wore dark suits. Standing between them, Laura looked like a jazz performer with her back-up singers. Thomas felt even more uncomfortable as they all made small talk about the artwork on display and their mutual friend who had invited them. Patrick managed to slip in that he had graduated from Harvard and worked for a law firm downtown. He specialized in contracts and also enjoyed sports and had played on a team in college. Thomas was not surprised to find out that the man played *golf.*

But the polished gentleman knew exactly what to say to disarm the elementary teacher's hostility and make him feel more at ease. "I remember that UCLA game a couple of years ago. Helluva touchdown catch you made."

After that, the two men talked energetically for another fifteen minutes while Laura slipped away to mingle. After a polite disagreement on the outcome of the play-off game, Thomas whispered that he had to get home to catch the last quarter. He and Patrick shook hands again.

Thomas said good evening to all the necessary people, then moseyed to the door. While buttoning up his coat, he was approached by one of the attractive sisters, the tallest of the three—and the prettiest, by his taste. Thin with hazel-colored eyes, she had a voice that was soft and sultry. She invited him to visit her church one day and handed him a small brochure with the address and number. She mentioned to Thomas that she always attended the late service at 11 a.m. He assured her that he would visit in the near future and left the event reasonably unscathed.

He fought with the tuner of his car's radio, struggling to locate the football game. Unsuccessful, during the drive his thoughts drifted to his museum visit. He was pleased that he had actually survived the confirmation of Laura's new relationship quite well. While it stung a little, by no means had he been crushed by the sight of them together. She would indeed be happier with Mr. Patrick Harvard Grad, who played golf with people who had monikers like Vincent Blah Blah Blah, the Fourth. Thomas admitted that, as stuffed shirts go, she could have done a lot worse.

He got home in time to catch the last half-hour of the game. Unfortunately, it turned out to be a blow-out.

The following Monday morning Thomas peeked into Glen's room. The place was decked out in the usual assortment of colorful decorations befitting the month. The first-grade children had colored pictures of Dr. King. Huge student-drawn book covers were taped to the walls. The title of a tot's favorite book had been scribbled on each cover in shaky print. The fifth-grade teacher chuckled at the single-digit subtraction homework pinned to a bulletin board, each accented with red happy-faces. He walked by other marvels and approached Glen, seated at his desk cutting out a set of teddy bears. The two friends brought each other up to date on the events in their lives. Thomas told Glen about running into his ex and the student trade to take place in a few minutes. They exchanged views about the recent play-off games and made predictions on the upcoming Super Bowl. Their conversation covered the same topics but did not possess quite the same spirit. Mercifully, the "notice bell" interrupted their interaction. Glen had duty that week so he excused himself. Thomas wished he could have stayed longer with his friend. He believed that somehow, if he and Glen had kept talking, they would have eventually hit their old stride.

The rookie teacher went back to his room, grabbed his coat and walked down to the upper-grade gathering area. Because of the cold, the students were allowed to congregate inside near a storage room. The third-, fourth- and fifth-grade classes, all eight of them, crammed downstairs into an area the size of a small classroom. The exposed metal pipes above, which constantly leaked water, produced entertaining and inventive games of what the students named "water dodgeball." About one-half of their number preferred to stay outside, the cold notwithstanding.

Thomas was surprised that his new student simply hung out with the class—no office visit by a parent or formal introduction. The boy appeared to be somewhat animated, apparently telling stories about his exploits during the fall. Freddy was a tall boy, very light-skinned with short, wavy hair. Perhaps some Anglo or Spanish blood in his veins, Thomas speculated. He felt a little apprehensive about Tyshaun, Maurice and Asa, the three tallest boys in his class, being in the midst of the conclave but dismissed his feeling as foolish. The bell rang and Thomas took charge, instructing the entire group—his students and others—to form single lines with their respective classmates and file to their rooms. He turned to Janet and instructed her to take his class upstairs quietly.

Once inside, Thomas showed Freddy where to hang his coat, found him a desk (too small for him) and gave him a copy of the ground rules. "Get to know those rules. They're the Bible here, son," he admonished.

Thomas introduced Freddy to his buddy, Janet, and explained the purpose of the buddy system. The boy seemed attentive enough. The couple endured a few seconds of teasing from the class. Because Janet also served as Student of the Week, Thomas asked for a volunteer to act as "second buddy." Freddy chose Asa.

The morning was uneventful. Thomas noticed that his new student did not raise his hand even once during math or reading. Not at all unusual, with it being his first day and all, Thomas reasoned. After lunch he gave Freddy two assessment quizzes. The results indicated that the eleven-year-old was at least one full grade level behind in both math and reading—by beginning of the school year standards.

The next morning after math, Thomas prepared the class for the usual first bathroom break. Janet selected Asa to escort the boys. The Student of the Week instructed everyone to quietly line up. They did so in an orderly fashion, as they always did. Asa walked slowly to the front of his line. Suddenly, Freddy jumped in front of him and pushed him out of the way, exclaiming, "Move, nigga!" He laughed and looked around, expecting several classmates to laugh with him, as they certainly would have done the previous year. Instead, he was greeted with expressions of horror at his bad manners. Every student looked away from him and at Mr. Payne.

"Is there a problem, Asa?" Thomas asked from behind his desk.

Asa pointed at Freddy. "Mr. Payne, Freddy just pushed me and got in front."

Thomas remained seated and furled his eyebrows. "Freddy, this year, we do *not* push each other in line." His face slightly softened. "Go to the end of the line, please."

Freddy pouted and sucked his teeth. "I was first."

Thomas took a deep breath but stayed at his desk. "No, you were not first, Freddy. And even if you had been, it would have made no difference because the monitor goes first. In this case, it's Asa. Now to the end of the line, if you please."

"No," Freddy replied, his face all scrunched up.

Shock permeated the room. Several students put their hands over their mouths as if they had just heard something terrible. Thomas rose and stepped from behind his desk.

"What did you say, young man?" He stopped at the edge of his desk about six feet from the start of the boys' line. "I know I didn't hear you tell me 'no' after I just told you to do something." His voice rose with the last few words.

Freddy looked away, unsure what to do. "I was here first. I ain't goin' nowhere."

Thomas slowly move closer until he was about a foot away from the front of the line. Several boys directly behind the obdurate student backed up out of harm's way.

The tall man took another deep breath and decided to try reasoning with his new student. "Freddy, because you're new, I'm going to give you a third chance to try out for the team. He turned to Asa and pointed. "Take the boys to the center of the room, please."

Asa pointed and ordered, "Gentlemen, if you please." All of the boys except Freddy moved several feet to the left. Thomas and his defiant pupil stood isolated, face-to-face.

"Now, son, the boys' line is over there. I'm giving you still one last chance to do the right thing," he cautioned. "You can stand here with me and wet your pants if you want to." Thomas folded his arms across his chest. "What's it gonna be?"

Total silence engulfed the room. Every eye rested on the new kid. Without uttering a word, he stomped his feet, once each, and headed for the back of the boys' line.

After a thirty-second delay, Thomas decided to take a peek into the boys' bathroom to guarantee that there were no further problems. Besides the fact that the bathroom stank with the smell of urine—the place had gone significantly downhill since J.J.'s December 1 retirement—no significant incident occurred.

Two hours later, with the class downstairs at lunch, Thomas stepped into the office to check his mailbox. He exchanged a few pleasantries with the school secretary and discovered that she and his LaShonda Walker were cousins. Marilyn Walker mentioned to Thomas that she was in the market for a new car and suggested they take a ride together in his. He stated that she would be more than welcome when the snow cleared up further. He reached into his full mailbox and scooped out a pile of paper, then exited the office, bidding the overworked woman a good afternoon.

The day's delivery from the Post Office produced interesting bounty. The Department of Social Services had received Thomas's response to their inquiry. Based on the answers to several questions he had been asked, an investigation would be launched to discover whether or not LaShonda Walker was the victim of parent abuse or neglect. A copy of the DSS letter had been forwarded to Mr. Dorn.

"He's gonna be shit-faced when he sees this," Thomas exclaimed to himself. Nothing made a principal more nervous that outside agency investigators snooping around the school, asking to see records, requesting copies of documents and interviewing people.

Another letter originated "From the Evaluation Team" of the Reading One-on-One Program, housed at Court Street downtown. It informed Thomas that his student, Douglas Berry, had been denied services due to his age. No signature appeared on the letter, no telephone number was provided, and no one else was slated to receive a copy. Plausible deniability for everyone but the homeroom teacher. Thomas simply shook his head in disgust.

Another notice, from the Adams's own evaluation team leader, listed an upcoming meeting to determine the special education classification for over half of the students in Room 217. Apparently, they were in need of special services due to their significant behavioral and academic problems. The request for special education had been made last spring by Ms. Patterson. Thomas surveyed the list. Seven youngsters allegedly displayed behavioral problems: one who no longer attended the Adams, one girl (Cleopatra) and five boys (Tyshaun, Asa, Maurice, Freddy and Vince). An additional eight pupils were earmarked for services due to academic challenges, including Doug. And three boys had managed to get on both lists. The letter evoked deep concern from Thomas. Local civil-rights activists routinely complained that teachers often referred difficult students of color for special ed to get them out of their hair. Judging from his mail, Thomas thought that the activists might be right.

A few minutes later Thomas sat at his desk listening to a Bach concerto while nibbling an apple and reading a student essay on protecting the environment. He wasn't hungry but wanted to be alone for a few minutes to think. Report cards were due again soon. He had sent out warning notices before Christmas, as required—not as many as before, but over half the class had received them. His thoughts leaped to a more promising situation. A retired gentleman from his church had agreed to visit once a week to teach chess—free of charge. Again his mind shifted. Two of his wards would almost certainly make the Honor Roll (Jonathan would have been three) and perhaps another would receive Merit honors. Thomas frowned as he flipped through his textbooks and charts. They were moving as fast as possible but still substantially behind grade level.

Suddenly the main door flung open and two students, Janet and Christine, rushed into the classroom, obviously excited and upset. "Mr Payne, Freddy's downstairs getting into a fight!" Janet breathlessly announced.

"What! Whatdoyoumean?" Thomas shot back, immediately standing. He frowned and put his hands on his hips.

Janet explained, spitting out her words. "He said some boy in Ms. Sanchez-Taylor's class skipped him in line. They started pushing each other." She caught her breath. "Asa and Tyshaun jumped up and grabbed him and pulled him away."

"Where's Ms. Flores?" Thomas asked.

"Umumhum," Christine answered, shrugging her meaty shoulders. "Nobody's down there but the lunch mothers. The kids, they be goin' crazy down there, Mr. Payne."

Thomas threw his apple into the wastebasket. He reached into the back of his desk and produced a yellow and red object. It rattled when he stuffed it in his pocket. "Let's go," he ordered and raced out the door with the two students following closely.

When the former college wide receiver entered the cafeteria, the place shook in absolute chaos. Students roamed out of their seats, screaming and running around. Food lay everywhere; on the tables, on the chairs and on the floor. The smell of some kind of cooked meat turned Thomas's stomach. Boys and girls ran in and out of the cafeteria bathrooms. Water flooded the floors of both. Two harried-looking senior women, one White and one Hispanic, yelled instructions to sit down or stop or wait—with no one listening. The lunch server, an overweight African American woman who always smelled of cigarette smoke, stood in one spot as though in a trance.

Thomas blew a whistle and yelled at the top of his lungs, "Everybody, sit down and shut up!"

About fifty students instantly hurried to their seats. The noise level immediately dropped seventy-five percent. It was generally known that Mr. Payne should not be defied. Thomas paused for a few seconds, then called out loudly again, clearly angry. "I said EVERYBODY sit down and shut up and I mean just that!" He walked over to the boys' bathroom and opened the door. "Get out of there, now!" he yelled. Five boys ran out and took their seats. The girls' bathroom was next. "Out, everybody, or I'm coming in. Don't think I won't do it!" Four girls appeared and quickly sat down.

"I don't know where you think you are, but let me tell you, this is a school!" Thomas growled loudly, visibly upset. Two boys started talking to each other.

"I said shut your mouths! I'm not going to tell you again," he warned. He scanned the faces of the room. "I mean it. The next person I catch talking is after school with me—and I'm working until 5 o'clock today." He paused and took a deep breath. "And if you think I'm playing, you ask anyone in my room if I mean what I say."

Several members of his class nodded their heads to verify his claim. A fourth-grade girl on the other side of the room slid out of her chair to throw away her half-eaten lunch.

"Sit down!" Thomas commanded. "I didn't say anyone could go anywhere."

"She don't know no English," a boy with an accent volunteered.

"I didn't ask you anything. *Callaté!*" the man roared. He looked at the frightened girl and pointed. "*Sientece, intiende?*" His voice sounded slightly softer but still angry. She nodded, her eyes as large as eggs and full of fear.

The room grew even quieter. Thomas called to Janet. "Captain, go find

Mr. Dorn. Hurry up!" he commanded, then returned to the subdued young-sters. "The rest of you, just stay that way until Mr. Dorn gets here. You can finish your lunch but if you so much as breathe too loud, you're gonna be sitting in a corner after school, keeping me company." He folded his arms across his chest and watched for the first victim to use as an example.

He didn't have to wait long. One of Ms. Patterson's students mumbled something to a girl sitting next to him.

"You!" Thomas shouted, pointing at the boy. "Get over there with my class."

The boy pointed at himself with a puzzled look on his face. "Me?" he asked, employing his usual routine. "I didn't say nothing. It was—"

"You better get over there like I told you, boy." Thomas interrupted. "Don't make me go over there and get you." He took a giant step forward.

The sad student slowly rose, walked over to a table hosting a group of fifth-graders and sat down.

"And how you get home is not my problem," Thomas declared in the student's general direction. "I'm not taking you. You were warned." The boy broke into tears, but Thomas paid no attention. He stared at the group of Ms. Patterson's students. "Anyone else wanna try Mr. Payne? You guys in 214 know how mean I can be."

They shook their heads. Just then several students muttered, "Uh-oh."

Everyone's eyes swung to the main cafeteria door. Janet entered with a stony-faced Mr. Dorn. Thomas sighed with intense relief.

"Thank you, Mr. Payne, I'll take it from here," Mr. Dorn assured him.

"Yes, sir," Thomas replied obediently. "Is it okay if my class leaves?" The principal just grunted, then started barking at the rest of the room's occupants like a drill sergeant.

Thomas cut past several students to get to Freddy. "I'll deal with you when we get upstairs, young man," he whispered, displaying his grinding front teeth. "And I better not hear that you so much as blinked your eyes too often on the way."

Freddy's face turned beet red but he said nothing.

Thomas blocked the path of Ms. Patterson's boy. "Go upstairs with my class. If you behave yourself, I might—I said *might*—send you back to your room after lunch."

The boy nodded earnestly, wiped the tears from his eyes and followed the fifth-graders upstairs.

Once the class returned from the bathroom and was seated, Thomas conducted his investigation. After listening to all accounts, he grounded Freddy for a week for fighting and disobeying the Student of the Week. The boy pouted and moped but wisely kept silent. Although upset, he recognized that this man was not Ms. Patterson. Thomas warned the class about poor behavior, especially in public. Surprisingly, he turned to Janet.

"Captain, can you handle this group or not?" he asked coldly.

"Yes, Mr. Payne," she answered.

"Then handle them!" he ordered. The angry man launched a stern warning about the severe penalties for disobeying the Student of the Week. "Janet's been chosen because she's done all seven of those things," he added, pointing to the seven criteria on the Student of the Week display. "She has my confidence and deserves your respect."

The remainder of the day proceeded uneventfully. After a lackluster performance during social studies and spelling, Thomas sat with the class for DEAR. He reviewed the next day's assignments, then sent them on their way home, grateful that the day had ended.

Thomas gathered his things quickly and headed for the gym. Glen had beaten him there by a half-hour. The two colleagues talked and worked out. Things seemed to be almost back to normal between them until the close of their workout. Thomas felt uncomfortable in the shower with Glen but hoped his friend did not notice.

The rest of the week was difficult for the class, especially for Freddy. It did not take the other students long to resent him for upsetting their routine. Complaints surfaced about the boy every day. Multiple small rule infractions were the norm. Thomas moved the boy's seat to the back of the room. Besides not commanding much self-control, Freddy seemed terribly unhappy inside. Thomas spoke to his foster mother on the telephone twice that week and heard the story of the lad's unfortunate childhood. Over the months the first-year teacher had listened to several sad tales, but this was the most disturbing he had ever heard. While sitting at his desk one afternoon he recapitulated the account in his mind.

When Freddy was just a child, his father was convicted of murder. Tragically, he had killed his ex-girlfriend, Freddy's mother. The boy lived with several different relatives, producing little stability in his life. His various aunts and grandparents all fought to take him in, hoping to be beneficiaries of a generous monthly state check. Freddy saw through their venal motives and responded by frequently getting into minor trouble with the law. Eventually, the Commonwealth of Massachusetts claimed him and sent him to live in a foster home.

Unfortunately, the matriarch of the foster family, whom he had grown to love, had recently faced a cancer diagnosis. All of her foster children had to be relocated. But Freddy faced additional stress. After a lengthy court battle, his father had won the right to communicate with him as long as he did not mention Freddy's mother. Subsequently, the man had apparently upset Freddy by sending him several letters. The current foster mother reported that the boy received counseling twice a week, but he fared no better at her home either. She confided to Thomas that she had considered asking the DSS social worker to find another placement for him.

Thomas sighed. He resolved that although Freddy had been dealt mostly low cards in his life, for his own good he would not be allowed to skirt the rules or get by without much effort in Room 217.

That Friday, concerned about Freddy's behavior at his first Student of the Week ceremony, Thomas sent the boy outside the room to serve as the door guard.

That Saturday Thomas received a call from his brother, who seemed in good spirits. He had found a place of his own and visited his daughters in Pittsburgh every other weekend. Of course, he complained about the amount of child support he had to pay his ex-wife, but he had found a new job as, of all things, director of security at a computer software research facility. A "friend" had recommended him for the position. He declined to offer more information than that. Also, he had filed a wrongful termination lawsuit against the Cincinnati Police Department. Edward assured Thomas that it was just a matter of time before the Department would settle up. Also, the former police detective had been contacted by a producer in New York about writing a book and selling the movie rights to his story. He would even be allowed to make a cameo appearance.

"You know, man," Edward mumbled after clearing his throat. "Um, maybe it turned out better that you didn't call April about the girls when I asked you to." It was his way of apologizing for their post-Thanksgiving Day argument.

"Well, I'm glad things turned out okay after all," Thomas replied, not wanting to rub his brother's nose in it. "Hey!" He exclaimed. "How's Mom's carpet? She never found out, did she?"

"You kidding?" Edward answered. The brothers again swore each other to secrecy upon pain of torture.

Thomas congratulated Edward on his good fortune. He told his brother about his new student and his current shaky relationship with Glen. He rejected Edward's suggestion to escort the boy somewhere, just the two of them, and "fuck him up good." He also decided against his brother's advice to forget about being friends with Glen, and chose not to seek Edward's perspective on his conflicting feelings regarding Heléna.

Later on the same day, Thomas also spoke to Glen on the telephone. Their talk lasted for about twenty minutes; a long discussion by recent standards. It was composed mostly of Adams humor and football analyses. Although he usually found an excuse to decline, Thomas finally accepted his friend's invitation to visit his church on Sunday evening. He would hear Glen's choir sing at a special service praising God for the ministry of Martin Luther King. The young mentee hoped that attending the celebration would restore their friendship to its former glory.

The following Sunday evening Thomas kept his word. Glen's church was a large place by Thomas's standards, recently remodeled, with huge stained-glass windows of Afrocentric Biblical characters. The young guest actually enjoyed the service, with its inspiring messages and wonderful choir. Glen was obviously a very talented musician. In spite of the cool indoor temperature, sweat poured from his forehead as he banged away on an electric piano.

After the service Thomas stayed for a buffet dinner, meeting several very kind church parishioners. Even at a congregation sprinkled with professionals holding college degrees, a teacher garnered considerable respect. Much to his pleasure, Thomas seemed to be a hit with the single ladies. One woman discreetly expressed an interest in Glen and asked Thomas if his colleague was involved with anyone. Thomas fought an urge to snicker and replied that he was not sure. Before leaving the parish, he had obtained the telephone number of one very lovely woman who had expressed an interest in visiting his classroom. She wanted to change careers from business to teaching.

While putting on his hat and coat, Thomas joked with Glen. "I'll definitely be back, man," he promised. "—If only to see more of these fine cutey-pies you've got here." He lowered his voice to a whisper. "Especially since you've got no use for them."

Glen playfully shook his finger at Thomas, and the two men laughed over the remark. It was the first time either of them had brought up the subject of Glen's recent revelation.

During the early part of the following school week, Heléna paid Thomas a visit. The two had been successful in re-establishing their friendship as it had been before the Adams's Christmas party. He informed Heléna that his application for Doug's inclusion in the Reading One-On-One program had been rejected. They agreed to surreptitiously continue the boy's tutoring.

Unexpectedly, Heléna disclosed an event from her weekend. "I had a date the other night," she announced.

To his surprise, Thomas became annoyed upon hearing about Heléna with another man but showed no emotion when he responded. "Oh? That's great. How'd it go?"

Heléna shook her head and frowned. "He was a real schmuck."

Thomas shrugged his broad shoulders. "Sorry to hear that." Actually, he wasn't. He brought up his own Sunday afternoon museum excursion. "Definitely an indication that I'm ready to get on with my life," he proudly added after he had finished the story.

After Heléna scampered out of sight, the young man scratched his head and asked himself aloud, "What the hell was I doing? Why did I say that?"

During the second to the last day of the month, Thomas decided to experiment with a new exercise for his entire class. An hour before lunch, the "Do Not Disturb" sign was hung on the outside of the door. First, he called a student's name and asked that he or she pick up his or her chair and carry it to a particular spot at the edge of the room. Thomas then carried the student's desk to the other side, out of the way. This ritual occurred twenty-eight times until every student sat in a chair with only a notebook or book in his or her lap. The students sat single file, stretched side by side into a wide inverted V-shape facing their teacher. Their numbers took up two entire sides of the classroom.

Thomas went to his desk and returned carrying a stack of paper half-sheets. Two underlined words appeared on top, typed a few inches apart:

"GIVER" appeared on one side and "TAKER" on the other. He held up the papers and explained.

"What we're about to do is called 'Giver-Taker.' It's an opportunity for each of you to give feedback on each other's contribution to the class." He recognized the puzzled expressions on more than one face and spoke slower. "One by one, a student is going to stand before you and give you your grade, so to speak. If he or she tells you that you're a giver, then I want you to put an X or check underneath the word 'GIVER' right here." He held up a sample sheet and slowly moved it from side to side for everyone to see. "If you're told by your fellow classmate that you're a taker, then put an X or check underneath that word." He demonstrated again. "When everyone's done, there should be twenty-eight checkmarks or X's in all. Okay?" He saw sprinkled head-nods and continued.

"When you stand in front of your classmate, you are to forget that you are friends or buddies and tell the truth. He or she is either a giver or a taker. That's it." He paused. "One more thing: Look each other in the eye; the speaker and the one being spoken to—and no mumbling. Tell the truth and nothing but the truth. Try to remember the person as a whole, not just what happened today or even this week. This is a grade for everything so far this year—and be sure to give yourselves a vote. Do that last. Any questions?"

"Mr. Payne," Christine inquired, with her green eyes reflecting the classroom lights. "How can *we* tell who's a giver or a taker?"

Thomas smiled. The girl did ask a lot of questions but mostly good ones. "Well, honey, the only thing I can say is think about what's happened so far. Does that person care about the class or only about herself or himself? Is the class better off or worse because that person is here?"

Several hands drifted downwards as Thomas explained. He answered two more questions, then walked to his desk on the other side of the room and fiddled with the classroom music box. A soft, contemporary song about friendship emerged. He went to the far right side of the room and motioned upwards to the boy sitting in the very first chair. "You've got the ball, Angel," he informed him. "Start here with Deborah."

Angel rose and faced Deborah, seated on his right but now on his left. Thomas stood directly behind the boy, watching both of them.

"Look each other in the eye," he reminded them.

"Giver," Angel reported to Deborah.

"Louder," Thomas ordered.

"Giver," Angel repeated, twice as loud.

"Record the vote," Thomas instructed, pointing at the paper in Deborah's lap.

Next came Connie. Angel loudly determined that she was also a giver. Akeem too. And Carmelita. And Hernando. Angel approached Francine and paused. Her eyes revealed uneasiness.

"Taker," the boy declared and moved on.

"Record your vote," Thomas directed the girl, pointing at her paper. Francine did so without displaying any emotion.

Angel voted on over half the class until he reached the bending corner of the V. At that point Thomas took hold of Deborah's hand and told her to begin, while Angel finished the second half. She obediently stood and hand-ironed her blouse. Now presentable, she placed a yellow notebook on top of the paper in her chair and stepped directly in front of Connie.

"Giver," she told her buddy and continued. Her teacher wandered closer to Angel but could still hear Deborah administering her votes. "Giver … Giver … Giver …" She came to Francine and paused for a few seconds, just as Angel had done. She looked over her shoulder at Mr. Payne, then turned back to Francine and broke the news, then continued with the next student. Francine lowered her head and added a checkmark next to her previous one.

"Wait, everybody," Thomas declared. He cleared his throat. "If you have to stop and think about it, that person is not a giver. Hesitation is a taker vote. If he's a giver, if she's a giver, it's clear in your mind." He waved his right hand. "Carry on."

Angel, almost done, continued. Deborah did likewise. Another song with a friendship theme began to play. When Angel eventually came around to his own seat, he was instructed to record a vote loudly for himself. He declared himself a giver, marked so on his paper, then sat down and waited for the next twenty-seven votes.

The exercise progressed with the background music continuing its gentle flow. Two students always stood far apart, voting. Occasionally Thomas forcefully reminded a pupil to speak up, look a classmate in the eye or stand directly in front of the seated student.

Angelica was the ninth person to deliver votes. She stood calmly before and spoke softly to the first five students on her left, all receiving giver votes. Thomas raced over to her.

"What are you doing, huh?" he asked with a frown on his face. The tall teacher hesitated and took a breath. "You scared that someone here isn't going to like you if you tell them the truth? Is that it?"

The young girl said nothing.

Thomas looked her in the eye. "That can't matter here, Angelica. Just like when I give you your report cards. It's what you earned. Now get off automatic pilot." He spoke to the entire class. "That goes for all of you. No selling out! Tell the truth." He placed his hands on Angelica's shoulders and spun her around.

The small girl stood in front of Pedro. "Giver," she said. Next came Freddy. "Taker," she informed him.

Thomas monitored the class. Twenty minutes later, after most students had voted, Cleopatra sat pouting. LaShonda closed her eyes. Francine's nonchalant facade had broken after her tenth taker vote. She scratched the words "I hate you!" over and over on the back of her paper. Tyshaun squirmed in his seat, visibly agitated. Carmelita seemed annoyed as well.

Finally, Gary, the last voting student, finished. Thomas stood in front of his team.

"Count your votes carefully. They should add up to twenty-eight. If you're short one vote, add one to the taker side," he ordered, holding up the sample sheet again. "If you have more than twenty-eight, take one off the giver side." Thomas walked around, checking the math. He reached Cleo as she erased a taker vote.

"How many do you have in all, Cleopatra?" he asked, sneaking a peek at her half-sheet.

After a long pause, she answered reluctantly, "I dunno."

Thomas took the paper from her and inspected it. His eyes widened. "My oh my," he commented, returning the paper. "Take one off the *giver* side if you're over." The tall girl changed her tally as her eyes became the color of crimson.

"Everybody out of your chairs," he sharply instructed, motioning upwards with both hands, palms up, "and go stand in the center of the room." A small rumble of noise surged as whispering escalated. "Todaaaay!" he commanded playfully. The entire class stood and walked past him. Some could be heard sharing good news.

Thomas stepped to the far right side of the empty chairs and patted the first few. "Everyone who received twenty-eight giver votes, have a seat here, one by one."

Several students looked at each other. Angelica slowly moved towards Thomas and sat down. Melvin quickly sat next to her. Gary joined them. Then Maria. Then Janet. Connie squeezed past a few bodies and sat down, smiling and beaming. Pedro did so as well. They looked at each other and rejoiced in their enviable positions.

"Okay," Thomas stated. "Now will those who received twenty-seven giver votes—all but one—please sit down here?" He pointed at the empty chairs to Pedro's right.

Several students maneuvered into those chairs. Deborah, Christine, Akeem, Melissa, Lakeisha and others. Thomas was surprised that Carmelita was still standing. Burning anger flushed her face.

"Hmmm. Very interesting," was his only observation. "Okay, how about twenty-six?"

Finally, Carmelita marched to a seat, joined by three other members of the class. Other pupils were scattered throughout the countdown. Asa had received twenty votes, to his pleasant surprise. Doug had garnered only nineteen. The numbers eighteen through eleven evoked no response. Thomas pointed at the last few seats.

"Well, how about ten giver votes?"

No one moved.

"Okay, nine." The six remaining students in the middle of the room stood still, embarrassed. LaShonda held her hands over her face. Cleopatra held her hands on her hips. The others displayed degrees of anger and dismay. Thomas felt sympathy for them, but he had privately reached the conclusion that after five months of such anemic effort, such feedback from their peers amounted to exactly what they needed.

"Alright then, eight giver votes."

Maurice breathed a sigh of relief and marched to a seat.

"Seven?"

Tyshaun sat down.

"Six."

Francine and LaShonda both tried to put themselves in the seat closest to Tyshaun, as though it offered more value. Thomas ordered LaShonda to sit in the coveted seat. Francine grunted and slung herself into the other chair.

"Five giver votes."

Cleopatra slowly approached the second to the last chair and fell into it, defeated.

Thomas stretched out his long arms and returned them to his sides. "Okay, four giver votes." He gestured towards the remaining chair and started towards the other side of the room, only to stop, look back and feign surprise that Freddy had not moved. Some students put their hands over their mouths, some with glee, some in sympathy. Thomas walked slowly backwards to the unoccupied chair and patted its back.

"Okay, let's try three then."

Still no movement. Loud, deep gasps and "Oh my God!" punctuated the air.

"Two giver votes."

Finally, Freddy staggered to his ignominious spot and slumped into it.

"Well, that's that," Thomas declared. He examined the faces of his pupils. "I'm very proud that you've performed this exercise as you always do, showing how cooperative you are. I've got bad news and I've got good news. The bad news is that some of you received very few giver votes today." He shrugged his shoulders, then pointed his finger. "The good news is that we're going to do this again in the future. So those of you sitting over there," he pointed to the section hosting the dejected students, "might decide that you'd rather be sitting over there." He pointed to the side with Maria, Melvin and company. Thomas strolled over to Francine. "How about it, Frannie? When we do this again in April, where will you be sitting, over here again or over there?"

Francine raised her head and wiped away a tear. "Over there."

Thomas stepped into Freddy's field of vision and lowered his head. "As long as you're in my class, I'm going to be on your team, supporting you in strength, not weakness." He pointed. "Go talk to Melissa—or Asa. They turned around." He pointed again. "My young brother, you can do better. You can give it your best. And your best is the *only* thing we accept in this place called Mr. Payne's Room 217." He straightened up. "Take your time, pal. I've got five more months."

Thomas approached Deborah, who smiled. He knew that she could be a top-notch student if she gave her all to the effort. He decided to challenge her and the others. "Isn't this the story of your life?" he growled, glancing at the others near her. "And the rest of you twenty-seven vote-getters? Always one short, huh? Always ninety-nine percent. Well, how about it? You gonna be sitting in the *almost-all* section again—or with the one hundred percent club?"

A mixture of voices, including Deborah's, answered, "One hundred percent club."

He walked past Carmelita and mimicked her dour facial expression. "What's the matter with you?" he asked.

She didn't answer.

"Ten minutes 'til lunch, Mr. Payne," Melvin warned, waving the discount-store timepiece.

"Thank you, Captain," Thomas answered. He confirmed the announcement with his own watch. "One last thing," he cautioned. "Those of you sitting at the right, smiling and giggling: It may be okay with you, but it's not okay with me if you're sitting over there, but your buddy is sitting on the other side of the room, *capisci?*"

The room grew quieter.

Thomas declared the January "Giver-Taker" exercise over and instructed Melvin to collect the papers for future reference.

While the students put the room back together, Thomas eased over to Asa and placed his hand on the boy's shoulder.

"You're on your way, son. Are you ready for the next step—leadership?"

"Yes, Mr. Payne," Asa declared proudly.

On the last day of school for the month, the temperature climbed into the forties, and raindrops fell. Snow remained but reduced in status to mere seasonal background. That afternoon Thomas counted the number of points and, according to January Jennifer, twenty-two students would be allowed to remain in the room and watch the movie, the same number as last month. He took comfort in the fact that, had Jonathan remained on the team, it certainly would have been one more. Appropriately enough, the six "outees" consisted of those who had received mostly taker votes during the previous day's exercise.

After distributing the snacks and starting the movie, Thomas exited with a group of melancholy students and returned alone. Not only was Asa present for his first Movie Day, he had points to spare. Thomas chose Janet, Pedro and Asa to be the event's official servers, an honor and a challenge. Servers distributed food to their seated classmates but could not speak unless addressed. And they were instructed to serve themselves last. Thomas watched Asa. On the first day of school, the boy had been chastised for stepping on the feet of several classmates while distributing paper. Now his performance definitely placed him in contention for the next step—leadership.

On the way home, Thomas stopped by a public library, a small building near the school, formerly a grocery store. It had large windows and a set of automatic doors that had been shut off. After returning a book and chatting with the librarian, the teacher prepared to leave. On the way to the door a little boy about six years old, wearing a worn, hand-me-down black winter coat intercepted him. The boy flashed a broad grin and waved, exclaiming to those around him, "It's Mr. Payne!"

Several youngsters abandoned their books, computers and games to enthusiastically greet and hug him. He put his finger to his lips and said, "Shhhh," then returned their affection. He did not recognize the tiny faces but assumed that the children were students at the Adams. He waved goodbye to them and pushed the front door open. Mixed with the blowing wind and the gentle patter of freezing rain, he heard one child declare to his mother, "I'm gonna to be a teacher when I grow up, just like Mr. Payne."

February

Thomas adjusted his body into the old, uncomfortable chair, composed mostly of cheap metal. He and Heléna took turns diving in and out of a plastic bag she had brought, stuffed with a crunchy snack. Glen had arrived late, so he was forced to stand behind them near the center window. Uncharacteristically, the teacher's lounge was warm. Heat poured into the small space with great noise and fanfare. The smell of spoiled food (neglected leftovers from classroom Christmas parties) emanated from the refrigerator each time its door opened, further contributing to the occupants' discomfort.

The monthly Faculty Senate meetings were held on the first Wednesday of every month. They offered an opportunity for the staff to meet and discuss issues, unfettered by the presence of school administrators. Usually minor issues surfaced but occasionally a significant matter would provoke an argument, then a vote. The results of this collective wisdom subsequently landed on Mr. Dorn's desk for his action—or inaction. The gatherings were cordial and open to all Boston Teachers Union members at the Adams, including paraprofessionals, the school nurse, the evaluation team leader and so forth. Sometimes, after a meeting concluded, Thomas overheard personal snipes about one union sister or another for a stated position during a meeting, the usual Adams pettiness to which the rookie teacher had grown accustomed.

They sat loosely divided by race, as usual, although no one noticed, not even Thomas. He focused on the game he and his friend had been playing. Each tried to elicit laughter from the other using the animal crackers at their disposal. Thomas bit the head off a horse (headless horse). Heléna bit the rear end off a bear (bare behind). She giggled, then reached into the bag, found two lions and positioned them so that one mounted the other.

Thomas covered his mouth but could not suppress his laughter. Neither did Heléna. Ms. Garcia turned around and hushed them.

Ms. Caine, the respected third-grade teacher, BTU building representative and president of the illustrious body, paused, then continued. "So we're all agreed to have the teacher's room painted blue over the April vacation, yes? Okay. The next item is …"

After disposing of several minor issues on the agenda, the group complained bitterly about the miserable squalor at the Adams. A few agreed that J.J.'s last year and a half had been less than stellar, but he had kept the place as clean as a hospital room compared to the efforts generated by the current guy. The new custodian, a gruff man with fiery red hair, eyes and nose, clearly hated his job and the kids. He frequently missed wastebaskets, rooms and coming to work altogether. The staff agreed that something had to be done lest they be menaced by their crawling nemeses again in the spring.

Thomas reminded his workmates that teachers likewise shared in the responsibility for keeping the building clean. He cautioned against allowing students to visit the bathrooms unsupervised, reporting that more than once he had apprehended unchaperoned boys stuffing urinals with paper, producing water-soaked floors. He also disclosed that the custodian complained about the state of the rooms after parties (food on the floor, overflowing wastebaskets, etc). Thomas added that in the weekly staff newsletter, Mr. Dorn had written vehement objections about children and teachers keeping food in their desks overnight. The staff listened politely to their young colleague and agreed, then resumed their litany of complaints against the custodian, deciding to present the matter to Mr. Dorn in the strongest terms.

Ms. Caine continued with the next agenda item: the potentially explosive situation during lunch. Several teachers charged that it was not uncommon for neither administrator to be present to supervise the youngsters. Everyone generally agreed that the lunch mothers, God bless them, were ill-equipped to control that unruly crowd. Thomas relayed his recent experience in the cafeteria the previous month and suggested that all teachers do their part by routinely reviewing the cafeteria rules with their entire class. The discussion closed with a resolution to take the faculty's concerns to the principal for an adequate response.

Thomas and Glen exchanged "what the hell" glances. For some time, Thomas had noticed that he and his Adams coworkers did not share the same approach to problem-solving. After attending several committee meetings such as the Faculty Senate and the Testing Committee, it was apparent that he spoke a different language than the others. He believed in self-empowerment and personal responsibility. They, in his opinion, invested in blame and passing the buck. Thomas postulated that major improvements at the Adams would never occur until the staff abandoned their commitment to victim status and recognized that they had more control over their personal and professional lives than they cared to admit.

After disposing of other trivial matters, the group arrived at the highlight of the day: recommending one of their own for the annual citywide Golden Apple Award. Its very mention sparked moderate enthusiasm from the previously underwhelmed audience. The Golden Apple was a very coveted prize; the highest honor bestowed upon a teacher in Boston. In all, twelve teachers eventually received the honor out of scores of nominations. The recipients acquired a gold-plated, apple-shaped statuette and five hundred dollars. Also, their pictures appeared in almost every major newspaper in the metropolitan area. No Adams teacher had ever won.

After a warm debate the staff agreed that everyone in the building would support the nomination of one candidate, thus bettering his or her chances of success. Thomas nominated Glen, only to be stabbed by a dirty look from his friend. Virtually every teacher agreed. They praised Glen's obvious talent and his dedication to the profession. However, Glen balked. He thanked them for the flattery, then announced that he respectfully declined the honor of a nomination, offering some feeble excuse about his belief in not judging a professional as better than his peers. The group begged him to reconsider but he was adamant. Eventually, they moved on and settled on Ms. Mustafa, who had left the meeting early.

Ms. Valdez stood and asked the Faculty Senate to submit a teacher's name for the Junior Golden Apple Award. This was an award for five outstanding first-year teachers. "Several of us have been talking about this for the last two weeks," she declared. "I think we all agree that Mr. Payne here has done a tremendous job with that bunch of kids up there." She gestured upwards. The members applauded. No one offered an alternative.

Thomas blushed and grinned. He had not been aware that such an award even existed. He struggled to find something meaningful to say. "Well, guys, I'm very honored by your sentiments. But perhaps you might consider Heléna here," he said, pointing in her direction. "She's doing an important job down there—"

"Oh shut up, Tomaso," Heléna interrupted after rolling her eyes, bringing scattered laughter throughout the lounge. "False modesty is not your strength." She got on her feet, flipped her increasingly long hair away from her forehead and addressed the group. "He accepts the nomination." She held up her hand to thwart any further comments from the man chewing the last of her animal crackers. "Mr. Payne is our nominee." She sat down and received a playful pinch on the arm from Thomas. Having run out of animal crackers, she threw the plastic bag at her friend.

Ten minutes later, the meeting adjourned. People commented on how well the assembly went—for a change. Glen, Thomas and Heléna paraded together down the hall, laughing and joking. Heléna, in the middle, grabbed the arms of her two escorts and began skipping and singing, "Weeeeerrree off to see the Wizard, the wonderful Wizard of Oz!" Thomas and Glen joined in. Because Glen knew all the words, while his companions did not, they did not get far before stopping and laughing. The trio separated at the first-grade teacher's room. Thomas asked Heléna if she needed a ride home. She declined, saying she had a ride. He was tempted to inquire for further details but decided against doing so and climbed the stairs to his own room.

Room 217 showcased decorative changes befitting the time of year. Several new posters of African American heroes and heroines received prominent display. A U.S. Supreme Court justice, a choreographer, an astronaut, a scientist, an inventor, a cabinet secretary and others provided testimony to what could be accomplished with hard work and determination. Affixed to the student-closet doors were fourteen red paper hearts with personally autographed names of a different buddy pair. Pasted to the side of the file cabinet was a display entitled, "History Makers of Tomorrow!" composed of photographic headshots of the entire class. Also, twenty-eight red hearts inside larger white ones dangled from sporadic locations throughout the room, with a pupil's name signed at each center. A list of individuals loved by the titleholder surrounded the name. Angelica, Maria and others included Mr. Payne among their loved ones.

Thomas checked his watch. It was nearly 4 o'clock. He marched down the center gauntlet of the empty room and stopped at Melissa's desk. He recalled her unique Student of the Week ceremony the previous Friday: As he had done before with Maria, he had found an excuse for Melissa to be out of the room and had informed the class that she would be the new

captain. Because of the nominee's weight, Thomas had suggested that besides himself, the biggest and strongest of his students would be the main
lifters during the second part of the ceremony. However, when presented
with the opportunity, Melissa had refused the cradle.

Thomas, always with a contingency plan, divided the class into two
lines. The room remained dark, and with Melissa standing alone and her
eyes closed, the class had paraded past her and whispered congratulatory
words in her ears. Half of the class stood on one side and half on the other.
The song, "You are so Beautiful," played in the background. The new captain's
tears had melted even Cleopatra's cold heart. (Other than the day she stayed
home ill, Cleo herself had earned a point for every day that week. Unfortunately, she came to school without her homework the following Monday.
"If you prefer to remain on ISP, we can do that too," the lanky girl's teacher
had informed her.)

Thomas returned to the present, approached the main board and
grabbed a piece of chalk. He became annoyed upon discovering that it had
been broken; the hazard of indoor recess and the relentless games of "hang-
man" the classroom-bound kids played after lunch. He turned away from
the board and let out a fierce sneeze. The amount of chalkdust accumulated on the metal chalkrack further irritated him. He wrote three of the
fifteen new spelling words on the board before Glen unexpectedly appeared.
His mentor had on his coat and clutched a briefcase in one hand and two
large tote bags in the other. He entered softly.

The host of Room 217 greeted him. "Hey, buddy."

"Is anyone around?" Glen casually asked.

"Are you kidding? Five minutes after the meeting this place became a
ghost town," Thomas asserted. Having lost his place, he scanned the list on
Doug's desk. Trying not to be impolite, he addressed his comrade. "What's
up?"

Glen spoke quietly but his voice was stern. "Just what do you think you
were doing?"

Thomas, shocked and puzzled, stopped writing and faced him. "Huh?
What do you mean?"

The visitor blinked twice slowly, then continued. "I mean that thing
with me and the Golden Apple." He dropped his bags and briefcase on the
floor. "You know I don't want a huge spotlight on me right now."

Thomas placed the chalk on the rack and took two steps toward his friend. "Look, I didn't mean anything by it—other than what it was. What you do with those kids, man, it's nothing short of a miracle. Everybody here knows that." He searched for the next spelling word, then gave up. "Hell, Glen, didn't you see how quickly everybody agreed? Take it as a compliment. You're great. We all know it. Now live with it," he commanded with a smile.

Glen, obviously still irked, bore no smile. "That's not the point. What I need is my privacy. I thought you would understand that."

Thomas opened his hands. "I do. I do understand, Glen." He started to become agitated himself. "Excuse the hell out of me for recognizing that you're a terrific teacher who should get some credit. God knows we're not gonna get it from Dorn." He caught himself and struggled to remove the sharpness from his voice. "Look, man, I'm sorry. I wasn't thinking. I just thought—well, I already told you what I thought."

The fire in Glen's eyes dissipated. Embarrassed, he checked the shine on his shoes. "Don't think I didn't appreciate the honor. But, you know, I've got to keep a low profile for now. You understand."

"Yeah, I guess so."

The veteran first-grade teacher bent over and picked up his belongings. "I better get going." He stopped and made a peace offering to his friend. "You going to Anthony's?"

Thomas shook his head. "Naw, I've got a lot to do here."

"Don't stay too late. See you tomorrow."

Thomas listened to his friend's footsteps as they grew more distant. He went back to the board and wrote the word "privacy."

The next day Thomas prepared to address his class regarding a much anticipated date—February 14, Valentine's Day. He had noticed that at least a week prior to February Ferdinand's posting, the males and females in Room 217 had begun sizing each other up and preparing for the day that they would declare their affection for one another. Girls and boys huddled separately during breaks to arrive at some agreement about who would be with whom. This created some conflict. Carmelita appointed herself arbitrator for her sex while Asa became the boys' negotiator. The two ambassadors frequently met to finalize tentative agreements.

As far as Thomas could tell, among those so inclined to pair off, the couples were as follows: Tyshaun and Cleopatra, Maurice and Francine,

Hernando and Carmelita (she and Jonathan had broken up the previous week but agreed that they would still be friends). Other arrangements were still being formalized. Carmelita had offered to fix Maria up with Brian but she refused, claiming that her Mami would kill her if she discovered that her daughter had a boyfriend. Brian rejected the notion as well, claiming that he already had a girlfriend, who did not attend the Adams. Several eligible girls expressed an interest in Melvin, but he reported that he wrote to a girl in Haiti. Some members of the class fancied students in Ms. Sanchez-Taylor or Mrs. Chang's class.

Of course, Thomas thought his children were far too young to think of such things. However, the restrictions on the little cupids' freedom (due mostly to indoor recesses) ensured that the situation would not get out of hand. He recognized that times had changed and attempted to be coopera- tive. In fact, that very morning he had chosen not to embarrass a student when he intercepted a note that had interrogated another, "I want to know right now. Do you love me or not?" At least, the teacher rationalized, all of the words had been spelled correctly.

"Next week is Valentine's Day, and the week after that we'll all be on vacation," Thomas announced. The class responded with whistles and noise. He raised both hands and curtailed their mirth. "Here's the deal in Room 217: We *will* have a short Valentine's Day party up here right after lunch." Shouts of rejoicing and thanks filled the room. Thomas asked that they listen. Melissa rose to go to the board, but the announcer told her it was okay.

"As I was saying, we'll have a party after lunch. A short one. Maybe twenty minutes." The news was greeted with playful boos and other sounds of disappointment.

Thomas raised his eyebrows. "If you're hurt by that decision, wait 'til you hear what else I've got in store." He cleared his throat. "First, if you're on ISP or grounding, that's too bad. Stay in your seats during the party." Young eyes surveyed the room as the fifth-graders silently predicted who would be glued to their chairs next week after lunch.

"Another thing," Thomas continued. "If you bring valentines—I can't make you do this—but I ask that you give one to every member of the class." This brought significant protests from about a dozen students, mostly boys. Thomas held up his hands again. All complaining ceased. "Listen, my dears," he teased. "We're not just a team. We're like a family now. I don't want one person with twenty-five valentines and someone else with two. You don't have to declare your undying love for the person. Just sign your name. Deal?"

After a few objections, the agreement was forged. Everyone received a sheet of paper bearing the correct spelling of every pupil's name. After being subjected to a merciless barrage of requests, Thomas reluctantly agreed to allow juice and dessert to be served during the event.

For a while he had trouble getting the class to settle down. The youngsters exhibited obvious excitement about the coming week's party. The resourceful teacher was forced to employ the old classical-music-identify-the-instruments exercise, so effective after the *Christmas Carol* production and on other occasions. Within five minutes the mood in the room became serene and peaceful. That Bach sure wrote some fine tunes, Thomas thought.

However, the next morning produced an unpleasant incident for Thomas and the Student of the Week. The day began auspiciously enough. Much of the snow on the playground had melted, so the Adams's children played energetically under the sun's generous rays. A kind wind caressed the faces of tomorrow's leaders as they laughed and pranced about. Thomas acknowledged the hugs and affection of the primary students when he appeared to gather his own brood. Melissa was not yet present at 8:25 to escort the class into the room. Following the line of succession, the task fell to the previous Student of the Week, Pedro.

Shortly after the homework check, Pedro announced that the rightful Student of the Week had arrived after all. Thomas stepped to the door and found a lugubrious Melissa accompanied by her mother, a heavy-set woman with piercing brown eyes. She was in her forties but looked far older. A sad-looking curly-haired wig covered her head. A simple discount-store black wool coat hung from her shoulders. She appeared to be tired and angry. They greeted each other cautiously.

"Mr. Payne, Melissa here's all upset. Says she left her homework in her desk, and you ain't gonna let her stay Student of the Week." The woman paused to catch her breath.

Thomas looked at Melissa. "What's going on?"

She took a deep breath. "I left my math in my desk," she whispered, sniveling. Thomas twisted his mouth from side to side and prepared to speak, but Melissa's mother interceded.

"I told the girl not to worry. That everybody makes mistakes, and she wouldn't lose her job over this, but the girl insisted. She fussed and cried all the way here."

Thomas twisted his mouth again. "Ms. Brown, thank you for coming." He folded his hands as he prepared to deliver the unpleasant news. "To be truthful, well, Melissa's right. She can't continue to serve as our Student of the Week."

"See?" Melissa moaned and hugged her mother. Ms. Brown became irate and raised her voice.

"I don't think that's fair! I don't think that's fair at all, Mr. Payne!" Her brown eyes glowed like hot coals. "Melissa works real hard doing all that homework you assign. You give her this job, and then you take it away for one little mistake. You wouldn't lose your job if you made one little mistake, would you?"

"You're right, ma'am, I wouldn't," Thomas replied calmly. "But my rules are very clear. The Student of the Week must earn a point every day during her term. It's a one day *suspension*, actually. She would be allowed to return to duty the next day if she came in with all of her work. But seeing that today is Friday, the day I choose a new captain, that won't be possible. I really am very sorry."

"I just don't think that's fair. I really don't," Ms. Brown fumed.

Thomas sighed. "Yes, ma'am, I hear you and I respect your opinion. This has happened once before with the same consequence. As a matter of fact, that person was chosen Student of the Week again recently and served with honor. I'm sure that Melissa will serve again herself in the future. But I'm afraid it won't be today." Just then they were interrupted by the sound of Pedro's voice.

"I'm at the board. Quiet please," the boy called out.

Thomas faced his students, then addressed Pedro. "This isn't September, Captain. This is February," he growled. "No warning. Just erase their check and let 'em stay in their seats during the afternoon recess. The snow's been melting pretty good. They might even let you go outside today."

"Yes, Mr. Payne," Pedro replied. The handsome boy brandished an eraser and scanned the classroom. Everyone buried his or her face in a book or reviewed the day's homework.

"Sorry," Thomas said, returning to Melissa and her mother. "Well, I have to get back to class." He nodded his head slightly and patted Melissa's shoulder. "She'll be fine." Melissa clung to her mother and whimpered. Like a mother sparrow, the rotund lady nudged her chick into the classroom. The man backed up.

"I don't know how you can be so cold, Mr. Payne. I really don't."

Thomas tried to sound calm and reassuring. "Thank you for bringing her to school, Ms. Brown. She'll be fine in a few minutes, I'm sure." Ms. Brown reluctantly turned and waddled out of sight. Thomas closed the door. Melissa wandered towards the closet while avoiding eye contact with her classmates.

"Nope, I don't think so," Thomas called to her, stretching out his long arm. "Straight to your seat. Give your things to …" he paused. Cleo could not get up either so she would be unable to help. Several hands sprang up, mostly girls. "Angelica," he called, motioning for her to rise. She climbed out of her chair and gathered the despondent girl's belongings. Thomas addressed Melissa.

"Honey, I know right now you think I'm being too strict. But you know I don't play favorites. Mr. Payne is tough but he's fair." He put his hand on her sunken head. "You've come a long way this year. Nothing has happened today to change the fact that I'm very proud of you." He straightened up and took Angelica by the arm and whispered to her, "Take good care of her today."

The small girl nodded. "I will."

Thomas went back to his desk. "Okay, everybody. Let's get back to work." He pried open, then closed the rickety drawers on his desk, producing loud squeaks. While digging in his center drawer, he sneaked a peek at Melissa. Her head was erect as she feverishly worked on her math. On the way back to her own desk, Angelica dropped off two brand-new pencils to her temporary buddy.

"You can keep them," she whispered.

That afternoon Thomas stood face to face with Asa and requested that the class be allowed to show him a token of their respect. He agreed and over two dozen of his classmates encircled him. Although the room was dark, Asa could see the spectrum of smiles on the faces of his peers. A soft song, his personal cradle song, began to play. The proud new Student of the Week remembered something. He produced a devilish smirk, suddenly raised his hand and asked if he could say just three words. Thomas agreed and gave Deborah a signal to pause the music. Asa smiled and shook his finger. "Don't drop me," he joked. Everyone remembered and laughed.

The cradle was performed smoothly. When his feet touched the ground, Asa sighed with satisfaction because Ms. Patterson had agreed to be the guest that day. He felt remorse at how badly he had behaved as a fourth-grader under her tutelage. Before leaving, she told Asa and the class how very proud she was that they were doing so well. Thomas nodded his head, and with great fanfare Vince gave her a huge computer-designed card, signed by everyone who had been in her fourth-grade class. It read, "Dear Ms. Patterson: We appreciate what you did for us last year." The veteran teacher was pleasantly surprised and left the room feeling joyful.

The following Monday Thomas cut the silent reading period known as DEAR short in order to present report cards. He requested that buddies sit together.

"There've been improvements since the first quarter, but we need to get in gear," the young man began. "We gotta put on the full-court press. That means significantly more hard work from everybody on the team." He paused. "And I do mean everybody." Thomas waved the cards in the air. "Now you've met the first challenge—bringing in your work, but just showing up with the work and behaving properly no longer meet minimum standards around here. I expect to see high-quality work from now on." Abruptly, he distributed the report cards.

The recipients devoured the hand-outs. They noticed subtle and incremental changes from the previous quarter. Failing grades to D's, C—'s to C's, B's to B+'s and so forth. Maria and Melvin did indeed make the Honor Roll; so did Pedro, although all three received many more B's than A's. Christine and Gary were awarded Merit honors for receiving only one C. Twelve students had not missed a day of school for the entire quarter, each garnering a certificate for perfect attendance. Others took comfort that they had earned nothing lower than a B- in all ten conduct and effort subgrades, guaranteeing them a "School Spirit" award. Angel, a previous honoree, raised his hand violently.

"Mr. P," he called out. "How come I get a C+ in Cooperation?"

"Because Ms. Nelson said you've been cuttin' up in music class. That's why," Thomas replied before directing his comments to the entire group. "This time, I did more than just ask the special class teachers to give me grades. I asked about your behavior. Some of you'll notice that your conduct grades are lower. That's for clownin' during computers, art, music and so forth." He shifted his weight from one foot to the other and continued. "If a teacher—any teacher—tells you to do something, I expect you to do it. Got that?"

His students chimed the familiar response: "Yes, Mr. Payne."

Thomas searched for a particular student and found him. "And Maurice, Ms. Poppocoupolis told me that during art class, you're always giving her backtalk when she tells you to do something. There will be no more of that. You hear me?"

Maurice lowered his head. "Yes, Mr. Payne."

The moderator shifted his gaze to the back of the room. "And Freddy, one more negative report about you, and you'll spend special class time with me—as well as recess. Do I make myself clear?"

"Yes, Mr. Payne."

"Well," Thomas said, examining his watch, "Go home and get your stories in first before I get on the phone tonight. I'm sure your folks will want to talk to me after getting these. Congratulations to those who improved this quarter." He pointed to Asa. "Captain, get 'em ready to go home."

The tall boy stood up and clapped his hands twice. "Okay, everyone return to your seats quietly, please."

The following morning Thomas awoke to hear a voice on the radio announcing school closings. The former athlete jumped out of bed and peeled back the curtains. The three automobiles in the small parking lot were blanketed by a thin layer of snow, nothing heavy. Nearby tree branches sported attractive white coats. Unimpressive ripples of gray, slushy snow hugged the street curbs. Thomas could see his neighbor, a single mother with two children of middle school age, brushing snow off her old subcompact Honda. The Cincinnati native shivered, grabbed his robe from the foot of his bed and listened further. The storm had turned eastward and raged harmlessly out in the Atlantic Ocean. Boston public schools were open as usual. Disappointment and relief settled in Thomas's heart. While in the shower, he hummed the song "White Christmas."

The drive to work took a little longer than normal but was uneventful. The temperature had climbed to three degrees above freezing. The sun declined to grace the morning commute and was not expected to make an appearance at all that day. Thomas stared at the leafless trees that only four months ago had displayed such spectacular colors. He enjoyed the outdoors but did not consider himself a winter person. Skiing, ice-skating and the like did not interest him. He longed for the return of warm weather and regular sunshine. Also, he missed his family in Cincinnati.

Upon arriving at the Adams, Thomas frowned at the dismal condition of the front-door steps, which obviously hadn't been swept in at least two days. At the bottom of the stairwell, kernels of popcorn a child had spilled yesterday had not been removed. He was relieved to push open the double-doors leading to the main corridor.

The teacher was greeted by the sight of Angel's mother sitting outside the office. She leaped off the squeaky wooden bench when she saw Thomas and grabbed his arm. She wore an open, short, black leather jacket, cut in an hourglass shape, accentuating her attractive form. The third button of her white cotton blouse strained to remain in place against pressure from her large breasts. A shiny pair of tall leather boots protected her feet. An almost new pair of blue jeans firmly squeezed the lower half of her body.

"Mr. Payne, I have to get to work, but I want to talk to you. Can you spare a minute?" she pleaded in her heavily accented English.

Thomas searched for a spot on the attractive woman's frame that would allow him to maintain a professional demeanor. Eventually, he stopped at her feet. "Of course, Mrs. Estevez. What can I do for you?"

"Angel showed me his report card. He didn't do so good, no?"

Admittedly, Thomas found teaching to be a job devoid of glamour, so he always relished seeing Mrs. Estevez, literally. With her curvaceous, top-heavy figure, high cheekbones and full lips, his prurient interests could be safely and secretly nurtured. Still, he took care to avoid even the appearance of inappropriate attention. He always found a reason to steer her into an open space, thus furnishing him with witnesses, and avoided prolonged eye contact. Thomas perceived Mrs. Estevez to be a caring parent. He applauded her hardworking ways (the woman worked two jobs) and admired her appreciation for the opportunities immigrants have in America. He also respected her insistence that her son take advantage of the country's free public education.

The short woman always acted "touchy-feely" and affectionate towards him. After surviving frequent visits to the Adams last year due to Angel's behavioral problems, Mrs. Estevez often expressed gratitude to Thomas for

Angel's improvement. She was not much older than the teacher of her only child. Once, early in the summer before he began working for BPS, Thomas had remembered seeing her out on the town with several big-haired girlfriends. The two of them had even danced together. He recalled that she had moved fluidly and smiled often. Fortunately, at the time, he still had the Laura blues and resisted making any advances.

"Frankly, Mrs. Estevez," Thomas responded, "Angel's schlupt off big time since the Christmas break. If he had invested half the time on his schoolwork as he spent trying to impress the girls, he would have done much better."

"Humph," the woman scoffed. "Like father, like son."

Thomas tried to keep a straight face.

The expressive Dominican Republic native assured him that she would see to it that her Angel studied more and stayed off that telephone. Caressing his arm, she thanked Thomas for his time, then released him and sashayed down the corridor. Although severely tempted, he fought the urge to watch her as she made her journey. He shook his head and recalled her comment about the boy's father. "Who'd be stupid enough to cheat on a woman that sweet and fine?" he whispered to himself.

A couple of months before, after such a visit, he would have staggered into Glen's room and whispered some mild off-color remark about his meeting. Glen always appeared to share the joke although, come to think of it, the first-year teacher mused, his buddy never offered any such observations of his own. Thomas wondered why he had never noticed that earlier. Since their Chinese restaurant conversation, Thomas had voluntarily ceased such antics. Glen never expressed reproach in any way, but Thomas simply assumed that such humor was now no longer appropriate between them. He bounded up the stairs, straight to his room.

A significant portion of the class returned their report cards. The suspicious instructor carefully checked each parent's signature. Three parents sent enclosures requesting that Thomas call to arrange conferences. Melissa's mother wrote that she thought too much pressure was being put on the students in Mr. Payne's class. LaShonda, who had only escaped another attendance-failure quarter because Mr. Dorn had granted her a waiver, turned in her signed report card without comment. Tucked inside was the note from her teacher strongly requesting a parent conference. A written reply did not accompany the parent signature. When Thomas asked what response her mother had exhibited to the host of D's and the one F she had earned, LaShonda removed her thumb from her mouth long enough to calmly offer a one word answer: "Nothing."

That afternoon during lunch Thomas stopped by the office to check his mailbox. He received three additional messages from parents desiring to meet. Mr. Dorn opened the door to his office and asked to see him after school. Thomas agreed. The junior staff member crept across the hall and opened the door to Glen's room. It was empty and the lights were off. Disappointed, he returned to his own territory.

A half-hour before dismissal Thomas called for a class meeting. Everyone knew why. A long-time ISP student, having earned her fifth straight point, had just become eligible to return as a member in good standing, according to February Ferdinand. Francine stood in the center of the classroom, about to give an account of herself. The cute, dark-skinned girl, obviously nervous, played with her fingers. She had witnessed the verbal assaults from classmates when others had assumed her position. Asa's encounter had been especially brutal. But Mr. Payne had spoken to her privately before the meeting and had coached her about her demeanor and language.

Thomas picked a piece of paper off the floor and threw it in the trash. Hernando and Melvin held up their hands, showing two fingers. After a playful protest that the shot was a three-pointer and not two, the instructor walked down the center pathway straight to Francine and held her face in his large hands. He gently lowered his forehead until it touched hers and whispered, "You'll be fine. Just answer their questions truthfully," then stepped back and spoke to the class from the other side of the room.

"Well, we know why we're meeting today. One of our lost sheep wants to return to the fold."

Christine clapped her hands. Asa, who sat next to her, joined her. Soon every pupil put his or her hands together for Francine. She blushed and covered her mouth with her fingers, hiding a broad smile.

Thomas resumed his opening. "Although there's no question that Francine is eligible to return, we take this opportunity to support her by speaking to her and providing feedback." He nodded his head twice and continued. "There are lots of ways to be supportive. Being supportive might mean calling your buddy to make sure she has her homework, like Christine's been doing." He pointed at the plump girl, who smiled. "It might mean praying for that person." Thomas shivered, realizing that he had allowed his personal beliefs to slip in and sought cover for himself. "—If you believe in that sort of thing." No one rose in protest, so he pressed on. "It might mean just telling him or her, 'Good work.' "

Free associating, he addressed Maria, calling her by the nickname he had given her. "Cookie, what did you say to Carmelita after you were chosen Student of the Week?"

Maria smiled. "I said, 'You will be next.' "

"That's right. And they've been Student of the Week four times between them." Thomas held his fingers in the air. "But being supportive also means telling your friend or your buddy when they've done wrong. It means helping them to get out of trouble and to stay out of trouble …" He shook his finger, lowered his voice and arched his eyebrows for dramatic effect. "Even when I'm not around."

"Mmm-hmm," Carmelita declared, cranking her neck from side to side. Several students giggled.

"Okay," Thomas announced. "Now it's your turn. You know the routine by now." He walked backwards and sat on a counter near the row of discolored windows, leaving the candidate to her inquisitors. "Raise your hand. I'll get to as many as I can. Speak directly to Francine and look at her." He pointed at the frightened young girl. "Frannie, answer their questions completely and loudly. Look them in the face. Speak up. No mumbling, okay?"

She nodded as hands sprang up.

Thomas watched the flagging arms and reflected on the process. In his opinion, subjecting a wayward pupil to the "feedback loop" was a demanding but necessary step to his or her full recovery. He believed that an expatriated student must accept the class's guidance and assistance after returning to their midst. In college he had read historical accounts about non-European cultures, like the Native Americans, Asians and Africans. Without naming it so, they had lived the Gestalt philosophy: *The whole is bigger than the sum of its parts.* Thomas held that African Americans especially suffered from adopting the European obsession with individualism.

He remembered his own experience with Revelations as the centerpiece of a feedback loop. His good looks and warm smile had fooled no one. "Yep, Mr. Hotshot, they sure had your number. They worked you over but good," Thomas thought to himself.

He inspected the class and chose a good friend. "Lakeisha."

"How come you been on ISP so long? You like it?" she asked with a haughty look on her face.

So much for gentle openings, Thomas thought to himself.

"I don't know," she answered.

"Not good enough," Thomas declared. He pointed to Lakeisha. "Ask her again."

"Why you been on ISP so long?"

Francine took her hand off her face. "Because I don't be bringing in my homework."

"Why not?" Lakeisha prodded further, clearly enjoying herself.

"Because I be playing and watching TV instead of doing what I'm supposed to do," Francine admitted.

More hands. Thomas called on Melvin.

"Didn't you see how you were hurting the team?"

"No. I mean, yes. I mean, at first I didn't understand but I do now," she replied.

Again hands shot into the air.

"Angelica."

"How do we know we can trust you now?"

Thomas shrugged his shoulders. Tough crowd today.

"Because I'm going to do my best and bring my homework in every day."

"Asa."

"Not good enough," he boy said. He stretched out his long grasshopper-like arms and legs. "I sat back there on ISP with you, Francine." Asa confessed, pointing at himself. "I remember the things you used to say about Mr. Payne and other people in the class; how you be calling them names and stuff. What I wanna know is, how do we know you gonna be better?"

Several classmates reacted to Asa's revelation with raised eyebrows. Francine thought for a few seconds. She didn't have a response. Asa had ambushed her by disclosing behavior few people knew about except those who sat in the back. She shook with fear. Her rescue came from the voice of her teacher.

"Francine, can you offer any proof that things'll be different from now on?" Thomas interjected. The room grew quiet. The tall man walked the gauntlet towards his frozen student but stopped about four feet away. He rolled his eyes and tossed his head to the left. "Look at the point count, honey."

Francine pointed at February Ferdinand. "I be getting all my points now," she offered.

Thomas breathed a sigh of relief and moved his head up and down. "Yes, you have," he affirmed, then resumed the program by calling on Gary.

"After all this time, what made you change?"

Francine put her hand in her mouth, then withdrew it. She stared at the scratches on the floor and muttered, "Giver-Taker."

"Louder," the man at the back of the room commanded.

"Giver-Taker," she called out.

Tyshaun had been patiently waiting with his hand extended. Although the boy currently sat in the back row on ISP, he had the right to speak during a class meeting. Thomas called on him.

"What's your contract?"

Francine did not hesitate. Mr. Payne had told her to be ready for that one. "I am a strong, kind and responsible young woman."

The questioning continued for an additional minute. Francine answered to the best of her ability. With a half-dozen hands still waving in the air, Thomas looked at his watch and called on the last questioner. "Christine, you've been working with her for some time now. Is there anything you want to ask or say to your buddy?"

Melissa lowered her hand and spoke slowly. "You can't go back, Frannie. Okay?"

She agreed.

Thomas stepped towards her. "Francine, before we vote, is there anything you want to say to the class?"

A long silence in the room was broken by the sound of footsteps and loud voices as a large group of students passed by. After a few seconds, the Room 217 audience turned back to the front of the room, waiting to hear the girl's final summation.

"I-I'm sorry it took me so long and that I hurt the team." She struggled to hold back tears. "I promise that if you give me this chance, I won't mess up."

Thomas asked if she had anything further to say. Francine shook her head. He walked near her and made a request, in accordance with the class practice: "Christine. Go stand next to your buddy. Here, nobody stands alone."

He addressed the class loudly. "When I count to three, you'll either stand to vote yes or remain seated to vote no." After counting the number of students present, he continued. "There are twenty-six students here today including you, Francine. You'll need fourteen votes. You and your buddy will vote by raising your hands or leaving them at your sides." Thomas pointed and addressed everyone a final time. "One more thing: stand or sit, but don't look around to see how the vote is going. Decide on your own."

He licked his lips. "Okay. One. Two …" The screech of dragging chairs already began. "Three!"

Thomas observed as every student either quickly or slowly rose. Francine and Christine held hands and raised their free arms high into the air. Thomas carefully inspected the results and declared, "Congratulations, Frannie. You've been unanimously restored with full privileges." Thunderous applause filled the room. Francine hugged her buddy. Angelica took a step forward but stopped. She looked to the left, her brown eyes fixed on her teacher.

"Go ahead," he told her.

She raced over to the two buddies and wrapped them both with the warmth of her small arms. Another pupil joined them, then two, then a dozen, then virtually the entire class. Thomas joined them as well. Francine became virtually invisible under mounds of pressing flesh. A few students shouted, "Group hug! Group hug!"

The remainder of the day progressed smoothly. A few minutes before dismissal, the Student of the Week chose Francine to help pass out various papers and notices before the bell rang. As they filed to leave, a few students stopped by the girl's desk and left small gifts for her. New, unsharpened pencils. Money. A new notebook. A highlighter. A ruler. Thomas had not requested such largess; it was a totally spontaneous display of kindness. He beamed with pride at the thoughtfulness of his children.

At 3:30 Thomas surveyed Mr. Dorn's office again. Not much really had changed since his previous visits. The computers hummed along. Boxes of books no longer blocked the door, but boxes of ancillary computer equipment had taken their place. A small stack of tools rested on the conference table. Thomas found himself in the office about once a month; always the same script: "Ms. So and So, the mother of So and So, called me today to complain about … I'll call her." Thomas still hadn't developed a thick skin since that first day in October.

He waited for his boss to get off the phone and kept his mind occupied by guessing who was the parent responsible for this audience with the principal. After an excruciatingly long period of time, the middle-aged man finally hung up. He offered no apology for the delay.

"Well, here we are again, Mr. Payne," he opened.

Thomas smiled. "Yeah, we've got to stop meeting like this. People are beginning to talk."

Mr. Dorn surprised his guest by laughing, then launched into the reason for their tête-à-tête. "As you probably guessed, I received a few complaints about you."

Thomas knew better but still became angry. "Shoot, Mr. Dorn. Why don't people just come directly to me instead of bothering you?" He immediately realized that he had said too much already. "I mean, you've got more important things to do."

Mr. Dorn scratched his gray head. "Well, some of these people have known me a lot longer maybe, I don't know. Anyway, Ms. Brown, Melissa's mother, called. She was upset about Melissa's report card. She said that Melissa stays up all night doing your homework and that you're never satisfied."

"That's just so untrue," Thomas whined. "Melissa's way behind in all of her subjects. She tends to catch on a little slower. She needs some extra help, and I've been trying to get it for her. But that's not what's really bothering her mom. Heck, the girl's last quarter grades were worse than this one, and she didn't have much to say then. The woman's mad at me for removing her daughter as Student of Week."

Mr. Dorn sat up. "Maybe you're right. She did speak at some length about that. She said Melissa cried the whole morning."

The telephone rang. Both men stared at it; Thomas dreading another long wait and the principal deciding on whether or not to pick up the receiver. It stopped after three rings. Thomas issued the standard line.

"I'll call her tonight."

"I wish that would do it but," Mr. Dorn replied, "she wants to meet with both of us."

"Fine," Thomas said curtly. He had been involved in two such gatherings. They followed a standard order of business: The parent would recite a host of nonsense reported by a student. He would volley with an opposing account, then would support his version with documentation (the point count, an incident report, his grade book, a recent test, etc.). The parent, thoroughly embarrassed for having jumped to conclusions, would promise that her child would improve. In this case, he would call Ms. Brown anyway, pacify her and report to Dorn that no three-party meeting would be necessary.

The two men agreed on a day and time. The principal mentioned another parent who called, unhappy with her child's grades. Thomas promised to call the parent that night, satisfying Mr. Dorn. The young man hoped that their business together had reached a conclusion, but the principal began anew.

"There's another issue that I have to bring up … for your own good." Unexpectedly, the usually stoic man actually displayed signs of discomfort. He adjusted his lumbering weight in his chair. "Mr. Payne, you're a single man. A single *Black* man. You have to be careful about what you say, what you do and how you act. I'm not saying that it's fair or right, but as a Black man I have to live with these restrictions too."

"I'm afraid I don't understand," Thomas replied. His eyes remained wide open, and his heartbeat began to flutter.

"Well," the principal elucidated. "It's like this: Separately, a couple of teachers told me that they saw you hugging and caressing some parent out in the hall this morning. They didn't identify the woman, but they reported that they've seen the two of you 'carrying on together' before." He waved his hands in the air and quickly added, "Now those aren't my words but theirs."

So much for the benefit of having witnesses when meeting with Mrs. Estevez. Thomas became furious but fought to control himself. "What kind of nonsense is this?"

"There's more," Mr. Dorn warned. "One of the teachers added that she's seen you with some of your female students, and you're too touchy with them. She said that someone else told her that she saw you hug and kiss one of the girls on the lips."

"What?" Thomas exclaimed. "Nothing like that ever happened!" He put both hands on his head. "I can't believe this!"

"Wait. Let me finish. There's more," the principal cautioned. "One of the paras told Ms. Flores that you were waiting for her by her car last week, and it made her nervous."

Thomas felt the explosion inside of him about to discharge but the last remark sparked his memory. His eyes moved rapidly from side to side as he struggled to recall the incident. He waved his index finger in the air. "Now that one I remember! You're talking about the woman in Ms. Marcos's room; the young, pudgy one. I noticed that her front tire was low on air so I told her about it."

"Yeah, that's her, Miss Cruz—and she's pregnant," the principal added, a little annoyed at the young man's description. He pointed to the ceiling. "One last thing …"

"Don't tell me," Thomas scoffed. "They found out about me being involved in the Kennedy assassination."

Mr. Dorn raised his eyebrows. "Not yet. But Ms. Flores also mentioned that there's word going around that you've been bothering Ms. Gutiérrez."

"You've got to be joking! She and I are the best of friends! She would never say anything like that." Seeing his supervisor raise his eyebrows and throw up his hands again, Thomas scowled. "Wait a minute here. Who are these people, anyway?"

"They asked me not to divulge their names."

"What the hell is this, Washington, D.C.?" Thomas fired back. "What do you mean, they asked not to give their names?"

Mr. Dorn shrugged his shoulders. "You have to look at this from my position. I'm sure there's nothing to it but I can't ignore something like this. Shit, if someone goes downtown about this, the first thing they'll ask is, 'What did Dorn know and when did he know it?' You know how it is nowadays. I've seen careers ruined over less, I'm tellin' you. I've got to look out for my ass, too. Not just yours."

He took off his glasses and took a deep breath. "You have to be careful, Mr. Payne. You're not from here. This is Boston, not Cincinnati. People here are uptight. You have to lay low and catch on to how things are here, man. I had to learn the hard way myself. That's why with me it's always strictly business." Thomas put his hand up to speak, but the principal refused to yield the floor. He shook his head and his finger. "Don't let these women here mess with your mind. Don't let anyone here know what you're thinking." Finally, he leaned back in his chair and tried to appear more relaxed. "Now you're young and full of ideas. That's good. You took a group of misfits and put them on the straight and narrow. You've got a brilliant career ahead of you. Don't get off on the wrong track because you weren't politically smart."

"I don't get it," Thomas whimpered. "Even if all of this is true, how come I see all those Spanish teachers hugging and kissing their kids and nobody gives a reservoir?"

"They're women and you're a man."

"That's not fair!"

"Life isn't fair, Mr. Payne."

A knock on the door interrupted them. Marilyn Walker excused herself and informed Mr. Dorn about an important incoming call. He told her to have the caller hold.

"Mr. Payne, um, Thomas, I tried to send word to you about this. I don't know if you got the message. Maybe I should've been more direct." He picked up the phone but didn't yet push the button flashing the green light. "I've been in this system some twenty-three years. Trust me on this one." He began hunting for the button, then put on his glasses to aid in the search. "Why don't you give all this some thought, and we'll talk again, maybe tomorrow?"

Before Thomas could respond, Mr. Dorn was holding a conversation with someone else not in the room.

Thomas departed from his trip to the woodshed very upset and agitated. He tiptoed out of the office, found himself standing outside of Glen's room and leaned forward. He could hear voices inside. Sensing that his mentor was not free to talk, he started downstairs towards Heléna's room. His footsteps reverberated in the echoing corridor, and his eyes burned with rage. He got about halfway down the stairs, then reversed his position, stomping all the way up to his room and slamming the door.

An hour later Thomas bench-pressed his limit at Anthony's and muttered unintelligible sentences under his breath. He thought of nothing but the meeting he had endured with the principal. The agitated teacher played the conversation in his head over and over again. He tried to generate a mental list of suspects who would spread such mendacious stories about him. All the while, he kept his eyes on the doorway leading into the free-weight section. He had left a note under the windshield wiper of Glen's car and hoped that his friend would arrive sooner rather than later.

Other members and guests came and went. Thomas usually found amusement in the various shapes and sizes he witnessed at such a facility. He noticed individuals who had made real progress over the months toward losing weight and toning their figures. Then there were others whose battles with their bodies would require smaller victories. The muscular former football player laughed out loud when recalling lunchtime at the Adams. The teachers fed on a constant diet of complaining about their weight while shoveling plateloads of fast foods into their eager, constantly moving mouths. Now, he had discovered, they had decided to complain about him—and for no reason.

Reaching the conclusion that Glen would not show up, Thomas roamed into the locker room. He opened his locker, dug out his mobile telephone and retrieve his messages. Heléna called—something about dinner tomorrow. The assistant manager of a bookstore reported that two special-order books had arrived. The last call came from Glen. He would be out for most of the evening but would try to call later. Thomas hung up, and for some inexplicable reason felt a little better just from hearing the voices of his two friends. Right now, home seemed the perfect place to be.

Once there, he called Heléna and informed her about the rumor that he had been "bothering" her. She immediately became angry.

"Just wait 'til tomorrow, Tomaso," she exclaimed, raising her voice. "First thing in the morning I'm gonna barge right into Mr. Dorn's office and set the record straight. You watch me." She paused to blow on her wet, peach-colored nails. "I'm gonna let him know that you and Glen are a couple of scrumptious guys who don't talk down to me like everybody else—especially him."

Thomas spent several minutes calming her down and eventually dissuaded her from the idea. Reluctantly, she agreed to abandon her plan. At Heléna's invitation, he agreed that rather than be alone on Valentine's Day, he and Glen would join her for dinner at her place. Heléna promised to dazzle her two male cohorts with her culinary skills.

On the morning of Valentine's Day, the clouds rolled in. Naked trees shivered against a chilly north wind. Thomas collected his troop and gathered them into the classroom. He reminded his hyper-stimulated group that it was still a school day, and that their parents had pushed them out the door to learn, not to find mates. He warned them to keep their valentines in their bags, threatening to confiscate all of them and cancel the party if he saw even one before lunch. The class, unfazed by their teacher's unromantic mood, buzzed about like bees. Everyone was so excited. Thomas commented to himself that it was going to be one of those days. It certainly started out that way.

According to a loose, verbal Room 217 rule, students had to attend to their business (i.e., pencils sharpened, coats hung, homework out, etc.) before "approaching the bench," unless an important matter required immediate consideration. However, the rule was not strictly enforced. Thomas employed it whenever he was assailed by several students seeking his attention.

While searching for his scissors on his battered desk, he was hemmed in from opposite sides by Maria and Angelica. They wore bright smiles and Sunday attire, and spoke nonstop about their plans. Apparently they would enjoy some big Valentine's Day event at their after-school program. The giddy youths reached into their book bags, produced huge handmade cards adorned with hearts and flowers and thrust them into his face. He thanked them for their kindness. Then it happened.

Maria put her arms around Thomas. Angelica, fearing that it was a sign that Mr. Payne might love his first cradler more than her, forcefully squished into him as well. She knocked his pen and pencil-holder to the floor, scattering its contents. Thomas looked out at the open door and ferociously bellowed at the two girls.

"No! Stop!" he screamed, pulling their arms from him. "Quit pawing on me all the time! I'm not your father!"

Instantly the room went from loud, incoherent banter to dead silence. The twenty-six other cupids were all dismayed. And they weren't the only ones. The second the words rushed out of his mouth, Thomas fervently regretted that he had uttered them, but he knew they could not be unsaid. He closed his eyes in pain, fearing what his selfishness had done to his precious girls. When he opened them, the sight before him upset him greatly. The shattered expressions on the faces of his two angels pierced his heart. They didn't say a word. They just stood there, eyes glazed over and swelling with water. Thomas reached out and clutched their hands. His head swung from left to right as he spoke.

"Sweeties, I-I'm sorry. I-I didn't mean that," he moaned.

Maria put her other hand to her face and wept softly. Angelica violently jerked out of his reach and stormed out of the classroom. Thomas turned the class over to Asa, proudly serving his second consecutive term as Student of the Week, and called for Carmelita to take her buddy to the bathroom. Carmelita put her glasses inside her desk, got up and led her weeping friend down the hall.

"Jessica," Thomas called, motioning with his right hand. "Go find your buddy and bring her back here in a hurry!"

The copper-skin girl in pigtails responded by throwing her book bag on top of her desk and walking out the door without question. Jessica, tall but shorter than Cleopatra, was well-behaved, quiet and responsible. She and Angelica had shared the same classroom at the Adams for years but had not been especially close. They had not been each other's first choice as buddies either but had developed a solid friendship over the past six months.

Jessica returned almost as soon as she had left, guiding Angelica into the classroom. The waif was silently crying. "She was right outside the door, Mr. Payne," Jessica reported.

Thomas thanked her and requested that Angelica join Maria in the girls' bathroom to recoup. Jessica grabbed two tissues from the box on his desk and exited with her buddy.

Five minutes later outside the classroom, Thomas faced the two girls. He held onto their hands. While they conversed, two adorably cute kindergarten girls walked by also holding hands, heading toward the Adams library. One carried a manila folder. They both raced to him for a hug. Their innocence and warmth rejuvenated him. They left and Thomas returned to his own children. The emotionally injured fifth-grade girls focused their attention on their shoes. They leaned against the wall next to a colorful bulletin board produced by the students of Room 217. It displayed warm-weather "winter" scenes from several countries on the other side of the world. Thomas, still very contrite, spoke gently.

"I'm very sorry that I yelled at you. It was very unkind of me."

Maria lifted her head. "Why'd you dog us like that, Mr. Payne?"

"We just wanted to give you the hearts we made for you," Angelica joined in.

Thomas frowned. "I know, Angelface, I know—and I'm sorry. You didn't do anything wrong. It was me. I've had a lot on my mind, and I was kinda mad about something else." He handed Angelica another tissue. "You see, this is my first year teaching and sometimes I make mistakes, too. The only thing I can do is admit it. You know that I love you, but sometimes—"

That was all Angelica needed to hear. She threw herself onto Thomas and wrapped her arms around him so hard he almost lost his balance. She sobbed, "I love you, Mr. Payne." Maria, then did likewise. Thomas silently thanked God that the heart of a child was so resilient, unlike an adult's. Had he damaged them permanently he would never have forgiven himself.

The sight of the three in an embracing triad generated some stares from adult and student passers-by. Thomas loosened his grip but Maria and Angelica, sensing that they possessed the advantage, refused to relinquish him. Out of the corner of his eye, the fifth-grade teacher saw the school librarian and the art teacher observing the three of them. Ms. Higgins and Ms. Poppocopoulis tried to avoid staring, Thomas remembered his meeting with Mr. Dorn just the day before and wondered if they had been the loose-lip culprits.

He felt the urge to ask the two women if they had a problem. Instead he tightened his grip around his girls and escorted them near the classroom door. When they finally separated, Thomas knew he had to settle one more matter. He addressed only one girl.

"Angelica, you must never leave the classroom again without my permission, no matter what. I must always know where you are. Do you understand?" His voice was serious but compassionate.

She agreed, keeping her head down. "I know, Mr. Payne. I'm sorry. It's just that you hurt me so bad."

"You broke our hearts," Maria contributed.

"Well, Cookie," Thomas whispered, "I guess that's a no point for Mr. Payne today, huh?"

The cheerful cherubs giggled.

"You're going to have to stay in your seat during recess," Maria quipped, shaking her finger.

"Yeah," Angelica joked. "And no privileges either." She put her hand over her mouth and exchanged smiles with Maria.

The remainder of the morning proved to be quite productive. All of the lessons had a Valentine's Day theme. The math Working Partners estimated the trajectory of Cupid's arrows in standard and metric units. They read stories about the history of Valentine's Day and how couples display love for each other in other countries. Spirited debates surfaced about polygamy in Saudi Arabia. And the students were especially fascinated by the concept of the dowry and arranged marriages in India. The latter generated vociferous laughter as "Dad" (i.e. Mr. Payne) theoretically arranged marriages on the chalkboard using the student pool at his disposal.

After school, Thomas parked himself at his desk and reflected on the day. In spite of an unfortunate beginning, events had actually gone well.

Every student toted home a bunch of valentines. Academically, it had been a productive day. His children seemed to enjoy the individually-designed cards he had constructed for each one on his computer. Thomas nursed a smile and a warm feeling as he picked up a stack of heart-filled cards addressed to Mr. Payne. He checked his watch, then stuffed his valentine treasures into a large envelope and placed it gently into his briefcase. He glanced at the wall clock out of curiosity. For the past six days, it had been 12:08. He had to hurry if he wanted to stop by Saint Mary's after-school program and surprise Maria and Angelica.

That afternoon Thomas drove home, showered and changed into his brown suit. At 6 o'clock sharp he patiently waited at the door of Heléna's fourth-floor apartment. He was apprehensive, given the scene the two of them had created the last time they were alone there. The intended presence of a third party had prodded him to accept Heléna's invitation, but poor Glen had rushed home sick right after school, a victim of some pesky flu bug. Thomas had entertained the thought of canceling his own appearance. Of course, his mother would have all but disinherited him if she ever discovered that her son had besmirched the Payne's honor with such poor manners. He straightened out the small bouquet of red and white carnations—something else his mother had taught him regarding proper etiquette. He knocked on the door lightly and heard rapid footsteps, then three clicks as someone inside unlocked and unlocked and unlocked the door.

"*Buenos noches*, Tomaso," Heléna declared with a broad smile. She stepped aside and motioned with her arm. "*Pasa adelante!* Come in!" She still had on her work attire, befitting the season—a satiny red and white dress underneath red, heart-shaped earrings. She had tied her hair up and wrapped an apron around her thin waist. Thomas extended his arm, which at its end contained the carnations. "For me? They're so beautiful! *Gracias.*" She stood on her toes like a ballerina and lightly kissed his cheek.

Thomas entered the apartment and sniffed the air. The smell was heavenly. Heléna took his coat, hung it up, then vanished into the kitchen, leaving her guest to amuse himself with the television, stereo, evening paper or his own imagination. A large, plush davenport occupied the center of the room facing a small color television. Simple, inexpensive wooden furniture—including several huge, full bookshelves—were placed at various locations.

The apartment, larger than Thomas's place, housed two residents. Heléna's roommate had gone out of town on some romantic excursion with her boyfriend. She too was Hispanic and a teacher—an English high school teacher. Most of the books belonged to her. They were recruited together from the University of California, Santa Cruz. The two women obviously loved photographs. Encased happy faces beamed everywhere. Although he had done so only two months before, Thomas scanned picture after picture and examined the subjects. He commented on the attractiveness of Heléna's family, from her grandparents to her three sisters and her.

Dinner turned out to be as delicious as Thomas had hoped. He feasted on an enormous meal, featuring lasagna as the main course. He teased his friend about being such a fine cook but admitted to having expected some exotic dish from her country. Heléna scoffed and reminded her guest that for the most part, she grew up in California. A familiar instrumental jazz song played in the background. Over dinner the two conversed easily about the Adams, their own families, past romances and the like.

After dinner Heléna arranged the dishes in the dishwasher while Thomas read the paper. He changed the music to a Spanish-language selection that had been perched next to the modest stereo. Two energetic numbers came and went, then a slower song flowed into the apartment. Heléna sang and swayed with the music. Thomas watched her move. She was graceful and sensual. Within a few minutes she sauntered into the living room and sat next to him. He showed her an article in the paper. Heléna slid closer to him so that they could read the piece together, prompting Thomas to separate her perfume from the other lingering aromas. While she read, he examined her profile. Suddenly, he struggled to get on his feet and announced that he had to go to the bathroom. When he returned, Thomas surprised Heléna by suggesting that they go out dancing. He knew a place, he reported, where Black music was featured on one floor and Spanish on another. She readily agreed. After a few preparations, they boarded his car for an evening of merriment.

A few hours later they returned to her place. Thomas watched Heléna as she progressed through the ritual of unlocking the door. After taking two steps inside, she clapped her hands twice and a bright light from a lamp as tall as her guest illuminated the spacious living room. Thomas plopped down on the overstuffed davenport and inhaled deeply. The wonderful smells still pleasantly played with his nostrils. He didn't plan to stay long but watched while the hostess turned on every light in the apartment and opened almost every door. It was nearly midnight, and he wanted to drive home unencumbered by drowsiness. Thomas stood and wandered towards the main entrance.

"Well, are you safe?" he joked.

Heléna came out of the bathroom after pulling the shower curtain all the way back. "I suppose so, *amigo.*" She took off her coat, sneaked over to the last unchecked closet, opened it and jumped backwards. She saw Thomas shaking his head and snickering. The woman made a face, then put away her coat. Although several feet away, she reached out. "Take off your coat."

"No, thanks. I guess I better get going. It's getting late you, know," he replied.

Heléna strutted closer to him, her red high-heel shoes meeting the glistening hardwood floor with a click-click sound. "I understand. After all, you're almost twenty-five years old," she teased. "You're not a kid anymore." She laughed and discarded her footwear, reducing her stature noticeably. She pointed to the carnations on the dining table. "Thanks for the flowers."

"Oh, its no big deal," Thomas replied. "My Mom always told me that if someone's invited you to eat, you should bring a bottle of wine or some flowers or something." He reached for the doorknob. "Thank you for dinner and a very enjoyable evening."

Heléna approached him. Thomas felt his heart beat faster—the way it had done all evening every time she came near him. He remembered their dancing earlier. When he took her in his arms, they fitted together as if they had been lovers for years. He knew that she felt something for him too. He remembered how red Heléna's face had become earlier when an attractive woman in a low-cut purple dress had flirted with him. He had felt the same way when she and some dashing gentleman had conversed with each other in Spanish, and the man had held her hand. In December in this very living room they had managed to stop in time. But then, Thomas had recently visited his friend Marlene in Worcester. Lately, he had been having trouble falling asleep. For him, two months without sex was a lifetime.

Heléna stepped even closer to him and covered his hand on the doorknob with her own. She tilted her head backwards and pushed her hair away from her face. Her eyes appeared sad and lonely. "I don't like being here by myself, Tomaso," she moaned, putting her arms around him. "And its Valentine's Day."

Thomas swallowed. "Heléna," he whispered and kissed her on the forehead. "I'm not sure about getting into something right now. I told you that I—"

"I'm not asking for a commitment, my dear Tomaso," Heléna purred softly, stroking his face with the back of her hand. "The next time I see you at work, this never happened." She reached into her pocket and pulled out a tissue. She wiped the lipstick off her mouth and slowly ran her tongue over her lips. "I just don't want to be by myself." She reached past his open coat for his tie and gently pulled his face closer to hers. "And I don't think you do either."

Their lips touched lightly for only a second. Thomas locked his fingers together and caressed her back with his thumbs. He felt the strap of her bra and hoped that it wouldn't be too difficult to undo.

"You're right. I don't," he admitted.

The following week provided Thomas with a welcomed vacation. Both Glen and Heléna had gone out of town, so he relied on the company of other non-teaching friends. He enjoyed staying up late and sleeping until 9 a.m. He watched movies, sometimes at home and sometimes at a theater. Almost every day he visited Anthony's for a long workout and flirted with the prettiest female members, just for practice.

Although he enjoyed time away from the Adams, every day Thomas missed his children. He would hear a song on the radio and chuckle, for it reminded him of some amusing remark by Melvin, Connie or another pupil. At the mall, grocery store or some other location, he would furtively pursue a pre-adolescent youngster, suspecting that he had happened upon one of his students. However, each time, upon closer inspection, he was disappointed to discover that it was an impostor. Sometimes his children even occupied his unconscious life. One night he awoke from a nightmare in which he had lost sight of the entire class during a field trip. They could not be found anywhere. Thomas was so upset that nearly thirty minutes passed before he found it possible to sleep again.

During the middle of the week Thomas received a funny postcard from Glen in New York. He laughed out loud and pinned the card to his refrigerator door with a football-shaped magnet. The next day he listened several times to a voice message Heléna had left him from California. It contained nothing provocative or romantic on the surface, but hearing her voice pleased him greatly. He missed her company. The night they had spent together burned indelibly in his memory. At night when Thomas retired to bed, he wondered what it would be like to have Heléna next to him.

Inevitably, the February vacation ended. The first day back to school was one of the coldest of the year. The temperature at 8 a.m. was only in the teens, even though the sun furnished deceptively bright light.

Thomas felt very pleased to see his children again. He was greeted with a major group hug from most of the class. That morning the fastidious instructor checked homework carefully, taking twice the usual time. Three students were absent, including LaShonda. Except for Freddy, every student had returned with his or her vacation homework, even Cleopatra, who needed only one more point to finally extricate herself from the clutches of self-imposed exile called ISP. Thomas assured her and her buddy Melissa that he would convene a class meeting before the day ended.

But that afternoon the atmosphere in Room 217 shifted from hopeful to disappointed. Thomas seemed powerless to stop the change. It seeped into the space like the fading light of a sunset.

The teacher held his hands over his face. The tension in the classroom was palpably heavy. Twenty-four students sat in their seats, several with their hands folded. Others bore frozen frowns on their faces. The class meeting had not gone well for Cleopatra. Unlike others before her, Cleo found it difficult to suppress her stubborn pride. She stood in the center of the room, recalcitrant and hostile, making little eye contact. After a ten-minute grilling, her answers to questions had become curt and flat. Melissa pressed both hands against her face in disbelief. Thomas tried once more to coach the tall girl out of the corner into which she had painted herself.

"Cleopatra, think about this, honey," he pleaded. "Are you sure you don't have anything to say to the class?" He waved his opened hands. "Anything at all?"

"No."

Thomas pushed both hands against his forehead and sighed heavily. "Very well, my sister. It's your call." He gave the instructions to the class and

asked Melissa to stand shoulder to shoulder with her buddy. "One, two ..."
A few chairs began to drag. Thomas closed his eyes and called the last
number.

He opened his eyes and counted. Cleo needed thirteen votes. She received ten. He sighed heavily and announced the results. "I'm sorry, honey.
You don't have enough votes. You must remain on ISP for two more days
and receive a point for both days."

Cleopatra wrapped both arms around herself, doubled over with pain
and screamed. The shrill sound erupted so suddenly that several pupils
jumped in their seats. The sight brought sadness to everyone's heart. The
fact that the girl actually had expected to receive the endorsement of the
class without asking for it astonished Thomas. He called for DEAR while
he and Melissa helped his agonized pupil to her seat.

Thomas whispered to the dejected, defeated child as she collapsed at
her desk. "Sweetheart, why didn't you open up and let 'em in? Sure, they
demanded a lot," he admitted, "but not more than you could afford to pay."
He stroked her face with his hand, but she turned away from him. The girl
shook her head but said nothing. Thomas put his hand on her shoulder.
"It's okay, honey. Wednesday'll be here before you know it. But I hope
you'll think about how you acted during the class meeting and bring a new
attitude."

The next day Cleopatra came to school with none of her homework,
which pushed the point count for her expected return back to zero with
five to go. Students complained about her skipping past them in line or
purposefully stepping on their feet in the bathroom. After three incidents
Thomas insisted that she wait outside of the bathroom until every girl but
the monitor had vacated. One morning Melissa reported that Cleo had
called her house and whispered profanities at her. Cleo denied the charge.
Later that day Thomas had to step between the sullen girl and Freddy to
prevent a fight.

On the last day of the month Thomas counted the checkmarks on February
Ferdinand and was very pleased to have picked up another "in" seat. Twenty-
three students remained to watch the movie. Eight pupils had earned Superstar status—a record. Thomas loaded a plate with snack food, filled a
cup with fruit punch and strolled to the tiny library with five of the "usual
suspects." Ms. Higgins was only too happy to watch them. For the first time

in the school year, Francine was not among them. She wiggled in her seat, anxious to partake of the goodies *her favorite teacher*, Mr. Payne, had brought. During the middle of the film, the tall waiter approached her desk with deference. Francine raised her head.

"Would my first-timer like a second cup of juice?" he asked.

Francine clapped her hands and squealed with delight.

Later that day Thomas filled his briefcase and tote bags full of papers and walked down the side steps into the office. Marilyn Walker had gone home. He went to the counter to sign out and heard his name mentioned by Mr. Dorn. He recognized the other voice in the office as belonging to Ms. Flores. He knew it was wrong to eavesdrop, but the temptation proved to be too much. He could only make out Mr. Dorn's strong voice.

Thomas tiptoed out of the office and quietly left the building through the front door. After crossing the street to reach his car, he waved to two Adams children boarding a van. Self-satisfied, he smiled and replayed Mr. Dorn's sentiments in his head.

"He's done a great job with those kids. He was the right man at the right time with the right class."

March

The enclosed area next to the main office served as the Adams staff meeting room and telephone station. Technically, everyone referred to it as the nurse's office. It was small, cramped and smelly. Drops of water fell onto the nurse's desk, compliments of faulty pipes from the upstairs girls' bathroom. A tattered black leather sofa and several beat-up chairs afforded meager comfort to a sick child or congregating adults. The shades, old and as thin as tissue paper, provided minimum protection from the sun. The windows reluctantly slid up or down only by applying considerable force. The room offered little privacy. Teachers stood in line to use the phone or competed for use of the bathroom. (The teacher's lounge lavatory could only serve two customers at a time, and frequently one or both were out of order.) An occupant had to slide a brick against the bathroom door to prevent embarrassment.

The school nurse spent only two days a week at the Adams and had become accustomed to the interruptions. A soft-spoken, middle-aged woman originally from Jamaica, she supported three grown children in college and considered herself fortunate to have a job. (The Boston Public School Department historically offered only lip service to the notion that every school should have a full-time nurse.) At the Adams, when faced with frequently nonexistent medical staffing, teachers did the best they could with the one-hour training session on first-aid they had received in October.

Hence the background as Thomas struggled to become familiar with School Department procedures for securing special education services for needy students. He fought the urge to yawn while listening to the jargon-laced reports of the school evaluation team leader, or ETL. Ms. Wagner possessed a polite manner and a relaxed style. She was a former nun who dyed her hair red, smiled a lot and measured barely five feet tall. She got along well with the White employees and was unaware that the staff of color disliked her. The latter claimed that she evinced racism by talking to them as if they were children. Thomas found her manner due less to racism than a desire to avoid unpleasant personal interactions. He recognized the irony that the diminutive woman inadvertently created the very situation she tried so earnestly to prevent.

Other Adams professionals also attended the afternoon meeting: Assistant Principal Abigail Flores; Ms. Pela, the school nurse; and Ms. Little, the Adams's lone special education instructor. The latter, although a year younger than Thomas, stated her opinions as often as she could. The ETL chaired the meetings, but Ms. Little always did most of the talking. The second-year teacher insisted on proving her intelligence to everyone. She enjoyed reminding Thomas aloud of his junior status at the Adams and his ignorance of "procedures with respect to special education policies." He observed the ridiculous-looking thick orange and red hair atop her dark skin and mentally joked that she and Ms. Wagner visited the same hairdresser.

The meeting droned on for two hours, and Thomas grew anxious to get back to his room. Of the twelve students referred by Ms. Patterson for special ed, he believed that only three actually required such: Doug, Freddy and Melissa. The others, as far as he was concerned, demonstrated virtually no behavioral problems anymore and had gotten considerably behind in their work mostly due to years of goofing off. Thomas insisted that they primarily needed after-school and weekend tutoring and a kick in the backside from time to time. They also, he thought to himself, needed a system that responded to requests for aid in a timely manner.

For example, for five months he had waited but his class had not been summoned by the nurse for a routine vision and hearing screening. Frustrated, two weeks ago the rookie teacher tested the entire class himself. Seven failed! Perhaps, Thomas feared, part of the reason some had displayed such poor reading skills had to do with poor vision. He sent letters to the caretakers of the seven students and received information that three of them had been fitted with glasses before the beginning of the school year. With the exception of Carmelita, who was not one of the seven, he had never seen any student wearing glasses.

The tall man returned his attention to the nurse's office. The afternoon had provided insight into the bizarre logic of the special education qualification process. A cumbersome system hindered needy students from receiving services and prevented students no longer in need from ending their involvement.

Eventually the subject turned to Douglas Berry. Thomas tried to remain calm, but after 120 minutes the dirty walls had begun to close in on him. "I've got an eleven-year-old kid in my class who can't read. Will someone please tell me what we can do about this?"

"Well, Mr. Payne, I've already told you that the school psychologist determined last year that he had no discernible learning disability," Ms. Wagner replied softly with a smile. "What have you tried?"

"Well," Thomas explained. "The whole class goes to the library every other Friday, rain or shine. Doug picks out books and tapes on his level. And me and his mother agreed that his older sister would read aloud to him every day. Also, I personally review phonics material with the boy almost every day. Um …" He squeezed his face with his hand as he pondered other activities. "Oh yeah! Doug goes downstairs to the second-grade classroom to 'help out' for the first half of their reading class every day. And the boy's in an after-school program where he's been getting one-on-one tutoring for reading. I personally check on his progress." He paused, then decided that he would have to reveal the clandestine activity hatched with Heléna back in November. "Um, and he's kinda in the Reading Triple-O program."

"With Ms. Cooke?"

"Um, n-no, actually," Thomas stuttered. "With Ms. Gutiérrez." Silence followed the disclosure. The women looked at each other, then at the young man.

"Mr. Payne," Ms. Little began. "You are aware that she is the *bilingual* Reading One-On-One teacher here?"

"Well, yes," he replied. "But I had to get some help for my boy. I'm telling you, my guy couldn't read a word. It was so sad. The saddest thing I've ever seen." He offered some protection for his colleague. "Don't blame Ms. Gutiérrez. I asked her as a personal favor. She said okay because we're good friends and she cares about these kids here." Thomas knew he was whining but didn't know how to stop. "And it's a good thing she did, too."

The sun appeared from behind a cloud and shone through the dirty windows onto Ms. Little's countenance. She squinted her eyes. Her chemically-altered, near shoulder-length hair breathed rings of fire. The expression on her face made her look somewhat menacing. The special education teacher rolled her eyes and got to work. "Mr. Payne, we can all appreciate your good intentions, but we just can't do our own thing. You and your … *friend*, Ms. Gutiérrez, can't let your personal feelings—about the kids I mean— affect how we're suppose to do business at the Adams.

Thomas winced at the last sentence. Rumors about Heléna's and his relationship had been floating around the Adams for some time, even though the two of them had been careful. As agreed, after their blissful Valentine's rendezvous, they had subsequently acted as if the event never occurred, and had sworn each other to absolute secrecy. Heléna had even raised her right hand and placed her left one on a box of graham crackers as she took the oath.

Ms. Flores broke into Thomas's reflection, speaking in her usual unassuming way. "Mr. Payne, the program is divided between Spanish and English for a reason. Ms. Gutiérrez provides special assistance for the bilingual students here. The program is paid for with tax dollars. We have to justify its existence every year."

Thomas paused and bit his lower lip. He did not want to reveal that his friend had an extra non-duty period four times a week. "Yes, I understand. But Hel—Ms. Gutiérrez sees Doug on her own time."

Ms. Flores seemed satisfied with his explanation. She eased back into her chair and folded her arms. "I'll take this up with Mr. Dorn and get back to you. Perhaps he can pull some strings and get the boy into the program with Ms. Cooke."

Thomas could see that she wanted to be helpful. As long as Doug's tutoring didn't hurt the Spanish students, he surmised, the assistant principal's shapely ass would be sufficiently covered.

But Ms. Little proved to be more difficult to mollify. "Mr. Payne. I hope that you understand that we all have our jobs to do. I don't give eye exams, and Ms. Pela doesn't teach math. There's a way to do things here. Sometimes one can do more harm than good if he just goes off and flies solo."

Thomas waited to see if anyone in the room would come to his defense. After an uncomfortable silence, he tightened his grip on his shaky chair and decided to resort to the educator's standard line of platitudes. "You've all made some good points. I'm sorry if my efforts to obtain services for Doug has resulted in compromising any existing programs. We all want what's best for the kids. He's a good kid. I just couldn't let him fall through the cracks."

"None of us want that, Mr. Payne," Ms. Little replied.

The sister just had to have the last word, Thomas assessed.

Before the meeting adjourned, the group agreed that the students in Room 217 would get an *official* eye exam from Ms. Pela by the middle of the next week, and Melissa and Freddy would join Ms. Little's three other pupils for one hour of tutoring in her room during the reading period. They also agreed that for the time being, Doug could continue to be tutored by Ms. Gutiérrez. The other students would continue to be "monitored."

Thomas painted a smile on his face and conveyed to everyone how much he enjoyed working with them. Ms. Wagner accepted his invitation to be a guest at the next Student of the Week ceremony on Friday. She told him that she had heard such wonderful things about his class and looked forward to visiting. Thomas slipped out of the room and took several deep breaths.

The frustrated man reflected on the misanthropic special ed teacher and why she had been so difficult. He remembered that when they had first met in September, Ms. Little had told him how much he resembled her former boyfriend. The sister was actually quite attractive—if you didn't notice the one-hundred-pound chip on her shoulder. And she just plain talked too damn much. Twice Thomas had heard the young woman make scornful remarks about the White teachers at the Adams, especially Ms. Patterson and her "Uncle Tom" husband. He had overheard her talking to the Black teachers at the Adams about how she despised Black men like her ex who dated White women. Thomas hypothesized that because of his friendship with Heléna, a Venezuelan of light complexion, Ms. Little harbored hostility towards him. Come to think of it, her attitude had soured right after the Christmas party. As he walked down the littered second-floor hallway, he resolved to simply stay out of the woman's way.

Thomas opened the door to his room and observed over two dozen students seated, each holding a book. He visually surfed the enclosed space, re-examining the new classroom duds. He had hung fresh role model posters. A United States Supreme Court justice, a member of the President's cabinet, a newscaster, a novelist, a college president, a recording star and many others all offered silent encouragement to the students in Room 217. However, in the spirit of Women's History Month, the gallery consisted only of women.

A photograph of a distinguished-looking older gentleman, Mr. Davenport, had been added to the group of "coaches" on the wall above the main chalkboard. (He visited the fifth-grade class once or twice a week to instruct them on the noble game of chess.) Fourteen large green shamrocks hugged the student-closet doors. Each buddy pair had signed his or her name to one. And Thomas had adapted an idea stolen from his mentor: sheets of paper hung in many spots around the room. On the top half of each, a student had drawn and colored the cover of a favorite book. Underneath it, one could read a short paragraph explaining why he or she had chosen the book.

Thomas turned his attention to the back, near the classroom's woefully outdated computer. Doug, surrounded by a set of earphones, listened on an ancient cassette recorder to a book being read to him. The boy kept an unmarked package in his desk containing an audiobook or computer software. The primarily second-grade material often had pictures of smiling puppies or titles such as "Our Day at the Circus" in big letters. During DEAR, he carried the inconspicuous package to the back, donned earphones and either inserted a tape or a disc in the appropriate machine. He followed along with the written pages, which always rested snugly in his lap.

Thomas's eyes finally rested on his desk. A small-framed, dark-skinned Hispanic man with gold, wire-framed glasses and long hair sat quietly studying. He wore a black turtleneck sweater and blue jeans. Thomas read the man's name, Mr. Hyde, printed on the board in capital letters. The students had gotten quite a kick out of that, since they had just finished reading the last chapter of *The Strange Case of Dr. Jekyll and Mr. Hyde* the previous week. However, this Mr. Hyde was a master's-level student in art, who frequently served as a substitute teacher.

The substitute turned his head when the door opened. He stood and approached the chair's rightful owner, speaking with a slight accent. "Mr. Payne," he said reverently, with a smile on his face. "What delightful young brothers and sisters you have!"

Thomas beamed. "Thank you, Mr. Hyde. They are a great bunch." He inspected the man's attire. It would take some time to become acclimated to teachers dressing in such a manner, substitute or not. Still, the man seemed good-natured enough.

"Yes indeed, sir. We finished all the work you left us," the guest instructor exclaimed, pointing around the room. "They work hard. They raise their hands before they speak. You are to be congratulated for what you have done." He lowered his voice. "I had this bunch once last year; the longest day of my life." The little man spoke further. "Listen, this morning I was in another classroom; the fourth-grade down the hall." He shook his head sadly.

"Talk about kids with no respect! Something should be done about them. I had to send three of them to the office before lunch." He tapped his host on the arm. "I bet you'll make short work of them next year, eh?"

Thomas winked. "By Halloween you won't recognize them."

Mr. Hyde concurred, then grabbed his huge, dark-blue book bag and stepped to the door. Thomas walked with him and they shook hands. The artist commented on the meaningful decorations throughout the room, especially the contracts. He said good-bye to the students and closed the door.

Thomas praised his children. "Thank you for being so good while I was at my meeting. Maybe you deserve a few extra minutes added to recess tomorrow."

The youngsters immediately agreed.

Spotting something amiss, he wandered over to a student's desk. Hernando tilted his head upwards and recognized the signal—his teacher lightly tapping the side of his own face. The lad frowned, then reached into his desk and produced a small brown case. He freed his new glasses and put them on.

That evening Thomas sat on a chair folding the last pile of warm clothes from the dryer. Stacks of underwear, socks and sheets covered his large bed. A few feet away atop a four-feet-high Gabriel Payne-designed table, the Boston Celtics and the New York Knicks chased each other back and forth inside the frame of a thirteen-inch color television. A muffled sound prompted Thomas to search under a stack of towels to find the phone.

"Hey, dude. It's your brother," Edward opened. The two men talked while Thomas continued matching sock and sheet combinations. Edward reported that the FBI, Cincinnati Police and the Treasury Department had all sent flunkies out trying unsuccessfully to pump his friends and family for information about him. He sent word through his lawyer that if they wanted the straight dope, they'd have to spend cash on his book, due out around Christmas. "The Cincinnati Police doubled their original settlement offer after they heard that!" he declared with a hearty guffaw.

Thomas chuckled. "How's your new job?" he asked.

"So far, so good," his brother replied. "Some fine, lovely women there, too. If I wanted to, I could have any one of them there, no lie."

Thomas closed his eyes and shook his head nervously. "Now, Edward, don't go—"

"Don't worry, little brother," Edward assured him. "I said I *could*. I haven't and I won't. Now that doesn't mean that I've been lonely, by any means." He described the current two women with whom he was involved down to their measurements. "And how about your love life?"

"With work and all, there hasn't been much time for romance."

"There's always time for romance," Edward insisted. They both laughed. "Um, Thomas," he continued. "I suppose it's time for me to fly to Beantown and see how my favorite brother's faring on his own." He didn't wait for an answer. "It'd only be for the weekend. I can't go taking off work yet."

"Edward, I'm really glad that you—"

"You know, Thomas, I'm really proud of you for getting the hell out and striking out on your own."

Thanks, man. You know, I—"

"So how 'bout it?"

"Of course, Edward, I'd be thrilled." Thomas said sincerely. The two men made plans for the visit two weeks from the next weekend.

Finally, Edward spoke proudly about his daughters. "Guess what? Ebony's playing the violin like a pro, and Erika's taken up ballet. Man, you should see 'em. They're growing like weeds."

Thomas listened patiently and fought the urge to bring up a sensitive related subject. He decided that it could wait.

After the two said goodbye, Thomas reflected on his brother's words. The family man had reappeared at the end of their talk. Initially, "Big Ed" sounded more like his old self: arrogant, ambitious and lusty, the same attitudes that had gotten him into trouble. Thomas felt concerned. He looked at the clock on his bookshelf and decided against calling his parents. He resolved to call the next day and advise that everyone keep a close eye on Edward. As he opened drawers and closets to tuck away clothes, Thomas recognized that two-and-a-half years ago, he would have enjoyed Edward's description of his two female friends. He was ashamed to admit it, but he had been very tempted to match Edward's tales with details of his February 14 night with Heléna.

The following day Thomas sat at his desk taking attendance. Outside, clouds sprawled across the sky but upon close inspection, one could glean the round outline of the sun. As usual, the classroom required more heat than it received. Half of the students wore sweaters. After three days of neglect the

battered floor was reasonably clean, having been swept that very morning—
by Thomas Payne. He looked up and finally caught a glimpse of movement
near the infamous back row. LaShonda waved a note in the air. Thomas
instructed the Student of the Week to bring it to him. He read why LaShonda
had missed the previous day of school and frowned.

"Captain," he said, facing Angelica's buddy, Jessica. "Go hang the sign
on the door." He abruptly stood, threw the note on his desk and stared at
the area near the student closet, pondering his next move. The man slowly
waved his hand from side to side as if he were applying paint to a fence.
"The rest of you, clear your desks. I'm calling a brief class meeting right
now."

Chairs and desks rattled, shook and clanged as surprised students prepared for the event. The prospect of breaking up their routine invigorated
them more than the impending exploration of polygons. Low whispering
surfaced as the sound of heavy footsteps stopped at the center of the room.
Thomas rubbed his fingers on the corners of his mouth and further pondered his options. He faced the class, poised to speak. "I've decided to make
a few changes in the buddy situation after all," he declared, searching the
room. "Cleopatra," he pointed. "Your buddy is LaShonda now."

The class produced noise like rapid-firing thunder. Cleo put her hands
over her face. LaShonda put her thumb in her mouth. Thomas took several
deep breaths and continued. "Tyshaun, you've got Freddy now." Turning
from one side of the room to the other, he pointed again. "Doug, your buddy
is Melissa."

More noise erupted. A few students cackled and congratulated Doug on
his recent engagement and inquired as to the exact date of the wedding.
Doug simply put his head on his desk and ignored them, but a smile formed
on his lips.

Thomas delivered his final pronouncement. "Lakeisha, you and Janet
are buddies now. That oughta give you a shot at being Student of the Week
in the near future."

Lakeisha grinned and extended her short arms into the air. "Hallelujah!
Thank you, Mr. Payne!" she shouted.

Several members of the class applauded. After waiting for a few seconds, Thomas raised his hands to quiet them. Tyshaun, obviously upset over
the change, raised his hand. Thomas called on him.

"Mr. Payne, how come I get Freddy? I've been doing better."

Thomas put his hand on his mouth again and thought for a moment. He approached March MaryAnn and surveyed the evidence, then turned back to his concerned student. "True, Tyshaun, and I'm happy about that. But Maurice has shown more. We've waited for you all year." He opened his hands and called to the class. "Hey, you wait long …"

"You wait wrong!" they all shouted back at him.

"Sorry," Thomas said matter-of-factly as he stepped behind his wooden fortress. "I had to make a switch based on where everyone is right now." He shuffled some papers on his desk. "If you continue to improve, I'll do what I can for you, I promise. But I just couldn't allow things to continue the way they had been."

Tyshaun lowered his head.

Lakeisha sought and received permission to speak. "When do we start, Mr. Payne?" she inquired, hoping for a propitious answer.

"Right now."

"Thank you, Jesus! Thank you, Jesus!"

"That's enough, Lakeisha," Thomas ordered calmly. He felt regret for the students who had lost responsible buddies, but realized how unfair it was for solid students like Lakeisha and Janet to miss being selected Student of the Week time after time. He would have to rethink the Buddy Rule for next year. He heard noises in the back of the room—Freddy and Tyshaun apparently debating the merits of their new partnership. Thomas spoke without much force.

"I don't want to hear another sound out of either of you," he commanded. Tyshaun opened his math book, but his new buddy pointed and insisted on offering closing remarks. Thomas, with his head still lowered, raised his eyelids. "Close your mouth, Freddy. You had the best buddy in the class, but you didn't appreciate it."

Freddy fired back some kind of rebuttal. A few students blurted out, "Oooooh."

Thomas stood, clearly annoyed. Freddy could be contained, but the boy insisted on these little pissing contests. From time to time it became necessary to squash the twelve-year-old's peasant uprisings. Not to do so, the provisional teacher believed, would send the wrong message to his other students. The irritated man gestured as he spoke. "Freddy, shut your mouth or spend the rest of the morning in Mr. Bennett's room, sitting in a corner. You've picked the wrong day to mess with Mr. Payne!" Even from where they sat, the occupants of the back row could see the fire in their teacher's eyes.

All heads turned toward Freddy. He lowered his. No further sound came from him.

"While we're at it …" Thomas added. "LaShonda, I want to see you at lunch."

All eyes shifted to the other side of the back row. LaShonda removed her thumb from her mouth.

The morning's math period came and went. As usual whenever new material was presented, most of the class struggled. Clearly, they had previously been taught nothing about geometry. They had no knowledge of terms such as octagon or quadrilateral. Thomas broke the day's activities into smaller pieces so that as many as possible could understand, and presented only half of the lesson he had originally planned.

The students showcased better aptitude during the reading period. For the past three days they had digested a thirty-page story from their textbooks. Back in November, Thomas had divided them into five groups, referring to them as teams. The students gathered into these permanent groups to read aloud the previous day's assignment. Thomas would flutter about like a hummingbird from group to group, watching individual students read, making notes in his grade book. One student from each group was appointed leader for the day. The teams contained a mixture of reading talent. Finally, each team had chosen its own name based on selections from the animal kingdom.

After allowing the class a half-hour to review as much of the story as they could, Thomas went to the board and wrote the names of each team, then launched right into posing questions. The rules were simple but challenging: all five or six members of a group had to raise their hands in order to be acknowledged. The first team with *every* member's hand straight up was chosen to answer the question. (This prevented the slower readers from being reduced to mere spectators during the game. It also nudged the better readers to assist their teammates in finding the answers.) The moderator would call the group's name and call on one member to give the answer. If he or she answered correctly, that group received a point. Thomas would record the point under the group's name on the board and move on to the next question.

By design, the day's ordeal had been tough. To keep the game close,

Thomas always manipulated on whom he called. If a team fell behind the others, he would wait a few seconds before calling on another to see if it could catch up. Melvin's group, the Lions, tended to always be in the chase for first place. However, Carmelita's gang, the Ducks, had won the last two out of three games. By the time Thomas came to the last question, three teams led with the same number of points. The Bears and Cobras had been eliminated.

Thomas wanted to finish soon. The activity had generated an unusual amount of window-shaking, raucous noise for the past twenty minutes. He had warned his neighbor a day in advance about "Animal House Games," but did not want to take advantage of Mrs. Chang's good nature. He spoke loudly.

"Okay, it's between Lions, Ducks and Elephants now, with six points each. The team to answer this one correctly is the winner!" Thomas cleared his throat. "Number twenty-eight: Why did the Princess decide to give the gold back to the poor family?"

Book pages swooshed as students searched. Within a few seconds, Melvin pointed to a spot on a page, whispered something to Hernando and raised both their hands. Hernando agreed and did likewise for a teammate seated next to him. Across the room, Deborah and all but two Elephants frantically waved their hands. The Ducks had gotten off to a slow start but one by one, Carmelita and company indicated that they had the answer.

Thomas coyly reminded the class of the rules. "*Every* hand on the team's gotta be up or no deal." He closed his book and took two steps toward his desk. "Maybe I should declare a three-way tie."

Shouts of "No! No!" filled the room. Eventually, every eligible hand pointed at the water-stained ceiling. Then Carmelita started to quack and was joined by her teammates. Melvin and the Lions answered with a roar. They were challenged by the trumpeting sound of the Elephants. Not to be left out, the Cobras hissed and the Bears growled.

Within seconds, the door to the adjacent classroom slowly cracked open, and Mrs. Chang's head and right shoulder appeared. She saw that the children all wore huge smiles on their faces and exhibited obvious excitement about something. The quacking and roaring and whatnot seemed to be good-natured.

"Are we disturbing you, Mrs. Chang?" Thomas asked sincerely.

The woman shook her head. Over the sounds of near-muted giggling, she answered. "No, not at all, Mr. Payne. I was just … curious, I guess." She disappeared and closed the door, withdrawing to the more sedate atmosphere of Advanced Work Class.

Everyone in Room 217 laughed hysterically. The ringmaster raised his hands. "Okay," he continued. "I think Lions, Ducks and Elephants got the answer at the same time."

The noise level exploded again as members of all three groups clamored that they had discovered the answer before the others. The Bears and Cobras offered their opinions as to which team had been first, thus heightening the atmosphere of enthusiasm. Thomas twisted his mouth. "Hmmmm, I think …" He looked around. All eligible participants waved their hands and yelled, "Right here!" or "Mr. Payne!" Thomas continued. "*Elephants* were a little ahead of you." The other two groups screamed, "No! No!" Thomas held up his hands and the room grew quiet enough to hear the man's voice.

"Well, how about it, Elephants? Do you know or don't you?"

The six students vigorously nodded and answered affirmatively.

"Okay, Thomas said. "I'll ask … *Napoleon* if he knows." A hush fell over the room. Brian, the former Tiny Tim in *A Christmas Carol*, had been struggling in reading. He tried, but previous years of being remiss about studying (and not wearing his glasses for the first six months of school) had repeatedly returned to haunt him. Thomas could have called on Deborah or one of the others, but he had noticed Brian's recent improvement. The teacher repeated the question. "Why did the Princess return all of the gold to the poor family?" Every contestant in the room took a deep breath.

Brian widened his eyes and spoke calmly. "Because she was in love with their son?"

"Ah-Ah-Ah! Don't ask me. Tell me," Thomas replied.

"Because she was in love with the oldest son," the boy repeated, his voice more certain.

Thomas blinked his eyes. His face showed no emotion, and his eyes drooped as if he had grown sleepy. He yawned, covering his mouth with his hand, then spoke. "Yep."

The Elephants broke into wild cheers and laughter, then got out of their seats and danced. Again they launched into their personal cheer—a high-pitched elephant trumpet sound—while holding their noses and shaking their heads. A few Lions and Ducks frowned. Some scowled at their fellow teammates, remembering the delivery of earlier incorrect answers against the advice of counsel. A classmate started chanting "Brian! Brian!" as was the customary honor for the pupil who had settled a tie-breaker. Eventually, almost everyone joined in. Thomas expressed admiration to each group for a job well done and gently chided the Bears and Cobras for not playing together as a team. As the students returned to their seats, Brian received several pats on the back.

Twenty minutes later Thomas leaned in his chair just enough to rock without falling. The sun shone more brightly. Several rows of empty desks witnessed the private meeting between the frequently absent girl and her frustrated teacher. LaShonda stared at his tie and anxiously waited to hear the reason for her summons. Thomas pushed his feet against the worn floor and rocked in a rapid jerking motion. He picked up a piece of paper with two sentences scribbled on it, read it and threw it back on his desk. Finally, the troubled man broke the silence. Due to the earlier reading-class game, his voice sounded a little hoarse.

"LaShonda, you've missed nineteen days of school so far this year. Nineteen!" he announced, tapping his grade book. "That's more than anyone else in the whole—more than my next three most absent students combined." He fumbled with papers on his desk. "You're falling way behind in your schoolwork. I don't know how I can send you to middle school. You're just missing too doggone much school!" His voice squeaked towards the end. He got up and pulled a chair next to his desk and beckoned the girl to sit. She did and he continued. "Honey, I've got to ask you: where are you when you're not here?"

LaShonda looked at the ground. Thomas pulled his chair closer to hers. "LaShonda, please. I don't like messin' in your business. You know I don't like to interfere, but I want to help." He took a deep breath and reduced his volume to a near whisper. "Please, tell me, where are you when you're not in school?"

The dark-skinned girl scratched her head. Fixing her gaze on the floor's many scuff marks, she parted her lips and mumbled a short reply. "At home."

Thomas put his hand on his chin and rubbed his smooth face. "Doing what?" he asked. "And please don't insult me by giving me that story about asthma." He knew he was taking a substantial risk to imply that LaShonda's health was not the real reason for her absences. He had just called her mother a liar. If the girl clung to her story and reported their conversation to her mom, he would have his head handed to him by Dorn.

"Taking care of my little brothers and sister—and my cousin," LaShonda confessed. Her face still displayed little emotion.

"Keep going, sweetie. I'm listening."

The child put her thumb in her mouth, then took it out again. "My mother and my aunt are at work. They work late. Sometimes they don't get home 'til late in the morning, so I have to stay home and take care of my brothers and sisters and my cousin." She shrugged her shoulders and the tone of her voice went up at the end, as if she had just explained a simple matter. Still no discernible emotion appeared on her face.

Thomas's eyes widened as he sat erect in his chair. "What time do your mom and aunt leave for work?" He was no longer annoyed but very concerned.

"At nine."

"At night?"

She nodded.

"And what time are they suppose to get home?"

"At around 6:30."

"In the morning?" Thomas watched his student wiggle her head again. He put his hand on his forehead as if he had a fever. "Sweetie, why don't they get home at 6:30 then?"

"My mom says sometimes Mr. Charlie makes 'em stay late."

Thomas rolled his eyes. The girl was obviously unaware that "Mr. Charlie" was a racial slur and not her mother's supervisor's real name. He reached in his desk and shuffled a set of three-by-five cards, separating one from the batch for review. Besides the usual family information—address, phone number, et cetera—Dolores Walker had indicated that she was unemployed. "How long has your mom been working there, honey?"

LaSahonda's shoulders moved up, then down.

Thomas paused for a few seconds, then continued. "LaShonda," he began gingerly. "Who's with you and your brothers, sister and cousin at night when you're asleep?" His heartbeat accelerated.

No sound came from the girl's mouth. She brought her thumb to her face, then lowered it. After an entire morning of no activity, the heating system finally kicked in, forcing warm air into the uncomfortably cold room. LaShonda shook her head from side to side and pursed her lips. Finally, she answered. "Nobody."

Thomas took a deep breath and slowly arose. He prepared to ask another question but looked at his watch and motioned for his uncomfortable student to accompany him to the door. "Sweetie, you have to eat lunch, and I have to talk to Mr. Dorn about this."

LaShonda's faced tightened up like a head of dry lettuce. She jumped up, grabbed Thomas by the arm and pleaded with him. "No, Mr. Payne! My mama told me not to tell anyone. She said that she could get in a lot of trouble, that she could go to jail! Please. Please!"

Thomas put his arms around his frightened student and she responded by embracing him. He wasn't sure how to respond and struggled to find the right words. "Honey, I have to. Now you know I'm always honest with my kids. The truth is I've already been questioned by some people from DSS, the Department of Social Services and—"

Just mentioning the agency brought terror to the girl's heart. She squeezed him tighter and begged even more. "Please, Mr. Payne! My mama said that they would take us away from her and make us live with my father if they found out. I don't wanna live with my father, Mr. Payne. His girlfriend hits us. Please, Mr. Payne!" Streams of tears fell onto the scarred floor.

Thomas held her by the shoulders and pulled her at arms length. He stared at her water-filled eyes. "Honey, it's dangerous for you to be home overnight by yourself with four little children." He separated himself from her, went to his desk and returned with a box of tissue. "By law, I can't keep this to myself. I have to tell Mr. Dorn." He reached for her and straightened a few strands of her hair, then took her by the hand and walked her to the door. "LaShonda, you're going to have to trust that I'll do what's right. And I'll do everything I can to keep your family from knowing that you told me, okay?" He put his hand under her chin and gently lifted it. "Will you trust me?"

Her head moved a centimeter just once before she returned her gaze to the ground.

The two descended the stairs to the lunchroom. The children of Room 217 had just finished eating and cleaning their three tables. The Hispanic lunch mother gave the Student of the Week the signal to go ahead and line up by the backdoor. Over 160 energetic students were anxious to go outside. The smell of cooked food left a bad taste in Thomas's mouth. He could see Ms. Flores on the other side of the cafeteria, leaning over a wastebasket and pointing while a fourth-grader placed trash inside. Neither she nor the child looked very pleased. It was a purely symbolic gesture. Trash lay all over the floor. The noise in the cafeteria was deafening, as always. About a dozen students roamed about the area; some wandering in and out of the bathrooms. The custodian lifted bales of trash out of huge drums and lined them with empty bags. Occasionally he paused to tell a student to get out of his way.

Thomas and LaShonda walked toward the director of food services. He informed the tired woman that he had made his pupil late and asked that she be served. Then he directed the girl's new buddy to stay inside with her. Cleopatra, who hadn't earned recess anyway, plopped down next to LaShonda and opened a book. LaShonda ate quietly. Thomas put his hands on the child's shoulder and told her that everything would be all right. He inspected her lunch and made a face because he could not identify the brown and red food items on her plate.

The troubled fifth-grade teacher quickly walked the two flights of stairs to the office and stopped at the principal's open door. Mr. Dorn sat in the corner by the large window staring hypnotically at a computer screen. The place still looked the same except that instead of tools, several stacks of reports now rested on the conference table. The principal glanced at the intruder for a second and grunted. Thomas spoke emotionally about the events of the past few minutes. Mr. Dorn, surprisingly calm, told the young man to send the girl to his office after lunch. Thomas agreed, then marched across the hall and relayed his story to Glen. His mentor forcefully suggested that he speak to Mona Caine, the head of the Faculty Senate and the Boston Teachers Union building representative. Thomas found the building matriarch and briefed her on his student's plight. She calmly suggested what actions he should take.

Within fifteen minutes after the end of recess, LaShonda returned to the classroom looking relaxed and clutching a chocolate bar. For the remainder of the day, Thomas watched the girl as he taught. She showed no sign of distress.

An hour after school had closed, the tense rookie teacher crept into the office. Ms. Walker giggled while whispering on the phone. Mr. Dorn's door was ajar, but Thomas could not muster up the nerve to interrupt again. Instead he gave Ms. Flores two letters, one for her and one for the principal. They chatted for a few minutes about its content. Upon hearing Mr. Dorn's voice and seeing the back of the man's dark-brown suit through his slightly opened door, Thomas excused himself and hurried out of the office.

He spent an unusual amount of time at Anthony's, then wandered around a very well-lit local mall to shop for new clothes, something he had put off since Christmas. He finally drove home, reaching the stairs to his apartment at nearly 8:30 toting an armful of shopping bags. The tired man nearly stumbled into the ironing board he had left standing that morning. Yesterday's dishes lay submerged under several gallons of stale dishwater. Thomas investigated a low humming sound. Although its screen was black, he had inadvertently left his computer running after faxing a document. He turned it off, then threw the mail on top of his dinette table and checked his calls. Among other familiar voices, the principal of the Adams had called and left his home number. A little after 9 o'clock, the telephone rang. The apprehensive teacher read the number on his caller-ID box and recognized it as belonging to Phillip Dorn. He did not pick it up and the headmaster left no message.

The following morning as he took attendance, Thomas felt a sudden draft as the door to his classroom swung open. Mr. Dorn offered no greeting but motioned for him to step into the hall. Ms. Flores stood behind him. The older man's face was tight and strained. The assistant principal looked worried. Thomas took a deep breath as fear tapped his heart. Still, as impassively as possible, he turned the room over to the Student of the Week, then slowly marched out into the hall and greeted his visitors. The spot where they stood was chilly and shadowy. The string of lights on that end of the hall had blown out on the previous morning. The smell of urine from the unkempt boys' and girls' bathrooms permeated the corridor. Ms. Flores made sniffing noises, but Mr. Dorn ignored her and produced a piece of paper.

"What's the meaning of this?" he inquired with clenched teeth.

Thomas glanced at the paper and immediately recognized it. He felt nervous and uncomfortable but attempted to appear unfazed, answering softly. "It's a letter."

"I can see that it's a letter, Mr. Payne. Don't be cute." Mr. Dorn snapped. "I mean why did you write it?"

Thomas excused himself and informed the Student of the Week that he would be just outside the door. He asked the students to go over their math or review the play they had been assigned to read. Then the apprehensive young man returned to his unexpected company. He tilted his head to catch a glimpse at Ms. Flores, crouching slightly behind Mr. Dorn. Her eyes revealed resigned helplessness. After school yesterday she had thanked him for being so concerned about one of his students. Today she was conspicuous for her reserve and deference. Thomas attempted to provide a coherent reply to his supervisor's question.

"Well, after we talked yesterday, I wanted to follow up with a letter so that you could have as many details as you needed before you took action." He made a clumsy attempt to change the subject. "Is there any word? What's going to happen to LaShonda?"

"I'm working on it," Mr. Dorn answered coldly. "How come you sent a copy of the letter to DSS? I'm the principal here." His piercing eyes burned through Thomas's blank expression and melted his outwardly calm facade.

"Because I told him to," replied a confident voice.

The three educators turned and observed Ms. Caine approaching, her footsteps all but imperceptible. She wore a medium-length dark-burgundy dress and shoes with flat heels. She placed her five-feet, two-inch frame next to her colleague and looked up at him. From a distance they looked like a father and his daughter. Her eyes revealed poise and determination. "Does my union brother wish to have representation at this time?"

"Um, why yes, thank you," Thomas answered.

"Good morning, Ms. Caine. Where's your class?" Mr. Dorn asked. Thomas noticed that his voice had lost much of its harshness.

"They're having art and music. I'm on my planning and development time," she replied, rubbing her hands together to warm them. "I'm under the impression that my brother has been summoned without notice and without union representation during his active teaching time. There are two administrators present, but has he been informed that he could request to have the BTU building representative present?" She did not wait for an answer. "Although he recognizes that this is not a discipline matter, he's wondering if he might be allowed to postpone this conference and return to his room. He would be happy to answer any written inquiries you wish to make or sit down with one or both of you with proper notice." She stared at the two administrators, a slight smile beginning to form on her face.

Mr. Dorn looked at his watch. "No, that won't be necessary, Ms. Caine. I found out what I needed to know. You've been very helpful." His eyes moved from one teacher, then to the other. "You can go back to your rooms now… Both of you." He turned and walked towards the center stairwell with Ms. Flores following.

Thomas inhaled deep gulps of air and grabbed his savior's hand. "Wow!" he exclaimed softly. "You were wonderful! How do you get away with talking to him like that?"

Ms. Caine ran her fingers through her salt-and-pepper-colored hair. "Like what?" she replied stolidly. "I'm the building rep. That's my job."

"You won't get in trouble?" Thomas asked, a little concerned.

"Yeah, he'll make sure that I don't get some supplies or something later on, but I've been here for years, and I've accumulated everything I need, mostly by spending my own money. That's why he doesn't scare me. I don't need anything from him."

Thomas cracked the door to his room and peeked in on the class. Everyone sat quietly, at least appearing to be involved in some academic task. He continued with Ms. Caine. "How'd you know Dorn was up here bustin' my ba—I mean, giving me a hard time?"

The third-grade teacher scratched the side of her face and smiled. "Oh, a little bird told me." Abruptly, she changed the subject. "Has this happened often? You know, unscheduled meetings with him without a building rep present?"

Thomas grimaced with embarrassment. "Um, yeah. Lots of times."

Ms. Caine closed her eyes as if she were suddenly seized with pain, then opened them again. She muttered to herself, "These new kids today," sounding just like another seasoned teacher Thomas knew very well. She shook her finger at him half-seriously. "Well, from now on, if Dorn wants to see you, put him off and see me or call the BTU Office and ask for Gwen Letterman. She's the elementary field rep for BTU. They're good for union contract matters but not worth two cents on anything to do with race. This was a contract matter. If you do get cornered and he starts asking questions, ask for a building rep and don't say anything. Okay, hon?"

He nodded.

Ms. Caine looked at her watch. "I gotta go." She started to leave but suddenly stopped and pointed at the classroom door. "Your class really in there? I had them two years ago; the longest ten months of my life."

Thomas smiled. "Sure, they're in there. Go take a peek."

She cracked the door and spied on Room 217, looking very different than when Ms. Blufford occupied it. She liked the way the place had been arranged and decorated. Manly, but effective. And there they were, the source of such discomfort two years before, every one sitting quietly, reading or studying. Asa, who now sat near the door, caught the sight of his former third-grade teacher and waved. She waved back and closed the door. The veteran teacher reached up, placing her hand on Thomas's broad left shoulder. "Extraordinary! That man better hang on to you." With those words, she strutted down the hall.

The following week LaShonda did not appear at the Adams on Monday, Tuesday or Wednesday. On the third day of her absence, Thomas asked Marilyn Walker about her niece, but the secretary coolly informed him that she could not discuss the matter. After school that same day, when he presented her with a card for his missing student signed by the entire class, Ms. Walker reluctantly accepted the item, only offering to "see what she could do."

Thursday morning Thomas asked his class if anyone knew anything about the child. Connie, who sometimes walked to school with LaShonda, raised her hand.

"Ain't nobody seen her since last Friday."

Thomas spotted other hands. "Do you know anything, Freddy?"

The boy took a deep breath and shrugged his shoulders. "My aunt told me that all the kids at 'Shonda's house got put in a foster home." The boy shook his head sadly. "Sometimes foster homes are bad places for kids." Several students agreed.

Thomas called on the next student. "Go ahead, Angelica."

"Maybe you or someone else should call the police."

He approached the girl and put his hand on her shoulder. "I'll talk to someone. I promise."

It wasn't so much LaShonda's absence that concerned them, but not knowing the girl's fate disturbed the harmony in the environment. For example, every day Cleo had to be assigned a temporary buddy.

On Friday morning Lakeisha whispered to her classmates that she had called LaShonda's house, but the number had been disconnected. This caused further rumor-mongering about the girl's whereabouts.

Toward the middle of the next week, after LaShonda's eighth absent day, Thomas stopped by the office to check his mail, as he did every day during lunch. He discovered a short, handwritten note from Mr. Dorn requesting that he clean out the missing girl's desk and send her cumulative record folder to the office; LaShonda Walker would not be returning. The junior staff member personally questioned Mr. Dorn about his now former student.

The principal only revealed that the matter was out of his hands. The aloof man took a couple of steps away, then stopped and spoke in Thomas's general direction. "People have been advising you about doing your own thing, but as an impetuous newcomer, you just didn't take heed."

Thomas clutched his mail tightly and stepped closer to his supervisor. "What do you mean by that?" He pointed at himself. "It's not my fault about the girl's home life. I just did my job. Thank God for 'impetuous newcomers' who aren't afraid to stick their necks out for one of our kids!"

Marilyn Walker pretended to examine a supply inventory. Ms. Valdez stuck her hand in her mailbox again to ensure that she had collected all of her mail. Fortunately for both men, Glen had entered the office in time to witness their exchange and found an excuse to all but drag his mentee across the hall.

Later that same afternoon after every Room 217 pupil returned from a meal of chicken fingers and potato tots, Thomas broke the news. The class became upset and agitated that a member of their family, even one who had been less than exemplary, would simply disappear without any kind of farewell.

"How come LaShonda didn't stop to get her things or say good-bye?" Melvin asked.

"Sometimes when something bad happens and you have to go live in a foster home, you have to leave things behind and start all over," Freddy replied.

"Will she be back at all, Mr. Payne?" Jessica inquired.

"Last year 'Shonda told me she wanted to run away from home and go live with her grandmother in Virginia," Cleopatra reported.

The mood shifted significantly when Hernando pointed across the room and declared with a scowl, "This is your fault, Lakeisha, for being so mean and selfish to LaShonda. She was your buddy!" His castigation evoked similar sentiments from others.

Lakeisha protested over their clamoring. "I didn't do nothing! I tried to help her, but she wouldn't listen to me!" Her remarks generated even more hostile reactions from the distressed group.

"This isn't helping!" Thomas exclaimed, breaking up the fracas. Lakeisha and a couple of classmates continued quarreling. "Listen to me!" he commanded forcefully. "During tough and challenging times like these, the team has to stick together."

No said a word.

"I'll let you know if I hear anything. I promise," he assured them.

To provide closure for those now left behind, Thomas set aside time for everyone to write a farewell letter to LaShonda. He retrieved one of her pictures from a previous bulletin board display and erected it on her desk. With the song, "Unforgettable" playing in the background, each student paraded one by one past the girl's desk and delivered a personal farewell note. Thomas promised that somehow he would see to it that she got them.

"Can we say a prayer for her, Mr. Payne?" Angelica petitioned.

Thomas scratched his face. "A moment of silence would be better."

At home a day later, two weeks after LaShonda's disappearance, Thomas received a telephone call from a female friend who attended his church and worked for DSS. She confirmed to her Christian brother that a LaShonda Walker and her brothers, sister and a cousin had all been placed in foster homes. Thomas expressed gratitude for the leak and assured his fellow parishioner that no one would ever discover that they had spoken.

Although it was unreasonable and unproductive, he spent the rest of the evening blaming himself for writing the letter that obviously had resulted in the girl being separated from her mother. He lost his appetite and could not concentrate on his work. Eventually, the distressed teacher called California and requested from Peter, his Revelations, Inc. buddy, a few minutes of solid coaching.

That Friday evening Thomas bobbed and weaved through traffic after making a pick-up at the always busy Logan Airport. Automobiles of all sizes, shapes and costs lined the highway as far as the eye could see. The long, parallel lines of winding taillights and headlights indicated that the journey would be tedious. An unseasonably warm temperature accompanied the raindrops splattering on the windshield of the red sportscar. The wipers, rocking in unison, did not mix well with the sounds of the constantly changing radio stations. At 7:30 the shifting music inside and bumper-to-bumper traffic outside gave Thomas a headache. He reached under his seat, retrieved a music disc and slid it into the player. Sarah Vaughan belted out a sassy tune. Edward frowned but relaxed in his seat.

Thomas felt such pride that his big brother had taken the time, trouble and expense to visit for the first time. Edward had not paid such homage during Thomas's early college years, and by the time he had donned an OSU football jersey, trouble in Cincinnati had begun. Now, Big Ed was in town—and in top form, too. Been back to the gym. Thomas sighed with relief that his brother had survived his ordeal and landed on his feet. It would take more than a few years in the can to keep Edward Payne down, thank you very much. And the two looked quite dashing together in their suits and ties. Edward's combination was especially dapper—a charcoal-colored number cut with a silver tie (imported Italian silk, of course).

Edward sat next to his brother, taking in the environment. That shenanigans with the radio was just his attempt to test the territorial boundary lines. He tapped the dashboard and commented on their father's handiwork. The men attempted to recall exactly how many cars their dad had restored and given away.

"There was Mom on her birthday," Edward recalled

"You on your birthday," Thomas remembered, pointing.

"Vanessa for college graduation—then Grandma for her birthday."

"You again after the accident," Thomas said.

"Then you after you graduated from Ohio State."

"Then Mom again for their anniversary."

"Then me last year after I got out," Edward acknowledged. He pointed at Thomas. "Guess what? He's doing another one!"

"For who?"

"You know Dad never tells."

The men knew their father well. Although he didn't say much in words, he sure said plenty by building and repairing things for the people he loved. Who could forget that backyard playground he had designed and constructed for their sister's kids?

After a short stop at the apartment to freshen up, Thomas took Edward to the Chinese restaurant where Glen had revealed his secret. The place was full that evening but still comfortable. Edward spent several minutes admiring the huge aquarium. He watched dozens of multi-colored creatures in their exquisite robes swimming about without a care in the world. Staring at the constantly moving fish, Edward looked like one of the first-graders at the Adams, Thomas thought. Eventually, a cute teenage female in low heels with a face like a bunny rabbit approached the gentlemen. Softly, she informed them that their table was ready. Edward awoke from his trance and vowed to have a similar tank installed at home when he returned to Ohio. The girls would get a kick out of it.

During dinner Thomas showed off his proficiency with the chopsticks. Edward gave the effort his best shot but reluctantly abandoned his quest and requested a fork. A few minutes into their meal Thomas decided to speak to his brother about a subject they had never previously discussed.

"Um, Edward," the youngest Payne said quietly. "Have you decided what you're going to do, uh, about your other daughter? You know, the one in the Netherlands?" He scooped up a clump of fluffy white rice and put it in his mouth, but had unexpected trouble swallowing it.

Edward continued to eat without breaking his rhythm. After getting out of prison, he had relearned how to eat at a leisurely pace. He looked at his brother indifferently. "What do you mean?"

"Well, you know. It looks like you've got a daughter in Amsterdam, and I've got a niece there. I was just wondering if she's been on your mind or anything, that's all." Thomas grabbed a bottle of soy sauce, turned it upside down and waved it over his food only once because his meal didn't really need any.

Edward shrugged his shoulders. "What? My little girls here ain't suffered enough, huh?"

Thomas immediately became defensive and apologetic. "Oh God yes, Edward. You know that I wouldn't want them to be hurt. But you know, Mom and Dad used to always say that if you brought a child into this world you had to do the right thing." He reached for the soy sauce again but just read the label and set it down. "Um, the little thing didn't mean to cause any trouble. And I know you wouldn't want her to be hurt either. But I've got to admit, sometimes I wonder how she's doing." Thomas said nothing further, fearing that he had gone too far.

Edward's face indicated no emotion as he laid his fork down. "Look, it's like this: When I was on the force, I got offered all the pussy a man could want. I'm talking about stuff that would make any man's mouth water. Young, beautiful stuff. Most of the time, I turned it down. Sometimes I didn't. It had nothing to do with April. She was a good wife and mother, but … I don't know. I spent so much time away from home. You don't know how it is when you're on the job." He picked up his fork and dragged a scallop into a shrimp. "I'm not saying it's right, but you know about cops and broken marriages. Anyway, contrary to the published reports, Breanna's mother—that's the kid's name—Breanna's mother was *not* my mistress. I only fucked her a couple of times. That's the God's honest truth. I swear." He raised his right hand, then lowered it. "Anyway, man, I'm tellin' you, no one was more surprised than me when that test came back and said that I was the girl's father. I thought, shit, what a rotten break! I'm fucked, now."

Thomas opened his hands. "So what you going to do about her?"

Edward took a deep breath. "It's already taken care of. I'm sending the girl money every month on the sly through a lawyer." He saw the shift in his brother's expression and fought to maintain eye contact. "Don't look at me like that. She's doing fine. The money I send goes a long way. It's a lot of money there."

Thomas rested his face on the back of his hands for a few seconds and took a sip of his soft drink. The ice had melted and the soda had lost its flavor. He made a face, then re-engaged with Edward. "I'm sure that the money helps, man. But don't you want to see her? You know, hold her in your arms and stuff? Have her meet her sisters?"

Edward's eyes grew huge. His thick eyebrows nearly met and a scowl formed on his face. "What? Are you fuckin' nuts? After all everyone's been through? I can't upset things here—Mom and Dad, you, Erika and Ebony—over what? Some stray?"

"Edward, she's your daughter."

"I've done as much as I can." His tone indicated irritation.

Thomas recognized the change and wisely let the matter drop. He did not agree with his brother's decision but understood that Edward had been through hell and back. As the baby of the family who had suffered little in his life, he felt he had no right to judge. Knowing exactly what to say to change the mood, he asked again about Edward's new job and held on to his seat.

The men spent virtually every minute of the following day together. They skipped breakfast and went to a gym, where a few of Thomas's friends, including Glen, joined them in a game of basketball. Edward aggressively held his own against men five to ten years his junior. Later, the two sat around the apartment, watching television and telling stories about their past athletic feats. Edward had been a college baseball star; an award-winning third baseman. Both men congratulated themselves for the sagacity to avoid pursuing the professional athlete illusion. They counted on two hands the number of former teammates now careerless, broke and bitter.

That evening they took out on the town, attending the dance club Thomas and Heléna had visited on Valentine's Day. It was a huge place with three dance floors. One could take in live jazz, Black dance music or Latin tunes. The door staff enforced a strict dress code, so the whole atmosphere evinced class and money. Dazzling women of all nationalities roamed everywhere. Dashing gentlemen posed and bragged about their occupations. Serious looking broad-chested male and female security guards, clad in tuxedos and carrying walkie-talkies, mingled with the crowd. Busy bartenders strained to hear orders shouted over competing voices and mixing songs. Spanish, English, Creole, French and other languages blended with the music. Lights blinked on and off, music thumped and patrons laughed. Interested parties sized each other up and plotted their means of capture or escape. Edward found the place to be absolutely wonderful. He wandered about aimlessly, approaching several women for dances. Thomas noticed that his brother almost always chose very young women, barely old enough to gain admittance to the establishment.

Almost a half-hour into their excursion, Thomas spotted Heléna and her roommate, Karen. He recognized the latter from the pictures in their apartment. Baby-faced, short but curvaceous, the English teacher wore a sexy red jumpsuit. Heléna was stunningly beautiful. She had thrown her hair totally to one side and wore a long, black dress exposing her silky-smooth shoulders and back. Men stared at both of them as they waltzed by. Thomas introduced the women to his brother. After a few minutes of obligatory small talk on how attractive everyone looked, Edward disappeared with Heléna for a spin on the Spanish dance floor. After a few minutes he returned and whisked away with Heléna's roommate. When they returned, the women excused themselves to freshen up.

Edward grabbed his brother's arm. "Thomas, anything goin' on between you and that fine, drop-dead gorgeous cutie-pie you work with?"

The younger Payne felt a surge of apprehension. "Um, well, kinda, Edward. We're just getting started, you know." He shrugged his shoulders. "I mean, we're slightly involved."

"No problem," Edward declared, patting his brother on the back. "I'll just take the other one then."

When the women returned, Thomas held onto Heléna's arm while the four of them talked. Finally, the two Adams workmates marched in the direction of the music. They swayed, twisted and laughed to a half-dozen energetic Latin selections, but upon hearing the first few bars of a slow number, Thomas took Heléna's hand and led her off the floor, explaining that they should find Edward and Karen.

After a thorough search Thomas spotted the pair on the other dance floor. Heléna suggested that the two of them cool off with a couple of cold drinks. Minutes later they returned to find the out-of-towner and roommate in the same location. A romantic slow song had been chosen, and Edward and Karen were locked in an inseparable embrace. Although they were not sure why, Thomas and Heléna did not like how they looked together but agreed that it was none of their business.

Time passed quickly. Thomas enjoyed being with Heléna, and she showed obvious pleasure in his company. Edward and Karen obviously also had hit it off. Twenty minutes before closing, the two gentlemen escorted the women to their car. While standing in the parking lot, Thomas looked at his watch and suggested to Edward that they call it a night, too. After a mild argument, his brother agreed to leave.

The next morning Thomas crawled out of bed groggy and dazed. He wandered into the kitchen to find Edward fully-dressed in a dark-blue suit reading the Sunday paper. The two men barely arrived in time for the start of the 10 o'clock service at Saint Phillip's African Methodist Episcopal Church, a medium-sized, recently remodeled place. Thomas and Edward giggled like children as they squeezed in the middle pews of the structure, joining about 120 souls. The minister, about the same age as Edward, possessed an eloquent voice capable of moving the sternest of hearts. The choir of nine sang in perfect harmony, directed by a young woman, a graduate student in music at Harvard University.

Thomas was amazed at how easily Edward adapted to the situation, Bible in hand, praying and affirming the messages with well-placed amens. Of course, the man was a hit with all of the females. Edward assured them that he would return soon. In the car, he hummed one of the hymns that the choir had sung and thanked his younger brother for bringing him. Thomas blinked his eyes in astonishment and admiration for his brother, a classic chameleon.

The following morning Thomas drove to work in a daze, the memory of his brother's visit, now history, still fresh in his mind. He hummed the same tune Edward had chosen in the car on the way home from church and attempted to make sense of his brother's visit. Spring had arrived, but one could not testify to such by the sights that morning. A mild nor'easter had deposited wet, heavy snow on the roads overnight. Thomas drove past his neighbors, their arms in violent motion as they fought to free windshields from the bounty of the storm. The frozen water clung to trees, creating picturesque scenes. However, given the time of year, the images failed to make a positive impression on the Cincinnati native.

The superintendent had decided that all Boston public schools would open one hour later than their usual times. Massachusetts schools further to the west and north had been ordered closed. John Adams students arrived very late. Teachers complained about holding classes on such a day when five snow days had been built into the calendar. At the Adams virtually every teacher reported attendance of fifty percent or less. In an unusual move Mr. Dorn visited each classroom to tally the number of students. He counted twenty-two in 217, by far the highest percentage at the Adams.

During lunch Thomas stopped on the first floor to get a cup of water. While walking he examined the floor planks of the long corridor, which had long ago lost their shine. Halfway into his stroll from one length of the chilly first floor to the other, he jerked his head backwards, astonished to see a familiar student planted on one end of the bench facing the office. At the other end rested a larger boy. Both looked angry and worried. Thomas remembered that the second boy had also been a student of his—for about five minutes on the first day of school—before being sent to Ms. Patterson. The harsh, bright illumination from the office shone directly on them like floodlights, drawing attention to their precarious status.

Thomas placed himself between the two and turned to his right. He spoke over unintelligible voices coming from the office. Ms. Walker and Ms. Sanchez-Taylor conversed on the telephone; the former in English and the latter in Spanish.

"Whatcha doing here, Jonathan?" Thomas asked.

The boy squirmed, lowered his head and mumbled something.

"A fight?" the man said. "With whom?"

Jonathan pointed. His former teacher turned to the left. The large boy leaned forward and spoke forcefully. "He started it! I—"

"Shut your mouth, boy!" Thomas commanded. "Did I ask you anything?" The boy responded by slamming himself against the bench and folding his arms above his protruding stomach.

Jonathan started to offer his defense, but Thomas waved his hand. "That goes for you, too. I'm sorry I asked. If I want to hear a story, I'll go upstairs to the library." He stood and entered the office. After checking his mailbox, which was empty because he had already retrieved his mail ten minutes earlier, he stepped across the threshold and approached the two boys.

"I suspect the principal will suspend both of you—which suits me just fine."

"Jonathan was disrespecting Mrs. Chang," the large boy volunteered. "He told her to get out of his face."

Thomas stepped closer. His eyes burned as he stared at Jonathan. The man tossed his head in the heavyset fourth-grader's direction. "That boy better be lying."

Jonathan said nothing.

Thomas shook his head and tisk-tisk-tisked the air. "I thought you told me you were going to make me proud, huh?" After a long silence, he pushed further. "How could you do this and hurt your mother so? You know she just got called back at work, and now she has to take off and come here to pick up your hard head."

"But he—"

"I don't wanna hear nothing about that boy!" Thomas retorted. "What did you learn in 217? How many does it take for a fight?"

Jonathan raised his hand, displaying his index and middle fingers. "Two," he replied softly.

The man continued his cross-examination. "Are you in Advanced Class or not?" he asked.

"Yes."

"Then act like it!" he ordered.

"Yes sir."

Thomas took a few steps down the hall before spinning around and returning to his former pupil. "One more thing," he cautioned. "When your mom gets here and Dorn comes for you, do them a favor: act like a young man and admit you made a mistake." He didn't wait for a reply but left the two combatants. He felt saddened at the sight of his former captain and all-star awaiting almost certain suspension. He remembered his mother's warning that after a student leaves your domain, you have to let go because sometimes they turn back into pumpkins.

Movie Day finally arrived, and Thomas found that he had picked up still another seat in Congress, as he privately joked. Twenty-four students were eligible to stay and enjoy the day's festivities. Only Freddy, Cleopatra and Tyshaun had to park themselves in Mr. Bennett's first-grade room. On the next school day Tyshaun would have enough points to stand before the class. Thomas told the sad boy how proud he was about his improvement and how much he looked forward to seeing him return to the fold.

On the way home Thomas sat in his car only three blocks away from the Adams, waiting for the light to change. Perpendicular to his field of vision, he spotted the thin profile of a dark-skinned young girl with wavy hair. She wore a familiar-looking blue coat and appeared to have her thumb in her mouth. Next to her stood a smaller child, presumably a younger brother. The excited teacher rolled his eyeballs as far as they could travel but only turned his head slightly. He did not wish to frighten the pedestrians by being too obvious. The girl stood calmly at the bus stop, reaching into a bag of potato chips and stuffing a handful into her mouth. Small crumbs fell onto her coat. She was a pretty child, but not LaShonda.

Suddenly, everyone's attention diverted to a white van sounding its horn behind the red sportscar. Thomas tilted his head upward at the shining amber light, then at his rearview mirror and frowned. Disappointed, he lifted his left foot off the clutch while applying pressure to the accelerator. Thank goodness, in a few minutes he would be home.

April

Thomas heard the echo on his left and stopped. Behind him and to his right, Ms. Sanchez-Taylor, in her classroom and out of sight, conversed in Spanish with another teacher, both sporadically laughing. Nothing unusual there. The suspicious man hesitated by the door of the boys' bathroom. The putrid smell repulsed him. Due to budget cuts, the Adams only had one custodian—and he had called in sick for the past three days. The school received part-time morning help for the first two days, but yesterday a substitute arrived during the late afternoon. The short, reticent man emptied the trash in all the classrooms. He took a look at the boys', then the girls' bathrooms and left the building in a huff.

Earlier in the day the John Adams's boys had produced some of their most offensive handiwork, urinating on the floor and radiator. When the heat finally kicked in a little before first lunch, everyone on the second floor was treated to the smell of rewarmed piss. The girls' lavatory fared even worse. Not equipped by nature to easily mark their territory on the bathroom radiator, they settled for pouring milk on the pipes, urinating on the floor near the toilets, spreading feces on the walls and tearing down one of the sinks.

Thomas checked his watch. At 8:05 it was too early to hear the voices of children in the building. Lately he had maintained early-morning vigils on his floor. Twice the previous week he had apprehended students upstairs before school opened and escorted them out of the building, and had scared off a few from a distance. Recently the second-floor staff had complained about items disappearing from their classrooms. Mrs. Chang discovered thirty dollars missing from her purse just the previous week. The week before that, Ms. Valdez, the fourth-grade bilingual teacher, had to replace a new electric pencil sharpener. Poor Ms. Patterson had nothing left to steal. Someone even had the temerity to invade Room 217, making off with the teacher's stapler and some computer software. Thomas had taken the violation very hard. Like his colleagues, he refused to believe that any of his own children had been involved.

The young sentry slowly pushed open the battered lavatory door. Water puddles, some yellowish in color, covered over half of the filthy floor. The area underneath the sinks and urinals was drenched. Opposite the door, the grapefruit-size cardboard that had covered a broken window had been removed. The window was raised wide open. The morning's forty-two-degree air rushed in, preventing Thomas from becoming too nauseous. Still, the place brought sharp pains to his nose and eyes. A dozen wall tiles lay broken in the corner by the window. Only one of the four overhead lights produced illumination; over the course of the school year the other three had been shattered.

Thomas grimaced, then assessed that the boys would have to reap what they sowed. If they insisted on relieving themselves in a ravaged, malodorous facility, they could do just that. He stepped inside and lowered his head, examining the floor under all four toilet stalls. Nothing. He ventured further. Between the urinals and the last stall lurked a short, plump Hispanic boy wearing a Boston Red Socks baseball cap and jacket. Their eyes met. Thomas extended his right index finger, beckoning the student to come closer.

"*Venga aquí,*" he commanded softly. The room magnified his voice just the same.

The boy shrugged his shoulders and complied. They carefully stepped toward each other as Thomas began to interrogate the student about his name and teacher. Suddenly, he heard the sound of something falling to the ground behind him. Another boy, tall and thin, flung open the door to the second stall closest to them and attempted to run, but the wet floor made his pivoting difficult. The two seconds subtracted from his takeoff provided Thomas with all the advantage he needed. Employing his wide receiver skills, he beat the student to the bathroom door and pushed it closed, foiling any escape. He positioned himself in front of the door.

"Going somewhere?" he asked.

The attempted runaway, a very tall boy clad in an oversized pair of black jeans barely hanging on his behind, spoke forcefully.

"Move!" he ordered as he tried to sidestep out of the bathroom.

Thomas widened his eyes in surprised. "No, son, you don't give the orders here. I do. What are you doing in here?"

"None of your damn business!" the skinny student replied angrily. He stepped left, then right, then left again, determined to leave, but Thomas cut him off, mirroring his movements. The two continued their dance for five more paces, moving quickly but going nowhere. The impudent boy had little chance of leaving the bathroom unless permitted and he knew it. Pride and machismo pushed him into his futile ploy.

Thomas recalled having seen his dancing partner before. He was a student in the fifth-grade bilingual classroom. More than once during recess or before school started, he had broken up a fight or near fight involving this particular student. Come to think of it, Thomas remembered chasing him and some others out of the building just last week. In the teacher's lounge Ms. Sanchez-Taylor frequently grumbled about problems she had with a tall, older troublemaker in her room named Carlos. Although thirteen years old and obviously able to orally communicate in English, she reported that he could barely read or write in that language or in Spanish.

The desperate pupil reached up and put his long arm on the twenty-five-year-old man's thick shoulder and tugged. Thomas barely moved.

"I know you speak English well enough to understand this, so I'm only going to say it once: Take your hand off me, now!" He knocked the boy's hand aside with his left forearm. The boy looked back at his friend, who said nothing. The stocky classmate seemed embarrassed to witness such an exhibition. Locked in an obviously losing battle, the frustrated teenager became enraged.

"Black motherfucker!" he yelled, lunging with both hands extended. Thomas stepped aside and allowed the student to slam into the door. Now behind the boy, he raised his arms and put him in a full nelson, locking his hands behind the combative student's neck.

"Please, don't make me hurt you," he pleaded. The boy struggled, but Thomas refused to let go. The exasperated teacher turned to the shorter accomplice. "Go get Mr. Dorn. *Apurase!*" he ordered while backing up, dragging his load with him. The short boy stepped past them, opened the door and ran. Thomas whispered into his opponent's ear as he tightened his grip.

"I don't want to hurt you, but I could if I wanted to, see?" He tightened his grip and felt his adversary become less animated. "Now, this contest is over. I'm gonna let you go but if you try anything funny, even your own mother isn't going to recognize you after I'm done. *Comprende?*" He listened but no sound came from his prisoner. "Be smart, *intiende?*" With the last word, he constricted his hold even more.

The boy winced in pain but stopped struggling altogether and nodded his head as best he could. "Okay. Okay," he whimpered.

"Good," Thomas said, relaxing his powerful arms. He released his captive and patted him on the back. "Now let's get out of this place. I can't stand the smell." He reached for the door and motioned for them to leave. "To the office, son. I'm afraid you're in some trouble." The two walked out of the bathroom.

Low rumbling sounds echoed from the first floor as scores of rambunctious elementary students journeyed to their classrooms. Thomas reached the top of the stairs, then stepped to the side, allowing two third-grade classrooms of potential learners to pass. Several spoke to him as they did. He waved but said nothing. He and his companion met the principal and the other boy at the bottom of the stairs. Thomas spoke over the clamoring youngsters racing by.

"Mr. Dorn, I caught these two in the bathroom upstairs. When I blocked the door so they couldn't run, this one," he said, taking a deep breath, "tried to get physical. I had to restrain him, but he's not hurt."

Both students stared at their shoelaces. From the corner of his right eye Thomas spotted Ms. Sanchez-Taylor awkwardly climbing the stairs with her class. Surprised, she stopped and asked the boys in Spanish what had happened. The clearly annoyed woman struggled to balance a stack of notebooks in her arms as she listened. Carlos pointed at his wrestling foe and started to say something, only to be interrupted by the principal.

"Close your mouth, Carlos. I've had enough of this!" the middle-aged man growled. "You and Hector go down and wait for me at the office." He turned to Thomas. "Why don't you go get your class and write up a report and give it to me as soon as you can."

"Okay, Coach," Thomas said. "You might want to check their bags. We've had some trouble with missing items upstairs." He turned to his colleague to show her the respect she had been denied by the principal. "I'll give you a copy of the report and tell you later what happened."

Embarrassed due to the way she had been treated by Mr. Dorn, Ms. Sanchez-Taylor readily agreed. Thomas continued slowly down the stairs while tucking in his shirttails and straightening his tie. His heartbeat had accelerated from the ordeal and still fluttered in his chest. "What's wrong with these kids?" he asked aloud.

Later that morning, during his forty minute planning and development period, Thomas stopped by Glen's room. His mentor had taken to his knees, tying the shoelaces of a caramel-colored, long-haired girl holding onto a teddy bear sporting an apron. When the tot saw Mr. Payne, she broke into a huge smile and waved. He waved back and called her by name. Glen looked up and saw his mentee towering over him. "Good morning, Mr. Payne," he called aloud in a sing-songy voice.

"Good morning, Mr. Payne," nearly two dozen first-graders responded in unison. Several children raced over for a hug, grabbing onto his legs or hands. Late-comers settled for unclaimed parts of his shirt and belt loops. The visitor acknowledged their affection and inquired about their well-being, addressing most by name.

Glen clapped his hands twice. "It looks like we're in luck, children," he announced. "If you all go very, very quietly to the reading corner, I think Mr. Payne might agree to stay and read a story."

The children expressed muffled glee at the suggestion. They placed their fingers over their lips, marched to the other side of the room and sat down on a shaggy brown carpet. They smiled at Thomas and waited.

Thomas looked at his watch. He and his friend whispered back and forth for a few seconds. After they finished, Glen handed his understanding buddy a book and asked him to take a seat in the hallowed Reader's Chair. Thomas tried to make himself comfortable on the short stool in front of the carpeted area. Eager eyes engulfed him with anticipation.

"Oh my!" the fifth-grade teacher exclaimed in a high voice while opening the book. "It looks like Mr. Payne came to visit his favorite first-grade class on just the right day. *The Very Hungry Caterpillar* is my all-time faaaavorite story…."

Thomas returned to his classroom, sat down at his desk and wrote an account of the morning's event. With the door closed the place could actually be peaceful. Because of the chilly temperature in the room, the windows remained closed, preventing the infiltration of disturbing noises. The sun kindly donated its gifts. Thomas looked out at the empty desks and nodded in appreciation that none of his students would dare provoke such outrage. Freddy's behavioral problems had been reduced to merely an annoyance.

Returning to his report, Thomas saw no reason to disclose more than the fact that after Hector left the bathroom, he had insisted that Carlos calm down, and the boy had complied. He carried the report to the office and hand-delivered it to Mr. Dorn, who directed him to stop by after school to discuss the matter. Thomas said that he would.

He returned to Room 217 and sat in his chair. Thomas extended his arms and spread apart his huge hands. With thumbs touching like a movie director planning a scene, he imagined the positions of his future classroom decorations. The door swung open, and Heléna strutted in like she lived there. She wore a dark-colored plaid skirt, a plain white blouse and black shoes—her "Catholic outfit," she joked.

"I heard about your adventure this morning," Heléna reported, closing the door behind her. "Did the kid really have a knife?"

Thomas watched the senior citizen maneuver his way around the room. The astute guest concentrated on the intense activities captivating a horde of willing participants. Chessboards rested between thirteen pairs of students, their eyes fixed on the cardboard objects and meandering soldiers.

The old man enjoyed coming to the class. He complimented his host on the changes to the decor. New posters graced the area, consisting of only Hispanic role models: a musician, a cabinet officer, a businesswoman, a tennis star, an Olympic gold medallist and more. Thirteen computer-designed images of dinosaur pairs had been taped to the student-closet doors with the name of a buddy at the feet of each extinct animal. The students had chosen their designations by chance. Pedro and Hernando garnered representation as a pterodactyl and stegosaurus, respectively. To the great envy of every other student, Deborah had drawn the powerful tyrannosaurus. Her buddy, Connie, had picked the mighty three-horned triceratops.

Mr. Davenport was an impressive-looking man, with thick gray hair. He wore a dark suit with a striped tie, just as he had done for over forty-five years when he had practiced law. Now semi-retired, he just did a little volunteer and consulting work here and there—considerably less than when he was working, but enough to "keep from being underfoot," according to his wife of nearly half a century. The students in Room 217 had taken to him right away. At first they stared at him, not actually at him but at his metal crutches, called Canadian crutches. Attached to his forearms, they helped him walk. He explained that he had been very ill when he was about their age, leaving him partially paralyzed. The gentleman added that he considered himself fortunate to have survived the ordeal. Others during his time had not been so lucky.

Mr. Davenport walked around observing the children as they played the grand game of chess. He would hover over two students for half a minute or so and make notes on a yellow legal pad. Sometimes the former chess champion would offer a suggestion or compliment. His favorite line that invariably evoked blushing pride was, "You sure you never played this game before?" When the student would answer no, he would reply, "I don't believe you." He offered patience and kindness to every pupil, regardless of talent—or paucity of it. He told the novice learners that this year he would simply teach them the fundamentals so that they could have fun. Frequently, he compared his observations with Thomas's, a pretty fair chess player himself.

Mr. Davenport looked at his watch. It was nearly time to go. He eased over to Thomas and adjusted his glasses as he whispered. "Well, we've got to start deciding about who's going to be on the team for the tournament in June." His voice sounded raspy from age. "You've got some good kids, here, Mr. Payne."

"True, a lot of good players," Thomas agreed. "And you know what? I've got to *make* half of them go out for recess. They'd rather stay inside and play chess." He looked around. "But to get it down to six. Hmmm … Definitely Melvin over there—and Gary."

"I agree," Mr. Davenport said. "And that spitfire one you got over there. That's one chess-playing number." He pointed.

"Oh, Carmelita? Yep, she plays to win, but she gets frustrated easily when she loses."

"She'll learn how to improve from her mistakes," the old man suggested while adjusting his glasses and perusing his notes. "And I like that one over there. The tall one."

"Thomas looked to the back of the room. "Who? Cleopatra? I don't know. She just got off punishment—what we call ISP—a little while ago. She's unpredict—" He suddenly shrugged his shoulders. "Okay, it's your funeral," Thomas conceded. "Anyone else?"

"The kid sitting next to her."

"That's Tyshaun. He just got off punishment a little before she did. A good player, though." Thomas thought for a few seconds. "Okay." He counted in his head. "One more to go. Anybody else?"

"The quiet one with the gray patch of hair."

"Pedro? Yeah, he's good. And focused, too. A tornado could blow in here, and the boy wouldn't even blink his eyes."

The men announced that the chess period had come to a close. The class murmured and begged for more time.

"Sorry, my children," Thomas said, overacting, "but we must see to that social studies test, remember?"

Mr. Davenport smiled. "Mr. Payne and I have been talking, and we've decided who's going to be on the chess team and go to the tournament in June that we told you about. All of you've been doing very well, but," he opened his restricted arms, "we can only take six." He announced the chosen team.

The half-dozen named pupils giggled as they received reluctant, polite applause. Eventually, the hand-clapping grew louder. A few unselected students raised their hands to appeal.

Thomas offered faint hope to the disappointed ones. "Like Mr. Davenport said, we could only bring six—although so many of you are doing so well. And remember," he added, "I'll replace anyone immediately if you fail to keep up with your schoolwork or get back on ISP."

Everyone stared at Cleopatra. She sneered and put her hand over her face to shut them out.

"Chess team," Thomas called out to the six proud students. "I'm going to need you to sacrifice your recess a few times a week to practice, okay?"

Pedro, Gary, Carmelita and Melvin readily agreed. Tyshaun and Cleo, who had only recently seen the light of day immediately following lunch, also agreed but with slightly less enthusiasm.

Several pupils not selected for the team immediately objected. They made comments such as, "That's not fair!" and "How come we can't play, too?" and "Please, Mr. Payne!"

After listening to their complaints, Thomas acquiesced. "Okay, okay. Tell you what," the assistant chess coach replied. "Anyone who wants to stay in for recess and play chess can do so."

Several students cheered. A few challenged others to a game.

Mr. Davenport expressed his pride in the group as a whole, collected his overstuffed briefcase and ambled off to another appointment—some pro bono work at the county jail.

That afternoon Thomas found himself in familiar territory—Mr. Dorn's cluttered office. The substance of the reports, computer software, boxes, etc., were different, but the room had maintained the same appearance throughout the school year. Thomas felt relief that his supervisor spared him the customary anxious wait while he conversed on the telephone. Tension hung in the air. Neither had forgotten their unpleasant exchange over LaShonda Walker, nor would either speak openly of their mutual distrust of each other. The principal opened with an announcement.

"First," Mr. Dorn began, "Douglas Berry is to be seen by Ms. Cooke, effective immediately. I pulled some strings and got the boy into the Reading Triple-O Program," the man announced smugly. "He's to go during the reading period. Had you told me that he had been denied, I would have gotten him in sooner."

"Thanks for helping. I'll send him down, starting tomorrow," Thomas replied. He remembered that Dorn had received a copy of the boy's denial from the central office. Obviously, Ms. Flores had kept her word and spoken to him.

The principal continued in a formal tone. "Mr. Payne, thank you for giving me the report about this morning's incident with Carlos Ramirez and Hector Peña." He skimmed over the document.

"*No problema,*" Thomas answered. "Don't be too hard on Carlos. I understand from talking to Ms. Sanchez-Taylor that he's had a rough go of it this year."

Mr. Dorn ignored the remark and pulled out a legal-sized pad of paper and a pen. "Now, the boys claim that you grabbed Carlos and put some kind of choke-hold on him and slammed his head against the bathroom door. Can you tell me what happened?"

"What?" Thomas blurted. "What do you mean 'choke hold?' I gave you my report. I don't understand what this is all about."

"Boston Public School Department policy forbids the use of corporal punishment on a student unless it's to prevent harm to yourself, himself or another," the headmaster recited. "There's been an allegation made that you acted inappropriately toward a student, and as principal, I have to investigate it. Its purely routine."

Thomas felt his heart pounding as if it would jump out of his shirt. The room became warm. He felt his forehead and underarms grow wet. He did not know what to say or do. By sitting down with the principal alone, he had done the very thing he had been cautioned not to do. He felt like such a fool.

"C-coach," he finally stammered. "If its all the same to you, I'm not going to answer any questions unless Ms. Caine or Ms., um, um, Letterman, the BTU elementary field rep, is here."

Now there's no need to get all defensive, Thomas," Mr. Dorn responded. "I just thought we'd settle this informally. Like I said, it's just routine. If you bring in outside folks, I'll have to hold a formal hearing. You don't want that, do you?"

No, Thomas thought, he did not want that. His head spun around in circles. The heavyset man sitting across from him became a surreal blur. The rookie teacher tried to organize the advice he had secured over the months from his mother, Glen and Mona Caine. The charge of inappropriately touching a student could end a teacher's career. He recalled the saga of a college friend—an African American male—who had taught at a high school in Cincinnati right out of undergraduate school. He faced an accusation of touching a female student inappropriately. Eventually, it was determined that the girl had made up the charge to get back at him for some discipline matter, but it took the whole school year to clear his name. After that the man left the field of education.

His supervisor raised his voice. "I'm waiting, Mr. Payne."

"I've said as much as I'm gonna say, Mr. Dorn," he finally replied. "Is there anything else?"

The principal took off his glasses. "You disappoint me, Thomas. I thought you were smarter than this. I tried to be helpful to you, but you had to go siding with Ms. Caine and that crowd."

"What crowd?" Thomas whined. "She's the building rep, that's all." He pulled his shirtsleeve up and looked at his left wrist. Contractually, he was under no obligation to stay. "It's 4 o'clock and I'd like to go." He reached for his briefcase and stood.

"Fine."

That was the last word he heard before storming out the door.

Thomas drove to the back of the gym and searched the area. A busy day at Anthony's, he surmised from the full parking lot. Glen's white compact car could not be found, so he sped down the narrow street behind the building, cutting off a man with red hair in a red BMW. The driver of the German car offered scathing and profane criticism about the teacher's intelligence, as well as an opinion about his family lineage. Ignoring the insults, Thomas raced on, unsure of his destination. The traffic lights seemed interminably long and drivers in front of him excruciatingly slow. Also, out of sixteen stations programmed on his car radio, not one offered anything agreeable to the agitated man's ears. The stack of music discs under his seat had outlived their usefulness. Thomas sorted through them and, one by one, threw them onto the passenger's seat. Abruptly, he recognized the white house with a young tree barely reaching the second floor. Mercifully, he had arrived.

The distraught first-year teacher slammed the car door and opened the swinging gate to the new metal fence. He climbed the steps to the front door and rang the doorbell. To calm himself, he slowly counted backwards from ninety-nine, a trick he had learned on the football team in college. Inspecting his surroundings, he noticed that the tree to his right, still a child by nature's standards, had begun to exhibit green pebble-sized buds. Thomas appreciated its beauty, but in doing so lost count somewhere around ninety-four. He became impatient and rang the doorbell again. Finally the door opened with a creak.

"Thomas? You look terrible. What's the matter?" Glen inquired. He was dressed in blue jeans and a New York University T-shirt. "Come in. I'll get you something to drink." They walked through his living room on a clear vinyl runway protecting a very thick powder-blue carpet. Thomas admired the wide, off-white sofa, loveseat and recliner encasing a sprawling entertainment center. That forty-two-inch color television and stereo system sure beat his modest furnishings, he admitted to himself. Huge mirrors covered one wall, making the large room appear even larger. The two men finally reached the brightly-lit kitchen.

Thomas remembered that three years before, the Buckeyes had whipped NYU's behind mercilessly during their own homecoming game. During the first quarter, he had thrown a block that knocked two men to the ground and put fullback "Mountain" Mike O'Toole in the end zone. Upon seeing the T-shirt, he usually teased Glen about the game, but at the moment he saw little humor in anything. "I'm sorry to disturb you, buddy. I—" He stopped abruptly.

Sitting at the table sipping a cup of tea and surrounded by five empty chairs, Thomas suspected right away, was the real "Jena," the person whose picture Glen should have carried in his wallet, if society was more tolerant. The man, of lighter complexion than Thomas, took to his feet and extended his hand. He was close to Glen's age. He stood straight and broad-shoulder. A thin, sharp mustache spread above his full lips. His suit, conservative and expensive, spelled stock broker or something like that.

"Hi, I'm Felix," he said calmly, extending his left hand.

Thomas expected to hear a higher tone, but the man's voice had a clear, low sound. "Nice to meet you. I'm Thomas Payne." He thought it wise to make his relationship to Glen clear. "Glen and I work together at the Adams." The two men shook hands.

"Of course. Glen's told me about the terrific work you do."

Thomas smiled. He wanted to fire back with, "Well, he hasn't told me shit about you, pal!" but fought the urge. "I'm afraid I'm intruding," he muttered, squinting his eyes and turning towards his friend. "I'm so sorry, buddy. I should have called first."

"Oh no. You're not interrupting anything," Glen and his guest said together.

Felix walked to the doorway between the kitchen and the living room. "As a matter of fact, I was just heading home," he announced.

Thomas glanced at the full cup of steaming hot tea the man had left behind and felt guilty.

"Help yourself to whatever you need in the kitchen while I get the door for Felix," Glen told Thomas. The two men left him alone.

Thomas opened the refrigerator, its door littered with first-grade artwork, and inspected the contents inside. He retrieved a carton of orange juice and a glass from one of the shiny cabinets, then stood still and listened. However, he could not hear the conversation in the living room. He wondered if the two men would kiss on the mouth and if so, if he would be able to hear it. He felt ashamed at his fascination with Glen's personal life.

Thomas wondered how one became homosexual. He wondered what Glen's childhood was like. Not good, he imagined. Maybe if his dad had been there for him, Thomas theorized, Glen wouldn't have to bear the burden of an "alternative lifestyle." He heard the door open and close, then footsteps as the home's owner trekked back across the kitchen's checkerboard linoleum floor. Glen offered no clarification about Felix, and Thomas did not ask for any. Instead, he subjected his mentor to three apologies before being persuaded to explain the reason for barging into his home.

Thomas took a deep breath and recapitulated every detail about his visit with Mr. Dorn.

After ten minutes of virtually nonstop talking, the first-year teacher took a deep breath to signal that he had finished. Glen shook his head from side to side. Thomas imagined his mentor's thoughts: "I told your dumb ass to NEVER go into the boys' bathroom!" but the man was too much the gentleman and supportive friend to state the obvious. Instead, he asked his mentee a few questions, then disappeared into the living room and returned with the White Pages telephone book.

"We better call Gwen Letterman at BTU before they close."

The following day after a fitful night's sleep, Thomas returned to the Adams. The sun's rays fell generously that morning. The temperature held in the mid-forties but was expected to climb to nearly sixty. A few dogwood trees nearby bore off-white flowers while other types only displayed green buds. At the house across the street from the school's front door, a six-feet-wide row of rhododendron bushes sprouted dazzling purple flowers. Still, Thomas's mood remained pensive. The kids had not changed, the structure of the building had not been altered and the staff looked no different than they had the day before. But everything seemed different. The sight of children laughing and playing failed to evoke the usual smile or chuckle. Pint-sized kindergartners and first-graders received their allotment of hugs and well-wishes but without the customary warmth and enthusiasm. After signing in, Thomas resolved not to enter the office again until signing out.

His mind wandered during the middle of math class. Twice he lost his place and had to refer to his plan book. He judged his performance as abominable, but no one seemed to notice. By late morning his guilt forced him to employ the pitiful adult line to his students that he had a headache. Throughout the day Thomas avoided contact with people, especially Mr. Dorn. While in the classroom, he continuously kept one eye on the door, expecting the principal to enter and deliver news that his services would no longer be required. Although he had spoken to his brother on the telephone before turning in for the night, he still felt very much alone. He wished he had a special woman in his life. He had been so tempted to call Heléna but didn't want her to "see" him while wounded and unsure of himself.

For some inexplicable reason the Ohio native reflected on his relationship with his father. He hadn't realized it, but his dad, a good and decent but quiet man, had not taught him much about emotions, especially what to do when afraid or anxious. He remembered seeing his father cry only once, upon hearing that his mother had died. The sight of tears on his father's face had shocked him and his brother, but not their sister Vanessa. True, Dad listened well—a lost art—but he seldom dispensed advice about personal matters. He usually helped Thomas to arrive at his own conclusions. He never yelled or displayed strong anger but preferred to say much by saying little.

One Friday night, Thomas remembered, when he was sixteen, he came home an hour past his curfew. Upon quietly easing open the front door to the living room, he detected his dad's still figure in the dark, reclining in his plush easy chair—an anniversary present from Mom—with the telephone nestled in his lap. Thomas remembered how his heart stuck in his throat as his father slowly struggled to get on his feet. The first words spoken conveyed concern: "Everything okay?" When Thomas assured him that he was fine and apologized, his father asked rhetorically, "You worried your mother. We can't have that, can we?" Thomas assured him that they couldn't. The next two times Thomas wanted to go out, he asked his mother first, who told him that he had to get permission from his father. Both times Gabriel Payne declined his request with the same line: "No. We can't have your mother worried." He said it in such a way that Thomas knew better than to argue.

The Ohio native's memories were interrupted by the sound of the door moving. Glen entered and sat on a bench in front of the teacher's desk.

"Any word?" he asked. Seeing his friend shake his head, he offered a game plan. "Don't let Dorn mess with your head, man. Walk around like you haven't got a care in the world. Don't change your routine." He thought for a second and decided to be more helpful. "Did you talk to Mona Caine?" Thomas nodded, so Glen continued. "So you're covered here. How about Gwen Letterman?"

"She's supposed to call me tonight after 6 o'clock."

"Okay, so let's get to Anthony's and get you out of this mood."

"I don't feel like it."

Glen stood up and placed his hands on his hips. "Is this Thomas Payne, the former wide receiver for the Ohio State Buckeyes? The man who caught a touchdown pass against UCLA and the University of Wisconsin—and threw a block that knocked two men to the ground for Mountain Mike O'Toole against NYU? The man who made short work of the Wild Bunch? The man who tells his students, 'Get your head on!' when they cry or pout? The man who doesn't know the meaning of the word defeat? The man who—"

"Okay! Okay! Let's go to Anthony's and work out already!" Thomas conceded, smiling.

The next day brought no further inquiries about the bathroom incident. Thomas relaxed and eventually rediscovered some enthusiasm for his job. Taking Glen's advice, he resumed his routine and at lunchtime stopped by the office to check his mail. Marilyn Walker's icy wall had melted by then. She greeted him pleasantly, and they exchanged mutual appreciation about the increasingly warm weather. Mr. Dorn, present but with his back to the couple, searched through the office-record cards for a student's home telephone number. The rookie teacher eased over to his mailbox and grabbed a couple of new school supply catalogs. He walked out into the corridor but two seconds after clearing the office, heard his name called.

"Oh, Mr. Payne?"

Thomas felt his pulse rise. He put on his nonchalant face, pirouetted and stepped into the threshold of the office. Rather than actually cross into the supervisor's home field, he merely leaned in, holding onto the edge of the doorway, thus breaking the imaginary plane while maintaining a distance of about eight feet. As a sign of authority, Mr. Dorn never moved towards a teacher, but Thomas chose not to come any closer. "Yes, sir?"

Mr. Dorn leaned against the counter, anchoring himself. "Ms. Colón called earlier. She wants Maria to come straight home instead of going to her after-school program."

Thomas nodded. "Okay, I'll tell her." He spun around and strolled down the hall. Once out of sight he took a deep breath and released about ten pounds of pressure.

Several days later Thomas and the children of Room 217 stayed in the building for less than an hour. As part of their reading unit on plays, they boarded a city bus to the Wang Center to see a theatrical production of *Beauty and the Beast.* Thomas enjoyed being away from the stressful atmosphere at the Adams but could not escape invasive thoughts. During the performance his mind wandered to the incident in the bathroom and his meeting with the principal, attempting to anticipate the next phase of his real-life drama. He feared the unknown and wished the entire episode had never happened, even though he believed that he had done nothing wrong.

He reflected on what several of the senior Adams staff had admitted to him regarding how they protect themselves from such accusations. Most refused to go into the children's bathrooms, no matter what they heard. Several teachers confessed that at the first sign of a fight between students, they turned around and quickly walked in the opposite direction—even if one of their own pupils was involved. When Thomas expressed his discomfort over such behavior, almost universally the veterans assured him that he would think differently after a few years. He feared they could be right.

After returning from the field trip and getting settled in, Thomas examined his watch. "Well, it's too late to start science now." He paused, fighting the urge to smile. "We have twenty minutes before DEAR," he coyly announced. Hands shot into the air. It would be the same request, regardless of whom he addressed. "Angel?"

"Mr. Payne, can we do an acting stretch?" the boy eagerly asked with a smile on his face and his eyes lit up like hot coals."

Thomas paused, then replied with exaggerated listlessness. "Okay."

Cheers erupted as the students pounded on their desks and stuck their hands into the air. They had begun performing acting "stretches" in December. Thomas had borrowed the exercise from his encounter over two-and-a-half years before with Revelations, Inc. (Hidden beneath the darkest crevice of the bottom drawer in his bedroom were two photographs of him standing alongside a construction worker and an investment banker; all three wearing ballerina costumes.) The exercises produced noticeable changes, especially for the quiet students, like Maria, Janet and Gary. The more they took risks by participating in the stretches, the more they took risks in their academic endeavors.

Thomas went to the board and drew a pair of long parallel lines about thirty inches apart. He wrote two words in the middle and tapped the board with his knuckles. "What's inside here?" Hands raised again. He made eye contact with a student and pointed to the side of his face. She understood the signal and put on her glasses before he called on her. "Christine?"

"Your comfort zone," she replied confidently.

"That's right," Thomas said. "And where is most of your learning going to take place?" He stared at one of his more reticent pupils. She responded by unbending her raised arm and extending it straight into the air. "Please, Janet."

"Outside of your comfort zone."

"That's right," the teacher declared. "So by accepting these assignments in the class, you get to stretch. You get to go outside of your comfort zone." He stopped to sneeze, received a blessing from several pupils and continued. "The more you stretch, the more you learn." Up went his index finger. "The first rule is: the stretches are totally voluntary. But what else?" Again, a sea of hands sprung up. "Akeem?"

The boy pointed, performing a near-perfect impression of the man standing ten feet away. "If you volunteer, you have to see it through to the end." Muffled giggling ensued.

"That's right." Thomas agreed with a laugh while rubbing his hands together. "Now, we won't do a new one today. So which one would you like?" He pointed and heard suggestions.

"How about the one about the crew on the spaceship?" Gary requested.

"Let's do the stretch where the girls ask the boys to dance to that Pat King Cole song!" Carmelita demanded. Thomas snickered at her mispronunciation of the great crooner's first name. Several students joined him. Carmelita shifted her head from left to right and widened her eyes. "What? What'd I say?" she asked.

"How about the one where the boy has to stand on top of the desk and sing 'You Are So Beautiful' like Pedro did with Lakeisha last time?" Everyone laughed. Pedro blushed.   ·

"Can we do Dr. Jekyll and Mr. Hyde?" Several students shouted "Yeah!" That had become a recent class favorite. No one could touch Melvin's performance on that one.

"Not today," Thomas said. "We'll do one that several of you can be in." Expressions of disappointment floated through the room.

"Mr. Payne, why don't we do the one with the gang and the grandmother?" Cleopatra suggested. The entire class enthusiastically seconded the request.

Thomas became uncomfortable. It was a great stretch, but the subject seemed a little adult for his taste. Over the past month he had been encouraging his pupils to invent their own stretches. The gang scene, created by Akeem, was powerful but unnerving.

"Okay," he said reluctantly. Several students shouted, "Yeah!" and volunteered.

Thomas chose five actors. As he pointed to each one, he or she came to the center of the room to create a character name. Volunteers widened the center gauntlet and brought a chair to the front. Another "stagehand" closed the shades. Thomas walked the actors through their lines and cues. He grabbed them by the shoulders and twisted them left and right, demonstrating how he wanted them to perform. After a few minutes he retreated to the back of the room, bent down and waved to Doug, who turned off the lights. The man pointed sharply and only the set of lights in the front part of the room came on, drawing the viewer's attention there. Gary, Brian, Melvin and Angel began talking and laughing at the same time.

"Cut!" Thomas called out. The boys stopped talking and looked at him. "Too soft," he said. "Waaaaay too soft. Remember," the director instructed, "you're high school boys, on your own time and up to no good. I want a lotta noise and spirit." He singled out one of them. "Especially you, D.J. I want five times more out of you." Gary nodded as Thomas walked back to his spot ten feet away and bent down a second time. "Okay, let's try it once again … Lights!" With a click the room instantly became dark once more. "Quiet everybody!" The front lights beamed, and the boys again exploded into overlapping conversation about unintelligible things. They were all much more animated and energetic, including Gary.

After several retakes, the scene began to take shape. Time passed quickly, and the Student of the Week reminded everyone that only five minutes remained until DEAR. Thomas stood. "Okay, folks, we've just got another couple of minutes. Let's try it one more time. No more interruptions from me."

Again, darkness, a pause, then a flash of light over the heads of the boys. They spoke loudly and animatedly about sports, school, girls, clothes, cars, etc. All four boys displayed machismo and confidence, including, if not especially Gary, who occasionally punctuated his sentences by snapping his fingers.

"Hey! Hey! Hey! It's time!" Brian, clearly the leader, announced loudly, silencing the others. He turned and motioned for Gary to come closer. "DJ, m'man, there's one last thing you gotta do to be in," Brian whispered, looking back at Melvin and Angel. "The next old lady who comes by, you gotta go grab her purse. We'll split the money between us."

Gary frowned. "I-I dunno guys. We ain't never done nothing like that."

"Yeah we have! You just ain't been with us!" Melvin announced, pointing his finger and sneering.

Angel waved his hand. "Yeah, ain't nothing to it. You just run up behind her, grab the purse and run."

"But what if she don't give it up?" the apprentice inquired.

Brian grabbed the boy forcefully by his shirt. "Then you gotta, you know, *persuade* her." He let out a menacing laugh, joined in by his friends.

The tension "D.J." felt as he scanned the faces of the chuckling boys carried into the audience. Thomas watched as the veteran gang members knelt down a few feet behind the nervous candidate, waiting for a victim. The room became quiet. In a few seconds, Janet, underneath a faded red scarf, slowly wandered on "stage." Her manner manifested the appearance of a senior citizen. When she reached the center, Gary leaped at her from behind, yelling, "Gimme that purse, lady!"

But the old lady did not surrender her purse. Instead she said no and clutched onto it, struggling with her attacker. The other three boys poked their heads up, emphatically demanding that their clumsy colleague hurry up. Gary, still behind the old woman, pulled at the leather handbag screaming, "I ain't playing, lady. Just give me the purse!"

The audience watched in horror as the old woman suddenly stopped struggling and clutched her chest with her right hand and grew limp. Gary carefully helped her onto a chair, symbolizing her fall to the floor. The three boys stood up.

"Whatcha do?" Brian asked, his voice shrill and angry.

Gary looked at the leader. His voice broke as he answered. "I-I-I think she's dead."

Uh-ohs could be heard throughout the room.

"Man, we told you to get the purse, that's all!" Angel shouted.

"Yeah," Melvin confirmed. "We didn't tell you to kill her! We don't be out here killin' no old ladies!"

The frightened main character was near tears now. "I told her to give me the purse but she wouldn't!" he shrieked. He looked at the figure slumped over a chair, removed her scarf and turned her face towards his. Janet's eyes remained closed. She breathed only through her nose, as Thomas had instructed her.

"Grandma?" Gary muttered quietly, his sad eyes bulging. "Grandma?" he called again. He took her in his arms and stared at his accomplices helplessly. "It's my grandmother!" he declared. With that announcement, the three boys fled in different directions, uprooting several chairs in their paths.

Gary, holding onto his victim, tried to stand and feebly reached for them with his right hand. "No! Don't leave!" Alone within seconds, he hugged the lifeless woman and cried, "What am I gonna do?" The terrified boy held the woman tightly in his arms. "I'm so sorry, Grandma. Please wake up. Please." he begged. "Please." His voice grew faint.

"Cut!" Thomas yelled. "Very good!" The class burst into wild applause and cheered the performance. The actors smiled and took deep breaths. Several students asked to be next on stage, but Thomas promised that he would see what he could do on another day. Several pupils exclaimed, "Aw, man!" The director praised each student individually, and within five minutes the entire room became totally quiet save for the sound of book pages turning.

That afternoon Thomas stopped at his mailbox after signing out for the day. A single envelope occupied the cheap wooden multi-layered structure. He retrieved it and turned it over a few times. His name was typed on the front. Gathering his briefcase and tote bag, the tired teacher walked down the stairwell leading to the back door. A short letter from Mr. Dorn stopped him before he stepped outside. On Friday at 11 o'clock he would be provided with coverage for his class. At that time he would attend an investigative hearing to determine if he had choked one Carlos Ramirez and pushed the boy's head into a door, in violation of the Boston School Department's policy on corporal punishment.

"Shit," Thomas exclaimed. He opened the back door and scampered to his car. It had started to rain quite heavily.

The nervous man attempted to make himself comfortable in the wobbly chair, the same one in which he had sat on the day of his interview over eight months before. How ironic, he thought. Of course, the reason for his appearance now was more somber. No one wore smiles on their faces as on that hot day back in August. The principal's office displayed its usual array of disarray. Mr. Dorn rambled about, searching for something as he ushered in all parties having business before him. The amenities hastily dispensed with, he removed books, folders and computer software from chairs so that the three visitors could be seated. The four participants, including the host, carried fresh yellow legal pads.

Mr. Dorn spoke nonchalantly. "The purpose of this hearing is to determine what occurred last week in the bathroom between Mr. Payne and Carlos Ramirez. This isn't an inquisition or a court of law. We just want to find out what happened, okay?"

Ms. Flores, seated next to her boss, nodded. Thomas looked at his invited guest and concurred. Gwendolyn Letterman smiled and said, "Of course." She sat with her wide shoulders slightly above the worn-out back of her chair, adjusted her trademark huge black glasses, then wrote on her legal pad. After talking to her on the telephone the previous week and meeting her that morning, Thomas had liked and respected her right away. A no-nonsense elementary teacher in her day, she had served as the Boston Teachers Union elementary field representative for only two years.

Letterman thought that the BTU had grown out of touch with its membership, so she had filed papers to run for the office just one day before the deadline. Her purely symbolic move was ridiculed as a gesture guaranteeing public humiliation. However, her predecessor, Maureen "Mo" Finnegan, a chain smoker with eighteen years on the job, had dropped dead of a heart attack a few weeks before the election. The incumbent's untimely death brought the forty-year-old daughter of Russian Jewish immigrants an overwhelming victory against several write-in candidates. Because of her background, Ms. Letterman entered the office of the Boston Teachers Union—a formidable structure adjacent to a convention center—fearing that she would not be accepted by her mostly male, mostly Irish colleagues. She was treated personally with respect and collegiality, but her ideas about confronting racism in the Boston School Department encountered benign neglect.

His authority as rule-maker and landlord firmly established, Mr. Dorn continued. "Now, Thomas, why don't we start by you telling us what happened that morning." He placed his left foot on the leg of Ms. Flores's chair.

Thomas resented his supervisor's rude and supercilious action. "Well," he offered. "First, I'd like to see any documentation about the incident other than the report I gave you, if any exists." He looked the administrator right in the face.

Mr. Dorn squinted his eyes towards Ms. Letterman. He knew that a provisional teacher would never have thought to make such a request on his own. He cleared his throat and straightened his tie. "Well, Mr. Payne, there isn't anything other than your statement."

"So neither boy has submitted anything in writing nor have their parents?" Ms. Letterman inquired. "And you have not submitted a request for an investigation to the BPS school police, the Department of Social Services, the BPS Office of Human Resources or to the superintendent?"

Mr. Dorn became annoyed. "No, I have not, Gwen. As I told Mr. Payne before, I'm required to investigate any allegation against a teacher of improper physical contact. Whether or not it goes any further or stays right here is up to me." His voice grew louder. "Now, if there are no other questions, I would like to hear what happened in the boys' bathroom, please."

Thomas, privately enjoying Mr. Dorn's agitation, reached into his briefcase and produced two sheets of paper containing a typed statement, along with three copies. "I'd like to read this expanded account of the incident to you, if I may, sir."

"Go ahead."

Thomas distributed copies to all parties in the room and read without raising his head. The statement provided three times the amount of details as his initial one-page handwritten report. He described the shamefully abhorrent condition of the bathroom and the recent problems with missing items on the second floor. He added that both matters had been presented to the Adams chief administrator after numerous Faculty Senate meetings. He mentioned that he had recognized Carlos from frequent problems with the boy during recess and having once chased him out of the building before school started.

Then Thomas provided details of his encounter with the two students in the bathroom—ten minutes before children were permitted to be in the building. He quoted the boy's profane and racist remarks to him. Finally, Thomas disclosed that, upon delivering the pupils to Mr. Dorn, he had asked the principal to check their bags. He stated that as of the time of his writing, he had not received any information from anyone about the consequences Carlos received for his racial epithets or physical assault against a BPS employee.

The first-year teacher finished his statement and raised his head to find Mr. Dorn clenching a tight jaw and breathing through flared nostrils. Ms. Flores looked very uncomfortable.

"As you know, Mr. Dorn," Ms. Letterman interjected, running her fingers through her short, black hair, "the Boston Teachers Union encourages its members to file criminal charges against all students who physically assault them, regardless of their age. Mr. Payne has been so advised."

"Well, that's his right, but I think that it may not be the best thing for the boy." Mr. Dorn replied, scratching his face. "The only reason I haven't held a suspension hearing for Carlos is because I thought that he was being transferred out of the Adams soon and because his family is hard to reach. They don't have a phone, so we have to send them notices in the mail—and they don't speak English either." He paused and nodded once to confirm his own statement. "In fact, I'm expecting a call today about a new placement for Carlos." He pointed at the chair next to his. "Um, Ms. Flores here has been following up on that with our ETL, Ms. Wagner."

The assistant principal's face indicated surprise. She lowered her head and wrote furiously on her legal pad, avoiding eye contact with anyone.

"Of course, Mr. Dorn. I thought it had to be something like that," the union officer said.

Mr. Dorn looked at his watch and made a face. "Well, that's about all I need to know." He stood and shuffled the papers on his desk into a neat pile. "Mr. Payne, thank you for taking the time to explain all this. I'll let you know if there's anything more." He turned towards Ms. Letterman and expressed similar sentiments.

Thomas and the BTU representative conversed with Ms. Flores as they left. Ms. Letterman told the assistant principal of her parents' history: how they had fled Russia with little more than the clothes on their backs. She revealed that as a little girl, she had actually attended the Adams. Ms. Flores, described her own parents' journey from Ecuador. The two women chatted like next door neighbors for a few minutes, then separated. Ms. Letterman and her client walked upstairs and stopped in front of the Room 217 door.

"Well, what do you think?" Thomas asked.

The short woman waved her hand. "You're in the clear. Dorn doesn't want anyone to read that letter you wrote. He won't let it go any further than his office." She paused, took a whiff and scrunched up her face. "Everything you said is obviously true. He wouldn't have done anything with it anyway. Mr. Power Principal just wanted to hold what happened over your head until the end of the year to keep you in line."

Thomas agreed, then whispered apprehensively. "Gwen, do you really think I should file assault charges against that kid?"

"Yep," she replied. "Look, BPS doesn't care if a kid shoots you in the ass with a cannon. Since the system won't protect you, you have to protect yourself." She paused and pushed her glasses closer to her eyes. "Besides, it'll give you even more leverage against Dorn. I wouldn't trust him any further than I could throw him."

She stopped talking after spotting a passing teacher and informed the woman that a reimbursement check the School Department owed her would arrive shortly. The teacher repeatedly thanked her while shaking her hand, then entreated that they excuse her for interrupting. Thomas smiled as he and his guest assured his colleague that she had caused no difficulty.

Ms. Letterman looked at her watch and turned back to Thomas. "I'd better get going."

Thomas shook her hand also. He felt as if a huge chain had been lifted from his neck but regretted that words could not fully express his gratitude. He feebly repeated what had been offered by the teacher before him.

"Keep your chin up, kiddo. It would be a shame to lose you," Ms. Letterman replied. "From what Ms. Caine tells me, you can walk on water." She shook her finger at him. "But don't get a big head," she joked. "I heard that a Jewish guy pulled that trick off first." They both laughed. She waved and headed for the stairs.

Thomas enjoyed the luxury of sleeping late on a weekday, then traipsed about in his pajamas and bath robe for an hour after finally climbing out of bed. He stood in his tiny kitchen, awaiting the microwave oven's notice that his cereal had been thoroughly cooked. He hadn't shaved yet and with no plans for the day, entertained the thought of skipping the chore altogether. During the third week of April, considerably later than Easter Sunday, all public schools in the Commonwealth of Massachusetts closed for one week. Thomas did not understand why children in the state received a one-week vacation in December, February and April, then languished in stuffy, hot classrooms until the end of June.

Thomas heard the familiar beep from the corner of his kitchen but ignored it as he stared at his New England Patriots calendar, compliments of his John Adams Secret Santa. The 280-pound defensive lineman posing for the current month had been traded right after the season ended. Thomas chuckled and flipped through a few pages until he reached June. He frowned. The last day of school appeared as a half-day on June 26.

The vacation sailed by quickly, and when school resumed, Thomas exhausted himself chasing special class teachers for third-quarter grades. It annoyed him that some could be so lax with their reports. The art teacher, Ms Popocoupolis, always distributed letter grades, but the music, computer and physical education teachers simply directed the junior staff member to "give them all A's." Thomas believed that such an approach to teaching lacked integrity and commitment. Of course, he suspected that he might think differently if required to calculate grades for over three hundred students.

That week, the first through the fifth grades prepared to take biannual standardized tests to determine their progress for the school year. In October they had undergone similar exercises, which, among other matters, helped decide who would be invited to Advanced Work Classes. The anticipated results of the tests always generated controversy, and this venture did not escape its share. Local news stories critical of the education provided by the city of Boston began to surface. Community activists and politicians took their usual positions: not enough money budgeted for the schools; too much money being spent improperly; racist, uncaring teachers; family poverty adversely affecting learning; unruly, disrespectful students; et cetera, et cetera.

Thomas interpreted the discord as the usual "them" against "us" nonsense. From his experience with Revelations, Inc., he had come to believe what his religious faith had taught him; "them" and "us" did not really exist except in the mind of an individual. Such divisions based on race, income, skin color, religion and so forth, he concluded, created wars, prevented countries from cooperating to discover cures for diseases and led to hostility among neighbors.

The idealistic young man served on the Testing Committee at the Adams, which met more frequently as the impending exercises approached. The Committee existed to recommend strategies for improving the school's annually dismal test performance. Every week Thomas listened patiently as his colleagues complained about the racist nature of the tests, complained about the parents, complained about the schedule, complained about everything. Because of his junior status, at first he was reluctant to offer suggestions. Eventually, he shared his beliefs that more classwork and homework from the teachers, and student involvement in after-school *academic* activities would result in substantially improved scores.

Thomas mentioned to his fellow committee members that only half of his students had been enrolled in after-school programs the previous year, but this year, because of his insistence, twenty-four of his twenty-seven students participated in such programs. He added that he called the program directors personally to check on his students. He revealed that he stayed after school for one hour twice a week, providing extra help to any student from his class bearing a note from home. He distributed a research article from his college days to every teacher at the Adams. It stated that students possessing their own library cards who regularly visited the library to choose their own books demonstrated significantly improved academic performance in all areas, especially reading. His colleagues responded to his suggestions with polite indifference. He and Heléna, who also served on the committee, shrugged their shoulders in resignation. Her stark advice for less Spanish and much more English in the bilingual classrooms received open rebukes.

Since the beginning of the calendar year, Thomas had prepared his students for the April ritual with test-taking skill-drills and openness about its arrival. On the Tuesday after vacation, the first day of testing, Thomas explained to his students what they already knew.

"Class, for the next few days I'm afraid we're going to have to skip reading and math in the morning in order to complete these tests. "I'm very sorry." He waited patiently as they cheered, clapped their hands and beat on their desks with glee. "You've taken these tests a buncha times before, so it shouldn't be any big deal." He stopped and acknowledged the usual questioner. "Yes, Christine?"

"Are we gonna get a grade for these tests?"

"No, honey. They will not be graded, or affect whether of not you go on to middle school or show up on your report card."

Thomas spent several minutes explaining the procedures for the rest of the week. He asked the students to spread out and assume their normal test-taking positions. Rumbling, scratching and creaking ensued for less than a minute as students dragged their desks, chairs and themselves into familiar locations. After directing traffic, Thomas asked for their attention.

"Before we get started, we better get a few things straight," he announced, imitating a stereotypical fired-up Baptist preacher. Several students chuckled. Familiar with the routine before a test, they prepared to play their parts.

"Aaaamen," Christine offered, her eyes closed.

"These tests," Thomas said, pointing at the stack of booklets on the table next to his desk, "don't bother us." He looked around. "Can I get a witness?"

More "Amens" surfaced, joined by a "That's right!"

"I said," the preacher paused and waved his hand, "these tests don't bother us."

"Well?"

"Um-hum."

"Go ahead, Mr. Payne. Preach!"

Thomas reached into his back pocket, pulled out a white handkerchief and wiped his brow. "We have made changes and moved mountains because we believe in ourselves, have respect for our leaders—living and dead—and care about our people." He paused to accept the affirmations from the congregation, then continued. "We have gone from the Wild Bunch to the Smart Bunch!" he exclaimed, touching his temples with his index fingers. He pointed to the door. "The other fifth-grade classes here are good, we admit that, but as long as Room 217 is around, they're always gonna be …"

"Second best!" everyone shouted.

"We've got the talent. We've got the drive. We've got the intelligence!" Thomas announced, hopping up and down once with each attribute. "We can't be stopped by anyone or anything." He paused again and exaggerated wiping his forehead. "School is no problem. Good behavior is no problem." He stopped, then started on the familiar call-and-response. "Bringing in homework is …" He put his hand to his ear.

"No problem!" they exclaimed.

"Setting a good example for the little kids is …"

"No problem!"

"Leadership is …"

"No problem!"

"And I say again, these tests are …"

"No problem!"

Thomas stopped and listened as the class broke into applause, then pressed on. "Here in Room 217, we do it neatly. We do it completely. We do it …"

"Sweetly!" they replied, almost in a hush.

Thomas nodded and smiled as he folded his handkerchief and placed it back in his pocket. He went to the table at the back of the room and pressed the button to the familiar music box. The class heard the song "I Believe I Can Fly" by R. Kelly. Thomas turned to his pupils and motioned for them to stand. They did.

His voice returned to normal. "Seriously, you've all made significant progress this year, and I'm very proud of you." He gestured into the air and glanced at the decorations. "Every month I put up posters of famous and influential people who have done fantastic things." He pointed upwards. "I remember asking one day during African American History month: What was the difference between you and Dr. Martin Luther King that enabled him to do great things? Between you and Rosa Parks or Harriet Tubman— or George Washington Carver?" Thomas smiled. "I remember that I must have called on half the class before …" He hunted for the right person. "Asa here, gave me the answer I was looking for."

The two-time Student of the Week accepted the acknowledgment with a grin.

Thomas continued. "Asa said, 'Nothing.' That's right. Nothing." He paused and moved his head from side to side. "They were all just ordinary people— just like you and me. Don't let anyone tell you that you can't do what those historic figures did because they had something special that you don't have! Some had far less than you do right now." He shook his finger at them. "One day, years from now I might be standing here in this classroom, putting up posters of famous role models." He walked closer to the window near his desk. The sky produced clouds and the threat of rain. Trees, not yet fully attired in their dress greens, swayed against a powerful wind. Thomas stepped near a student. "And I might just be holding a photograph of you, Gary." He put his arm on his pupil's shoulder.

The boy smiled. Thomas turned to face another learner.

"Or you, Angelica." He did the same to her. She responded by pressing her cheek against the back of his hand. "Or you, Pedro—or any of you." The tall man pointed around the room as his voice grew softer. "Remember, you're up for great things. You've already taken the first step. Keep up the good work." He searched around. The positions of the desks momentarily confused him. Having located his pupil, he patted the stack of materials on his table. "Captain, please pass out the answer sheets and choose another to distribute the booklets."

Lakeisha, clearly enjoying her first term as Student of the Week, smiled as she arose. "Yes, Mr. Payne."

That Friday Thomas was relieved to have finally finished testing. He looked forward to resuming the normal routine when May began next week. Still, the aberrant few days provided him with less work to correct. He drove home with the windows down. The temperature held at sixty-five degrees (according to the sister with the sultry voice on the all-jazz radio station). Trees had become greener and fuller. Tulips (and even dandelions) had begun to appear. Thomas passed by two ice cream trucks on the way to the Post Office.

Once there, the rookie teacher took a deep breath as he pinched the envelope between his thumb and index finger. He re-examined the mailing address to ensure that he had written it correctly, then took the letter to a box-like glass table. Encased inside were official-looking forms and advertisements for decorative stamps.

Thomas set his briefcase on the counter, snapped it open and snatched a manila folder containing the parent/guardian names and mailing addresses of each student. He checked the name again, then grabbed his copy of the letter and reread it: *Dear Ms. Berry … This is to inform you that your son, Douglas Berry is in danger of nonpromotion to the sixth-grade due to academic difficulties … Please call me at … Sincerely, Thomas Payne*

Thomas closed his briefcase, approached the mail chute, and opened the metal door. He suddenly became curious about its workings. As he examined the contraption, opening and closing it, a plump senior woman wearing a long, thick sweater excused herself. Startled, Thomas released the letter. He apologized for being in the way. The woman returned his smile, indicating his absolution.

Upon reaching home and retrieving his mail, Thomas climbed the winding stairs to his apartment. With every shade up, the sun shone through the opened windows of his living room. The smell of insecticide still hung in the air. (His landlady, a garrulous widow who lived on the first floor, had seen a roach in her unit a few days before and demanded that the entire building be fumigated.) Thomas dropped his belongings near the door and hung up his jacket, then poured himself a tall glass of orange juice.

Falling onto the sofa, he turned on the television and read the paper as he watched a cartoon based on a comic book crime-fighter with super powers. The show was the second episode of a two-parter. Thomas had become a secret fan of the program and watched religiously at 5 o'clock or recorded it. He remembered having been quite a lover of comic books when he was a kid: Batman, Spiderman, Superman, the Incredible Hulk—

all the ass-kickers. As a cover story, he told his friends that he watched the show just to connect with his boys.

Thomas opened the *Boston Globe* and read about the usual subjects: complaints about taxes, a Justice Department investigation into some official in the President's cabinet, the opening of a long-awaited movie, an earthquake in some foreign country. He made a mental note to send a check to the Red Cross and turned the pages. He stumbled on an announcement of the Golden Apple Awards in the *Metro* section. The pictures of twelve teachers were displayed along with a one-paragraph description about each. Thomas noticed that one awardee, an African American woman in her thirties, had very sexy eyes. Unfortunately, Ms. Mustafa had not made the cut.

He turned the page to finish the article, trying to appear blasé to no one in particular. On page twenty-one he skimmed over the names, pictures and descriptions of the five Junior Golden Apple winners. They almost all appeared to be hardworking, idealistic—and young. Several winners from both groups were people of color, so he assumed the selection procedures had been fair. He had actually forgotten about having been nominated. No big deal, he told himself. He went back to his program. A villain had just discovered the hero's secret identity.

"Uh-oh," Thomas said aloud. Turning his attention away from a commercial for some ugly, violent toys meant for pre-adolescent boys, he reached for his mail. The usual: bills, requests for money from worthy charities, advertisements. One fancy envelope with two recognizable names on the return address intrigued him. He hadn't seen Dr. or Mrs. Newman in almost a year. Reading their names evoked a feeling of apprehension.

Thomas cut open the envelope, freed its contents and read the invitation. The twenty-five-year-old man stood and paced in his living room. Sounds of a fierce battle between the forces of good and evil emanating from his television received little attention. He read the notice again, then went to the calendar. On the last Saturday in June, Laura, his former fiancée, and Patrick, the baritone-voice, golf-playing, art-loving attorney, would be married.

"Life goes on," Thomas thought to himself. He threw the invitation on his center table and stared at the last few minutes of his program but found himself distracted.

On the last day of the month Thomas double-checked April Anastasia and walked only one student to Glen's room during the Movie Day festivities. Unlike previous occasions, Freddy appeared disappointed about his exclusion. Thomas praised his pupil for his progress and expressed his desire to see the boy included next month.

Upon returning to the room, he witnessed a jubilant atmosphere. Cleopatra, Tyshaun and two other students had survived their flirtation with the "Danger Zone." That is, they had made it to the movie with no points to spare. Thomas and the rest of the class cheered the two first-timers. He asked that the class make a special effort to include *everyone* next time, especially Freddy. After some arm-twisting, they all agreed.

That afternoon right after school, Thomas met with Doug's mother and explained her son's situation. Armed with pages of documentation, such as previous grades, class work and standardized test scores, he built his case. He praised Doug and his family for the boy's apparent improvement in behavior and effort from the previous year. He reported that for the past several months Doug had been receiving long overdue special help and had begun to show signs of improvement. Still, the first-year teacher confessed, he did not believe it would be enough to carry him into the sixth grade.

Ms. Berry, a thin woman with a long face, listened intensely. She accepted Thomas's evaluation but expressed anger at "the system" for not doing more for her son. "Look, Mr. Payne," she said quietly. "I wanted Douggie to repeat the fourth grade last year but Ms. Patterson talked me out of it. She said the same thing you saying—he's been improving. Now just what does that mean?"

"Well, Ms. Berry, it means th—"

"I admit that I ain't been much help," she interrupted. "I ain't never got past the ninth grade. And I had to raise Douggie and two more boys and two girls by myself. Their dads took off."

Thomas lowered his head. "It sounds like things have been—"

"Since I don't have awholelotta booklearnin', I gotta depend on educated people like you and Ms. Patterson to help my boy ..." Her voice trailed off. "But all I know is that my baby's been going to school for six years and he can't read no better than his seven-year-old sister." She lifted her head. Her eyes glowed with anger. "How could something like that happen, Mr. Payne?" she demanded to know, her voice raised. The angry mother stopped talking and placed her hand over her mouth. Embarrassed, she abruptly stood. "I'll have to think about this," she announced and raced out of the classroom.

Thomas thanked her for coming. His heart melted at the sight of the helpless woman as she left.

Thomas drove to the gym and worked out. As he lifted the heavy weights, his mind rested on thoughts of Laura and her impending marriage. He shook off the thought that he felt jealous, then admitted that he probably did feel regret. He wondered why he had received an invitation anyway. Probably a warning notice, like at the Adams, so he wouldn't get blind-sided finding out about it from someone else. Of course he would not attend.

The first few bars of a dance tune familiar to his children jarred his attention back to the huge, noisy, brilliantly-lit room. Thomas strained and grunted, struggling to complete his last set, then grabbed a towel to wipe his face. Lots of lovely women frequented the gym, he told himself. He also recalled his father's rare advice. Nevertheless, he thought, he had violated Dad's Rule with Heléna and had survived.

Thomas inspected his surroundings. Mostly males in the immediate area, but dozens of well-packaged females usually assembled in the southern wing, utilizing the stair-climbing machines, bicycles and aerobic classes. Men hanging out there other than for warming up received ridicule from the other men as wimps. And women there resented men hanging about and leering at them.

For the two years he had been a member at Anthony's, Thomas had noticed a few of the ladies checking him out from time to time. Maybe, he thought, he could float a few trial balloons and see who grabbed at one. Of course, he couldn't be too obvious. He looked at his watch. Time to hit the showers. But before doing so, perhaps he might visit the south wing and spend a few minutes on one of the stair-climbers.

May

"Next is Mr. Payne," the principal announced.

Thomas clutched his folder and took a deep breath. He nodded, then strolled on stage in front of the auditorium, replacing Mr. Dorn. Now the center of attention, the young man opened a manila folder and raised his head to address the two hundred mostly black and brown faces staring at him. Among the fidgety third-, fourth- and fifth-graders were his students, who sat to his left on the worn, stained carpet, quietly awaiting his pronouncements. Melissa, after forfeiting the revered position in January, once again had earned the designation of Captain. She crouched like a lioness, observing every member of the class, poised for the opportunity to repay those who had regaled at her previous ignominy. Toward the back of the tiny auditorium, some of Ms. Patterson's students rolled around on the floor. Other classes contributed their fair share of noise. Near the barred, opened windows behind the children, a row of parents and teachers chatted in Spanish and English.

Thomas generally disliked Adams's assemblies. He thought they ran far too long, taking time away from the job he was contracted to do: educate children. Less than two months of school remained, but from what he observed during the standardized tests the previous month, they had no time to spare.

He put up his hands to quiet the antsy children and waited but recognized the futility of his efforts. Outside, rain fell against the opened windows as damp air filtered into the stuffy area. The dark sky brightened only from occasional flashes of distant lightening. Thomas took two steps forward, his toes resting just inches from the edge of the platform. The dry, faded wood of the small stage creaked underneath his feet. The heavy, open black curtains served as the frame to his promulgation of award-winners. The dirty walls, twice his height, mixed his words with the static of competing voices. He eyed his supervisor, expecting a word of admonition to the unruly children, but Mr. Dorn waved impatiently for him to proceed. Thomas cleared his throat and forced a smile on his face.

"Good morning, everyone."

"Good morning, Mr. Payne," a few dozen children responded.

Two third-grade boys in Ms. Bishop's class sitting directly in front of him began kicking each other. Their teacher made no attempt to stop them. Thomas closed his eyes and wished he were somewhere else. His scene would be the program's final one. The senior classes always went last. Ms. Sanchez-Taylor and Mrs. Chang had already announced their February-through-April awardees. The presentations started with the youngest grade, in this case, the third. (The primary-grade assembly would commence later that same morning.) Thomas forced the edges of his mouth to curl up.

"I'm very proud to announce the third-quarter award-winners for Room 217," he declared.

Mr. Dorn, a few feet away, discussed a matter with Ms. Flores. The children from the other classes, having already received or not received their awards, found no reason to focus on someone else. Thomas glanced at his students. Their faces displayed embarrassment for him. They flung their heads from left to right, observing the casual chatter in the room and recognizing the unfairness of it all. They had sat quietly while their schoolmates received acknowledgment, but their consideration would not be reciprocated. Heléna had sneaked into the room a few minutes earlier to catch her friend's act. She quietly scoffed at the lack of respect shown a colleague by his co-workers and their pupils. Thomas wished she had not come to witness his powerlessness. He spoke rapidly, attempting to quickly put the matter behind him.

"First, we have perfect attendance …" He announced seventeen winners, the highest percentage in the school. One by one, they marched to the front of the auditorium and accepted a gold-laminated certificate about the size of a five-by-seven index card. Next, Thomas announced his twelve School Spirit awardees, about the same percentage as the other rooms. Finally, he zipped through his three Merit winners and his two Honor Roll students. His numbers in the last two categories never came close to any of the other teachers. The honorees crowded on stage, a few balancing multiple certificates. After the last student shook the principal's hand, Thomas smiled and swung his arm in the vicinity of his proud group.

"Congratulations to all of you and thank you." About half of the seated, restless audience lethargically applauded. Thomas and his bunch stutter-stepped over reclining schoolmates to reclaim their spots on the floor. Mr. Dorn provided additional closing remarks and thanked the children for being so good. He announced the end of the assembly and scurried out the door of the auditorium, leaving the teachers to fend for themselves.

Thomas placed his hands on his temples. His head ached and his mouth was dry. He watched the other classes jousting to exit the room and sighed. Once again his class had produced the fewest purely academic honors in the school. He felt regret but considered his evaluation of student work to be fair and accurate. His pupils possessed no less talent than the others. His grades simply reflected brutal honesty.

Once he remembered, while passing through the teacher's lounge during lunch, he overheard a few of his colleagues, huddled around a cache of fried foods, donuts and diet soda, discussing their grading policies. Virtually every one admitted that her grades received some level of inflation—although they never uttered the word. Several teachers confessed that they never put an "F" on a report card, even if the student deserved one. One instructor stated that to do so would "discourage the child from trying his best." Thomas was surprised to hear Mrs. Chang admit that, to avoid unpleasant exchanges with the parents of her ostensibly high-achieving students, she avoided placing anything lower than a C on her quarterly reports. Ms. Rogers, the fourth-grade Advanced Work teacher agreed, reporting a C+ as her cutoff.

Thomas remembered reading in college that parents routinely berated public school education but spoke favorably of their own children's teacher and classroom. After listening to the staff, he understood why—because of the promiscuously disbursed, inflated grades. He had also come to recognize why standardized tests had become so vilified at public schools in general and at the Adams in particular—the tests provided glimpses into the ugly truth. Parents virtually never received the results of the tests. In fact, Mr. Dorn expressly forbade disclosing the results of the standardized tests to the parents or children.

Teachers received a written report, with scores broken down by student, subject and sub-subject. The test-taker's scores were recorded on a self-adhesive label to be attached to the individual's cumulative record folder. Yet, the results remained a secret. That way, Thomas realized, parents could continue to hold onto the delusional notion that even though public schools were going to hell, their own children were performing quite well.

Parents associated with Room 217 had encountered "sticker shock" upon receiving their child's first report card. Virtually every student received marks significantly lower than the previous year. Parents had complained, although none as vociferously as Cleopatra's mother. Thomas heard variations on a familiar theme: "But she made Honor Roll last year!" or "He received Merit Award from Ms. Patterson!" Even the Conduct and Effort grades could not escape gratuitous inflation. The previous year, Tyshaun and Asa had once each received School Spirit awards; so had Cleopatra.

Thomas recalled his internship at another elementary school as part of his master's training in educational administration. The school, twice the size of the Adams, was a sprawling multiracial structure a few blocks from his apartment in Jamaica Plain. Three years before his arrival, the principal and teachers had decided that only Attendance and School Spirit certificates would be awarded on a quarterly basis. They had made the change because the Honor Roll and Merit winners tended to be disproportionately White and Asian! The faculty, a mixed-race group about sixty percent White, considered their move to be academically sound. Thomas carried out his duties at the school without questioning his superiors. However, when offered a teaching position there, he declined.

After the John Adams awards assembly ended, Thomas escorted the class back to the sanity of Room 217 and praised them for their good behavior. As a reward, he extended an impromptu ten-minute indoor recess to the entire class—except those who had not returned homework or had otherwise not taken care of business. That afternoon the class participated in its second "Giver-Taker" exercise. With the exception of Freddy, every student received more giver than taker votes.

The following day at the beginning of reading class, Thomas made a familiar request. "Take out your journals," he instructed. As his students complied, he opened an additional window. After three cloudy days in a row, the sun finally stroked the faces of the pupils who sat near the glass. The humidity had declined from the previous day. Armies of birds could be heard negotiating over territory. A wide row of yellow and orange tulips stretched against the basement wall of the house across the street. In front of it, the tallest tree on the block sported its new coat of leaves.

Thomas peered down into the schoolyard. A truck carrying school lunches beeped repeatedly as it slowly reversed itself towards the back door.

On the other side of the playground, two teenagers competed in a spirited one-on-one basketball game. The taller one was being bested by his shorter and quicker friend. Thomas longed to challenge the victor to a duel; he'd make short work of the boy, he thought to himself.

He reached at the wall between two windows to press the corner of a poster secured by masking tape. All of the posters featured black and brown-skinned Americans who had achieved great success. However, the politician, writer, musician, painter and others had also overcome severe physical challenges (blindness, paralysis, etc.) to achieve that success. Thomas checked the buddy-pair pictures of flowers on the closet doors. Angel (a lily) and Melvin (a petunia) had accidentally been crumpled during the morning rush hour. He would replace them later.

The usual array of flapping, shuffling and swooshing slowed to a trickle as twenty-seven students manipulated their school-issued powder-blue notebooks, donated by Boston University. Each homeroom teacher had been given a set of six-by-nine-inch booklets with the explicit instruction that they were solely for journal writing. No further details followed, so teachers assumed that they could develop their own journal programs. Thomas decided to initiate a regular diary-entry activity, with everyone writing purely for private personal development. He correctly guessed that a writing ritual with no evaluative aspect might encourage similar pursuits for their own sake. Over the school year, several students reported that they had purchased locking diaries for home use.

At the beginning of the year, Thomas introduced the journal exercise as a semi-confidential matter. He assured his students that he would neither ask to see nor peek into their journals. He cautioned, though, that no absolute security from parental eyes could be guaranteed. The students agreed to leave the notebooks in their desks and that no classmate would peek into the journal of another, whether buddy, best friend or whomever. Once, Maurice read an innocuous entry written by his neighbor, Cleopatra, and brought on himself five days grounding with no chance of time off for good behavior.

Over the school year a routine had gradually developed: Journal entries were recorded during the first ten minutes of almost every reading class. Thomas would write the "stem" (the first few words of the entry) on the board, and everyone would copy it and continue writing for five to seven minutes or until time was called. Most of the openings were quite innocent: "On my last birthday, I…." or "The most fun I ever had was when I…."

Sometimes, however, the entries offered opportunities for more serious contemplation: "The last time I had a nightmare, I dreamt that...." or "Our roommate, Jonathan, is being transferred to Mrs. Chang's room and I feel...." Students routinely submitted excellent topic suggestions. About once a week Thomas asked if anyone wanted to share, then he would accept volunteers to go to the front of the room and read his or her entry.

That day Thomas decided to focus on a serious topic, potentially upsetting to some. He hung the "Do Not Disturb" sign on the door and returned to the center space at the front of the room. Standing at the chalkboard, the teacher spoke slowly. "Today, we're going to write about something we all have. As you know, this month we will celebrate Mother's Day, so I want you to write about your mothers." He faced the aging board and neatly wrote, "When I think about my mother, I...." and read the words aloud. Hands shot up.

"Yes, Angelica?"

"What if you don't have a mother, Mr. Payne?" she inquired, her small eyes showing discomfort. Her grandmother had braided her dark-brown hair into two pigtails, causing her to look much younger than nearly eleven years old.

"Everyone has a mother, Angelface," he answered. "She may not be with you right now, or maybe you don't remember the last time you saw her, but she's still your mother." He pointed at the board. "I'm talking about the woman who gave birth to you." He removed his eyes from Angelica and asked, "Don't you think about her sometimes?" to no one in particular. Several students nodded, including the young girl.

"All the time," she whispered.

Thomas opened his hands and wiggled his fingers. "Okay, go ahead. Remember, no one will see it but you. We won't share today." He went to the back of the room and pressed the button to the music player. Softly, "A Song for Mama" by Boyz II Men began to play. A soft breeze entered the room, stirring a few papers on the teacher's desk. At first, the boys and girls just stared at their notebooks. Eventually, a few students began to write. Gradually, the hand of every student moved furiously.

Thomas walked back to his desk and restacked a few papers. Staring at a small picture of his parents, he thought about his own mother. He remembered when he was about seven years old and had gotten sick. His mother had taken such good care of him. She had brought him soup and held him in her arms. He had tried to be tough but had felt so bad, and her embrace had felt so good that he cried. She had even scolded Edward for making too much noise in the next room. Thomas remembered the pleasure he had derived from hearing their uneven exchange. His condition had improved slightly the following morning, but Mom had insisted that he remain in bed for another day. She read him a story, bought him new comic books to read and played cards with him (Mom had let him win). Yes indeed, he thought, his mother was a saint.

The song ended, summoning the Ohio transplant back to his classroom. He eased over to the other side of the room and changed the music to a soft, instrumental piece. Disturbing sounds came from the children, not unexpectedly, but Thomas chose not to visit anyone unless called. Maria raised her hand and he gingerly walked to her desk and leaned in.

"Yes?"

"Mr. Payne, Angelica and Freddy are crying," she reported.

He put his hand on her head. "I know, Cookie. It's okay." The music and soft weeping muffled the sounds of adult footsteps that stopped at the teacher's desk and returned to the middle of the classroom. Separately, Thomas presented his two sobbing, still-writing students with a box of tissue. Each stopped writing long enough to pull the article from the box before returning to the assignment. Two additional pupils received tissues also. Thomas went to the board, erased the stem and, facing the class again, inquired as to their readiness to proceed. "Anyone need more time?" he asked. Half of the entranced children raised their hands. "Okay, another minute or so." He went back to the music box and waited until the selection faded into nonexistence.

"Thank you for your honesty and for being so brave," Thomas exclaimed. "I was going to do this one next month for Father's Day but I think it's best if we do them together." He went back to the board and wrote a few words, then he rotated and addressed the class slowly. "This one says, 'When I think about my father, I....' He set the chalk down, brushed his hands and tried to sound casual. "Same as before. Write whatever comes to mind. Write about the man who gave you life, whether you last saw him this morning, yesterday, last week, last year or never. Questions?" Seeing none, he traveled to the familiar area in the back corner and inserted another music piece into the machine. After a haunting piano introduction, Billy Joel sang "Goodnight, My Angel."

Thomas went to his desk as his thoughts again turned to Cincinnati. For some reason, he remembered a particularly difficult time in high school. His calculus instructor, an uptight woman with a master's degree from the Massachusetts Institute of Technology, apparently thought the popular wide receiver had little chance of achieving a passing grade in her class. She had a reputation for being especially hard on African American male jocks. She refused to call on him when he volunteered to answer questions and took pains to address him when his hand was lowered. His mother had insisted that he transfer, but his father had offered to help him.

That semester the two Payne men frequently stayed up well past midnight. One morning Dad came late to breakfast. With red, droopy eyes, he joked that he had gotten too old to be pulling "all-nighters." Thomas remembered his father's patience and encouragement while they attacked equations. The man was nothing short of brilliant. Later, the teacher accused him of cheating on his final exam because he had scored an A-. His dad went to the school and asked the teacher to produce her toughest question for Thomas to solve right there. She did and Thomas "knocked it out of the ballpark." He remembered the satisfied look on his father's face when she apologized.

The disquieting sounds erupting throughout the room abruptly brought the teacher back to the present. He watched with compassion as tears fell onto Carmelita's desk. Thomas approached her and held out the tissue box. She took one, then another and quickly blew her nose, anxious to resume her task. He was surprised to find Lakeisha noticeably upset. She lived in one of the few households with married parents and obviously adored her father. He had met them several times. Still, he extended the box and she accepted its relief. Thomas went from student to student, distributing tissues and words of encouragement. After travelling to the back table to play another instrumental piece, he raced to the closet to open another box. All around him, he heard crying, sniffing and blowing as if he had stepped into a funeral. Finally he went to the board. "I guess we should finish up," he announced.

Another minute passed before he addressed the melancholy group. "I said that we would keep these private, but perhaps some of you might want to talk. Reading can wait." He waved his finger in the air and bore a stern expression. "But what is said here stays right here. Nobody goes out and blabs what was said among us, okay?" Heads nodded and hands slowly inched upwards. Thomas looked around. "Carmelita?"

"My father's in jail, Mr. Payne," she reported, trying to catch her breath. Her face had turned brown, and her eyes, now blood-red, had swelled. "My mother said I'll be a grandmother before I ever see him again."

Thomas's own eyes filled with sadness. "Where is he, sweet pea? Here in town?"

She shook her head from side to side. "No, he's in Puerto Rico. I haven't seen him since I was in the second grade. He told my mother that we should forget about him. He won't let anyone come to see him. He said to tell everyone that he's dead!" She put her hands over her face and wept again.

Thomas thought for a second, then offered a suggestion. "Have you ever thought about writing to him? People in prison need to get letters from someone they love." He stepped closer and put his hand on her cheek. "Know what they do? They read the letters over and over again. Maybe you could ask your mother for the address."

Carmelita sat up and blinked her eyes repeatedly to clear her thinking. "Okay."

Hands filled the air. Thomas looked by the window. "Napoleon."

Brian spoke with clenched teeth. "My dad used to drink and beat my mom. I hate him!" He balled his fist and pounded it on his desk. Tear rolled down his face. Every eye was fixed on this usually stolid boy. "How come he had to be no good, huh? How come he couldn't be a great guy, like you, Mr. Payne?"

Thomas stepped closer. "You don't have to tell me if you don't want to, son," he replied. "But is that what you wrote today? That you hate your dad?" He waited.

The boy's face scrunched up, his eyes closed and his chest heaved as he struggled to catch his breath. "No." He put his hands over his face. Tears flowed freely from almost every boy and girl in the room. Some felt the pain of their own situations, while others sympathized with their friends. Brian removed his hands. "I wrote that I miss him. I don't know why, but I do. Why should I miss him, Mr. Payne?"

Thomas brought him the box of tissue. "Have you told your mom this?" The agitated boy shook his head. "Why not?" Brian shrugged his shoulders. The teacher leaned in and put his arm around him. "Yes, you do know why not. Tell me. It's okay."

Brian lowered his hands. His nose had started to run, so he reached for the box and wiped. His voice seeped out hesitantly. "I think that, you know, maybe my mother'll get mad at me. I don't wanna hurt her. She's been hurt too much."

Thomas put his hand on the boy's head as if to bless him. "It's natural to miss your father. Even if he's done wrong, he's still your father." He removed his hand and placed both elbows on the boy's desk, holding his own face in his hands only a few inches from the face of his distressed student. "You've grown up a lot since your dad left. Maybe enough time has passed for you to talk to your mom about how you feel."

Brian nodded in agreement.

On and on it went. Suppressed pain and uncertainty reverberated throughout the classroom. It became clear to Thomas that the subject of an absent mother or father more often than not had developed into a "don't ask, don't tell" issue at many households. The youths spoke of long-held feelings about their biological parents. Some disclosed shattered homes due to substance abuse. Others described homes with no clear excuse for a parent's truancy. The feelings expressed toward a mother or father varied from intense love and caring to deep-seated anger and resentment. Most anguished over missing fathers. Thomas felt sadness that the majority of his students came from homes without one or both parents.

The family of Room 217 talked and shared with their confessor for a half-hour. The group, including Thomas, grew hoarse and drained emotionally. After bringing their session to a close, he lined them up at the door for a break and suggested they visit the bathroom, dry their eyes, then replenish their fluids with the bottled water downstairs. He told them to take as much time as they needed and recommended that they keep a close eye on their buddies. Melissa, still trembling but trying to appear in control, stood in line with the girls and Brian with the boys.

Students continued to wipe their eyes. Several girls hugged each other and their teacher. Lakeisha whispered to him that she knew that her father at home wasn't her real father, but her parents didn't know she knew. Thomas agreed to see her privately right before lunch. Almost everyone was still wheezing and gasping for air when they lined up. Tyshaun tugged on the tall man's sleeve and reported that his buddy would not move. Thomas dismissed the class and advanced to the back of the room.

"You okay, Freddy?" he asked.

The boy lifted his face. His eyes appeared puffy from weeping as he struggled to speak. "M-m-my father …" he stuttered before stopping to wipe his face on a tattered tissue and tried again. "My father …" He collapsed his head onto his desk, defeated.

Thomas positioned himself behind the boy and lowered both hands on his shoulders. "I know, son. I know and I'm very sorry." He fought tears himself. "But what can you do? What can anybody do? It won't change what's happened." He realized he was talking to avoid his own discomfort and stopped.

"I miss my mother, Mr. Payne," he moaned. "But I'm too old to carry on like this."

His pained voice pierced Thomas's heart. He rubbed the top of the boy's head gently. "Says who?" he demanded to know. Freddy kicked the legs of his desk. Thomas struggled to find a response, something he could do to relieve his student's suffering. He searched around the room until his eyes rested on LaShonda's former desk. Aware that he could get himself into serious trouble for articulating such a suggestion, his voice quivered. "Have you had a chance to say good-bye to her?"

Freddy lifted his head. "Wh-What do you mean?"

"That's what funerals are for, my little brother," Thomas replied. "People get to pay their respects to a loved one who's gone." A slight smile formed on his face. "I remember my grandma's funeral. We all got to say good-bye."

"I-I was just a kid when it happened, Mr. Payne. They wouldn't even let me go. I don't even remember what my mama looked like anymore." Freddy closed his eyes in an attempt to shut out his guilt. "That's terrible, ain't it?"

Thomas pulled up a chair and sat down. He rested his elbows on the fifth-grader's desk, supporting his face with the dark side of his hands. "No, Freddy. Like you said, you were just a child." Thomas lifted his head and searched the room for a response. He studied the newly displayed paintings of flowers hanging all over the room from art class—daffodils, marigolds, tulips and such—but could not conceive a feasible plan. Then he stared at the set of student photographs still spread above the center chalkboard. "Do you have any pictures of your mom?"

The boy sat up. His eyes slid right to left. "My grandmother does," he answered.

Thomas pointed. "Okay, I'll tell you what. The next time you visit her, ask to borrow a picture of your mom for school. Give it to me, and I'll go to this place I know and have a color copy run off and laminated for you. Hell, I'll make two of them for you. What do you think?" Thomas realized that he had uttered a swear word but suspected that Freddy had not noticed. He gave the boy's ear a tug.

Freddy sat up even straighter, and his voice cleared somewhat. "Why would you do all that for me, Mr. Payne?"

Thomas smiled. "Because you're one of my boys, Freddy, and I'm on your team. I've been telling you that for months." He looked at his watch and stood erect. "Now go downstairs. Tell your buddy to stay with you. Take your time." He pointed and put on his tough teacher face. "Now that don't mean you and Tyshaun come waltzing back in here tomorrow, hear?" A smile broke across the boy's face as he got to his feet. They walked together to the door with Thomas's hand resting on the lad's shoulder.

The recuperating fifth-graders stood in the hallway. Melissa rumbled out of the bathroom to the front of the line and gave the hand signal for the group to head back. Freddy walked by, going in the opposite direction and motioned to Tyshaun. Several eyes turned and followed as the two boys clomped toward the bathroom. Thomas stepped aside so that his students could re-enter the room. Their faces still displayed some signs of strain, but generally everyone appeared to have recovered from their ordeal enough to resume their academic tasks. He smiled at them as they crossed the threshold, then closed the door after pinching Vince, the last pupil in line, on the shoulder.

"Is Freddy alright, Mr. Payne?" Angelica asked.

Thomas smiled at her. It was just like Angelica to care about someone else's well-being, he thought. "Freddy'll be alright but he's going to need a lot of support."

"Okay. We'll help him," she assured her teacher.

Thomas nodded and checked his watch. Silently, he walked to the back of the room and fiddled with the music player again. A few clicks later, a rapid drum sounded, then a lively Jamaican-style dance tune blasted away. Recognizing the song immediately, several boys and girls started bopping their heads up and down while waving their arms about. A few began singing.

Thomas smiled and waved his hand. "I'll give you a reading assignment later. Let's clean out desks, relax and jam for a few minutes!"

Everyone applauded to indicate full agreement.

That afternoon after dismissal, Thomas sat at his desk alone. A sudden gust of cool air swept into the room and struggled futilely to scatter a nearby stack of spelling assignments. Having earlier gone to the table and picked several papers off the floor, Thomas had securely anchored them with a music disc. He watched the battle for a few seconds, then resumed his task of doing nothing.

He thought about the events during and immediately following the journal exercises. He felt pride that his charges had reached deeply within themselves to explore disturbing areas. Thomas admitted privately that he had not been prepared for the avalanche of emotions that poured from the hearts of his sometimes spiritually troubled children. He assumed that several would speak to their caretakers at home about what had transpired, and suspected that he might even receive a follow-up telephone call or two about the matter. Hopefully, Dorn would not be involved.

The Cincinnati native reflected again on his own feelings about his parents and his family. He regretted not having spent more time with his sister, Vanessa. A creative and talented artist, she designed everything from dresses to wallpaper, selling her ideas freelance. Thomas had recently come to understand that he had avoided getting too close to her because of her tendency to be overemotional. She cried easily. Until a few years ago, Thomas had been quite uncomfortable with tears. He and his brother had declared that tears were for sissies. "A brother has to be strong," they repeatedly affirmed to each other. Such attitudes had led to their insensitivity toward women.

Thomas remembered the look on Dora Jefferson's face at their high school prom when she caught him kissing that older girl with the round ass (he no longer remembered her name). To avoid dealing with how he had hurt her, Thomas had expressed anger at Dora for not believing his lies and having stormed out of the party. He never disclosed the details about that night to his parents, but he and Dora never spoke to each other again. During his involvement with Revelations, as part of an assignment to seek another's forgiveness, he had found Dora's number, called her and apologized. She had responded graciously towards him and had conveyed genuine respect for his gesture—after she got over her initial shock.

Maybe, Thomas thought, Vanessa had become involved with that church because she had not found fulfillment for her emotional needs. Edward's legal problems had occupied everyone's attention at the time. Sis had always required a great deal of love and attention. She had reached out to her youngest brother for support, but he hadn't recognized it. Fortunately he had learned that it was never too late to develop a close relationship with a family member. Thomas resolved to spend more hours at Vanessa's the next time he visited Cincinnati. She and her husband didn't seem like such drips anymore. Funny thing, he mused. He had thought of Jerry as an uxorious wimp because he didn't like sports, never refused Vanessa anything and liked working on computers. And he had formerly viewed his two nephews as a couple of brats. Soon, he would welcome the opportunity to construct a more charitable evaluation.

He thought about someone else too and arose from his chair to see if she had gone. He left the day's projects on his desk and descended the back stairs to the basement. The temperature dropped five degrees downstairs but did not make him uncomfortable. He avoided several puddles of water from the pipes overhead and proceeded past a set of double fire doors into a smaller hallway. Two storage rooms stood adjacent to one another. The larger one was filled with various textbooks and assorted school supplies, the smaller one with the scent of perfume.

Thomas looked at the bottom of the second door and saw a band of light. He heard the sound of music inside, Spanish music. He knocked twice and received permission to enter. Upon opening the door, he saw Heléna seated in a small chair, reading a catalog on available literature books. On her small table, a plastic vase held an attractive, hand-picked bunch of lavender lilacs. She lifted her head and greeted him. Thomas admired how lovely she looked.

"*Hóla*, Tomaso. Haven't seen you down here in ages," she exclaimed with a smile.

Thomas noticed a few decorative changes since his last visit—besides the flowers. She had hung a few of the posters he had loaned her. Also, student-drawn pictures of favorite books occupied the walls. He put his hands on his hips and tried to look annoyed. "Hey, what's the big idea, stealing my ideas. I oughta sue!"

"Ha!" Heléna replied, tossing her booklet on the tiny table. She took to her feet and mimicked his pose. "Glen schooled you! Don't think I didn't know where you got the idea." She cranked her neck a couple of times.

"Well …" Thomas offered in feigned embarrassment. "I'll let you off the hook this time." They both giggled. Changing the subject, he flexed his elbows outwards a few times. "How can you stand it in here?

"What?"

"It's too frickin' small, that's what."

Heléna advanced closer to him. "Not really. The kids are small. It gives us an opportunity to look each other in the eye," she replied, arching her dark, thinly-honed eyebrows. "That way, I can tell what's on their minds." Characteristically, she switched subjects. "Speaking of which, what's on your mind, *mi amigo*?" Before he could answer, Heléna focused on the sound of a Spanish ballad coming from her palm-size radio. "Oh! I love this song!" she cooed.

She turned up the volume, reached for her friend and squeezed his arms while oscillating her attractively sculpted body. Thomas relished the sight, then responded by putting his hands on her waist and shuffling his feet back and forth. She gazed at his face. Hers displayed tenderness and caring. She threw her head back and closed her eyes, enjoying the perfect moment.

Lately, he noticed, they had been touching each other occasionally when alone. The fondness the two had for each other could be controlled in public but not in private. Thomas felt his skin getting warmer. Standing close to Heléna could have that effect on him. The music eventually faded, so he backed up and fell onto a student-sized chair, extending his long legs halfway across the floor. Heléna turned off the radio. They resumed their conversation. Thomas described what had occurred that morning in his room. Heléna listened with fascination. She sat down and the two talked for a few minutes about the awards assembly. The subject then shifted to their own families.

"Did your brother tell you that my roommate, Karen, flew to Cincinnati and spent the weekend with him? She broke up with her boyfriend a couple of weeks ago, you know."

Thomas was surprised. His eyes grew large and he shook his head. "No. I didn't know anything about it."

"I don't think it's a good idea, you know, the two of them together. Karen doesn't know a lot about men."

"True," Thomas replied. "But let's face it, they don't need our permission." He frowned. "I don't know why Edward didn't tell me about his plans but …" He shrugged his shoulders and threw his hands up in resignation.

They moved on to discuss their other siblings. Thomas mentioned his recent resolution about his sister.

Heléna stared at a poster of a lovely Spanish singer holding a book while surrounded by a group of small children. "You know, I was always kinda jealous of my three sisters. I really was afraid that my parents loved them more than me. And they were all so much prettier." She sighed. "One of them had even been voted second runner-up as Miss California."

Thomas raised his eyebrows. "Oh? I didn't know that."

Heléna pointed to her face. "A few months ago, I paid an obscene amount of money for electrolysis to get rid of my thin mustache." She wiggled her mouth. "What do you think? Looks better?"

Thomas stared at her. "I never noticed you had a mustache," he lied. "You're very pretty, Heléna. What are you talking about?"

She reached into a copper tin, seized a round piece of peppermint candy and threw it at him. "You're such a terrible liar."

They both laughed. Heléna inhaled deeply and descended into deep thought. The subject of her sisters suddenly consumed her.

"You know, Thomas," she confessed, "it wasn't easy growing up with three beautiful sisters. My family's from Venezuela, and there it's every little girl's dream to become Miss Venezuela, then Miss Universe—or Miss Something."

"I read that somewhere," Thomas remarked.

Heléna continued, barely aware that he had spoken. "When I was a girl, I wasn't very pretty. I was skinny and wore glasses and had braces on my teeth. I was so ugly. All my girlfriends got their periods and their tits sooner than me. I was a late bloomer. Around sixteen or so I started filling out in all the right places. But I didn't know nothing about boys. My dad was real strict."

Her eyes opened wide as she steamed ahead. "You might not believe this, but I used to be real shy. My only boyfriend in high school was really interested in my older sister." Thomas snickered and Heléna added, "The bastard." She grabbed a peppermint and switched it from one hand to the other as she expanded her account. "I went off to college with my virginity intact just like my parents wanted. Once I got to UC, I went kinda wild for a couple of years, you know what I mean?" She hung her head. "Maybe God is punishing me for it. You know, now all I meet are jerks, losers and married men trying to get a little something on the side."

She spotted the look of sympathy on her friend's face and shifted into her usual high-spirited demeanor. "Jesus, Tomaso, I don't know why I'm going on like this. You didn't come down here to listen to me confess my sins." She put her hand over her mouth and dropped the candy back into the tin. "Come to think of it, why did you come down here anyway? Not that I'm not always glad to see you. I know you've been pretty busy."

Thomas stood up. His mouth became dry and his pulse accelerated. "Um, I just wanted to see how you were doing, that's all." He checked his watch. "Well, I better get going." He took a step, then another, but turned back. "No, that's not all," he confessed. A little nervous, he paused, then reached for Heléna's hand and gently pulled. She stood and put her hands on his chest. He feared that she could feel his heart pounding. He kissed her on the forehead and looked into her eyes. "Heléna, you are so beautiful in every way. I can't understand how you wouldn't know that. If you're not involved with someone, and if you're interested, I would like for us to start seeing each other."

Smiling, she tilted her head back and put the back of her hand on her forehead. "Shoot, Thomas. We see each other all the time." Her giggling did not elicit its usual accompaniment from him. She shook her head playfully. "Oh I don't know, Tomaso. What would Daddy say?" She put her arms around his neck and giggled again, clamping her tongue between her perfect teeth. Her expression and voice became serious, her eyes revealed endearment—and fear. "Are you sure this is what you want? Are you over that other woman? What was her name? Laura? The one you were going to marry?"

Thomas held onto her. "That's all in the past now. I'd like for us to suit up and see what happens. You game?" Their lips met lightly for just a second.

Heléna smiled. "Sounds yummy to me, Tomaso. But if we're going to do this, we should keep this between the two of us, you know—and you can't be fuckin' other women, *entiende?*" She shook her finger at him, complete with burnt-orange nail polish.

Thomas winced. One day he'd have to talk to her about her mouth. "Agreed," he replied, raising his right hand. "You want to shake on it—or can we do better than that?"

Just then, the outer door banged as the custodian stomped into the corridor. He brutalized an old Frank Sinatra song as he fought with a set of keys to the boiler room door across the hall. The two teachers released each other and looked embarrassed, as if they had nearly been caught in some wrongdoing. Thomas put his hand on Heléna's cheek and whispered, "I'll call you tonight."

When he arrived at the Adams the next morning, Thomas inconspicuously wandered downstairs to Heléna's room and inspected the lock on her door. He had always been concerned about her being in the basement of the school without adequate security. He had broached the subject a few times, but Heléna reported that she had spoken to Mr. Dorn and to the custodian about putting a working lock on her door. Each had assured her that he would look into the matter. The last such conversation had occurred back in January. Thomas resolved to remove the old lock after school and replace it with a new one the next morning. He wanted his girl to be safe. He delicately opened the door and searched for possible witnesses. Seeing none, he scampered off to his own room.

That afternoon during recess Thomas stayed in to practice with his chess team and several additional players. Eventually, a solid group of ten enthusiastic competitors met during the early afternoons. The team continued to improve in skill and discipline. Virtually every day right before lunch, they set up at least a half-dozen chess boards, went to lunch, grabbed a quick bite and returned to the classroom. Thomas observed the games and coached, but he often played as well. He could still defeat everyone in the class—although games against Gary took longer than the others.

After recess the class reassembled, and Thomas stood stoically in the hall near the teacher's lounge. He waited for his students to finish quenching their thirsts at the "watering hole," as he liked to call it. One by one, they filled their paper three-ounce cups with water and drank. The Student of the Week supervised, enforcing the two-cup maximum. Getting water this way took forever, but the station upstairs had been broken—by an unknown group of students. While waiting, he saw Heléna exit from a nearby classroom and strut towards them. Seeing her made the young man's heart jump. She wore a pair of olive-colored pants with a white long-sleeve blouse. Her breasts pressed against a pair of dark braces holding up her slacks. Thomas thought she looked very sexy. He noticed Freddy and Tyshaun staring at her. The latter poked the former and made an almost imperceptible head move in the woman's direction. They smiled and nodded in agreement. Thomas frowned.

"Hello, Mr. Payne. How are you today?" Heléna asked.

"Fine, Ms. Gutiérrez. Thank you," he replied, barely turning in her direction.

She continued on her journey. Thomas stole a glance at her derriere and fantasized about his plans for the next time they saw each other.

His carnal thoughts were interrupted by the sight of Mr. Dorn exiting the office, carrying a set of manila folders in his right hand and his reading glasses in his left. Thomas had stayed out of the man's way since their meeting with the BTU rep and had received no further summons since then. The two men exchanged slight head nods as the principal passed by. Suddenly, Gary, at the end of the line, raised his hand. Thomas waved to the boy, granting permission to speak. The boy stepped into Mr. Dorn's path.

"Sir, I would be pleased to meet you on the field of honor at your earliest convenience," he declared. Teacher and students suppressed giggles.

Mr. Dorn smiled and looked at Thomas. "Can you translate for me, Mr. Payne?"

Thomas approached the two. "I noticed a chess board in your office. I told the class that you probably play. You've just been challenged to a game." He smiled and put his hand on Gary's shoulder.

The principal smiled again and lowered his eyes to the dignified pupil. "So, think you're ready for the big time, do you?"

"Yes, sir. I promise to defeat you quickly so that you can get back to your important work here."

"My, my. Confident too! I like that," the man replied. Now, if that's not a serious challenge, I don't know what is." He looked at his watch. "How about tomorrow at the start of lunch?" The boy agreed and returned to his line. Melvin and Hernando patted him on the back. Mr. Dorn chuckled and put his hand on Thomas's shoulder. "I'll have him back soon. It won't take long."

The two laughed, and the older gentleman continued on his journey. Thomas felt relief that their exchange had lifted the dark cloud over their heads, at least for him. After escorting the class back to the classroom, he summoned the Student of the Week.

"Make sure Gary gets to pass out papers today," he whispered.

On Friday after school Thomas called his brother and scolded him for not divulging his recent weekend plans. Edward offered as sincere an apology as he could and defended his actions, saying that the decision occurred at the last minute. Thomas considered telling his brother about his recent conversation with Heléna but decided not to, fearing that Edward would spoil his good mood by asking locker room-type questions.

After Thomas said good-bye he spoke to his sister, her husband and their boys. Vanessa was surprised that her little brother seemed interested in her work and her well-being. She admitted to being disturbed by recent developments at the church; some revelations of "peculiar" bookkeeping discovered by an auditor. Now the pastor was under fire. She confessed that she didn't know what to believe. Her concern dissipated when Thomas asked if he could stay at her home for a couple of nights when he visited in the summer. He had never stayed there overnight. Vanessa enthusiastically agreed. Thomas heard his nephews cheer when she announced that "Uncle T" would be staying with them in July. He promised that he would pray for her family and their church, then hung up.

He checked his watch and became angry at himself for spending so much time on the telephone. He had to hurry if he was going to finish the task he had started the day before—cleaning his apartment. He took out the garbage, washed the dishes, vacuumed the living room carpet and changed the sheets on the bed. He opened all the windows to completely air out the

place. It was such a wonderful day. The temperature had climbed to sev-
enty-eight degrees with predictions for similar weather for the entire weekend.

Thomas went to his stereo and played a collection of slow-tempo classical nocturnes to relax. He didn't understand his excitement. Heléna and he
would go to a movie and then to dinner at that Chinese restaurant with the
aquarium—that's all. Heléna had stopped by his place more than once on
work-related business. He had helped her type a new résumé just a couple
of months ago when her portable computer went on the fritz. They had
behaved themselves quite admirably then, but this was the first time she
would visit as his ... his ... whatever.

He inspected his surroundings. Now he regretted not having bought
plants to help the place look more homey. Thomas checked the clock in the
kitchen, then ran into the bedroom and started to undress so he could shower
and change. He stopped to hear his messages and discovered that a woman
named Tyisha, a young sister with an absolutely gorgeous body who worked
out at Anthony's, had returned his call. He'd have to get back to her and
hint that he only wanted to work out together. At nineteen, she really was
too young for him anyway.

At 5:30 Thomas surveyed his castle a second time. With its dustless
furniture, spotless floors and fresh linen, it hadn't looked so good since Easter. He couldn't wait to see the look on Heléna's face when she saw the red
rose he had bought for her. Enough already, he thought. Thomas sat down,
turned on the television and swore because he had missed his superhero
cartoon. He tried to relax by watching the local news. About fifteen more
minutes passed and his anticipation changed to concern. He never should
have agreed to Heléna taking the train. While observing the weather report,
Thomas glanced down at the pile of movies beneath the television and
gasped! He jumped up and grabbed a movie with pictures of scantily clad,
big-breasted women on the cover and ran into his bedroom. He stuffed the
contraband securely into a suitcase on the closet floor and slammed the
door shut. On cue, the doorbell rang.

Thomas felt his heart jump and scolded himself for acting like such a
schoolboy. He walked down the recently swept stairs and all anxiety turned
into enchantment when he opened the door. In the background a six-feet-tall
azalea bush showed off a dazzling bouquet of pink flowers. In the foreground,
Heléna held open her arms and smiled. She had changed into a pair of black
jeans under a loose-fitting top, exposing her shoulders and svelte midriff.

"Hi, handsome," she said.

"*Bienvenidos*," he replied. *Te miras bonita!* You look beautiful!" He stepped back, allowing her to enter and took her in his arms. Holding her felt wonderful. He examined her lovely face and noticed that she had applied a generous amount of red coloring on her full lips. Remembering how he would respond to Laura, he kissed his guest lightly on both cheeks. Heléna frowned.

"What the hell was that? What are we, French diplomats?"

"You've got a half-gallon of lipstick on," he said, laughing.

"Oh, sorry," she apologized. "It's been a while since I've had a boyfriend, you know." She reached into her jacket pocket, pulled out a yellow tissue and wiped her mouth clean. "Better?"

"Much better," he answered.

The next Monday at the beginning of social studies, Thomas prepared the class for a challenge. The morning had been chilly, but after lunch the sun had managed to maneuver past the clouds. The classroom had begun to get comfortable. Thomas stood at his familiar spot at the center of the gauntlet.

"For the past three weeks we've been studying the deeds of brave men and women who struggled to form a great new nation called the United States of America," he began. "We've read simple versions of the Declaration of Independence and the Constitution, and watched a movie showing us how such historic documents became a reality." He held up his hand, showing his index and middle fingers. "For the next two days, the great assembly of Room 217 will likewise come up with a declaration that identifies our beliefs." He lowered his middle finger and pointed at the class. "And you will have to confirm your declaration," Thomas announced, "by coming up with a giving project that the whole class will be involved with for the rest of the school year."

The students began to whisper among themselves. Christine raised her hand. "Mr. Payne? Mr. Payne?" she called out.

Thomas gave her a sour expression. She put one hand over her mouth and kept the other in the air.

"Wait, there's more," he said. "You can take about an hour or so today and another hour tomorrow putting together this declaration. It has to be written and signed by every one of you. The document only has to be about a paragraph and it must begin with the words: 'We, the Class of Room 217,' then go on."

More hands waved at him. Thomas ignored them.

"One last thing," he offered with a smirk. "You'll have to create the document on your own. I'm going to be outside the door correcting papers." Raised voices scattered throughout the room.

"What!"

"You're not even gonna help us?"

"Come on, Mr. Payne! That's not fair!"

"Yeah, how we gonna do all this on our own?"

Thomas laughed. "You'll be fine, my children. Play together like a team and don't get too loud. And the rules for those who are grounded or on ISP, and the rules for getting out of your seat and talking without raising your hand first will be temporarily turned off."

The class burst into applause and began talking aloud to each other. Thomas held up his hands and the room grew silent.

"Now I'll be back during the last ten minutes to help mop up. Any questions?"

Five minutes later Thomas gathered an armful of papers, pulled a chair outside the room and left the assembly to its own ingenuity. The rookie teacher made himself as comfortable as he could out in the noisy hallway. Students from other rooms constantly wandered back and forth. One little boy, the child who had greeted him in the public library a few months ago, proudly displayed his Student of the Week badge. A rumble of noise emanated from the other end of the hall—Ms. Rogers's fourth-grade Advanced Work Class returning from their scheduled school library jaunt. Her brood conversed as if they were outside. Thomas lowered his head and closed his eyes, hoping they wouldn't take too long to clear the area.

The group spotted Mr. Payne sitting outside his room, immediately cut their noise level in half and stumbled by without incident. (Back in February, while his pupils sweated over a "killer" math test, the fourth-grade AWC had drifted by, generating so much noise Thomas had stepped outside of his room and scolded them. Ms. Rogers, a haughty woman from Louisiana who identified herself not as Black but Creole, said nothing. But she never forgave her colleague for his forwardness and barely spoke to him for weeks.)

Although outside his room, Thomas had not closed the door completely. He made efforts to grade papers but what he overheard made him shudder. His team argued and fought like members of English Parliament. The rudeness and uncooperative spirit evinced by his often difficult students did not surprise him, but statements coming from the mouths of his usually congenial ones shocked him.

"Shut up, Melvin!" Maria yelled.

"You shut up!" he replied.

"That is so stupid," Pedro told Gary.

"Yeah? But not as stupid as what you said."

"You don't know what you're talking about," shouted usually quiet Janet to Jessica.

With the assembly having accomplished nothing after a half-hour of infighting, Akeem, the current Student of the Week, ran to the door. "Mr. Payne, they won't listen to me!" he whined. He was joined by a handful of classmates with similar complaints about the misdeeds of fellow students.

Thomas shrugged his shoulders and spoke calmly. "Captain, it sounds to me like *you've* got a problem. But I'm not going to interfere. Now you really do have to keep the noise down, though." He went back to placing scores on the morning's math seatwork. "Bye," he said without looking up.

Akeem ran back inside. "Mr. Payne said you guys better keep the noise down and do what I say!"

"He didn't say that!" Carmelita screamed, closing the door.

The second half-hour produced few tangible results. By the time Thomas returned to the group, the assembly of fifth-graders had exhausted themselves with infighting and bickering. Several students sat flushed-faced and defeated. More than one buddy had threatened to petition Mr. Payne for a trade. Cleopatra had even broken up with Asa. Thomas snickered and commented on how tired, beaten and hot everyone looked.

"Nobody even thought to open the windows?" he asked smugly.

No one replied.

A welcome breeze from four just-opened windows sought to revive the worn participants. Thomas strutted down the walkway to take his center stage position. He listened to griping and blaming for about a minute before steering the discussion towards the theme of individual responsibility. He especially chastised those like Cleopatra, Hernando and Angelica, who obstinately withdrew from the process altogether.

"Would a player on a sports team be allowed to sit on the bench sulking while the team was struggling?" he asked.

Abruptly, he sent two students to retrieve the aging school video equipment and showed a clip from a recent college women's basketball game, focusing on the bench of one particular team. The tall, athletic women seated with the coach cheered and encouraged their teammates on the floor. When a player scored a field goal or even a free-throw, her teammates on the sidelines enthusiastically applauded. After the film ended he asked his students to retrieve their journals and gave them a few minutes to write on how each as an individual had failed the team and how he or she would be different the next time.

The following day the class demanded that Thomas allow them to commence their important deliberations for the Class Declaration right after homework check. He agreed to switch math to the afternoon so that they could get to work. The teacher again gathered his things and resumed his position in the outer hall. The fracas that ensued was spirited and contentious but productive. After an hour Thomas entered the room.

"I'm afraid that your time is up," he announced.

The assembly expressed regret; they had come very close to a statement and project but could not quite nail down the appropriate words. Thomas asked to see both, and after a few minutes of fine-tuning, Room 217 had its declaration and giving project proposal completed. He wrote them on the board:

We, the Fifth-Grade Class of Room 217, will set a good example for the young children at the John Adams Elementary School. We will be Givers, helping those who need help, and Leaders, doing positive things to improve life for everyone at the Adams.

To show that we mean it, we will go to Mr. Bennett's first-grade class during DEAR at least once a week to read stories to his children.

Thomas stepped back to re-examine the words. He went to the back table and prepared a music selection. A slow, intoxicating South African song, originating from the days of protesting Apartheid, spread across the room. Thomas wrote both paragraphs on a sheet of paper, then erased the second part from the board and asked everyone to read the first paragraph itself aloud three times. On his signal, the assembly arose from their chairs and slowly, deliberately spoke the words to their declaration. Upon finishing for the third time, they erupted into wild applause and, filled with class pride, repeatedly cheered, "Two-seventeen! Two-seventeen!"

A few days later at 2:35 Thomas sat at his desk waiting for the last summons for bus boarding. He prepared a list of parents to call that evening because a few students had begun to slack off on the quality of their work.

The sight and scent of unidentified, hand-picked red flowers, compliments of Jessica that morning, lightened his sour mood due to a very warm, less than satisfying day. Most of the student chairs had been turned upside down and placed on top of their desks. Three pairs of chess players sat opposite each other near the window, eyes glued to the game before them.

"Bus 061. Bus 061," a female voice on the crackling loudspeaker announced. Two students grabbed their book bags and exited among goodbyes from Thomas. Only two more bus passengers remained. Suddenly the adjoining door to Mrs. Chang's room swung open, and Mr. Dorn entered, surprising everyone. He wore short-sleeves, baring meaty, hairy arms. He asked the students to step out into the hallway so that he could speak to Mr. Payne alone. They gave puzzled looks to their teacher, then slowly complied. Thomas was embarrassed by his supervisor's bad manners. If Dorn wanted his students to leave, he should have addressed him first.

But that wasn't the only problem. Once again, he had no union representation. The young man glanced at his watch and resented the intruder for putting him in such a position. If worse came to worst, he could hide behind the contract and end their talk in eight minutes. The principal sat in a student's chair and motioned for company. Thomas stepped from behind his desk and sat in an adjacent chair. His feet shook nervously.

"I have your evaluation, Mr. Payne," Mr. Dorn announced calmly, brandishing two copies of the document. The man paused to read the large banner hanging near the American flag, avowing the Class Declaration. He read it but said nothing afterwards.

Thomas froze with trepidation. He had heard little over the year about evaluations. In September, Mr. Dorn had entered the room with a day's notice and sat down in the teacher's chair. On top of the desk lay a magazine featuring swimsuit models Thomas had confiscated from one of his boys, the embarrassed young man nervously mentioned later. After observing a math lesson and taking notes, Dorn had told him that if he heard nothing further, he could assume that everything was fine.

Subsequently, the principal virtually never entered his room except to participate in a ceremony. Twice Ms. Flores had observed a lesson for about twenty minutes, both times with notice. Last month, Dorn had paid an unannounced visit and stayed for a few minutes before being paged. Thomas obsessed about the visit but again, hearing nothing, assumed the best. Dorn was known for two things: hiding in his office and holding petty grudges about "loyalty." Mona Caine had informed the provisional teacher that if he was in any trouble, he would have heard about it a long time ago.

The principal handed Thomas a set of papers stapled together. "This won't take but a few minutes," he said. "In general, you got passing marks or better in every category." He opened the document, pointed to a page, said a few words, then turned the page and continued. Thomas simply nodded and said "Uh-hum" for five minutes. Mr. Dorn flipped to the last page and read his comments.

Mr. Payne has been a welcomed addition to the staff at the Adams School. He possesses wisdom and insight that would cause any principal to doubt that he is actually only completing his first year. The success he has had with his fifth-grade class is noteworthy and admirable. Initially, parents balked at his tactics and style but after some guidance and suggestions from the school administrators, they were uniformly converted to support his approach. Mr. Payne's class presented virtually no discipline problems inside or outside of his classroom. His innovative and creative ideas take some time to get used to, but are effective. Other teachers have incorporated some of his ideas in their own classrooms. His students are excited about learning and about school. This is manifested by the fact that he has the highest attendance of any class at the Adams.

He handed Thomas a pen. "Sign here. We're a little past the technical deadline so if you don't mind, date it for last week," the gray-haired man suggested with a frown.

Now in a quandary, Thomas did not make eye contact with his supervisor. He was somewhat pleased with the results of his evaluation but uncomfortable with the request to backdate it. And he didn't agree with that crap about "guidance and suggestions from the school administrators" at all. Once again, he was paying for meeting with the man without representation. Dorn had played him perfectly. By barging in at the last minute with students still present, he had gambled that he would have no problem securing coverage for his derelict ass. He had gambled correctly.

Thomas shrugged his shoulders. "Sure," he replied. The rookie teacher signed both copies—one to keep and one for the principal. In a few seconds Mr. Dorn had left and the chess combatants entered to resume their contests. Thomas felt a little confused and dazed. He considered checking to see if Glen had gone home yet but decided against leaving his pupils alone. Besides, he was in no hurry to admit to his mentor how Dorn had snookered him.

The following week Thomas and Heléna sat together in his living room, watching a movie. She claimed most of the space, her long legs stretched across the sofa and her head on his shoulder. He held onto her with his left arm. Besides the flickering television, only the six-feet-tall halogen lamp posted in the corner illuminated the room. For the past ten minutes the pair had been engaged in a sticky discussion about future transportation arrangements. They had agreed that from time to time, he would pick her up at her apartment and bring her to his place to stay the night. However, Heléna requested that in the morning he drop her off three blocks from the school to make it appear as if she had caught the bus.

"I don't know why such a ruse is necessary. I really don't," Thomas complained. "After all, we're not in high school."

Heléna closed her eyes, then opened them. "You don't understand what it's been like for the past year," she explained, staring into his eyes. "I'm not well-liked by the other teachers."

"That's not true, honey. They just—"

"Listen, to me, Thomas," she pleaded. "The women there—they don't trust me. They're suspicious of me. They think I dress too provocatively. They think I'm coquettish and too opinionated. They don't want me around their men." She leaned in and whispered. "Over the school year, three times I've had to fend off unwelcomed advances. Once from the father of a student, another time from Ms. Garcia's fiancé, and once from the husband of Ms. Enriquez—you know, the second-grade bilingual teacher with the shaky marriage."

Persuaded, Thomas agreed to deliver less than door-to-door service.

Negotiations successfully completed, the two lovers sat snuggled on the sofa to enjoy the rest of the movie.

"I don't know about this movie," Thomas joked. "Too much talk and not enough action or sex for my taste."

Heléna leaned closer. "Ummm, I'd thought you'd never ask," she whispered, and began to flick her tongue in his ear.

Thomas closed his eyes and slowly moved his head up and down. Unexpectedly, the telephone rang. He cursed and grabbed the receiver, answering without bothering to check the number. To his surprise he heard what would have been a familiar voice during the day and bristled. Once in October a student had obtained his number from the local phone book and called to ask about an assignment. The next day he made it clear that under no circumstances should any student call him at home unless something drastic had occurred. He had never received another call—until that moment.

Thomas waved his hand and pointed at the television. Heléna responded by fighting with the remote control. She pointed and pressed buttons, frantically trying to mute the sound. The channels changed, and the menu appeared and disappeared on the screen. Thomas's face twisted with concern. "Maurice? What is it? What's the matter, son?"

Heléna sat up. "What's wrong?"

Thomas put his finger up to quiet her and listened. "Yeah, I know your brother—Kahil, right? He's in Ms. Patterson's room. What'd he do this time? Is he in some kind of trouble?"

"What is it, Thomas? Tell me," Helena begged.

He cast a stern look at his girlfriend and opened his hands to indicate that he did not know, then put his finger up again trying to end her questioning. His eyes widened and his jaw dropped as his expression changed to shock. "He's dead! How? What happened?" He arose and paced the floor.

Finally Heléna managed to shut off the television. She climbed off the sofa, raced over to Thomas and put her arms around him. She held onto him as he listened, trying to glean information. She couldn't hear much, only bits and pieces.

Thomas spoke rapidly. "Where's your mother? What? Who's there with you? Okay, give me your address. Okay, I've got it. I'm on my way. Stay in the house. Don't go anywhere, hear?" Still flabbergasted, he hung up and stared at Heléna.

"Tell me, honey," she begged, shaking him a bit.

Thomas shook his head in disbelief. "Maurice's brother's been shot and killed."

"*Hay Dios mio!*" Heléna exclaimed, making the sign of the cross.

"Oh my God is right," he replied, rubbing his forehead before explaining further. "He was out riding his bike, and some men in a car shot at a house and killed him by accident, they think. Poor kid was just at the wrong place at the wrong time." Thomas broke from his trance and wandered into the bedroom. He sat on the bed and began putting on his sneakers. Heléna followed and sat next to him. He continued. "Maurice is home alone."

"What!"

Thomas scoffed, "I guess when they called his dad, and he came over, the fool ran out the house, saying he'd find the sonsabitches and kill them himself. Maurice told me that his dad keeps a revolver in the trunk of his car." Before Heléna had a chance to say anything, he held up his hand.

"Wait. There's more. Maurice's mother ran out to stop his dad from doing something stupid. She called her sister to stay with Maurice but that was an hour ago. Someone called the house and hung up. Maurice got scared but didn't know what to do, so he called information and got a hold of me." He reached down to tie his shoes. "I've gotta get over there."

"Okay. You want me to go with you?"

"No. Stay here and maybe call Glen and tell him what happened. Watch the news and see if there's anything on about it." He grabbed his keys and walked to the door. They kissed and he left after promising to be careful.

Five days later the entire Adams Elementary School family formed a tight circle in the schoolyard. In the center sat Maurice and his family. Members of the school community gathered to pay their respects. The circumstances notwithstanding, it was a beautiful afternoon; seventy-five degrees and hardly a cloud in the sky. Teachers stood with their classes. Angelica slid near Thomas and held his hand. Maria saw them. She squeezed past everyone and grabbed his other one. Thomas gazed at the morose family, sitting in battered folding chairs: Maurice, his mother, a few aunts and uncles, both sets of grandparents and his father. His dad never found the men involved, but the police did. According to the news, the whole episode involved a dispute over drug-selling turf. The gunmen had meant to warn the family inside the house to stay out of their territory.

Maurice's mother sat in a daze, exhausted from sleepless nights, crying and recently, anger. The news stories had already begun to shift, questioning why a ten-year-old had been riding his bike after 9 o'clock in the evening on a school night. Thomas wished he could go to Maurice and say something comforting. He noticed that for the first time, Ms. Patterson's kids were quiet and still. She held her husband's hand and wept silently. Many of her students also cried. Thomas opened his arms and embraced his own two angels.

Mr. Dorn addressed the crowd. "What a tragedy to gather here because we've had to bury one of God's children," he lamented.

Angelica started to cry, even though in her last encounter with Kahil, she had warned him to stop bothering her. Thomas hugged her and kissed the top of her head. She looked up at her teacher, then pressed her face against his side and closed her eyes.

He looked across the playground at the sea of sad faces and spotted Heléna standing in the vicinity of the paraprofessional staff. She had informed him just the other night that she would not return to the Adams next year. She was sick of being treated like a leper. Besides, she came to Boston with the promise of having her own class, not some converted storage closet and a handful of kids. She told Thomas that after seeing what he had done, more than ever she wanted "a shot at the title," as he would have described it.

Mr. Dorn spoke well, Thomas admitted to himself. After a few more remarks the principal nodded, and Thomas pressed the button to the huge portable music box he had brought from home. Everyone heard Wee Gee's hauntingly beautiful song, "Hold On to Your Dreams." Mr. Dorn asked the student from each class holding a balloon to step forward. Fourteen children came to the circle's center. Each clutched a balloon filled with helium. Maurice's buddy, Akeem, represented 217. Mr. Dorn spoke a few more words and asked that they release their balloons into the air. They did. Thomas followed the multicolored objects as they soared upwards and blew across the sun-drenched sky. He felt so sad for his boy, Maurice. He wondered how he himself would react if he ever got a call saying Vanessa or Edward had been killed, then shook the thought from his mind.

The ceremony ended, and Mr. Dorn dismissed the group. Thomas took his students back into the school and allowed them to write about the experience in their journals.

Things eventually returned to normal at the Adams. Ms. Patterson's students resumed their activities befitting the Dog Pound. If anything, they displayed worse behavior than before. Thomas did not accept the conventional wisdom that they were just acting up out of grief.

One day he caught two boys trashing the boys' bathroom and turned them over to Ms. Patterson. Later, when he asked what punishment Mr. Dorn had imposed, the fourth-grade teacher insisted that "under the circumstances," she had chosen not to take them to the principal. Thomas delivered a stinging rebuke to his colleague, wrote an Incident Report detailing his apprehension of the boys and gave a copy to Dorn and Ms. Patterson. The boys were suspended for a day and ordered to assist the custodian with cleaning up after school for a week. Ms. Patterson complained to Mona Caine, saying her union brother had been "cruel." Ms. Caine offered to mediate, but both sides refused.

Maurice eventually returned to school. He surprised everyone by bringing all of the homework Thomas had sent, saying that doing his homework helped keep his mind busy.

On the last day of the month, May Myisha revealed that once again every student in Room 217 except Freddy could enjoy the festivities. Freddy had come two points short of the required number needed to stay with his classmates. Thomas inspected the last two weeks on the calendar and told his disappointed pupil that he had come very close and would almost certainly be included on the last movie day. He chose Cleopatra and Brian to work together as servers, and made a joke about how amusing they looked together—with with her a foot taller than him. To his astonishment and amusement, he discovered from Carmelita that the odd couple had recently become an item.

Later that afternoon Thomas and his mentor worked out at Anthony's with only about three dozen customers. The teachers marveled appreciatively at their good luck at having free run of the place. Thomas spoke effusively about his students for the first half-hour of their visit, prompting Glen to break the spell.

"Um, Thomas, maybe it's time to start preparing for you never seeing them again," Glen advised. "You know, I'm going to see my kids next year as second-graders—a couple of inches taller, maybe. But you? You're never going to lay eyes on most of your group again—ever." He took a deep breath and waited for a response.

His words dug like a dull knife into his mentee's heart. "That's a hellavu thing to say. You're suppose to be my friend," the rookie barked half-heartedly.

Glen added weight to the leg-press machine so that his training partner could use it next. "I am, man. That's why I'm warning you about this." He twisted the huge metal disks clockwise to secure the weight and added, "I know how much you care about those kids. Sometimes, I think maybe you care too much." He shook his head left to right. "You don't want to be caught flat-footed on the last day of school when they leave and you go back into the room to clean up and face the fact that they won't ever be back." He double checked the machine and pointed at it. "It's all yours."

Thomas adjusted himself into a forty-five-degree angle and put his feet up. He pushed lightly against the six hundred pounds of weight, testing its construction. Everything had been set properly. His best friend, now nearly upside down, watched him with intense, concerned eyes. He recognized that Glen offered wisdom worth heeding. "Thanks for setting the weights," he said clearly.

Glen knew what he meant.

June

The sky had cleared after the late-night downpour. The local newswoman on Channel 8 with the dyed blond hair and surgically enhanced cheekbones reported a couple of tornado sightings in western Massachusetts. But Boston merely received a thorough dousing. By the time Thomas entered his car, the sun had emerged in time to dry the sidewalks and streets for the a.m. commute. According to Ms. Blondie's grinning meteorologist colleague, the day would become warm and humid by the afternoon.

Thomas jiggled the coins in his right pocket as he stood watch, alone as usual, over the hordes of children running inside the John Adams playground. A few of the younger tots sported shiny raincoats as they chased each other, jumped rope or discussed the latest television cartoon adventures. On the other side of the schoolyard where the older kids played, several boys competed in a game of touch football. Near the battered south-wing fence, two boys threw a softball back and forth. Two groups of girls jumped rope. Still another bunch of fourth- and fifth-graders played basketball.

Cleopatra scored a basket against a boy from Mrs. Chang's class, who had allowed too much distance between them in spite of Melvin's warning that she had the "eagle eye." (Thomas had informed the boys that they could not exclude the girls from the game since the basketball hoop belonged to everyone.)

The first-year teacher noticed that generally the bilingual children played together, conversing in Spanish, while the students in the monolingual classes associated with each other. He wondered what the Adams staff could do to integrate the children.

Thomas also observed a peculiar sight about twenty feet away: Asa, clad in an oversized New York Yankees T-shirt, meandering through a maze of yelling and screaming children. He held the hand of a little boy wearing black tennis shoes and short pants. Thomas recognized the small companion as one of Glen's first-graders, named Marquee.

The young man rang the bell for everyone to line up by class. "Let's go, everybody! It's a school day!" Thomas called. "There's still plenty to do and only a few days left to do it," he reminded the disappointed children. As Asa passed him to get in line, he tapped the boy on the arm. "What was going on with your little reader?" he asked.

Asa shrugged his shoulders. "Marquee asked me to help him get his ball back. Some second-grader had taken it from him."

Thomas patted him on the back. "You did your good deed for today, huh?" He could not help but snicker at his Good Samaritan.

For the past few weeks he and his class had visited Glen's room during DEAR to read stories to the first-graders. They performed their duties twice a week. Thomas kept the same dyads together during every visit for continuity. (He placed Doug in charge of book distribution.) Mr. Bennett's kids displayed excellent manners and obviously enjoyed the visits. Before leaving, their big readers always presented them with a self-adhesive sticker bearing the image of a broad smiling face or cartoon character, which the little ones promptly stuck to their foreheads. By the third session the two classes had settled into a routine. Big and little reader had grown comfortable with each other. Some first-graders even sat in the laps of their readers. Both teachers expressed deep satisfaction with the project.

Glen's children apparently took quite a liking to their unofficial big siblings. In the morning the tots frequently ran to greet the Room 217 students as the latter entered the yard in the morning. The fifth-graders at first seemed surprised at the intense affection shown to them by the six-year-olds. They reported that their little readers hugged and kissed them on sight and, with great relish, bragged to others that their big readers came to see them during DEAR. Sometimes they offered their older benefactors gifts of candy or money, which were graciously declined. One little boy who had fallen totally in love with Jessica presented her with choice selections of his mother's jewelry. With gentle words Thomas and Glen managed to persuade him to return them.

When passing each other in the hall, the first-graders—who were not allowed to speak without permission—smiled and waved furiously at their big readers. Occasionally in the morning a Room 217 student would be approached by his or her little reader for assistance with a problem—a lost book bag, a nasty fall or a problem with a classmate. Thomas had instructed his pupils to make the sacrifice and be as helpful as possible. The senior students murmured about all the attention they were given but exhibited huge smiles on their faces when doing so.

During the previous week, however, Heléna had reported to Thomas that in the teacher's lounge she had overheard one primary teacher's objections to the arrangement. The querulous woman reported to others that she had spoken to Mr. Dorn, complaining that Mr. Payne's visits evinced favoritism to Mr. Bennett's class, thereby damaging the self-esteem of her children. Thomas dismissed the criticism as not worth the spit of a reply.

The following day Thomas and his students watched a short film about endangered species due to habitat reduction and unrestricted hunting in Africa. Next week they would visit the city zoo to wrap up the science unit on wildlife. By one o'clock, the temperature had climbed to eighty degrees. The windows stretched open as wide as possible, but little air circulated in the stuffy space. The youngsters attempted to remain erect because laying their heads down during instruction time was strictly prohibited. They had been allowed to refresh themselves at the downstairs watering hole a half-hour earlier and recognized that additional munificence from Mr. Payne would not be forthcoming.

Thomas watched the film with distant interest. His mind kept returning to the six members of the chess team. Hours earlier they had climbed into a rented van with Mr. Davenport; part of their day-long excursion to an elementary school in Wellesley, an affluent suburb outside of Boston.

Sitting near the window, trying to catch a breeze, Thomas inspected his darkened classroom. Large posters made to look like newspapers hung on the walls and dangled from the light fixtures. The newspapers, dated twenty to forty years in the future, carried bold headlines. Cleopatra, after a distinguished career as a dancer with the Boston Ballet Company, had just been named its director. Melvin, having served two successful terms as President of the United States, had seen his image added to those carved on Mount Rushmore in South Dakota. Carmelita, a successful research physician, had discovered a cure for diabetes in time to rescue her ailing mother. Deborah had received an appointment as Chief Justice of the United States Supreme Court. Other posters predicted similar noteworthy achievements.

Thomas cut his eyes over to the student-closet doors and snickered at the baby photograph of each buddy pair. He had color copied each one. Almost everyone had brought a picture of him or herself while still in diapers.

Thomas turned his head as he heard a distinct clickety-click sound. He became excited and beckoned a student to turn off the television. As the main door moved, light from the hall crept into the room and expanded across the floor. Pedro eased himself inside. He wore a striped tie and dark pants. All the boys on the chess team sported ties. All the girls had donned dark skirts. Each entered toting a ribbon and small bag. Another chosen pupil turned on the lights, and the class became galvanized with energy as everyone sat up, eager to hear the results.

"Welcome back," Thomas greeted them, trying to sound calm. The team members separated, allowing the chess coach and assistant coach to stand side by side.

"We didn't do too badly for our first time out, no siree," Mr. Davenport declared.

"What happened?" several seated students shouted. The room grew noisy. Jessica stood and pointed at the chalkboard.

"It's okay, Jessica," Thomas advised. He opened his hand, gesturing to Cleo, who had entered after Pedro. "You may resume your duties, Captain."

The tall girl pointed at herself and playfully addressed Jessica with the standard change-of-leadership proclamation. "Thank you. I'll take it from here," she decreed.

Thomas laughed with his first-time Student of the Week, then turned his attention to Gary, the team leader. "You do us proud?"

"Mr. Davenport said we did okay," the boy replied while untying his tie.

Thomas nodded. "Well, the most important thing is that you all had fun." He paused. "Did you?"

A burst of lightning seemed to strike the room as each member of the team reported the joy of his or her experience. Carmelita spoke rapidly, her accent becoming more pronounced, as it sometimes did when she became excited. "It was great, Mr. Payne. You shoulda seen the school. It was big and had everything!"

Tyshaun jumped in. "Um-hum. It had lockers and a huge gym!"

"You should've seen that library!" Melvin exclaimed. "Man, it was soooo big. No lie, you could've drove a tank through there."

Thomas scratched his head and smiled. "I'm glad you enjoyed your visit. It sounds like a nice place." He opened his hands and faced Mr. Davenport. "The chess tournament, remember? The reason they went. How'd it go?"

Mr. Davenport took out a handkerchief and began mopping his forehead. "Just fine," he replied. "Every one of them advanced at least to the next phase in their group." He propped his crutches against the teacher's desk and leaned against it. "You see, they divided them into beginners and experienced players. We were all in the beginners' section with a couple dozen other kids. There were six beginners sections and four experienced. If you won, you kept playing until you reached the top of your section."

"Gary won his!" Cleo announced excitedly. "He beat four in a row."

"Is that right?" Thomas asked. "Well, good work, son." The class broke into applause. Gary smiled and proudly raised a blue ribbon into the air.

"I took third place in my group," Cleo added, holding up a red ribbon with a large "3" printed on it."

"Me too!" chimed in Carmelita, Tyshaun and Pedro, displaying similar awards.

"I took second place." Melvin declared, extending a gold ribbon towards the seated children.

Thomas inspected the ribbons and clapped his hands. "I'm very proud of all of you. I guess we showed them that the Adams kids ain't no slouches, huh?" He nodded once.

Everybody applauded the group again. The team members beamed with pride.

Carmelita returned to her observations. "Mr. Payne, you shoulda seen that cafeteria. It was huge, and the floors were so clean you coulda eaten off 'em."

Tyshaun waved his hand. "And that playground! It wasn't all run down like here, Mr. P. It was big and had all kindsa designs for games and stuff— and they had this play area with ropes and tires and swings and all kindsa stuff. It was something!"

"They had a separate basketball court!"

"And a big ol' field for playing football or soccer or volleyball."

"And the bathrooms were clean! Not all messed up like here."

"And they had a big parking lot for the teachers and visitors."

"And the building was air-conditioned!"

"Man, we didn't wanta leave."

"How come we don't have nice things like that, Mr. Payne?"

Thomas felt everyone's attention shift to him but he didn't know how to reply. He read the expressions on the faces of his pupils. Their eyes had been opened to how the "other half" lived, those with money and access to the political system. The chess team acted as if they had been to paradise. The other twentysomething fifth-graders who had not been to Wellesley sat dumfounded at what they had heard. They wished they had boarded the van with Mr. Davenport, maybe not to play chess but to see all the wonders. They had no idea that people only a few miles away lived in what they considered to be such opulence. Seeing it on television wasn't the same as seeing it in real life.

Thomas inhaled deeply from the warm, muggy air. For most of his students, next year would bring more or less the same as the current one. The desks and chairs would be bigger, but they still would not have enough textbooks, computers, library books, etc. Thomas didn't know how to explain why some of God's children with white skin had so much more than those with brown.

He coughed and cleared his throat. "Well, kids, um, some cities have more money than Boston so they can, um, afford to buy more—just like some people have more money than others." He thought for a minute, then continued. "Um, the people who live out there, well, a lot of them went to college—just like all of you are going to do if what you wrote on your newspaper headlines is going to come true."

"If we do right and make something of ourselves like you said, Mr. Payne, will we get to live nice and send our children to a nice school?" Angelica asked.

"Yes, Angelface," Thomas replied. He shook his finger as his voice returned to normal. "But remember, there's more to being successful than having money. What good is it to be driving a nice car or living in a fancy house if your life's a mess?" He pointed to a newspaper on his desk. "Remember when we read about the baseball player who got arrested for drugs, or that rich family where the husband killed his wife? They all had plenty of money, but it didn't make them happy, did it?"

Several students answered, "No." Others shook their heads.

Mr. Davenport interjected. "Mr. Payne's right as usual, my brothers and sisters." He stood straight, aided by his crutches. "I've seen people with lots of money in jail because they got greedy. And others who thought that getting a quick buck would improve their lives. Too many talented Black folks with their whole lives ahead of them now sitting behind bars, hoping to get a second chance." He took a deep breath and added. "I'm telling you, the cards are stacked against you, so you're gonna have to work twice as hard to make it out there. But you can. At least now you've got a fighting chance." The lawyer clenched his fist, then suddenly checked his watch. "Listen, I gotta go," he abruptly declared. "It's been a pleasure and an honor serving you."

He continued to address the students, but pointed at Thomas. "You listen to that man right there and do what he says. I've never seen anything like that thing they did for you last week, Cleo, when they made you Student of the Week. I told my wife about it the minute I got home, I was so impressed."

Cleopatra smiled proudly. Angelica and Maria, seated on opposite sides of her, each grabbed one of her hands and congratulated her. She squeezed their hands. She had gotten used to being touched by her two openly affectionate friends. In fact, she rather enjoyed it. It was so different from her home, where everybody fought and yelled at everybody all day long.

Thomas went to the door and shook the old man's hand. "It was our honor to have you here, sir. The kids learned a lot—me too. And for you to pay us a special visit last week just to participate in our ceremony ..." He paused. "That meant so much to the kids and to Cleopatra." He put his other hand on top of Mr. Davenport's. Finally the two men separated, and the retired lawyer ambled to the door with sounds of thunderous applause behind him. Members of the chess team raised their plastic bags in the air and thanked him for the gifts he had given them.

"Oh, one last thing," Thomas added, pointing at his desk. "Captain, if you please."

Cleo went to the desk and searched for a few seconds before seizing a huge card. She approached the two men and extended the card to Mr. Davenport.

"The class and I, we all signed a card for you," Thomas mentioned. "It just says thank you for putting up with us."

The senior barrister opened the object, read it and perused the smiling faces of the children and the adult in the photograph. He raised his head to face the class again. A smile formed on his deeply lined face. "This is really nice." he said. The room remained silent. He looked at his watch again. "Well, I better get going."

Thomas turned to his students and motioned with his hand. "Rise, please. A great teacher is about to depart."

They took to their feet without speaking. Mr. Davenport smiled, tilted his head in half a bow and stepped out the door.

That afternoon after dismissal, Thomas visited Ms. Cooke, who had placed a report in his mailbox identifying Doug as the only student in Room 217 who had not passed the fifth-grade reading exam. Apparently, anyone with grade three reading skills could survive the Metropolitan Power Reading Test. According to Mrs. Chang, a student received three chances to answer sixty percent of the multiple-choice items correctly before being retained in the fifth grade. Thomas and Ms. Cooke both expressed doubt that Doug would be able to achieve a passing score. She advised that the boy would have to take the test again a few days later and could take it one final time the following week if he did not pass. She mentioned that a parent could appeal to the principal for a waiver based on some "damn good reason" for promoting the pupil on to middle school anyway. An example of such a reason was a recently diagnosed learning disability. Ms. Cooke scoffed and added that obtaining a waiver from Dorn was easier than buying candy at the corner store.

Thomas returned to his room and began writing new spelling words on the board, stopping just long enough to loosen his tie. Even though sunlight no longer directly struck his windows, the room had grown hot and sticky. Three of the paper birthday cakes had unattached themselves from the grimy walls. Thomas borrowed a ladder from the new custodian and retaped them. He pulled his undershirt away from his body, trying to cool off.

That morning he had bristled at a remark from a student indicating that the warm weather prevented him from concentrating. He quoted his mother's favorite saying in such circumstances: "The air is the air. We can't do anything about it." With only sixteen school days remaining, Thomas promised himself that he would continue to push his students to the limit of their endurance. Earlier he had scolded Angel for complaining about the continued weighty homework assignments.

"Man, this ain't no Advanced Class," the boy had whined.

One veteran teacher Thomas had met at the dentist's office during the April vacation, a very pleasant brother with a head full of curly gray hair, had advised him that "after Memorial Day, we're just putting in time." The former football player rejected such talk. Out of sheer pride, pro teams that had clinched their division titles still played to win their remaining games. Their fans would not accept having bought expensive tickets just to witness their favorite team lie down on the job. Thomas believed that as long as he received a salary to impart knowledge, he would do just that.

He rolled up his shirtsleeves and wished he had visited Heléna downstairs earlier. He had barely caught a glimpse of her at all that day. By now she had reached her gym and was shaking and gyrating to loud dance music with about three dozen other women of various shapes and sizes panting alongside her. He found himself thinking about her constantly. It was probably just as well that they tried to maintain some distance, especially since they found it so difficult to keep their hands off each other.

Heléna obviously enjoyed sex. She confessed that her caring for him really enhanced her pleasure. Thomas felt the same way but still thought that Heléna's recent Friday afternoon proposition that they make love in her room with the door locked would have been too risky. Maybe serving at different schools next year would be better for both of them. Thomas hadn't said anything aloud, but he suspected that they were falling in love. The thought terrified him.

For some strange reason he recalled that his last love, Laura, had constantly obsessed about her appearance but had shown little interest in exercising. Sure, she had been blessed with her mother's small frame, but it never hurt to help nature out a little. Thomas had found her reluctance puzzling. But she had made it clear that she preferred to date muscular men. Her boyfriend before him had been a starting basketball player at Boston College. Laura had confessed to Thomas that her stuffy parents had no interest in athletic contests. She told him that they judged athletic men— especially athletic Black men—as dim-witted buffoons being used by the White man. Thomas surmised that the attraction for well-built men by Little Miss Silver Spoon was her modest way of asserting her independence from her parents.

With each passing day he became more relieved that they had gone separate ways. Nevertheless, as the date of her wedding approached, he was surprised that he actually considered attending. Twice the other day he had nearly summoned the courage to ask Heléna if she would accompany him. He would, of course, not attend the event without her.

Thomas finished all of his classroom chores and packed his bags. He checked the room clock. It had been 7:17 for the past three weeks. He dismissed the clock with a wave of his hand, grabbed his things and strolled down the hall.

That Friday evening Thomas stomped his feet and yelled at Glen's television set, prodding the players of his favorite basketball team to fight for their lives during a crucial National Basketball Association championship game. Glen's spacious living room appeared neat and clean, as always. The old lady from his church, who insisted on being paid in cash, certainly kept the place in good shape. (What the government didn't know wouldn't hurt her, she liked to say.) Humid air surrounded the home outside, but thanks to a one-year-old central air-conditioning system, the air inside remained dry, cool and comfortable.

During a time-out Thomas inspected the area directly within his reach. On the center table, two tall glasses holding melted ice cubes the size of marbles had been propped snuggly into coasters; one contained residue of soda, the other, beer. A huge bowl, empty except for a dozen darkened popcorn seeds, rested in front of the two armchair competitors. Thomas read the titles of the neatly arranged magazines, generally of interest to African Americans and music lovers. He saw nothing that would indicate Glen's secret proclivities. He wondered if a small movie container with bare-chested, good-looking men on the cover had been crammed into the dark corner of his good buddy's bedroom closet.

After engaging in an internal debate, Thomas decided against tattling on a fellow teacher. Earlier that day in the lounge, he had heard big-mouthed Ms. Little make a remark about the handsome copy machine repairman being "one of Mr. Bennett's boyfriends." It had marked the third time in the school year that Thomas had heard a remark from an Adams staff member about Glen's private life. Also, a few days earlier Heléna had told him that she had overheard a group of Hispanic teachers speculating about Glen's sexual orientation. Thomas saw no reason to upset his friend by mentioning such mindless gossip.

Glen expressed his views about the basketball contest less loudly than his friend, but made his opinions well known. Both complained about the abysmally poor officiating but disagreed as to which team had profited from the situation. The sweating, long-legged giants on television ran back and forth across the screen, oblivious to the supplemental coaching bellowed to them from Boston. By the end of the fourth quarter Thomas's vanquished choice, burdened by too many turnovers and poor free-throw shooting, crawled off the court. After the inevitable interviews and analyses finally ended, Thomas agreed that on Monday morning, Glen would receive the Room 217 copy card for twenty-five free copies. The two men laughed at their gentlemen's bet.

As the theme song to the local news show played, Glen picked up the glasses and walked into the kitchen. Thomas followed him, carrying the greasy popcorn bowl. In a few minutes with the dishwasher groaning in the background, the two men drifted into a discussion about the Adams. They praised the new custodian who had started in mid-May. Both admitted that because he was a young, White male sporting earphones, a long beard and tattoos on each arm, everyone had assumed that he would be a slacker. The fact that he also drove a motorcycle aided in that consensus. In fact, "Bobby" worked hard all day and considered his job to be an important part of the school's mission. Thomas mentioned that the man had told him he was "born again," happily married, with his first child on the way, and listened only to Christian rock or Gospel music.

Moving on to other aspects of the work environment, Glen mentioned that some staff members had floated the idea of an end-of-the-year get-together. Thomas asked his mentor if he would attend such an event. To his surprise, Glen said that he would.

Thomas cleared his throat. "Would Felix come too?" He avoided eye contact by examining the magnets on the door of the refrigerator, his finger scanning the number of a nearby pizzeria.

"No," Glen replied. "We're through."

Thomas scratched his head and turned towards his friend, who had stunned him by readily disclosing such a personal matter. He recognized the look of pain on Glen's face and sympathized with him, having borne the same expression nearly a year before. He stepped closer to his host.

"Oh? I'm sorry to hear that," he offered sincerely. "He seemed like a sharp brother." Thomas couldn't believe that he had just complimented Glen on his choice of a boyfriend. If the guys on the football team could hear him now!

Glen shook his head. "It's for the best. We were just at completely different places." He washed his hands in the kitchen sink and spoke in a discouraged voice. "This closet stuff is fucked up. It really is."

His earlier words struck a nerve for Thomas. "What do you mean about being at completely different places?" he asked.

"Felix is sharp, just like you said. Smart as hell. He's some kind of insurance manager for one of those big companies downtown," Glen stated proudly. He parted the refrigerator door, reached in and picked up a can of soda. The first-grade drawings clinging to the door fluttered. He adjusted the magnets holding them in place with one hand while raising the can towards Thomas with the other. "Want another?" Thomas politely declined. "Anyway," he continued, "we couldn't do anything or go anywhere. He was so scared that he might be seen. It was okay at first but shit, man. How many movies can you watch or dinners can you eat at home?"

Thomas nodded. "So you wanted to get out a little more?"

Glen laughed. "A little more? I couldn't even go to his house! We snuck around like a couple of unfaithful spouses. I couldn't call him at work or nothing. He just came over here, so we could fuck, you know what I'm saying?"

"Thomas cringed at the thought, and his eyes lit up like flares. He shook his head violently and covered his mouth but started laughing out loud. "No, not really."

Glen joined his laughter, then paused. "I'm sorry, partner. Does this make you uncomfortable?"

Thomas regained his composure. "No. It's okay. Hey, how many times have you been there for me? You say whatever you feel like saying. Hell, this is your house."

Glen took a sip from his soda. "Thanks, buddy. I don't really have a lot of people I can talk to about this—other than my therapist." He contemplated the wisdom of adding to his story and decided against testing the limits of his young friend's tolerance. "Naw. You know what? I'm done with it. Like you said a few months ago about your ex-fiancée, what's over is over."

Thomas felt mildly relieved that Glen's narrative of his personal misfortune had ended. He still had not recovered from the shock of his mentor's casual revelation about seeing a therapist. Glen? Mr. Together? Of all people!

At one time he thought shrinks were just con artists skilled at taking money for doing nothing more than listening to other people's problems. Recently, he had changed his mind. Through his involvement with Revelations, Inc., he had come to understand that a lot of people lugged around a lot of pain. And Lord knows from what he witnessed a couple of weeks before while his students wrote in their journals, kids like Freddy needed someone to help them put their world back together.

He remembered one evening during the first training at Revelations: He and his group had been brought to tears when one beautiful young woman confided that her father had sexually molested her two sisters and her throughout their childhood, then had started on their daughters before she finally turned him in. While anyone with decent eyesight would have viewed her as extremely attractive, she hated how she looked. Another participant, a silver-haired, middle-aged businessman wearing a very expensive suit, confessed that a generation ago he had served three years in prison for killing a teenager while driving drunk. Others had shared similar accounts of past and present demons.

"You can talk to me about anything," Thomas assured him.

"Thanks, man. I really appreciate it," Glen replied.

The two discussed other matters. Thomas raved about Heléna for a while. (She had given him permission to share their happiness with Glen— but only if their friend agreed to take the graham cracker oath of secrecy.) Then like a couple of proud fathers, the men swapped stories about their students.

The following Monday morning arrived with a favorable sea breeze from the east, cooling off most of Boston. While dressing for work, Thomas watched the usual sophomoric duet on the local news for the extended forecast. They consumed a considerable amount of time giggling over an inane story about a deer that had somehow wandered within the city limits of a small New Hampshire town. Finally, the meteorologist predicted pleasant weather for the next three days, with a gradual warming trend by the weekend.

In Room 217, once the class had settled in, Brian's buddy, Vince, serving his first term as Student of the Week, announced the previous week's all-stars. He read the names of twenty students who had been present and produced all homework, a new class record. And the homework check resulted in the second All-Star Day of the month. Citing the classroom ground rules, Thomas agreed to set aside time for an extra recess later in the morning. He applauded the class, and they themselves.

At the end of a very productive day Thomas announced that everyone would have to leave right away because Ms. Flores had requested a private meeting with him. He added that he could not allow any more "hanging around" after school, since one student had recently worried his mother by stopping at a friend's house for several hours without calling home first. The mother's frantic calls to the Adams forced both administrators and Thomas to consume a considerable amount of time on the telephone. Everyone in the room stared coldly at Angel, who lowered his head.

After the last student left the room, Carmelita returned and positioned herself at the door's entrance. Thomas reminded her of his announcement about no hanging around after school, but she argued that her numerous attempts to speak to him had been rebuffed by Vince, who had repeatedly enforced the "no fly zone" near the teacher's desk. Carmelita pleaded for permission to "approach the bench." Thomas motioned for her to enter. When she reached his desk, she dug into the pockets of her short pants and proudly, displayed a crinkled envelope.

"I got a letter from my father last Saturday," she reported.

Thomas widened and blinked his eyes in astonishment. "Really? How is he?" he inquired.

"He's okay," she answered. "He said that he was surprised to get my letter."

"What letter?" Thomas inquired.

"The one you told me to write, Mr. Payne," she answered. "Anyway, he said that he cried for hours after reading it. He said that he was sorry; that he had been wrong to cut off his family. He promised to write as often as he could."

Thomas smiled and stepped from behind his desk to put his arms around the proud girl. He touched her chin with his index finger and looked into her eyes. "You were so brave to take that chance to reach out to him," he asserted. "Now you have your father back, and he's found his family again. I'm glad." They embraced.

Just then Ms. Flores appeared. She smiled and waited. Thomas saw her standing at the door and again told Carmelita how proud he was of her and suggested that she be off to her after-school program. She agreed and exchanged greetings with the assistant principal on the way out. Thomas did not feel the same defensiveness about Ms. Flores seeing him hug a student as he did with Mr. Dorn. The Ecuadorian native had expressed strong support for his affectionate manner with the kids.

Ms. Flores followed the girl down the hall with her eyes until she disappeared. The woman turned to Thomas, who leaned against his desk waiting to hear the reason for her visit. "The year with you has been good for her, Mr. Payne," she commented. "I remember more than one recess or after-school incident involving that young lady last year."

"Who? Carmelita?" Thomas asked, feigning surprise. "Oh, she just needed someone to show her what was underneath that facade." He moved towards his guest and motioned for her to sit on the bench in front of his desk. She did and the young man grabbed a student's chair and sat next to her. "To what do I owe this honor?" he asked, fixing his eyes on the manila folder in her hand.

"I wanted to talk to you about your test scores, Mr. Payne," the unassuming woman replied. "They came in." She opened the folder, handed him several sheets of paper and pointed. "The improvements for virtually every one of your students was very noteworthy. It's not to say that they all reached the sixth grade—or even the fifth for that matter. But almost every one showed marked improvement in reading and math. Some jumped nearly two grade levels in one year!" She pointed further. "The only one who did not show much change was—"

"I know. Doug, right?" Thomas interrupted, then promptly offered a defense. "He really hated taking that test. I had to practically force the boy to take it. Anything to do with reading, and he just freaks."

Ms. Flores shook her head. "No, it wasn't Douglas Berry. In fact, he jumped from no score—because he couldn't read at all—to a second-grade reading level. Normally we wouldn't be too proud of that, but given where he started, that's actually quite good."

Thomas looked bewildered. "Not Doug? Then who?"

Ms. Flores searched the paper. "Freddy Wilson. He showed very modest improvement but," she added, "he came to your room very late in the year."

"Yeah," Thomas agreed. "And he didn't start really showing up ready to work until a few weeks ago."

Ms. Flores provided the him with an overview of how to read the results of the tests. Thomas listened and visually scanned the report. He did not fully understand all of the notations but decided against admitting his ignorance. Inside, his heart jumped for joy. He remembered his conversation on the first day of school with Mrs. Chang and Ms. Sanchez-Taylor. He had actually done it! He had tamed the Wild Bunch and had documented proof of his success.

He looked at his supervisor and unsuccessfully fought the urge to smile. "They did that well?" he asked, lowering his head, concerned that the sin of pride might be evident on his face.

"They did better than well, Mr. Payne. You are to be congratulated on the fine work you did," she answered.

His expression suddenly became serious and he tilted his head to the side. "Wait a second," he ordered. "Mr. Dorn know about this?"

Ms. Flores could not meet his gaze. She stood and began to pace. "Of course, Mr. Payne. He *is* the principal here." She struggled with her words. "He too was very pleased." She took a deep breath. "To tell you the truth, we didn't do very well again. The Advanced Classes did fine—they always do—and a couple of other classes, but overall the scores were very disappointing." She turned her profile to him as she inspected a poster of a student who, fifteen years in the future, had become an all-star professional football player.

Thomas cautiously took in the view. That woman sure kept herself in good shape, he thought. Her ass would literally stand up to any twenty-year-old's. He wondered how she accomplished such a feat. Mr. Flores sure was a lucky guy, he mused, then shook off the thought and responded. "I see. I'm sorry to hear that."

"You have to understand that Mr. Dorn is under a lot of pressure. The superintendent keeps putting so much on the principals."

"I'm sure being a principal is not easy nowadays—nor is being an assistant principal, huh?"

Ms. Flores closed her eyes and sighed. "No," she whispered. "It isn't." The short woman started to comment further but stopped herself. Instead, she returned to the second reason for her visit. "To tell you the truth, Mr. Payne, it wasn't good news for Freddy, but it was lucky for you that he showed so little improvement. Mr. Dorn asked me whether I thought something improper had occurred in your room. You wouldn't know about this, but last year there was a cheating scandal at a school, and a respected senior principal ended up losing his job. Everybody's a little suspicious these days. I spent some time with your figures over the weekend and noticed the one blip on the screen. There's nothing to worry about now."

A burst of anger filled Thomas's heart for a few seconds, but it quickly dissipated. Dorn could be a son-of-a-bitch but not stupid enough to kill the golden goose, he thought, as he reached for his supervisor's hand. "I guess I owe you one, Ms. Flores. Thank you."

She shook his hand. "No, thank you, Mr. Payne. It's been a pleasure working with you. I don't know where you learned what you did with this class, but it obviously works and we need to find out more about it. One day I'd like to sit down with you and talk about your training."

Thomas smiled at her. "I would enjoy that, but you'll have to promise to call me Thomas, deal?"

She returned the smile and pointed again, this time at herself. "Only if you agree that it's Abigail."

Just then, the principal called over the loudspeaker for Ms. Flores to report to the office. His voice broke the spell between them. Becoming tense and stiff again, she said good-bye and hurried away. Thomas watched her leave, then picked up the folder containing the test scores and sat behind his desk to examine them. "Well, how 'bout that!" he exclaimed.

When he reached home and opened his mail, Thomas discovered a form letter from the Human Resources Office of the Boston Public School Department. He read the notice informing him that he had become a permanent teacher, a status similar to tenure. He felt proud and relieved about the appointment. Glen and Ms. Caine had explained to him that such a possibility was just about the only perk for an African American man who taught at the elementary level. Years before, with the threat of a federal lawsuit hanging over both heads, senior administrators for the School Department and the Teachers Union had reluctantly approved changing the traditional definition of seniority, and its benefits. The adjustment would grant early tenure to some preferred groups, including Black men, who in turn, would serve as role models at schools such as the Adams, where so many children grew up without fathers. Glen had also received a similar letter at the end of his first year. During a recent after-workout dinner, he had suggested to Thomas that if he did become permanent early, not to broadcast the fact too widely. Apparently, some White teachers expressed less than total support for the initiative.

Heléna called him later that evening, and the two sweethearts spoke for several minutes about their day. Eventually, Thomas prepared to raise the subject of attending Laura's wedding. He felt slightly nervous about asking her to accompany him. So far, they had never quarreled. He did not want to break their magic, but common courtesy demanded a reply without further delay. His voice broke, and his words slowly poured out like old molasses.

"Honey, um, you got any plans for the last Saturday of the month?"

"No, Tomaso, *mi corazoncito*," Heléna replied. "Why?"

Thomas staggered on. "Well, um, you know, I was thinking that we might go somewhere together. It's no big deal … Um, we don't have to go if you don't want to. It might be nice, but—"

"You want to mail your request to me? I'd get it faster," Heléna teased, demonstrating that she did not have Glen's patience.

"I've told you about using my material," Thomas joked. Hearing no rebuttal, he swallowed and pushed the words out in one surge. "Anyway, I thought that we'd go to, um, go to Laura's wedding. I mean, it was very kind of her parents to invite me and everything—and I'm sure it'll be a nice event. I-I thought you might enjoy it." He stopped talking and waited for her response.

It came swiftly.

"You want me to go with you to your ex-fiancée's wedding?" Her voice sounded irritated.

"Um, well, yes, honey."

"Why?"

Thomas heard the hurt feelings in her voice. He started to apologize and withdraw the request, but Heléna spoke again.

"I mean like, do you miss her? You want to see her one last time? Maybe give her a nice, slow visual fuck as she walks down the aisle. Is that it?"

"No, baby. It's just that—"

"So you want me to go out and buy a new dress and get my hair done and look real nice, just so you can say to her, 'See what I had to settle for since I can't have you?' Is that it?"

"No, honey, just listen to me, *por favor*?" Thomas pleaded. "I don't have any feelings for Laura any more. I've told you that." He switched the phone to his other ear. "I just thought that … that you would like to go to this thing. It's going to be real fancy. I don't really go for all that mess, but you seem to like it. Besides," he took a deep breath, "you're partly right. There *is* a part of me that wants you two to meet. It'll be like me saying, 'You did me a favor, Laura. I've met this beautiful, intelligent, *emotionally expressive* woman. Being with her makes me happy. Thank you very much.' "

The other end of the phone was uncharacteristically silent.

"Well … I-I don't know." Heléna finally whispered. "Let me think about it, okay?"

They made small talk about their families for a few minutes before winding down their conversation. Heléna's voice had lost its buoyancy. Thomas felt terrible for having hurt her and did not want them to stop talking, but it was getting late. As with Glen, he believed that if they kept talking, they would eventually return to normal. After saying goodnight, he heard the click on his earpiece and placed the receiver down.

"Well, that didn't go too badly," he said aloud to himself.

School dragged on tediously for Thomas and his class. In spite of the hot days and constant interruptions, they managed to continue learning. The rookie teacher peppered them with new material in every subject. The youngsters eventually resigned themselves to the fact that escape from this despot would arrive only after the last day of school. Thomas sent a note home with every student to stave off the inevitable requests for early report cards due to early summer vacations. His letter unequivocally asserted that report cards would be distributed only after the commencement exercise.

He made only one exception—to Doug's mother. The boy had indeed failed the third "power" reading test and tentatively would not be promoted to the sixth grade. Thomas agreed that since Doug would not attend the graduation ceremony on the last day of school, she could pick up his report card the day before. Ms. Berry had requested and received a waiver from Mr. Dorn, but Thomas refused to co-sign the form. According to School Department policy, two out of three signatures could still produce a waiver, but the principal had to indicate in writing why the third signature had been withheld. Mr. Dorn sent Ms. Flores to persuade Thomas to sign the waiver, but again he declined.

Three days before the last day of school, Thomas received a call at home from Doug's mother. She informed him that the entire family had decided to move to Pennsylvania, and since Doug would get a fresh start there, she was willing to allow him to repeat the fifth grade. She surprised Thomas by thanking him for doing the right thing for her boy. Thomas praised her for her bravery and Doug for his improvement over the year.

On the morning before the final day of school, Thomas met with his class. A steady rain fell, and thunder rumbled enough to be noticed but not enough to alarm anyone. Most teachers had not employed a "no early report card" policy, so most classrooms were only half full. Only Doug had not come to school in Room 217. Thomas bragged to the class about how they continued to show the other classes which room was "top dog" at the Adams. Still, in spite of his bravado he was filled with sadness and apprehension at the thought of not seeing his children ever again. He collected the final homework of the year and announced the Movie Day participants. Every student had earned the required points! Thomas and the class burst into tumultuous applause.

He reviewed the schedule for the day: shortly, they would walk downstairs to participate in their last awards assembly, then they would hold the last rehearsal for the graduation exercise. The afternoon would be reserved for the movie and other farewell activities.

Thomas read aloud the words written by a student in Ms. Rogers's room on behalf of the entire class—her pupils had been the last fourth-grade group to receive a Whispers ceremony.

Dear Mr. Payne,

Thank you so much for the Whispers ceremony your class did for us, and thank you for the notes they gave us. We will never forget the wonderful words your kids whispered to us that day. We cried so much because we really heard every word that was spoken. What you said was true. Now that your students will be leaving, we will be the new senior class. We promise to take good care of the school and take good care of the younger kids here.

Sincerely,

The kids in Ms. Rogers' Room 211

Thomas placed the card on top of his desk next to the ones written by Ms. Patterson and Ms. Valdez.

Later that morning the Room 217 fifth-graders returned from the awards ceremony carrying armloads of goodies. Besides the usual classroom honors, eight students toted statuettes for perfect attendance all year. And the class received an award for the highest attendance percentage of all classes at the Adams; each student received a two-pencil-and-eraser set. Thomas was one of only two teachers who received a fifty-dollar department store gift certificate for having never missed a day of work. And the previous week, the special class teachers had given his students a pizza party as part of their annual "Most Productive and Best Behaved" group.

Thomas distributed one additional honor—to Melvin, for having been selected Student of the Week five times, more than any other student. He handed the boy a certificate to purchase a movie or electronic game of his choice at a local store.

That afternoon after the movie Thomas prepared the class for one final exercise. He stepped into his familiar center-stage position and spoke deliberately, trying to mask his distress. "Well, tomorrow is it, folks. You'll come in the morning pretty much for the commencement exercise and for report cards. Be on time. We'll meet up here as a class for one last group cheer and to say good-bye privately among ourselves." He struggled to hold down the lump in his throat. "Right now, we'll do one more thing together." He instructed Maria to distribute a lined sheet of paper to each pupil.

"Put your name on top of the paper in big capital letters," he directed, and waited until everyone complied. "Keep your pencils, get up and spread out over the room. Leave the papers where they are." The bewildered youngsters hesitated as they turned their heads to look at each other. Eventually one, then two, then six, then every student rose and went to the perimeter of the classroom, carrying a pencil.

Thomas resumed his instructions. "What you're going to do is go to every desk in the class and write a little message to that person whose name you see. It doesn't have to be a lot. It just has to be positive and sincere. Try to say something positive and try to get to everyone. This is kinda like Whispers, only it's in writing, so instead of trying to remember what everyone said, you get to keep it forever." He stopped and opened his hands. "Take the paper home and put it in a safe place. Next year, if something goes wrong at your new school, take out the paper and read it again and remember how your classmates believed in you. Then get back out there and kick some butt!"

He walked to the back of the room and primed his reliable music box. "I want you to make a special effort to get to that person who you've been avoiding all year. You know who. Tell him or her that wonderful thing about himself or herself you've always wanted to say. Or find that person you've had trouble seeing good in, and allow yourself the joy of being a giver one more time by sharing a positive word. This may be the last time you get to do it." Thomas shuffled discs in his hand as he continued. "Now from my spot back here I'm going to talk to you while you do it. Any questions?"

He fielded two inquiries, telling them not to worry about spelling and not to sign their names. He returned his attention to the music box and pressed a button, filling the room with the song, "That's What Friends Are For" by Dionne and Friends. Thomas looked at his students, each standing ready, pencil in hand.

"What are you looking at me for? Go ahead."

Like a squadron of soldiers ambushing another company, they descended on the empty desks. Thomas watched pupils wander aimlessly, scribbling comments on the papers of various classmates. "Don't stand around waiting for someone to finish," he cautioned. "Move on to another empty desk." He could not see what they wrote but noticed that the desk of some students received considerably less attention than others. "Stop!" he called and shut off the music.

Everyone froze and stared at him.

"Still doing it, huh? Still saying, 'I'll get to them later after I take care of my friends,' huh?" He shook his finger at them. "That won't do! His voice became gentle, and he placed his hand on his heart and gestured towards them, as if tossing an object in their midst. "Class, you've got to unload yourself of the belief that some people in our family deserve less. Did it ever occur to you that your attitude was the reason they didn't go as far as they could have?" He shook his head. "Don't carry that stuff with you any longer. Share the love. Give it away. Like a waterfall, you will not run out. In fact, you'll see it return to you many times over." He shifted his eyes back to the music player. "Go ahead."

The song resumed, and students roamed about, sometimes bumping into each other as they moved from desk to desk. Thomas spoke to them, his voice, firm but supportive, carrying over the new song being played, Mariah Carey's "Anytime You Need a Friend."

"Don't hold back. Get to everybody!" Thomas prodded. "Don't be afraid. They don't have to know who it is—just that someone in the room noticed their specialness." Moments later he called out, "We supported and believed in you. Won't you do the same for someone who's been part of your other family for the past year?" The young man looked at his watch. "We're almost out of time. Please get to that person who really needs your attention!"

The pupils chased around frantically. Some looked harried while others displayed little emotion. After another thirty seconds, he called to them again. "Stop. That's it. We're done. Please return to your seats and take a minute to read your messages."

The youngsters calmly did as they were told. A few showed signs of fatigue. Thomas switched the music to a slow, instrumental piece. He walked to his desk, sat down and made last-minute entries in the report cards. (Ms. Nelson, the music teacher, had only that very morning directed him to give A's to every student.) A few muffled sounds of gasps and giggling surfaced as the children examined their papers. Angelica's eyes filled with water. Many students had written to her that they would always be her friend and would never leave her. Cleopatra smiled broadly because at least six students indicated how proud they felt to be her friend. Freddy shook his head from side to side and muttered, "No!" several times under his breath, afraid to believe the messages of friendship and respect bestowed on him. Maria closed her eyes, pressed her paper tightly against her heart and rocked as she absorbed the written embraces of her classmates. Thomas watched unobtrusively. The behavior of the satisfied students symbolized their new-found inner strength and fortitude. They believed in themselves and each other.

Thomas stood and stepped to the center of the room. "Take them home and keep them in a safe place. There'll be times when you'll need them." He looked at his watch and said nothing further.

For the last fifteen minutes, instead of DEAR, the students cleaned out their desks for the last time. Thomas played fast, spirited music to snap them out of their trance and dismissed them with a word to dress sharp for the final day of school.

The final morning of school at the Adams arrived with dark skies and a light but steady drizzle. Girls and boys coming to school gathered in their classrooms, lest they disturb the decorations for the fifth-grade honorees and their families. Some students arrived holding umbrellas or wearing rain gear. Others received a ride from their parents. Several of Thomas's pupils came late but he said nothing about it.

In the auditorium Heléna and her crew raced about pell-mell as they applied finishing touches, attempting to enliven the room in spite of its dirty, gray walls. They draped streams of colorful crepe paper across the low ceiling and taped balloons to the stage and door entrances. They pried open rickety metal folding chairs and spread them over most of the floor space. Next door the custodian hummed "Precious Lord, Take My Hand" while folding and putting away the last of the cafeteria benches. The three fifth-grade classrooms were all but full, but every other room hosted less than half its normal student population.

By 9 o'clock every student in Room 217 had arrived—except Doug. Instrumental jazz music overshadowed the distant echoes of thunder. The room bore none of the markings that had distinguished it all year. The walls were bare, and the desks had all been pushed to the left side of the room. The chairs remained accessible so that the dressed-up pupils could sit. Mountains of papers and cardboard items covered Thomas's desk and table. He estimated that it would take at least six hours to clear everything, so he would have to return the next day.

In his black pinstriped suit, the handsome young teacher greeted parents and reacquainted himself with family members, charming them. The older sisters of more than one student made a point to introduce themselves. Angel's mother, dressed in a red silk top revealing ample cleavage and tight black slacks elevated by high-heel shoes, hugged him fondly.

"How come such a wonderful, beautiful man have to be my son's teacher?" she lamented.

Thomas winked at her. "Perhaps it was God's way of keeping both of us out of trouble."

Mrs. Estevez laughed and touched his face. "I hope to see you again, Mr. Payne," she whispered, before turning and strutting out the door, leaving her son to enjoy his last day with his classmates.

The rookie teacher surveyed the iridescent colors of the clothing worn by his students and smiled at the well-dressed brood. "You all look very nice today," he declared. "Don't worry, the whole thing downstairs will be over soon."

Thomas thought that some of the girls had adorned themselves in attire a little too adult for his taste but said nothing. He did, however, send Carmelita to the girls' bathroom to remove a modest patch of make-up and lipstick. All of the girls wore dresses or skirts, and all of the boys had hung ties around their necks.

Deborah avoided close contact with anyone and continuously hand-ironed her purple dress. Akeem looked especially noble in his bow tie. Three boys had come to school toting neckwear in their pockets because no one in their family could tie them. One of the three, Brian, bore a note from his mother asking Thomas to help the boy one last time. He gladly obliged. While standing behind the lad in front of the storage cabinet mirror, Brian whispered to him.

"My mom said she might let me go see my dad in Florida next month, Mr. Payne," he said.

Thomas lifted his eyebrows. "Oh? Well, if that makes you happy, then I'm happy." He double-checked the knot. "All done."

The excited group chattered to each other and to Thomas about everything and nothing. A little after 9 o'clock Ms. Flores announced via the loudspeaker that all fifth-graders should proceed to the auditorium.

Thomas gathered his troop in the center of the room. "Don't forget who's the senior class, the champions around here," he reminded them. "Make your families and me real proud today. We'll meet back up here for your report cards and one last hurrah." He noticed brave smiles on the faces of a few students and understood. He would miss them, too. "Alright," he exclaimed. "Let's go!"

The ceremony itself progressed along smoothly. A few crying babies occasionally drew attention away from the activities on stage, but generally everything went well. Ms. Nelson provided musical accompaniment on an old, recently-tuned piano. The children sang the school song in perfect unison, if not in perfect pitch. Mrs. Chang's class and Ms. Sanchez-Taylor's—absent Carlos, her oldest and tallest student—all behaved well. A guest speaker from the local chapter of the Urban League spoke eloquently—too eloquently. Her vocabulary did not reach down to most of the students—and many parents. She received polite applause at the end of her presentation. At the appointed time Thomas stood and, amid a few whistles from the audience, presented his students with a certificate generated by computer software he had purchased and donated to the school.

After the program the families schmoozed and consumed light refreshments laid out in the cafeteria. The fifth-grade students returned to their rooms for distribution of report cards and farewells.

Once back in 217 Thomas took pictures of his pupils and distributed the report cards with little fanfare. There were no surprises. Those slated to attend summer school—over half of them—moaned over the confirmation letter enclosed with the report card. Several pupils asked about Doug. Thomas only admitted that, to his knowledge, the family had moved to Pennsylvania, then ended the discussion to answer the door.

Mr. Dorn and Ms. Flores entered. The two men shook hands, symbolically declaring a truce. Thomas air-kissed Ms. Flores on both cheeks. Carmelita and Asa jetted over to the principal and assistant principal and pulled them away, transferring them to the other side of the room. Thomas found their behavior to be quite strange, but another knock on the door prevented him from making a proper inquiry. Melvin cut him off and opened the door. Glen greeted the boy. Thomas knew that Glen normally stayed holed up in his room during his lunch. "I was summoned," was all he managed to explain before being whisked off to the back of the room by Melvin. Thomas put his hands on his hips.

"What's going on here?" he asked.

Everybody turned towards him, then glanced at each other and snickered. Thomas felt slightly uncomfortable. Mr. Dorn looked at his watch and suggested that they get started. Ms. Flores advanced towards Thomas and stopped a few feet away.

"Mr. Payne, would you come outside the room with me for a minute, please?"

Thomas surveyed the impish faces of his children and cautiously walked alongside the assistant principal, who closed the door behind her, once they had reached the hall. She calmly explained. "The kids met with me and Mr. Dorn and asked us to be here."

Thomas could make out sounds of children prattling excitedly, chairs being dragged across the floor and Melvin shouting commands to everyone. The tall man leaned to his left trying to sneak a glimpse, but Ms. Flores blocked his view, smiling. "You'll see in a second, Thomas," she said.

Just then the door creaked open and Asa waved his hand. The lights had been turned off. "We're ready," the boy announced.

Ms. Flores stepped aside and Thomas cautiously marched into his dark, very quiet room. His students had formed a bending line facing him in the center of what remained of the floor space. The first-year teacher immediately recognized the configuration as their Whispers line. He felt his heart beat faster and his breathing require more effort. Angelica slowly approached him and took her teacher by the hand. Clothed in a white dress, she looked like an angel. "This way, please," she mellifluously requested, escorting him to the front of the line facing the participants before returning to the front spot. Thomas looked down the sea of smiling faces. Mr. Dorn, Glen and now Ms. Flores had assumed positions at the end.

Asa waved to Deborah, who occupied the corner of the space where the reliable, often-employed music player rested. She nodded and pressed a button.

"We know how much you like old movies and old songs, Mr. Payne, so we thought you might know this one," Carmelita called out from her third-place spot.

A few notes from a piano sounded, followed by a soft set of violins, and Thomas recognized the voice of Gladys Knight as she sang the opening lines to one of his favorite songs: "Wind Beneath My Wings." He smiled and put his hands over his face, then clapped them together twice with pure delight. The first whisperer approached him. He stood quietly and reverently so she could come as close to his ear as possible.

"I love you, Mr. Payne. I'm going to miss you so much," Angelica started off. She desperately wanted to hug him but fought the urge and moved to the left.

"Thanks for making us winners instead of losers," Angel declared, then he was gone.

"You have done so much for us."

"I won't forget what you taught me."

"I'm glad you were my teacher."

They passed by one by one, and Thomas listened as tears rolled down his face. Each child's acknowledgement brought deeper feelings of love and pride. For a brief flash he felt selfish and wanted the moment to last forever. He recognized that in a few minutes he would not see most of them ever again. They had grown both physically and emotionally, and he had been a part of the latter. They were not just children but *his* children; his Pedro, his Maria, his Gary. And in a few more minutes he would have to do the most difficult thing all good teachers and parents have to do—let their children go.

The line grew shorter. The music faded briefly before Janet, who had replaced Deborah so that she could join the line, inserted the selection her grandmother had given her. Thomas immediately recognized the harmonizing violins and base beat, then heard the English performer, Lulu, sing the words to the theme song from an old movie he had just watched the previous week: "To Sir With Love."

Thomas felt his heart overflow with love and longing. He wanted to embrace each one of his children and thank them for their thoughtfulness.

"Oh, my God. This is so wonderful!" he cried. Eventually, the children all finished. Thomas reached into his back pocket, pulled out a handkerchief and wiped his eyes.

Ms. Flores was next. She held his wet face in her hands. "You are a wonderful teacher," she said.

Next, Mr. Dorn. Thomas held his breath. The man leaned closer. "You did a good job here, Mr. Payne. Thank you." He sounded sincere. Thomas nodded to him with half a smile.

Finally Glen approached. They had been through so much. Glen held his mentee by the shoulders and announced, "You taught me more than I taught you, my friend."

Thomas shook his head from side to side. Not true, of course, but what a wonderful thing for Glen to say. Then it ended.

Everyone broke into applause. Thomas pressed his fingers firmly against his mouth to keep from making even more of a scene over his surprise than he had already. He was about to thank them when the youngsters encircled him. He broke into a broad smile and his mood lightened. They always did this after Whispers or a cradle to lighten the mood, so that the event did not become too mawkish.

"Group hug! Group hug!" everybody shouted. Thomas felt his breath becoming sparse as the children laughed and squeezed in on him. He laughed, his spirits ebulliently soaring. The mass of pressing flesh eventually expanded again, and Thomas caught his breath. He held up his hands and spoke while wiping his eyes.

"Thank you," he said, scanning the faces of the participants, including Mr. Dorn, who now inched towards the door. "All of you so much. You have honored me more than I can say." He looked at his watch and instructed his class to form a circle for the last time.

The three adults took the hint and departed. Thomas walked to the back of the room, inserted a disc in the player, then went to his desk. He returned with a stack of large brown envelopes and distributed them to the class. While Boyz II Men sang "It's So Hard to Say Goodbye to Yesterday" in perfect harmony, he informed them that the packages contained their contracts and photographs from the wall. He had also placed inside a short personal note and a gift.

"Remember the day you filled out a form to win a free book that came with a catalog? I said it was a contest?" Dozens of heads moved up and down in remembrance. Thomas smiled. "Well, I lied. The book you selected as your first choice is in the package. It's a gift from me to you."

Children started to cheer and offer thanks. Some opened their envelopes. Thomas asked them to wait and raised his hands.

"You earned it. You worked very hard this year, and you should be proud, just like I am. I'm proud of each and every one of you." He looked at their faces. His voice quivered as he spoke and his eyes filled with tears. "Well, good luck in sixth grade. Stop by and see Mr. Payne some day."

The group cried and told him how much they would miss him. Thomas put his hand in the center and cleared his throat. "Hey, which class is the greatest?"

"Two-seventeen!" they all shouted.

"Who?" he asked, putting his hand to his ear.

"Two-seventeen!" they clamored again.

"God bless you and watch over you and your families," he said.

That following Saturday morning Thomas checked to make sure that he had turned the light off in the bedroom closet. He examined himself in the mirror. He hadn't worn his white suit all year and looked quite dashing in it, if he did say so himself. He waltzed into the living room and turned off the air-conditioner while calling for Heléna to hurry up. He wanted to get on the road. She stepped out of the bathroom.

He could not get over how marvelous she looked. She wore a lavender backless dress with a plunging neckline and little make-up except her usual heavy lipstick. God had blessed her with a lovely countenance. He whistled and clapped his hands. "Honey, you're not supposed to be prettier than the bride at a wedding. It's impolite."

"Well, what can I say?" she joked, opening her arms. "I gotta let the chips fall where they fall." She frowned and crinkled her nose at him. "Of course, if I would've got proper notice, I could've really set myself up right."

They both laughed. Thomas grabbed the box containing the gift; a set of champagne glasses with the bride and groom's initials and the wedding date imprinted at the bottom of each one. He juggled it on one hand. Heléna snatched it from him.

"Give it to me. It's not a football, you know." She strolled to the door and waited.

Thomas thought about the previous night. Heléna had been somewhat quiet for most of the day—quiet for her. He remembered how intensely they had made love. Heléna always exuded passion, but she had shown even more so. She told him that she loved him and asked twice if he was *her* man. He told her that he loved her and that he was—and meant it. Now, in the light of day he wondered if she had regretted her words. He had not.

He opened the door and turned on the light above the stairs. Standing right next to her, he wanted to check her state of mind—or heart—but wasn't sure how. "Baby?" he said.

"Yes, Tomaso?" she replied, looking in his eyes.

Thomas reached out and pulled her closer to him. "Are you, um, um, very sure …" He paused. "Are you sure about all this? You know, going to the wedding and everything else."

Heléna smiled and placed her hand on his face. "*Si,* Tomaso, *mi corazoncito,*" she said softly. "I'm sure about everything." Her eyes revealed a hint of fear. "And you?"

He nodded. "Me too."

She smiled and disappeared down the creaky stairs. Thomas followed but while closing the door, caught a glimpse of the area by his living room window. Two relatively new, tall, leafy plants rested on the floor, soaking up the sun. Heléna had given them to him a couple of weeks before. He had forgotten their technical names but liked how they brightened up his home. He promised himself that he would take good care of them. In fact, he was proud that he had remembered to water them that very morning.

Heléna, now out of sight, called for him to "shake a leg." Thomas yelled back that he was coming and promptly followed her downstairs and out the door.

Order Form

To order additional copies of *Rookie Year: Journey of a First-Year Teacher*, complete form below.

Ship to:

Name _____

Address _____

City _____ State _____

Zip _____ Telephone (____) _____

Quantity _____ book(s) at $21.95 each   _____

Postage ($2.00 each book)   _____

Shipping and handling (per order) $3.00

(MA residents add $1.10 sales tax each book)   _____

Total   _____

Send check or money order to:

Peralta Publishing Company
P.O. Box 35407
Boston, MA 02135-0007